The Lightworker Trials

R.S. O'Neal

The Quest for the Aura series: Book One

Books in the Quest for the Aura series:

- The Lightworker Trials

- Terra

- Aqua

- Caelus

- Incendium

Note to readers: The Quest for the Aura series is set in beautiful, sunny Australia, and all spelling and grammar is consistent with Australian English.

The Lightworker Trials print edition ISBN: 978-0-9954473-2-5

Cover design by Deranged Doctor Design

www.derangeddoctordesign.com

*To Mum and Dad
Who always walk Lightly*

*And Craig, Molly and Deck
The most stalwart fan club*

"Live with Courage and Light" – Alia and Rufus

"Walk Lightly and carry a big stick" –
Sergeant Tottingham

"May the Light guide your steps" – St Illuminado

"An interesting journey ahead indeed" –
Madame Overmantle

N
W
E
S
C.E.P Compound
Staff Quarters
First Aid
Earth Lodge
Refectory
Air Lodge
Meditation Hall
Lecture Theatre
Common Room
Lake Altum
Water Lodge
Fire Lodge
Training Shed
Runway
Therapeutic Pools

CHAPTER ONE

EYRE OPENED HER EYES, awake so quickly that her brain struggled to catch up with the rest of her body. Adrenaline was sparking through her veins and her heart pounded violently in response to it; ready for flight, as if her body knew something she didn't. The sound came again from outside her window, a high-pitched, eerie shriek that made the hairs on her arms rise. What *was* that?

In the dark room she could hardly see a thing, and she teetered on the edge of complete panic. But then she started to breathe slowly and carefully, helping her body to calm and her brain to take charge again. Finally her heart slowed and the awful fear began to subside a little. She hadn't heard anything else after the initial shock of waking so suddenly.

But still cautious, she took a breath and slid out of bed, crawling along the floor towards the window, feeling in some primal way that she absolutely *had* to remain unseen. She could only make out the dim outlines of the dressing table and chest of drawers in the bedroom and she manoeuvred around them silently until she reached the heavy curtains that hung in front of the window.

Her eyes were still adjusting as she peered through the gap between the windowsill and the curtain. The moon was only a sliver and she couldn't see much outside, just the usual layout of the Edmunsuns' back garden, the trees making shadowy shapes in the dim light. The fountain in the centre of the lawn threw up steady arcs of water, and the droplets glinted occasionally, but that was the only movement she could see in the backyard. Her eyes strained as she searched for any sign of what might have made that terrible noise, and then, drawn by some sense she had no name for, her eyes travelled closer in, along the window to the end of the windowsill.

What she saw made her heart stutter with fear, and her thoughts tumbled around in panicked confusion. A hulking, black shape, as large as a big dog, was crouched on the sloping roof below the windowsill, staring at the closed curtains so intently that she held her breath, fearful that any movement might draw the slanted red eyes towards her. She couldn't make out what sort of creature it was—but knew it was nothing she'd ever seen before, with its lumpy, hairless skin and bony wings. And whatever it was, its sinister presence filled her with a sharp and palpable fear.

As if it could sense her horrified gaze, the creature turned its head towards her and she dove back down to the carpet, scrabbling her way across to the bedroom door, her breath heaving painfully in her chest.

Ohmygodohmygodohmygod, she thought in a mindless jabber as she groped her way across the floor. When she reached the hallway she stood up, gasping in terror, but uncertain what to do. Who should she go and see? What would she tell them? What on earth *was* that?

The decision was made for her, because Mrs Edmunsun suddenly stepped into the hall, pulling on the green satin gown she always wore over her nightclothes. She strode over to Eyre, concern showing on her serene face.

"Eyre!" she said. "Are you okay?" Seeing that she was trembling, Mrs Edmunsun took Eyre's arm and led her downstairs into the huge kitchen. She pulled out one of the stools that fitted under the grey and white marble bench and guided Eyre on to it.

"Hot chocolate!" Mrs Edmunsun said decisively as she wrapped a large, soft blanket around Eyre's shoulders. Eyre was shivering uncontrollably despite the balmy spring temperature and she was grateful for the warmth. She knew that Mrs Edmunsun thought she was having another nightmare, and why wouldn't she? Over the past month Eyre had had enough of them, and cried so many tears; this was just one more "moment". But what could she say? That she saw a monster sitting on her windowsill? How mad would that sound? It would just confirm in Mrs Edmunsun's mind that Eyre was still in shock.

Eyre's thoughts were interrupted as a thin, lanky girl walked in to the kitchen, yawning. "Midnight feast?" she said. "I'm in!" Beatrice was pale-skinned with long dark hair and an intelligent face that usually sported glasses, but she wasn't wearing them now. She looked myopically at Eyre, sympathy on her face.

"Did you have another dream?" The compassion in her voice caused tears to gather under Eyre's eyelids, but she gritted her teeth against them, determined this time she wouldn't cry. The Edmunsuns must surely be getting sick of it.

"I'm sorry to get you up," Eyre said eventually. Beatrice gave her a hug and then pulled up a stool beside her, wrapping her hands around the mug of hot chocolate her mother passed her.

"Always happy to drink hot chocolate," Beatrice said, taking a noisy sip.

Eyre calmed down in the bright kitchen, and as she drank she began to doubt herself. Perhaps it *had* been a nightmare, and she had been sleepwalking, caught between wakefulness and slumber, just dreaming the dark creature she thought she'd seen on the roof. Mrs Edmunsun chatted away, trying to help Eyre settle down, and Beatrice went along with her as they talked about school.

"Beatrice said your first week back went quite well," Mrs Edmunsun said. "Except for Mrs Humphries' class." It broke the tension as the three of them laughed. Mrs Humphries was the English teacher at St Jeffrey's and possibly the most boring teacher at the school.

"Eyre did really well, Mum," Beatrice replied. "Stayed awake the whole lesson!"

"Mr Ray was nice," Eyre said. "He came and welcomed me back. It was pretty good overall."

A silence descended and Mrs Edmunsun smoothly filled the gap. "Well, Peter is back tomorrow morning, and we thought we'd go to the beach at Mooloolaba in the afternoon. Why don't you girls go and look at the Cotton Tree Markets in the morning? I'll get organised after breakfast so we can all head to the beach when you get back."

"Great idea," Beatrice said, grabbing Eyre's empty cup and taking it with hers to the sink. "The markets are cool."

Mrs Edmunsun looked at Eyre's drawn, pale face. "Do you think you can get back to sleep now?"

Eyre's stomach clenched, but she kept her face impassive.

"Yes, thank you, I'm fine now. Thanks for the hot chocolate."

They all headed back to bed again, but Eyre left the bedroom light off as she entered her room and sidled around the walls to the window, peering out at the roof again from behind the curtain. There was nothing there and nothing anywhere in the yard remotely like the leathery creature she thought she had seen earlier. Unsettled, she lay back down on the bed, telling herself it must indeed have been just a nightmare. But sleep took a long time to come, and when it finally did, she tossed and turned as a hulking dark creature lurked at the edge of her dreams.

CHAPTER TWO

EYRE STOOD IN THE shower, letting the hot water stream over her, trying to wake herself up after her disrupted sleep of the night before. Her eyes were gritty and she felt so tired. The last thing she wanted to do was go anywhere, but Beatrice was so excited by the idea of the markets that Eyre was pretending to be enthused as well. She turned the water off and grabbed her towel, sliding the bathroom door open into the guest bedroom; her bedroom now. She dressed quickly in denim shorts and a T-shirt and grabbed her backpack, a brightly coloured canvas bag that she took everywhere with her and headed downstairs.

Beatrice met her in the hallway, her long hair in dark braids this morning, her rainbow-coloured glasses firmly in place. Today she had put in a purple nose stud—she wore a tiny jewel in the corner of her nose that she changed according to her mood. It was the one characteristic that didn't fit Beatrice's overall nerdy image, and Eyre was still trying to work out exactly who Beatrice was.

"Come on then, my friend!" Beatrice said, motioning towards the door. "There are goods to be bought! Onwards!"

But then there was a sudden clatter of feet as Beatrice's seven-year-old brother, Lachie, raced down the stairs towards them. He wore glasses like Beatrice, but there the resemblance ended. At fourteen, Beatrice was taller than most fifteen-year-olds, and thin, whereas Lachie was a small, rotund kid, as sunny and anxious to please as a rollicking puppy. And his hair was fair like his dad's, whereas Beatrice was dark like her mother.

Lachie barged past Eyre and Beatrice, heading for the front door.

"Dad's home!" he said in excitement. Beatrice made a happy noise and followed him across the marble floor. Eyre lingered uncertainly and then headed upstairs to her bedroom, not wanting to intrude.

Her bedroom was a huge room with a queen bed and an ensuite bathroom. It was decorated with white bed linen and tasteful pewter ornaments—as different as possible from her old bedroom at home with its bright colours and patchwork bedspread. Mrs Edmunsun had said they would go shopping to find some decorations more in keeping with a young girl's room, but they hadn't had the chance to do it yet. Personally, Eyre thought they shouldn't bother. Nothing would ever come close to being like her room at home. It was gone forever, and no amount of new furnishings would bring it back.

She could hear footsteps coming up the stairs and then there was a light knock at her bedroom door. She opened the door and the large form of Peter Edmunsun stood there awkwardly, his kind face uncertain as he held something in his hand.

"Hello Eyre," he said, and gave her a quick hug. "Are you doing okay?" Eyre smiled noncommittally and Mr Edmunsun nodded, understanding. "As well as you can, I guess. Robyn told me that your first week back at school was alright."

Eyre nodded and Mr Edmunsun, looking apologetic, continued. "I've just got back from Canberra, and I, well I've finalised it all." He hesitated, and then continued. "I brought this back. . . ."

His voice trailed off and he held the package out to her. "I'm afraid that, well . . . it was all they could find. . . ." He handed the small wrapped object over to Eyre, looking like he wanted to disappear. This was obviously way too tough for him.

Eyre swallowed hard, trying to keep control as she looked at the white and orange post-pack, contemplating its horrible significance. Everything that had made up her life, reduced to the contents of this small envelope. Someone had written "Lightward effects" across the top of the envelope, obviously directing it to the next of kin. Such a stark title; two words that headlined the implosion of her life.

"Thank you," she said, a huge lump in her throat. Peter Edmunsun's forehead wrinkled, and he patted her shoulder awkwardly.

"You're part of our family now, Eyre," he said. "Your parents were dear to us too, and we hope that eventually you'll be happy here."

Eyre nodded, unable to reply, as yet more tears spilled out of eyes that had already cried buckets, waterfalls, oceans. She knew the tears would never run dry. Peter Edmunsun hesitated but could think of nothing more to say, and after patting her awkwardly on the shoulder, he left, looking troubled. Eyre shut the door, sitting on the bed with the small package in her lap.

Eventually she ripped off the top of the envelope and tipped out the contents. There was only one thing in there, but it caused the tears to come even stronger. Eyre picked up the silver necklace and stroked it, her mouth quivering as she remembered it around her mother's neck. A sturdy chain with a series of unusual charms on it, her mother's "special things", as she had described them when Eyre's childish fingers had grasped at the chain. When she was little Eyre had played with that necklace for hours, and she knew the contours of each beloved charm even with her eyes shut: the small ornate cylinder with the hole in it, the elaborate key inlaid with a bluish-purple gem, and the locket engraved on the front with a strange geometric symbol. . . .

Eyre carefully opened the locket, studying the photograph inside. Herself, aged about eight, and her mother and father; he, a huge man with intelligent eyes a deep sapphire blue like her own, and her mother, laughing merrily in the photo as she always did. As Eyre brought the image closer the photograph fell out of the locket, the backing sheet following. She picked up the backing sheet, not recognising the strange, shimmering paper.

But as footsteps approached she quickly returned the backing and inserted the photograph as a timid knock came at the door.

"Come in," she called, wiping her face, and the door opened.

Beatrice, a worried look on her face, came inside the room. "Dad said you were a bit upset," she said. "I thought I'd come and see how you were doing."

Eyre smiled crookedly.

"Your Mum and Dad are so nice, Beatrice," she said. "I'm okay, it's just—hard," she finished eventually. "This is my mother's silver necklace—it's all that was left after . . . the fire."

Beatrice sat on the bed beside Eyre and looked at the open locket. "Is that your parents and you?" she asked. As Eyre nodded, Beatrice studied the photo. "They look lovely," she said.

Eyre closed the locket and hung the necklace around her neck. "Mum never took it off," she said. "I'm so glad it survived the fire."

Beatrice leant over and picked up one of the charms on the chain, looking at it closely.

"It's not silver, Eyre," she said. "It's titanium. I can tell by the energy. That's why it survived when nothing else did. Dad said they found it in the ashes of the house." She hugged Eyre suddenly and said fiercely, "You've had a terrible time, but I'm really glad you're here with us! We all understand it's going to take you some time."

Eyre didn't understand what she meant about the 'energy'; it was sort of weird, really, but the empathy from this kind girl registered. Eyre's tears overwhelmed her again, but as she looked at the tall, gangly girl who stood in front of her with such a pained look on her face, she felt less alone than she had for the last, horrible month. Orphaned Eyre might be, but she was fortunate to be in this loving home with people who apparently knew her parents well and were great friends of theirs—but people who Eyre had never heard of until a month ago. She was still adjusting to her new reality, and so were the Edmunsuns.

"Thanks Beatrice," she said, breathing deeply to stem the tears. Then she tried to take the necklace off. She wanted to put it somewhere safe—like a bank vault or Fort Knox or something. She couldn't bear to lose it. But the clasp wouldn't open.

"Here," Beatrice said after she watched Eyre trying to open it. "Let me try." Eyre turned her back to Beatrice and Beatrice fiddled with the clasp for a while. Finally she gave up in frustration.

"It's stuck, I think," Beatrice said. "Maybe you should just leave it on."

Eyre struggled for a moment with that idea. On the one hand, she would be overjoyed to have this precious remnant of her previous life near her; on the other, the thought of potentially losing it was intolerable.

Beatrice's eyes were sympathetic. She understood this was a bigger issue than just a necklace. Then she stood up resolutely.

"Come on, let's go for that walk," Beatrice said. Eyre nodded and grabbed her backpack, and they headed for the door.

CHAPTER THREE

EYRE HEFTED HER BAG across her shoulders as she and Beatrice walked away from the house and across the deserted netball courts that backed on to the street where the Edmunsuns lived. Half a kilometre away Eyre could see marquee tops and brightly waving flags where the Cotton Tree Markets vendors had set up their stalls amongst the clusters of casuarina trees. Masses of people moved in and out of the area, and cars lined the streets, up on the curb and parked illegally when they couldn't find space. But here it was silent, the courts eerily empty once the Saturday games were over. Only a lone, grubby Labrador walked around lazily, scavenging for leftover lunch bits. Obviously a regular here, judging by its portly frame, Eyre thought, as she watched it riffle through a brown paper bag, its nose buried so deeply only its ears hung out.

They walked across the faded green expanse of the playing courts, pitted and scuffed from years of running feet. It was warm already, the late spring sun sending waves of heat upwards from the concrete.

A sudden breeze swirled leaves up in the air in a mini tornado, and the fat old dog leaped in fright, pulling its head out of the paper bag. Both Eyre and Beatrice laughed at its comical fear. But then strangely, the hackles on the dog's back rose and it drew its teeth back, snarling as it backed away from something they couldn't see. Eyre looked around, trying to see what the dog was frightened of. It seemed to be looking across the courts towards something in the distance, but she couldn't see anything other than a great crowd of people. She frowned as the dog continued to scrabble backwards, growling in a most un-Labrador-like way, obviously terrified. Then it turned and raced away, yipping in fear, as fast as its stout old body would carry it. Eyre looked at Beatrice, who seemed unnerved, her eyes following the dog intently.

"That dog is as disturbed as I am," Eyre said eventually, by way of an apology for the night before, and was rewarded when Beatrice huffed out a laugh. Beatrice finally took her eyes away from the disappearing dog.

"You're alright, Eyre," Beatrice said. "Let's go get some retail therapy. I find that's a great cure for insanity!"

The markets were humming with noise and colour as the girls arrived at the tangled maze of tents and tables. Eyre strolled through the crowd, stopping occasionally to look at something that caught her eye, but buffered as always by a dragging flatness that made it hard to raise any enthusiasm. She was browsing half-heartedly through new and secondhand books piled on a table and had just added her name to the mailing list for the latest book of the popular fantasy writer L.R. Onase, when she had the strong feeling that she was being watched. She looked behind her and spotted Beatrice three tables back. Beatrice had her nose to a bright pink candle as she listened to the vendor's animated sales pitch.

Eyre looked the other way up the aisle and was taken aback when she saw a tall, hulking boy staring at her with eyes that burned with dislike. He had a Morse code of acne tattooed across his cheeks and outsized ears that stuck out from the side of his head like ping pong paddles, and he stood in an odd, threatening way as if he was about to charge her. For someone slightly silly-looking, with those clown-like ears, he had a heavy, dark aura about him and an overbearing bull-like presence that was intimidating. Disconcerted, Eyre looked away and picked up another book, trying to ignore him. But he strode heavily towards her, fists clenched, and stopped at the book table. He looked at her name on the mailing list.

"Eerie," he said. "What a weird name."

"Actually—it's pronounced 'Air'," Eyre said, sighing. She'd had this issue for many years, especially from teachers at every new school she'd been to.

"Well, we don't like strangers around here," the large boy hissed as he leaned over her. The venom in his voice left Eyre speechless—uncharacteristically, she couldn't think what to say, so great was her surprise at his unprovoked attack. They stared at each other for a long moment until Beatrice's voice came from behind her.

"What's going on?" she said sharply.

The boy's mouth twisted, then he gave another hard look at Eyre before turning and walking off without replying to Beatrice. Eyre put the book back on the table, surprised to find her hands were shaking. She turned to Beatrice.

"Well, I don't know what that was about," she said. "But he obviously doesn't like me very much. I wonder if he's been around to every person at the markets that he doesn't know? Or am I just special?"

Beatrice looked at the receding form of the boy as he disappeared into the crowd.

"That's Ben Perrill," she said shortly, her eyes still on him. "Rugby jock and all-round bully. He's in our year at school, but obviously you haven't had the privilege of meeting him. He's a jerk for sure, but don't take it personally. He's awful to most people in general."

Eyre grimaced and shrugged. "Ah well, how lovely to meet one of the locals." Then she lifted a lock of her auburn hair up. "Or maybe he just doesn't like red hair? Some people aren't keen on rangas!"

Beatrice laughed, and they continued down the rows together.

The strangeness of the encounter lingered, but distracted by the hubbub of the crowd, she eventually forgot about it.

An hour later Beatrice looked at her watch and suggested they head home.

"It's getting really hot, why don't we take this stuff home and head to the beach? The others should be ready by now." 'This stuff' consisted of six bags of items Beatrice had bought from various tables around the markets— a bright green bikini with a pink hibiscus pattern on it, a pair of pineapple earrings, and various other things she just had to buy, including the pink candle she had been looking at earlier. Beatrice certainly enjoyed the lighter side of life.

"I'll just let Mum know we're on our way home," Beatrice said, pulling out her phone as she grappled awkwardly with her bags.

She dialled the number and listened for a moment, then started to leave a message.

"Hi, Mum, we're just on our way home—see you in—" Suddenly Beatrice stopped, and a horrified expression dawned on her face as she looked over Eyre's shoulder.

"BREACH! Oh god, Mum, BREACH!" she screamed at the top of her lungs into the phone, then threw it into her handbag and dropped all her shopping bags.

"Eyre, come on, RUN!" Beatrice screeched, grabbing Eyre's arm in a grasp that hurt and starting to drag her back down the side street they had been walking along towards the netball courts.

Eyre's stomach dropped in fear at the look on Beatrice's face, all the worse for not knowing what was going on. She looked back over her shoulder desperately, searching wildly for the source of Beatrice's panic. Unable to get rid of Beatrice's grip on her arm, she stumbled along behind, trying to keep up as Beatrice hauled her back down the aisle. Beatrice's long legs made it hard to follow her, especially as Eyre had never been known for her athletic skills. Strangely, the most frightening thing was that Beatrice had dumped her packages back in the aisle. What could possess her to leave in such an awful panic? The realisation that something had scared Beatrice so much she had dropped everything spurred Eyre to run faster.

Gasping for breath, she tried to talk to Beatrice as they pounded down the road towards the netball courts.

"What's going on, Beatrice?" Eyre said as she took another gulp of air. "What did you see?"

Beatrice shook her head and dragged her desperately towards the netball courts. "Eyre, you have to RUN, please! Just come with me! I don't have time to explain. HURRY UP!" She practically wailed the last words as she stumbled along the road, and Eyre's stomach lurched as she tried to run faster. Her chest was on fire, and her breath was coming in heaving gasps as she tried to suck oxygen into her lungs. They reached the netball courts and raced across the hot concrete, the access to the Edmunsuns' road seeming tantalisingly close.

Suddenly Beatrice looked behind her and slowed to a stop, turning around.

"Oh no," she breathed. The dread in her voice caused Eyre to stop and turn also.

Lurching across the courts towards them were three tall, thin men. At first Eyre thought they were in Halloween costume, they looked so strange. They wore dull, metallic suits that seemed to suck in the light as they approached, and their pale skin had a greenish tinge as if covered in stage makeup; ill-looking, emaciated. They all had dark hair—the tall, middle one with hair to his shoulders; the one on the right with a long dark ponytail; and the one on the left with a buzz cut. But despite their awful appearance, it was the way they moved that caused an intense foreboding to rise within her—they came towards the girls with a jerking, sideways-forwards movement like strange broken creatures, their joints snapping and cracking violently. It was an eerie and terrifying sound, and the peculiar way they moved caused Eyre to step away from them fearfully, edging backwards towards the road. Their eyes were fixed on Eyre, and a foul-smelling steam curled upwards from their jackets, smoking like they were on fire. A terrible dread crawled in the pit of her stomach as she tried to understand what was happening.

"God, Eyre," Beatrice said softly. "I'm so sorry."

"Who are they?" Eyre asked, looking from one of the strange men to the other, her eyes wild. "Or what? Why are they walking like that? What do they want? *For god's sake speak to me, Beatrice!* What is happening?"

Beatrice held Eyre's arm, pulling her away from the creatures as they jerked their way across the courts towards them.

"We're going to die," she whispered bleakly.

Eyre looked at her in disbelief.

"Well . . . *run*, then," she cried frantically. "Come ON!"

"It's too late," Beatrice said, her voice wavering. "We'll never get away."

Eyre looked from her to the men and back again, confused and terrified by the hopeless tone in Beatrice's voice.

The thin man with the ponytail stepped towards the girls and lifted his hand. Suddenly a dark plume of smoke blasted from his palm towards them. Beatrice must have been expecting it, because she pulled Eyre out of the way just in time, and the smoke hit the ground where they had been standing, blasting a deep hole in the concrete. Eyre gasped in shock, her mouth hanging open. Beatrice stepped in front of Eyre protectively.

"Go away," Beatrice shouted. "Leave us alone!"

"Impossible, I'm afraid," said the tallest man in an odd, rasping voice. "She was meant to be with the others when I dispatched them last month. An oversight I am about to rectify." He brought his hands up, and his eyes, as flat and lifeless as a shark's, focussed intently on Eyre.

Eyre heard his words and exhaled in shock. What was he talking about? Did he mean he killed her parents? It was supposed to have been a gas explosion, a house fire, a terrible accident . . . no one's fault. What was happening? Her brain was struggling to catch up.

"Kill them," the tall man said to the one beside him. The emaciated man with the ponytail lifted his hands again and hurled a searing flame of fire towards Eyre. She raised her hands defensively and cowered down as Beatrice screamed.

A sudden hum and buzz filled the air, and an acrid, metallic smoke blew across Eyre's face. She looked up in confusion, realising she had not been blown to dust after all.

Streaking between her and the blistering spear of fire was a shining golden light. It formed a wide shield that stopped the flames from reaching her and Beatrice, and it resonated with a high-pitched hum, hovering half a metre above the ground, unmoving, and so bright it was blinding. Eyre clambered to her feet and looked in confusion for the source of the light.

She gasped in surprise as she saw Beatrice's mother, both hands raised, palms facing outwards, her feet planted solidly on the ground. The golden beam of light was coming from the centre of her palms, forming a solid barrier of light against the onslaught of pitch and fire that the three men hurled towards the girls. She was maintaining the shield as the flaming projectiles crashed into it, but the edges were starting to waver, and Eyre could see the effort it was costing her—sweat poured down her face, and her hands were trembling. Suddenly the barrier of light disappeared, and Mrs Edmunsun's shoulders slumped in exhaustion. But she stepped forward and quickly sent a searing rod of light straight through the creature with the ponytail, and he exploded into black smoke, shrieking as he disappeared.

The tall man snarled in frustration and sent a retaliatory blast of scorching soot at Mrs Edmunsun, but she deflected it with a quick flick of her wrist, and it rebounded at a ninety-degree angle into one of the netball posts, cutting it in two. The pole fell over with a dull clang, the netball ring hammering into the grass at the edge of the court.

Suddenly there was a violent explosion, and Eyre watched in shock as the creature with the buzz cut was hit by a searing lightning bolt that came from behind her and Beatrice, incinerating the thin man instantaneously so that all was left was a ball of roiling smoke. Eyre looked around in desperation, her thoughts ricocheting around her head as she tried to work out what was happening and where the new source of light had come from.

Striding across the netball courts was Peter Edmunsun, a shining crystal blade in one hand and his other palm aimed towards the remaining creature, the tall one. Peter Edmunsun fired another blast of lightning from his palm, a jagged bolt of silver that streaked towards the tall man. The creature flew up into the air to dodge it, and the lightning crashed into the cement behind him, sending deep cracks radiating outwards, all the way across the ten netball courts. Undeterred by the fearsome creature, Peter Edmunsun twirled the crystal sword above his head like a gladiator and as the creature landed back on the ground, he took aim.

"KAAR!" he roared. "Get away from my FAMILY!" He threw the crystal sword at the gaunt creature, but it ducked and sidestepped with surprising grace. Eyre watched the sword spin in sparkling windmills until it hit the cement and dug into the netball court up to the hilt.

Hissing in rage, the creature named Kaar returned a blast of fiery black soot that only missed Peter Edmunsun's head by a sliver. Mrs Edmunsun stepped forward to her husband's side and together they hurled huge waves of shining light back at the horrible creature.

With a screech of rage, Kaar suddenly streaked straight upwards in the air and there was a deafening clap of thunder as he disappeared.

Eyre looked around in complete shock, shaking in fear. She took in the cracked netball courts, the metal pole of the goal hoop seared in half, and the huge holes blasted into the cement. What had just happened? Her mind could not process any of it, and she looked up at the sky in bewilderment.

Dark clouds were churning above them, completely obscuring the sun. A wild wind was howling through the concrete expanse, whipping the casuarina trees at the end of the courts into maniacal forms. It was an eerie, unnatural sound, and Eyre felt a prickling across the back of her neck. Far across the road she could see the coloured tops of marquees being blown violently upwards and disappearing into the sky, and people running in panic for cover. Something evil was here, that much was certain. The old Labrador had felt it coming, and she could sense it now: a dark, malevolent energy filled the air.

Peter Edmunsun motioned urgently to the girls. "Come here, quickly. Hold on to each other. Kaar will be back very soon—with more Gothak. We must go!"

Eyre blindly grabbed on to Beatrice, and they held hands with Peter and Robyn Edmunsun, forming a circle.

"Now, Peter!" cried Mrs Edmunsun. There was a clap of thunder and a blinding white flash of light enveloped them. Eyre had a terrible sense of vertigo and swirling brightness.

And then everything went white.

CHAPTER FOUR

WHEN THE DIZZINESS PASSED, Eyre opened her eyes. She looked around in confusion—where was she? The four of them stood in an open space, and in the distance she could see stands of eucalyptus trees along the edge of dense bushland. Squinting as the light hit her eyes, she could see towering cliffs at the other end of the clearing. Five small wooden cabins squatted in a semicircle around the clearing where she stood, and the Edmunsuns' car, a blue Holden four-wheel-drive, was parked in front of the second-to-last cabin at the far end. As Eyre looked around, her befuddled brain trying to make sense of it all, Lachie exploded from behind the car, his short legs pumping as he charged towards them across the clearing.

"Mum, Dad!" he cried. "Was it the Gothak? Did you blast 'em?" He did a one-two motion with his hands, making accompanying exploding sounds. If it wasn't so close to the truth, Eyre would have laughed. Peter and Robyn's eyes met, a worried look passing between them, but Peter picked up Lachie and swung him around.

"Yes, but we all got away, and we're safe now. We're going to stay here for a while until we can get things sorted."

"Yay!" Lachie cried, jubilant. "In the mountains! No school!" Beatrice smiled.

"How did we get here?" Eyre eventually asked, the first question of about a thousand she had. Beatrice hesitated then looked at her father, who stepped in.

"Eyre, I understand you must be very confused by all this," he said. "And it's a lot to take in at once—we had hoped to introduce you to everything more gradually. Beatrice will explain a lot of it to you in the coming days. There's too much to go into right now. And if you have further questions you can always come to Robyn or me." His eyes took in her white face and stricken expression, and he continued.

"Your idea of what is normal in the world is going to change quite drastically from now on. Your parents were part of a group of people called 'Lightworkers' who have special talents and gifts. We are also Lightworkers, and there are many of us amongst the people you encounter every day—in fact, all around the world. We actually knew your parents well—we went to school together, and so did the other people who own the cabins here, which we call 'Highlight'. A terrible struggle has been going on in the last century between the Lightworkers and the Gothak, the creatures that you saw just now. The Gothak live in the Underworld—they want to destroy our world as we know it, and they are particularly hunting the Lightworkers. We were lucky today. We didn't lose anyone."

Eyre looked at Robyn slowly. "So my parents. . . ."

Robyn looked distressed and nodded. "I'm sorry, Eyre. The Gothak blew up the house while they slept. Your parents didn't have a chance. It's lucky you were staying with us, or the Gothak would have killed you too. Your Mum and Dad knew you were all in danger, which is why they were organising to move up to the Sunshine Coast near us, and why they sent you up ahead. But they just weren't quick enough to follow. I'm so sorry."

Silence fell on the group. Eyre was too confused and disbelieving to say anything, half thinking this was a joke, that she was being set up in some way. But the grave expressions on everyone's faces and the soot that covered them all were the evidence that proved Eyre's life had just changed irrevocably, whether she understood it or not. And there was a new and dark hatred starting to grow in the pit of her stomach alongside the grief that had taken residence barely a month ago.

Peter wiped his blackened face, smearing soot further across his brow, and looked at the shell-shocked group. "We can explain more to you, Eyre, in the coming days, but for now we need to get you all settled." He turned to Beatrice and continued.

"Mum and I must go and consult with the Echelon tonight. The Gothak have never been so bold before—appearing in the middle of the day, in an Entis suburb. This is a terrible omen. They're obviously strengthening in force, and we must go immediately to discuss what to do. You will be safe here. Jengles will light the Mantle tonight, and some of the others will be arriving tomorrow."

Peter and Robyn looked at each other, and Eyre could see they were exhausted. She realised that she too was aching with weariness.

"Come on then," Peter Edmunsun said. "Let's get you into your cabin." Eyre started to follow him, but she felt a wave of intense nausea, and bright colours started to balloon in front of her eyes.

"Peter—quick! She's fainting!" Robyn shouted. And then the ground swallowed her up.

✕✕

Eyre opened her eyes blearily and sat up slowly. She had been lying on a very soft and large sofa, her head buried so deeply in the side cushion that she had a pattern ingrained into her cheek. She rubbed at it distractedly as she tried to collect her thoughts. Someone had covered her with a soft patchwork quilt, and with a start of recognition she realised it was one her mother had made. The bright colours were so familiar Eyre clenched it in her hand as if it might bring her mother back.

She sat up and took her phone out of her pocket, but then stopped. Who was there to contact? She put the phone on the coffee table, feeling like she might cry. The only people she knew now were here with her—*Lightworkers*, apparently.

She looked around, trying to work out where she was, taking in the cacophony of colour that surrounded her. The sofa she sat on was covered in a heavy fabric with thickly woven threads—a riot of reds, greens, and blues.

She was inside one of the cabins—that much was clear. It was constructed of wooden logs, and it had beautiful leadlight lamps that glowed brightly throughout the room. It was cosy and warm, and she felt comforted and disinclined to move.

Footsteps sounded on the wooden floor, and Beatrice walked into her vision, carrying an emerald-green pottery mug, steam wafting upwards from the rim. Sometime while Eyre had been asleep, Beatrice had had a chance to clean up, because she had changed her clothes and her face was no longer black with soot. She looked amazingly relaxed, considering the events of the afternoon. Beatrice headed for the sofa opposite Eyre and then gave a start as she saw Eyre sitting up.

"You're awake! That's good. How are you feeling? Or is that a stupid question?"

Eyre shrugged and looked around, feeling conflicted. Despite the tranquillity of the room, she felt a rising irritation that she had previously known none of this, not from her own family or Beatrice's, despite the fact she had been living with them for a month already. Was it not important enough for them to tell her the real reason for her parents' deaths? And why would Beatrice know about Lightworking or whatever it was called— even Lachie knew, and he was only *seven*—when Eyre didn't have any idea about any of it? She looked at Beatrice flatly.

"Where am I? Well, I realise this is one of the cabins, but where *are* we?"

Beatrice sat down opposite Eyre. "We're in the Blue Mountains, Eyre. Not far from the town of Wentworth Falls, actually, if you've heard of that?" She didn't wait for Eyre's reply and swept on. "These cabins belong to Lightworkers, and we call our settlement 'Highlight'. This cabin is your family's." She stopped and corrected herself awkwardly. "Yours."

There was a silence as Eyre processed this fact.

"So how long has my family owned it then?" she finally asked, hoping that it might be a recent acquisition, which might somehow excuse the fact that her parents had seen fit to withhold such a huge piece of information from her.

Beatrice realised the reason for the question and looked uncomfortable, answering after a slight hesitation.

"The cabins have been here for twenty years. Your parents had theirs built when mine did."

No wonder her parents loved the Blue Mountains! Eyre felt suddenly silly, wounded deeply that she had been left out of this secret, despite the times they had told her how much they loved it there. But always said in a hypothetical way, in a *"wouldn't it be nice to go there"* way, not in a *"we own a cabin there and do so love to spend time there"* way. Spending time without her, obviously. Suddenly all the business trips her parents had made together made sense. She tossed the patchwork quilt to the end of the couch, as if somehow this small act of rejection would hurt her mother back.

"How long have I been asleep?" she asked.

"It's been two hours, Eyre. We didn't think you would sleep so long or we would have put you on the bed. And then we didn't want to disturb you. You've had a big shock. We all have." Sensing Eyre's anger, Beatrice started fussing. "Can I make you a cup of coffee? Mum and Dad came back with some supplies for the cabins. Your fridge and pantry are stocked. Ha— here I am offering you a coffee in your own cabin!"

"Well, you might as well make it," Eyre answered, trying unsuccessfully to keep the sharpness out of her voice. "You obviously know your way around better than I do."

Beatrice said nothing and headed back to the kitchen, situated just to the side of the small living room. Eyre watched as she clattered busily with cupboards and mugs and teaspoons, placing them on the kitchen bench.

The bench was made from a slab of cedar and it glowed with a high red sheen in the light from the lamps. It was carved from an irregular piece of wood, the bark still attached along the edge, and Eyre's heart clenched as she took in the three barstools in front of it. Suddenly her wounded rage melted into a deep grief, a profound yearning for her parents to walk around the corner and sit with her on those stools, for them to explain why they would keep this beautiful place a secret from her.

Beatrice returned with the coffee and Eyre took it, holding her hands around the glossy green enamel and feeling the warmth through the pottery.

"The others arrived while you were asleep," she said. "Abby and her Dad —you know Abby . . . well, her family are Lightworkers too. But Lachie's gone to stay with Grandma and Grandad for a while."

Eyre thought about this silently. She had met Abby, a short bubbly blonde who was Beatrice's best friend. They were like mismatching bookends—physically the opposite of each other, but complementary in a strange way. Eyre had only been at the new school for a week before she had to go back to Canberra when her parents were killed, but she had already met Abby quite a few times by then and experienced her wacky sense of humour. And Abby had lost her mother to illness when Abby was young, so she had been kind to Eyre. She understood what it was like to lose a parent. Abby and Beatrice were always together at school, and now, knowing this other part of their lives, it made sense.

"Their cabin is the one next to yours. And Whittaker Ray and Nick have arrived at Highlight, just now. They're the next one along, then ours."

Beatrice noted Eyre's startled look and nodded. "Yes, it's Mr Ray from school. He's been at St Jeffrey's for a couple of years. I hadn't met him before St Jeffrey's, and I didn't realise he owned one of the cabins. I don't think you've met Nick, yet. He's in our year, too. Mr Ray is a Lightworker —but Nick is not his son. He was at St Jeffrey's for a long time before Mr Ray came—Nick's been there since grade two. Mr Ray became Nick's guardian when Nick's father—uh, left. . . ."

From the tone in Beatrice's voice Eyre realised there was a lot more to the story with Nick and Mr Ray, but there was *so* much going on that Eyre hadn't known about, this was just one more piece in an increasingly complex puzzle. She suddenly felt exhausted; her mind could not keep up with it all. So much to take in at once, so much information, and so much of it completely unbelievable. She stared into her coffee mug.

"So who's in the last cabin then?"

Beatrice shrugged. "That cabin has always been left empty for Lightworkers to use if they wanted. I'm not sure who owns that one. There's never been anyone there when we've been here. Usually the only people here have been Abby's family, my family and uh. . . ." Once again she looked apologetic. "Sometimes your Mum and Dad. Whittaker Ray has never been here when we were here in the past. This is the first time."

Eyre thought about the weirdness of seeing the science teacher from St Jeffrey's walking around in this new reality of hers. No wonder he had made a point of saying hello to her when she finally went back to St Jeffrey's—he knew exactly who she was. Once again a sliver of betrayal wormed its way into her thoughts, but she determinedly ignored it.

"So what about Nick? Does he know about Lightworkers? And about Mr Ray?"

Beatrice thought about it. "Well, I don't know for sure, but I think not. He's never given me any sign he knew about us. If he didn't know before, I think he's probably going to find it just as hard as you."

And then Beatrice picked up Eyre's phone. "Ah, we don't use phones at Highlight, Eyre. We're supposed to be priming our energy to use telepathy, so beyond Entis—ah, that's *Earth*—communities, we don't carry them." She spoke hesitantly—not wanting to annoy her further, Eyre supposed. But after the shock of this morning, not being able to use her phone was the least of Eyre's worries.

She sat quietly looking out the window. A sudden knock at the front door interrupted her thoughts. Before either she or Beatrice could move, the door opened and Abby flew in like a swirl of butterflies. Her short, blonde hair was coloured pink at the ends, and her pretty face was alive with excitement as she flung herself onto the couch beside Beatrice.

"Hi, Eyre! By the Light, Beatrice, get out of school free! We're not going back, apparently—we're here 'til the TEPs!" Beatrice and Abby did a high-five, and Beatrice laughed delightedly. Over the month that Eyre had known Beatrice and Abby, they often said 'By the Light', or 'BTL' for short. Eyre had just imagined that it was their own eccentricity—sort of like a handshake in a secret club. *Secret club* was right, she thought dryly.

Beatrice shared Abby's joy about staying at Highlight. "Fantastic! We'll miss finals! That's brilliant!"

Eyre had no idea what the TEPs were but she was happy she wasn't going back to the Edmunsuns' place. After the horrifying day there and the unsettling night before she never wanted to go back—ever. And missing school was just fine by her. There were too many sympathetic glances and whispered conversations as she walked down the corridor, long silences in the classroom as students struggled for things to say to the new girl, the girl who had just lost her parents. Abby turned to her.

"I'm *so* glad we can finally talk to you properly, Eyre," she said. "It's been so hard, knowing you are one of us. You'll be coming to the Academy, I guess."

Eyre could only look at her blankly, and then there was another knock at the door. This time the person waited outside for Beatrice to open the door, and Eyre saw it was Mr Ray standing there.

He was an old man, but he stood very straight, and he had very blue eyes with a direct gaze from under white eyebrows that could only be described as *beetling*. Eyre guessed he would be about seventy, but he had an unusually youthful bearing; he moved with an energy that belied his age.

"Hello, Eyre," he said, speaking past Beatrice. "May I come in?"

After a second of surprise, Eyre nodded awkwardly, feeling disconcerted seeing him here, away from St Jeffrey's. Following behind him was a slight boy with a shock of blond hair sticking out in all directions. From the wan expression on his face, Eyre realised that he had probably got here the same way she had and that obviously he was new to all this also. He had the look of someone just whacked in the face by a wet fish.

"Eyre, this is Nick Richardson," Mr Ray said. "I'm not sure if you met at St Jeffrey's or not. He is my Ward."

Eyre shook her head and said hello to Nick, who just nodded briefly back at her. He had watchful eyes, despite his obvious shock, and he looked like someone who was ready to bolt at any moment should the need arise. Right then he obviously felt the chances of the need arising were fairly high.

"I need to go and meet with the Echelon," Mr Ray said, speaking to Beatrice and Abby. "Your parents are there already. Nick unfortunately has had no time to process all this, so I would appreciate it if you would help him to settle in. I realise this has been very difficult for both him and you, Eyre."

Eyre and Nick looked at each other, and Nick, expressionless, raised an eyebrow. *That's an understatement,* the gesture said, and Eyre felt suddenly relieved that she wasn't alone in this strange new journey.

"No problem, Mr Ray," Beatrice said.

"Thank you," Whittaker Ray replied. "Jengles will be here soon to prepare the fire. Don't draw attention to yourself until the Mantle is lit.'"

Nick finally spoke. "Actually," he said, "I can light a fire. I've done it a lot."

Whittaker Ray laughed softly and clapped him on the shoulder. "Right you are. But the sort of fire you'll be needing out here takes years of practise to perfect. Jengles is a Master Fireweaver. He'll have it going quickly, which is essential today."

Beatrice grimaced. "He may be a Master Fireweaver," she said, "but he's a rude old curmudgeon. I don't think he's ever said two polite words to me in his life!"

Mr Ray smiled. "That's the Mimir, Beatrice. Brilliant at working with their hands, but not so famous for their social graces. Just help him if he needs it. Otherwise, leave him to it."

Beatrice looked disgruntled but nodded as Mr Ray turned towards Nick. "Well, I had better go. See you soon. I'm very sorry this happened this way."

There was a bright flash, and he disappeared. Eyre's eyes had spots swirling in front of them, and Nick looked like he needed to sit down. Obviously he was just as unsettled by all of this as she was. As Eyre looked at him, she realised with a shock that his body was covered in scars: all over his arms and legs, smooth and shining, all sizes and shapes, some of them obviously the result of a major injury. Had he been in a terrible accident? Eyre wondered as she tried not to stare. But Nick's eyes flickered, and Eyre realised he had noticed her looking—he was obviously used to it. She looked away awkwardly.

"I might head back to my cabin," Abby said, "and get ready for dinner. Shall I meet you when the fire is lit?"

Beatrice nodded. "Great idea, I'll show Eyre around here and catch you a bit later."

"I'll head back, too," Nick said, obviously relieved at an excuse to escape. "Nice to meet you, Eyre. I'll see you all later."

CHAPTER FIVE

AFTER ABBY AND NICK had left, Beatrice walked back over to Eyre, who was still sitting on the sofa.

"Such a lot to take in, I know. Why don't you have a look around while I grab some towels for you."

Eyre slowly stood up, not sure where to begin. She still couldn't believe this amazing cabin was *hers*. It was bittersweet to suddenly have something so wonderful but at such a cost. She looked around and just decided to head towards one end of the cabin and work backwards.

She discovered that there were two bedrooms and she stood in the room that was obviously meant to be hers. The walls were clad with timber, and there was a diamond-shaped stained-glass window to bring light inside. The light danced through the glass as if a rainbow had exploded and scattered luminous bits of itself all through the room. Eyre trailed her fingers across the coloured patterns on the wall.

She walked down the hall into the kitchen and looked around the area that Beatrice had seemed so comfortable in. It was a welcoming, warm space with so many curious objects to look at: crystal goblets, bright enamel plates, a line of carved stone ornaments on the windowsill. But most striking of all were the cupboards; they had doors that were carved intricately with animals and plants, vines weaving their way through bunches of flowers, magpies taking flight, brumbies galloping across the plains; the doors were magical. Around the edge of the cupboard doors was a decorative, ornate border made up of the initials AER repeating continuously to form a border. In between each AER were double horizontal lines, then a vine and a bee symbol, and the border was inlaid with precious stones and crystals.

Looking up at the middle of the three top cupboards, Eyre felt a ribbon of pain thread through her. Carved into the wood of the middle cupboard were two initials entwined: A and R. Alia and Rufus, her parents. But then her eyes moved sideways, and she saw that in the cupboard door on each side of the central door, the initial E had been carved. Eyre felt a slight easing of the knot that had settled in the pit of her stomach ever since she had realised the huge secret her parents had kept from her. She lifted her hand and ran her fingers over the E in the middle of each door. At least they had been thinking of her.

"We did wonder who 'E' was, Abby and I," said a voice at her shoulder, and Eyre nearly jumped out of her skin. She turned to see Beatrice there, carrying some emerald-green bath towels.

"It's good to finally find out who you are! Your parents never talked about you much, although we knew they had a daughter." Beatrice put the towels on the end of the cedar bench. "Here you go. There's more in the cupboard down the hall, and there's soap and stuff in the bathroom cabinet. But before you have a shower, let me show you the attic! You *have* to see it!" She dragged Eyre down the short corridor to a little spiral staircase at the end of the cabin. It twirled up through the roof, a narrow set of stairs made out of chunks of wood. Pulling Eyre behind her, Beatrice went up the stairs and into a small attic. Dominating the room was a window that stretched from the roof to the floor. It was shaped like a diamond turned sideways, a huge piece of glass cut and placed with loving precision into a lead framework. Suddenly Beatrice stopped the babbling and looked at Eyre with tears in her eyes.

"I'm so sorry," she said. "I'm blathering. I really don't know what to say to you about all this. I can't imagine losing my parents, and then finding out about all—*this*. I just don't know what to say to you."

After a moment, Eyre rallied, her own eyes glistening. "No, I want to know," she said, although the pain in her chest was intense. "Please continue blathering. At least now I will know."

Beatrice huffed an awkward laugh and continued softly. "Well, the five cabins were all built by the same craftsman—he's famous, Stephen Dorf—but there's slight differences between them depending on what the owners wanted to put in there, and your dad asked him to install this panel in your attic. I've only been in yours a few times—mostly to come and see this window. Isn't it amazing? None of ours have anything like this. Apparently your Mum loved glass so much that your dad searched the whole world to find this panel for her. It took him many years, my Mum told me," she said, looking at it in wonder.

The window was indeed incredible. The panel depicted an intricate scene of creatures and people, breathtaking in its colours and the genius of its construction. Eyre looked at it closely in amazement—she had never seen glasswork like it. It was luminous in its beauty, and she could see no seam in the scene, no sign of how the colours had been placed to outline the figures and the landscape. They looked almost painted on, or rather *into,* the glass. Beatrice spoke softly.

"It depicts important events in the history of Lightworkers," she said. "And it was made three hundred years ago by the legendary Glasscrafter, Jolin the Second. Jolin's father's work is sought after also—he was Jolin the First, obviously—but he's not as well known as his son. People scour the earth for a single piece of Jolin the Second's work. Even a small vase is hugely valuable, and here you have a whole panel of it! It's a rare treasure."

A couch covered in tapestry had been placed against the wall opposite the window—obviously so people could sit and admire the glass. Beatrice and Eyre took an end each and looked across at the panel as the afternoon sun shone through it.

The details were intricately wrought—a peaceful scene where two people were drifting down a beautiful stream in a canoe. Then as Eyre looked at the panel, it suddenly changed and another scene appeared. Her jaw dropped in amazement, and she looked at Beatrice, not believing her eyes.

"Yes, isn't it incredible?" Beatrice agreed. "Jolin the Second introduced the technique of Transitioning into his art. Nobody had ever seen anything like this until Jolin did it. And actually, no one has ever managed to create artworks like his again."

They sat in silence for a while, watching the panels as they rotated through scene after scene of shining, detailed images. A faun here, sea scene there—someone fighting a menacing red creature with a huge sword, meadows with strange looking and unidentifiable creatures traipsing through them, side by side with Australian animals as well. It was a peculiar mix. Eyre kept looking straight ahead as she processed this information.

"So who looks after the cabin then? It looks so well maintained."

"Jengles does that. He's always kept it ready for them."

Eyre watched the swirling patterns, saying nothing, but her jaw tightened imperceptibly.

Beatrice turned towards her. "You know, Eyre, your parents were both members of the Lightworking Echelon, which is like the Lightworking Government in Australia. Every country has an Echelon. Maybe they kept you away from here to protect you."

"Yes, but so are yours, and they told *you,*" Eyre replied, frowning.

"I know, but your parents were different. I'm not sure what they did. It was something very secret, and they travelled around a lot. Whatever it was, it was never spoken about, but it must have been really important in the Lightworking world. Your parents were very respected. And because of that, I guess they were an obvious target for the Gothak. They would have had to be careful."

Eyre felt a surge of frustration. "Well surely, I would have been safer knowing *what* was out there, rather than completely . . . *oblivious* to it all?" She shook her head and then gestured around the cabin. "And how wonderful it would have been to have shared all this with them over the years, like you have with your parents!" Despite herself, her voice hitched. "Now I'll never get the chance."

Beatrice shrugged and looked away. "I can't give you an answer to that, Eyre," she said softly. "I never really knew them. But I do know that they were smart people. I'm sure they had a good reason for their decision."

Eyre looked back at Beatrice and softened. Somehow it helped that Beatrice hadn't known her parents well—although it seemed that Eyre had hardly known them, either.

"Yeah," she said finally, "I'm sure you're right."

They sat silently, watching the beautiful glasswork transform into one magnificent scene after another.

Eventually Beatrice shifted on the sofa and looked at her watch. "It's very hard to leave here once you start watching—so mesmerising! But I'd better get going. I'll see you a bit later. If you need anything you know where I am."

She headed down the stairs, leaving Eyre to gaze at the moving window as if somewhere in there she might find the answers to everything.

CHAPTER SIX

EYRE SAT ON THE couch reading a book she had found on a bookshelf against the wall, *A Guide to the Blue Mountains and Surrounding Areas*. She felt so much better after a hot shower; washing the black soot from her body not only made her feel cleaner, it somehow made the events of the morning recede in her mind, washing the horror away. She was feeling better, and the book was interesting, so she engrossed herself in finding out the history of this area her parents loved so much.

There was a knock at the door, and Beatrice came in carrying a plate of chocolate chip cookies she set down on the coffee table.

"Thought I'd bake some," she said, plonking herself on the couch and taking one herself. "It's still a while until dinner."

"Thanks," Eyre said, realising that she was hungry. Beatrice grabbed a book from the shelf, and they sat reading companionably, neither of them inclined to make conversation. The peace of the afternoon was soothing after the terrifying encounter with the Gothak. Eyre was reading about the legend of the Three Sisters rock formations—named Meehni, Wimlah, and Gunnedoo, when there was a sharp rap at the door.

"That'll be Jengles," said Beatrice, looking over her shoulder at the door and making no move to get up. "He said he'd come over this afternoon, grumpy old goat that he is. Don't take it personally."

Eyre pulled open the door and then stopped in bewilderment. No one was there. She peered around the corner and then looked down, realising that there was an immovable object, about a metre and a half tall, standing on the step before her.

"Get out of the way," it said. "Let me inside!" Barging rudely past her, a short solidly-built creature the colour and texture of a walnut barrelled into the cabin and sat down next to Beatrice on the couch.

"Hi, Jengles," she said unenthusiastically.

"Still haven't shrunk any, have you?" he said back to her. "Most unattractive, a tall beanpole like you." Beatrice rolled her eyes in annoyance but said nothing.

Eyre shut the door and stepped back into the cabin. Her eyes widened in amazement at the sight of the little being sitting on the couch next to Beatrice. Stocky and muscular, his skin was burnished brown and the texture of leather. Large coffee-coloured eyes were made all the more striking by red hair tied back from his face, and sprouting from his chin and woven into a thick fishtail plait was a fiery red beard that matched his large, bristling moustache. The beard was so long that Jengles had tied it in a knot towards the end, and it swung back and forth as he looked around. His red eyebrows were drawn in a bad-tempered frown until Eyre approached the couch, intending to sit down opposite him. As she moved past Beatrice and Jengles, the light shone through the window and caught the red of her hair, turning it into a fiery halo.

Jengles' face underwent a sudden transformation, and his eyes widened. Uttering an expletive of some sort (Eyre thought it might have been "Dimmog!" or something like that) he suddenly jumped up from the couch and raced over to her. She stepped back in apprehension, hoping he wasn't going to bite her—Beatrice had warned her they were cranky creatures. But he flung his muscular arm forward with a flourish and went down on one knee, his nose touching the ground in an elaborate bow.

"Ah, by St Ria, I didna realise that were you!" he said, standing up again and staring fixedly at Eyre as tears coursed down his face. "Just like your mother you are! So luminous! Precious, beauteous one. . . ."

Eyre turned in bewilderment to Beatrice, who was looking like she'd just run into a brick wall at high speed. Not knowing what else to do, Eyre patted Jengles awkwardly on the top of his red hair.

Jengles wiped tears away, and then he started and looked over at Beatrice, who sat on the couch in dumbstruck silence. He scowled and a look of embarrassment crossed his face as he stepped away from Eyre. Recovering himself, he stood to attention and saluted Eyre.

"The Mantle must be lit!" he cried. "Eyre is here!" And then suddenly he was gone. If there'd been leaves in the house, they would have swirled out the door dramatically after him.

Beatrice looked at Eyre, speechless. She had several attempts at saying something and gave up, just shaking her head. Eyre looked out the front door at the little form marching industriously around the firepit.

"Can we go and watch?" she asked Beatrice. "I know you've probably seen this a million times, but I don't know what a Mantle is, and I'd really like to see what he does."

"Sure," said Beatrice. "Jengles would want you there, no doubt. He obviously thinks you're a goddess of some sort. I've known him fourteen years and he's never said a polite word to me. Ever. Go figure."

They made their way down the polished front steps and out to the middle of the courtyard where Jengles was busying himself gathering wood. He was muttering as he rushed around, his red beard swinging left and right at the speed of his actions. Now and then he would look up at the darkening sky, a serious expression on his face, and then continue intently with his preparations.

Eyre stood watching him and saw Abby and Nick coming across the clearing towards them. Nick started in astonishment at the sight of the short but muscular being, but didn't say anything and followed Abby as she walked up to join them. As they approached, Beatrice looked at her watch and strode over to Jengles.

"Let us help you, Jengles," she suggested. "It's getting dark." Jengles ignored her, and she shook her head in irritation.

Suddenly he noticed Nick, and a nasty look came across his face.

"What's that then?" he demanded, pointing a finger covered in red hair at Nick. Rather taken aback, Nick looked over his shoulder, not sure if the short being was talking about him or not.

"Yes, you," Jengles said rudely. "I'm not talking about the door post!" He stomped over to Nick and looked him up and down, difficult from his height even though Nick wasn't very tall. "Although it *is* probably smarter than you!"

Nick was speechless and looked over at Abby, who was struggling not to laugh out loud. Beatrice appeared mollified at the sight of Jengles behaving in his usual fashion. Jengles put his hands on his hips.

"Well, make yourselves useful," he said sharply. "Get some wood. I need to fill the Mantle Basin. Stack the wood by the side." He indicated a metal firepit in the middle of the cabins' courtyard area. Then he turned to Eyre, and his face softened, adding, "You, my lovely, might like to come and watch me while they gather wood. It's important for you to learn about these things. Your mother should have brought you out here a long time ago. . . ." His voice drifted off as he spied a sturdy branch that had fallen from a eucalyptus tree, and he dashed off across the clearing towards it, as if it might escape if he didn't hurry. Beatrice's eyes narrowed as she looked over at Eyre, her temporary satisfaction at Nick's treatment by Jengles completely gone again.

"*This* is going to take some getting used to," she said evenly, then broke into uproarious laughter at the sight of Abby's flabbergasted expression. "That's right, my friend, I can't believe it, either!"

Slightly relieved that Jengles had left them on his mission to find the perfect piece of wood, Eyre followed Beatrice around, picking up armfuls of branches. They skirted the edges of the trees where limbs had fallen in the wind, and there were plenty of broken bits to haul back to the side of the firepit. Gradually the pile grew higher and Jengles motioned them to stop. He surveyed the wood carefully, as if he was looking at a blueprint, then slowly he selected a piece out of it and placed it carefully in the metal basin, as gently as he would lay something fragile and cherished. Examining the woodpile from all angles, he took a piece here, a piece there and laid them in an intricate pattern at the bottom of the firepit, recreating it into a wooden matrix. While he laid the branches, he talked to them as he would to a beloved person.

"There, my beauty, lie down quietly. So mighty, you are. I thank you for the gift of safety you give us."

The four of them watched as Jengles, still talking to the wood, placed the branches in criss-crosses, creating a sturdy tower that grew two metres above the rim of the metal basin. In order to place new bits of wood in the matrix, he had to climb up the existing tower to add another branch. Eyre looked at it in wonderment; she couldn't see how the whole lot didn't fall down. She watched Jengles select another piece of wood and nimbly climb up the tower to put it at the top. As she stood there with Beatrice, Abby, and Nick, Jengles spotted her and waved.

"Hello, my lovey! Won't be long, I'm nearly done! Can't have you getting cold!"

Beatrice rolled her eyes. "Unbelievable," she said. "The years of abuse we've put up with from that crabby little walnut, and suddenly Eyre finds his sensitive side!"

Abby giggled. "Well, I think it's hilarious!"

They all sat down on large sandstone chunks that formed seats around the fire, watching Jengles as he placed each piece of wood in the stack. Eyre found it fascinating, like watching an artist at work.

Suddenly a large dark shape swooped past them so fast they almost missed it.

"What was that?" Beatrice said sharply. Another black form appeared from the night and dove towards Nick. Before he could react, the creature had sliced him deeply in the shoulder with its sharp black talons, screeching shrilly as it flew heavily back skywards. Nick shouted out in pain, and the girls looked up to see more shadowy creatures veering towards them. Jengles dropped the branch he was holding and ducked as a huge black form careered past him, almost tearing his back with its vicious claws. With a horrified start, Eyre realised that whatever the dark thing was that had flapped by her face, it was the same as the awful creature she had seen staring in through her bedroom window at the Edmunsuns' house. Dread filled her as she saw that there was a whole sky full of them, circling in black swarms above her.

"*It's the Zyx!*" Jengles roared, bashing his hands at one of the low-flying creatures. "*Get inside. Quickly!*" Crying out in terror, the girls helped Nick up off the ground as dark forms streaked past them. Eyre dodged the talons of one of the creatures, but its heavy, hairless body slammed into her, knocking her to the ground. She had a quick sight of blood-red eyes and leathery wings before there was a sharp thud and a screech as the creature fell off her, speared by a long piece of wood flung from above. Jengles stood on the top of the pile of wood, watching as the creature died in front of her.

"*Get inside!* Hurry!" he shouted, reaching for another piece of wood. The grumpy old dwarf had disappeared. As he stood atop the branches he was suddenly a fearless and ferocious warrior. Eyre scrambled to her feet and helped Beatrice and Abby drag Nick up the steps of the Edmunsuns' cabin. Halfway there a swarm of Zyx crashed into them, sending them sprawling up the wooden steps. Nick ended up on the veranda as Eyre, Beatrice and Abby fought the horrible creatures off. And then two sturdy Mimir arrived and despatched the Zyx with furious blows as the girls staggered to their feet. Eyre's shins were grazed, and Beatrice held her shoulder, but they grabbed Nick and hauled him inside before the next Zyx swooped downwards.

Inside they slammed and bolted the door, then helped lay Nick on the couch. He had a massive wound that stretched from his shoulder to his navel, bleeding profusely. Abby raced to the bathroom and grabbed a towel that she placed over the deep gash and pressed down hard.

The bleeding slowed, but Nick was starting to shake with terrible tremors.

"It's the venom," Abby cried desperately. "Get the anti-venene, Bea!"

Beatrice ran into the kitchen and opened a cupboard door. Eyre could hear a frantic scrabbling as Beatrice searched through the contents before she ran back into the lounge room holding a vial of bright green liquid. As Nick moaned in pain, she poured the glowing medicine into his mouth. He fell silent, unconscious.

Beatrice felt his forehead, concern furrowing her brow. "I think we were quick enough. We'll have to watch him."

"What about Jengles?" Eyre cried, staring desperately out the window. She could hardly see him amongst the twirling black forms surrounding him. "We've got to help him!"

Beatrice put her arm around Eyre. "He'll be okay, Eyre," she said. "The Mimir have fought the Zyx for centuries and he's immune to their poison. Jengles knows what to do, and help will be coming." Her words were confident, but her mouth tightened as she looked out the window.

Jengles suddenly leapt from the top of the wood stack to the ground, his feet making a sound like a clap of thunder. He stomped his feet again, and again the clap of thunder rent the air. He kept stamping, and the air rang with the booming sound, sending the Zyx flying wildly in circles. Each time he stomped, streaks of lightning shot from his feet in all directions, and whenever the lightning struck a Zyx it shrieked, burnt to a crisp in a second. But before Eyre's fearful eyes, the number of Zyx seemed to be increasing, and she couldn't see how Jengles would survive the deadly onslaught.

Then, at the corner of her eyes, she saw movement from the ground. In the fading light a circle of earth, about a metre across, lifted upwards from the ground like a lid. As the booming of Jengles' feet continued, more and more circles lifted up, and as Eyre watched in amazement, dozens of stocky creatures like Jengles exploded from the ground. The Mimir, Mr Ray had called them, and they swarmed across the clearing, shouting to each other as they looked up at the swirling cloud of Zyx.

A Mimir with a beard braided into two halves lifted a lid in front of Eyre, just below the window, and as he clambered out, she could see inside it. It was like a tunnel that stretched down beneath the earth, with walls that were lined with glowing crystals in a rainbow of colours that seemed to throb with light. The Mimir pulled a glinting, curved weapon from behind his back, and the lid slammed shut behind him. More Mimir burst from tunnels scattered near and far around the clearing, each carrying a sharp weapon like a scythe, and they headed for the Mantle, where Jengles was fighting the Zyx ferociously.

"Give me a Crescent Blade!" Jengles shouted to the Mimir as he swiped away one of the screeching creatures. Someone threw him one of the sickle-shaped blades, and it gleamed as Jengles caught it neatly in his hand. As the Zyx whirled around him, he swung the weapon expertly, slicing through the leathery forms. He had a strange grace for one so short and squat, and the grotesque creatures fell before his lethal blade, hitting the ground in a black circle around him. Dozens of Mimir fought wildly in the darkness, cutting the Zyx from the skies. But they paid for their successes dearly; many of them had gaping wounds from the razor-sharp talons. Eyre was distressed to see some of the Mimir lying motionless on the ground.

"Watch Jengles," Beatrice breathed, her eyes fixed on the stocky creature. "He's lighting the Mantle." Jengles had put his weapon down and now seemed oblivious to the wildness around him. A battalion of Mimir stood guard, their flashing blades keeping the Zyx away as Jengles approached the pyramid of wood. He stood by the tower of branches, his hands resting gently on the wood at the base. Suddenly a wisp of smoke arose from beneath his palms, and he drew his hands away. Then, with a blinding flash, the rest of the wood caught. Not in flames of fire, but a burst of silver light that travelled from the lowest branch along the lines of carefully placed wood through the entire lattice, until the whole matrix was lit up in brilliant tendrils of light. Then with a huge *Whoosh!* the whole stack ignited and sent luminous beams radiating in all directions, like a lighthouse. Eyre's breath caught at the fierceness and power of the light; it was the most astonishing sight. The bright rays emanated out over the cabins and then dropped, forming a protective shield above them, blocking anything from entering. The lattice of wood remained shining brightly in the middle of the beams of light, like a silver matrix, so bright it was hard to look directly at it. Eyre could see dark shapes flying above the Mantle, but if they got too near they disappeared in a flash of sizzling light. Nothing was getting through that shining barrier.

Jengles seized his Crescent Blade and started to attack the Zyx again, his strong arms slicing through the dark forms. Underneath the light the Mimir fought wildly with the remaining Zyx until finally the numbers started to reduce. Leathery black forms piled up on the ground, their eerie red eyes open and staring.

After a terrifying half hour, the last Zyx was slain. An unnerving quiet descended on the courtyard, and the exhausted Mimir slowly came together around the Mantle Basin, leaning up against each other and helping the wounded to the centre of the clearing where they rested against logs. A low humming filled the air, a tuneful murmur that was soft and calming but powerful. Farther out some of the Mimir were removing the dead.

Beatrice opened the door, looking out carefully. Then she motioned Eyre and Abby to follow her. Abby covered Nick with a blanket before they left —he was still deeply asleep.

The girls sat on the logs around the Mantle Basin, listening to the rising sound of the humming as the Mimir took away their fallen and stitched up the injuries of those who had been slashed by the Zyx. With deft hands, they used long curved needles and what looked like fishing line to pull the edges of wounds together tightly. Eyre mused sadly that their skill at repairing the injuries probably came from years of experience, and her heart tightened at the sight of so many lying still out on the ground.

Eyre walked over to have a closer look at the pile of slain Zyx and was shocked to see that some of their claws still had flesh attached, ripped from the skin of the Mimir. She shivered as she surveyed the hairless, misshapen forms. These creatures looked like they had come from the depths of hell.

She sat back down and contemplated the courage it took to face and fight the terrifying beasts. "The Mimir are very brave," she said to Beatrice as the sounds of the melodic humming washed over them.

Beatrice nodded, looking over at the little figures. "Their name came from the legend of a Norse giant who guarded the Well of Wisdom in European lore. Well, they may not be giants, but they are huge of spirit and committed to the fight against the darkness. The Lightworkers would not be here if it wasn't for them."

After a pause Beatrice added quietly, "The Zyx coming is a sign things are very wrong," she said. "We've never had a breach here before. And I've never even seen a real Zyx, let alone so many of them. They're terrifying."

Eyre fell silent in tacit agreement. She shivered as she stared at the quicksilver lines of the matrix, shooting up to form the Mantle. The memories of the past day were scorched into her mind, and an unsettling fear of the unknown was growing blackly inside her, like an unwelcome companion she could never get rid of.

Suddenly Jengles appeared and walked towards them, carrying something in his hand. As he got nearer, Eyre realised it was a guitar, and then as he handed it to her, she realised that it was her mother's. She thought it had disappeared forever. She wanted to weep with sadness and yet felt incredible joy at the sight of the beautiful instrument. The memory of her mother playing to her so many times over the years was so strong, and a pain pierced through her as she stroked the beautiful inlaid marquetry along its honey-coloured sides. She ran her fingers slowly over the strings and the mournful tones of a minor chord lifted above the humming. When she was young, Eyre's music teacher had told her she had perfect pitch—an unusual gift where she could identify and sing a note at pitch. But she'd never been particularly adept at playing the guitar, although she'd tried. Singing was more her forte.

"Play," said Jengles.

Eyre looked up at him. "I can't play like my mother," she said wistfully.

"Play!" Jengles repeated, his eyebrows drawing together. Hastily Eyre placed the instrument across her lap. There was a silence as the humming stopped and everyone turned to her. The faces of the Mimir were all different—the size of their noses and the proportions of their features differed from face to face. But they all had the same walnut skin and red hair, brown eyes, and fiery red beards. Unique but similar, variations on a theme. She felt a sudden warmth towards them, these brave small beings who had fought so ferociously. They had won today and destroyed the evil creatures, but there was an ominous feeling in the air, a foreboding for the future that reduced them all to silence.

A song came to her and she spoke hesitantly, feeling the weariness of the crowd. "My mother taught me this song when I was young. I've always loved it, but I'm understanding it more lately." She began to strum the chords gently. "It seems right for tonight somehow."

Eyre wasn't able to pick out the individual notes on the strings as her mother had, but the soft strumming had a haunting quality to it. Softly she began the lyrics to the song, the melody rising like a lilting Irish ballad.

> *"When the world is in a turmoil*
> *and the fighting just goes on,*
> *when the blackness threatens, and evil boils,*
> *and all lightness seems to be gone,*
> *I will look out to your eyes, my love,*
> *and head towards their glow.*
> *When the darkness passes, as it always does,*
> *we'll be together again, you know."*

She began the second verse, and the gentle humming started again as the Mimir joined in, their brown eyes, lost in their own thoughts, staring into the silver fire. As Eyre's pure voice rose into the still night, a sudden disturbance in the air made them all look up. There was a gasp of astonishment as even the Mimir were surprised into silence when a swarm of fireflies flew in and formed a bright nimbus above Eyre's head. This was hardly the most surprising event of the past few days, so Eyre ignored it and kept singing as the golden lights danced above her. Her hair blew in the slight breeze, catching the light from the silver matrix in gleaming red streaks.

> *"So don't give up, and don't despair,*
> *though times ahead be troubled.*
> *The Light will guide us over there*

till we rebuild the rubble.
Our spirit will soar high above
whatever foul wind rises.
And I will wait for you, my love,
till the Aura once more guides us."

Again the Mimir joined in, and Beatrice looked amazed to see tears running down Jengles' wizened face. As the humming faded away Eyre finished the song and put down her instrument. There was silence, and then all the Mimir bowed to her. They made an odd gesture with their hands, the thumbs and pointer fingers on each hand touching each other, and called out to her in unison:

"The Light will Endure. Inguz!"

Then slowly, one by one they slipped away, disappearing down the holes in the ground until only Jengles and the girls were left.

"The Mantle will protect us now," Jengles said, looking out at the darkness. "The Mimir will clear the carcasses of those foul beasts overnight. They will be gone by tomorrow." He turned to Eyre and came over to kiss her hand. "Inguz, Fair One," he whispered, and then disappeared. One minute he was there, the next he was gone. Eyre shook her head in bewilderment.

"Eyre, come and stay in my cabin if you like. We have an extra room," Abby said, understanding Eyre's confusion.

"Thanks, Abby," Eyre said after a moment, as she looked out into the unfathomable night. "But I think I'd really just like to be alone right now."

CHAPTER SEVEN

EYRE WOKE THE NEXT morning and stretched in her bed. Her arms touched the smooth, carved bedhead, and turning over she traced the form of a dingo embedded in the wood. Semi-precious stones and shards of coloured glass were set into the red cedar, and they glowed in the morning sun streaming through the panels of stained glass. Eyre wondered if anyone else had slept in this bed before her. So many mysteries, so much she didn't know. She sat up and pulled on her clothes, wincing as her muscles protested. She had scrapes and bruises from the night before—throwing herself through the front door to escape the Zyx, and to save Nick, had been unavoidable, but it certainly had painful consequences. She bent over gingerly and put on her shoes before heading towards the kitchen.

The kitchen was alive with a myriad of rainbow colours streaming through the windows, and she felt strangely peaceful. No matter the reasons her parents had never brought her here, this little cabin was a sudden connection with them that made her feel they weren't entirely gone. There were echoes of them everywhere: in the colourful art glass ornaments; the many books covering a wide range of topics that stacked the bookshelf— both her parents had loved to read; the large, sturdy chair under the window that Eyre knew must have been her father's; and, of course, her mother's guitar, which now stood in the corner of the room, glowing quietly. This cabin was *hers*, and she felt a poignant joy. She might not have her parents, but at least their memory was alive here.

She pottered around in the kitchen making toast and a cup of tea before settling down on the couch. A clatter up the front stairs outside announced a visitor, and Beatrice barrelled through the door and sat opposite her on the sofa.

"Hi, Eyre, how're you feeling? Are you as sore as I am?" Beatrice rubbed her shoulder tenderly. She propped her long legs up on the coffee table and surveyed the large black blotches on her skinny legs. "Gorgeous!" she announced.

Eyre nodded ruefully and displayed the motley array of injuries on her own legs. "I feel like I've been hit by a train."

Beatrice grimaced in sympathy. "Me, too, but I think Nick's feeling it the worst. He's okay but very slow this morning. Lucky though. If you don't take the antivenom within an hour it's too late—the toxin from the Zyx will kill you. Nick is resting this morning. It'll take him some time to recover."

Eyre grimaced, horrified to think of the pain Nick must have gone through.

There was a silence, and then Eyre held out her silver necklace. She had found that she couldn't take it off; it was permanently around her neck. Now that she'd heard about Light energy, she understood that this was something more complicated than just a faulty clasp. So she opened the locket a bit awkwardly, as the chain wasn't long, and showed the photograph to Beatrice. Eyre ran her fingers over it lightly. "I'd really like to know some more about Lightworkers," she said eventually. "I mean, what do we do? And how do you know someone's a Lightworker . . . and—" She broke off and looked at Beatrice. "I don't even know the right questions to ask."

Beatrice leaned forward. "I know this must be confusing. I'll try to help you understand. But where to start?" She thought for a moment. "Well, Lightworkers have been around since people have been around. We have always been part of the normal population, but no one knows about us. Our goal is to keep Light energy flowing, to make sure that good prospers in the world, and that the Dark forces do not take control.

"And the Gothak—the Dark side—" Beatrice continued, "equally wants destruction and mayhem in the world. They want disease and pestilence and wars and pain. They feed on those things, and the Zyx are just one of the many foul creatures—Strigis—that they breed to help them achieve that.

"The Dark Forces have been ascending this century because of a terrible treachery. The Aura—a powerful Light force—once stretched around the world, a source of hope and positive energy. But it was destroyed after one of our own betrayed us to the Gothak, and the Aura was broken up, scattering light around the world. Remnants of the Aura are still here, but they are now so rare. Those of us who have one, protect it fiercely. So now Lightworkers are working to figure out how to reform the Aura, while fighting to make sure the Gothak do not continue to rise." Beatrice looked out the window sadly. "It's been a terrible battle, and many people have been lost over the years. I'm sorry that your parents were amongst them, Eyre."

Eyre was silent for a long, dark moment. Finally, she spoke. "And the Mimir? Jengles? They're part of this?"

Beatrice nodded. "Fortunately, the Lightworkers are not alone. There are magical beings in the world, the Mimir included, that fight for good alongside us. The Mimir are ancient earth creatures, guardians of the soil and its treasures. They have allied with us to try and prevent the Gothak from rising. Jengles hates them so much! He would dance on their carcasses if he could. Actually," she added dryly, "I thought Jengles hated everyone—until you arrived, that is!"

Eyre leaned back, her head so full of questions it was hard to get any out. "So can you make light come out of your hand like your Mum can?" she finally asked.

Beatrice shook her head. "You don't get your Light energy—we call it Viq—until you're a bit older. We go to a school called The Academy of Light to learn how to use Lightworker skills. But not everyone gets Viq, and you're not automatically accepted into the Academy. It's complicated. We have to go through an assessment program first. School—the Academy—officially starts in February next year, but students who will be in first year go to orientation and assessment at the beginning of December. There're a few Light Institutions around Australia, but our families have always gone to the Academy of Light. A lot of people want to go there, so you have to apply. Abby and I are really hoping they'll accept us. You undergo assessment while you're at orientation, and if they want you they'll offer you a place for next year. My dad will take us there when it's time for orientation."

Beatrice smiled apologetically at Eyre, who was playing with the locket distractedly. Eyre's face reflected the confusion she felt.

"I know this sounds unbelievable," Beatrice said softly, "but there's no other way to explain it It just *is*—and you're part of it."

Suddenly the photograph fell out as it had once before. The silver backing followed, fluttering to the ground beside it.

"I'm going to have to fix that," she said, reaching down.

Beatrice leaned forward suddenly. "Wait, let me see that!"

Eyre picked up the photograph and handed it slowly towards her.

"I've already showed you this. . . ." But Beatrice shook her head and Eyre put the photograph on the coffee table, not sure what Beatrice was talking about.

"No, not that, the silver backing," Beatrice said, reaching down for the shimmering oval of paper. She looked at it intently, turning it over. "I think it might be—" She looked up, eyes shining. "It is! It's a Peragro! Wow." She passed it back to Eyre, who looked at it carefully. It was definitely pretty, but it just looked like a shining oval of silver paper to her—nothing unusual about it that she could see.

"It's a message, Eyre. Only the person it's intended for can read it, and only when they're on their own. You have to look at it when no one's around, but you have to hold it for a few seconds. If it's meant for you, you'll be able to read it. It's made out of Light Paper—it's very special. Mum and Dad receive them occasionally from the Echelon. Light Paper is used only for the most secret messages. But don't put it down until you're ready—once you put it down it disappears."

Eyre held the pretty paper in her hand like it was a priceless document. A *message* for her? She scarcely dared to hope, and joy sparked in her eyes. "I hope so," she whispered. She put it carefully on the coffee table beside the photograph of her parents and sat back, trying to process all this information.

Beatrice stood up and gave her a hug. "I'll leave you to look at the Peragro—and I know you'll need to think about all this. I can't imagine how you're feeling. I'll go and check on the others, then I'll come back shortly." She looked at the expression on Eyre's face. "I really hope there's a message for you, Eyre," she said. "Inguz. It means blessings. I wish you blessings in your life with us—and I'll help you with everything."

Beatrice waved at Eyre and headed out the door. Eyre watched her go, starting to believe that kindness could indeed be a physical force in the world.

CHAPTER EIGHT

AS THE DOOR CLOSED, Eyre held the photograph, thinking about all the information she had been told. She studied the faces of her parents, feeling like she'd never known them. So many secrets. And to have everything outlined so matter-of-factly only increased the weirdness factor. She put the photograph back in her locket and closed it, her head spinning.

Beatrice talking about Dark forces, and magical beings, and a broken Aura in that pragmatic tone was more than unsettling; it made Eyre wonder if she was actually out of her mind and imagining everything. But the silver paper on the table sat in witness to the authenticity of her conversation with Beatrice, and Eyre picked it up, turning it over to see that both sides were definitely blank. A surge of disappointment ran through her, and she was about to put it down when the paper suddenly started to heat up, almost to the point of burning her fingers, and Eyre gasped as black writing appeared on one side of the paper. With a pang, she recognised her mother's handwriting and she ran her finger lightly over the words.

Cabin Lightkeeper

She turned the paper over, but there was nothing else written on it, so she put the paper on the table and sat back, trying to think. Suddenly the silver oval began sending off rays of light until the Peragro was shining so brightly the message was obscured, and Eyre could barely look at it. Then the rays began to dim and when eventually the light snuffed out, the paper was gone.

Eyre concentrated on the words she had seen, trying to work out what they could mean. Cabin Lightkeeper. What sort of message was that? And why was it such a secret, worthy of the 'very special,' as Beatrice called it, 'Light Paper'? Well, she was undoubtedly at the cabin already, so that parwas clear. But what on earth was a 'Lightkeeper'? How could she look for something when she didn't know what it was? She considered calling Beatrice back, but decided to have a look through the cabin first; perhaps something might be obvious—maybe a candle holder or a torch of some sort. She stood up and wandered through the halls, checking each room as she went.

Finally, down the end of the hallway she found a small doorway that looked like a broom cupboard, but when she opened the door she saw that inside the cupboard was a small staircase spiralling downwards, similar to the one that had led up to the attic. Eyre slipped in through the door and stepped into the gloom. As she went through the doorway she felt an intense cold wash over her, a blast of frigid air that stopped as soon as she reached the first step. She continued downwards, and a line of blue crystals lit up along the walls, glowing brightly enough to light her way. Eyre looked at the pretty lights, wondering whether a 'Lightkeeper' might actually refer to the row of blue crystals. Perhaps the Peragro's message was intended to help her find the basement?

She reached the bottom and squinted into the shadows. Then, as she stepped off the final step, more crystals above her and on the walls lit up, and the room was filled with the light from glowing blue crystals, dotted around like stars. It was pretty and peaceful, and Eyre relaxed as she looked around.

She could see that the basement was filled with cardboard boxes, and against the walls behind the boxes, there were the irregular shapes of chairs and furniture packed tightly together. Walking to the nearest box she opened it and saw that it contained a pile of her mother's clothing. Opening the next box, she found familiar kitchenware, and then another that was stuffed with the contents of their linen cupboard. With shocked recognition she realised that these boxes had come from her home in Canberra. But how could that be when her house had burnt to the ground? She looked more closely at the stacked cartons and realised that there was writing on the sides of each box. Her mother's neat writing listed what was inside each box—confirming that the basement contained all the contents of her old home. Eyre felt a huge joy take hold of her. She had moved around so much in her life that her possessions and the well-loved furniture were hugely important to her every time they moved to a new area: *they* were the infrastructure of home, rather than the house they occupied. Even her old oak sea chest was there. And to her delight she could also see the shape of her ancient piano sitting behind the pile of boxes. The boxes and the furniture must be what her mother had wanted her to find—her parents must have transported everything here before the Gothak burnt down their house.

As she looked at the labels on the stacked cartons, Eyre's heart contracted; the familiar handwriting that reminded Eyre so painfully of what she had lost was ironically now cataloguing all the things she had suddenly found.

She sat down amongst the boxes, intense emotion spearing through her. It was a searing mix of anguish and joy—a terrible grief at the pain of losing her parents mixed with the inexplicable joy of finding these precious possessions and memories intact. Tears ran down her face as she cried for her parents and for herself, for the life they would never have together.

Eventually the tears stopped and, her heart heavy, she decided to head upstairs. But she stopped at her old chest and ran her hands over it lovingly —an old friend who had suddenly reappeared, risen from the dead. It was a family antique that had been handed down for generations in her family, a solid old sea chest from the 1880s, made with curved panels of wide-grained oak that glowed golden in the light. When she was younger she had stored all her most special things in it: photographs, seashells, special letters, her battered teddy. She opened the chest, expecting it to be empty, but was surprised to see a small octagonal box about ten centimetres wide nestled in the bottom. There had always been a strange depression constructed into the base of the chest, an octagonal hole that Eyre had often wondered about. She noticed that the little box fit perfectly into the depression; the cavity held it snugly so it couldn't move. Lifting the little box out, she marvelled at its beauty. It was cut from crystal with many sharp facets that sparkled in the light. The lid and bottom were an unusual purple-blue colour, and inlaid into the lid was a strange symbol made of shining gold:

Eyre looked at the symbol closely, wondering if it meant anything, or if it was purely decorative. The centre of the intriguing symbol was filled with sparkling white crystals. Holding up the glowing little box, Eyre turned it around and around, marvelling at the craftsmanship that had created this beautiful thing. She'd never seen it before and wondered where her parents had kept such a treasure.

Eyre worked out that she had to swivel the lid to open it and peered inside expectantly. She was a little disappointed to find it empty, but as she went to shut the lid again, a voice reverberated around the basement.

"Eyre," the voice said softly. With an explosion of disbelief, followed by incredible joy, Eyre realised it was her *mother's* voice, and she looked around frantically.

"Mum?" she cried desperately. "Where are you?"

"Eyre," said the voice, "sit down and put the box on the ground." Confused, her heart soaring, after a moment Eyre obeyed, looking around desperately for her mother.

The blue crystal box began to glow, and Eyre gasped as bright light radiated outwards from it. The rays began to form a shape; eventually the image of a person emerged on the ground beside the little box, about a metre high and completely made of light beams. It was her mother, but it wasn't . . . and she realised with astonishment that it was a hologram of her mother's image, brightly lit and moving, a haunting 3D ghost from her past.

Eyre stared dumbfounded as the figure turned around in slow circles. Then it stopped, facing towards her. Her mother's image spoke.

"If you're seeing me here, then I guess I am dead." Eyre's breath caught in her throat, and a tear coursed down her cheek. The hope that her mother was somehow alive was extinguished, and the crushing pain was immense.

"I am so sorry, darling," the small figure continued. "I had hoped you would never see this message, but it seems that we have gone to the Light earlier than we expected."

Eyre rubbed her eyes and watched the hologram image desperately. It might not be her mother alive, but it was still an image of her beloved face, and the voice was totally her mother's. Another form suddenly emerged from the light and joined her mother.

"Hello Eyre," said her father's voice, "we wanted to tell you this in person, but recently events have been dire, and we knew we must put this together in case the worst happened. Obviously it has, if you are seeing us here. I am sorry that we're not with you. But we knew you would work out the Peragro."

With help, Eyre almost answered, but stopped, realising there would be no reply.

"Eyre," her mother said, "do you remember the cylinder on my necklace?" Eyre reached automatically for the chain and looked at the hollow silver object. She ran her fingers over the ornately carved surface and waited for her mother to speak again.

"It's called a Tone Blow. You can take your necklace off when you're near your Lightkeeper. Blow the Tone Blow." Surprised, Eyre tried to undo the clasp of her necklace and found she could indeed take it off now. So she picked up the cylinder and blew tentatively through it. A pure note sounded through the basement and suddenly on the ground before her an object materialised—not a hologram—a real *book*!

About half a metre square, it was very worn and covered in ancient leather, with designs of creatures and vines inlaid into the dark cover. Pieces of irregularly shaped gold and semi-precious crystals studded the design and formed a frame around the edge. She saw the book had many pages, and she sat down in anticipation to read it. But frustration flitted across her face when she realised that a brass lock bound the book; it needed a key. Gritting her teeth, Eyre turned the book around and over, seeking a way to open it. As she huffed in frustration, her mother's hologram spoke.

"Don't smash the book, Eyre," her mother laughed softly. "The key on my necklace will open it." Eyre smiled ruefully as she wiped more tears from her eyes. How could she forget the key on her mother's necklace? She had looked at it so many times over the years. She took the silver key, the one with the strange purple-blue gem set into the end of it, and realised that whatever the stone was, it was the same as the crystal used to craft the crystal box. Obviously they went together, and now that she looked at it more closely, she could see that it was indeed a functional key. She had always thought of it as a strange old piece of ornamental jewellery.

Eyre's father spoke again.

"We want you to know that we love you so much, and you are so precious to us. You are a special, clever, loving girl, and we know how brave you are. You will need that courage in the months and years ahead."

Her mother nodded. "The Lightworkers will look after you and help you find your way. Be strong, my girl, and when you need to escape or gain strength, come in here and talk to us."

"Use the book," her father said, "to find out the truth and the history of our family and the Lightworkers. It is the Lightward-Tyson Wisdom, your heritage. We wanted to tell you some of this ourselves, but the book will help you to understand, now that we are unable to illuminate you.

"You are now the guardian of the Lightward-Tyson Wisdom. The book will reveal its truths when you are ready for them and when the time is right for the journey. You can't force it or rush it. Treat it with reverence— it is priceless beyond words. And you must *never* remove the Lightkeeper from the basement. We have used the strongest wards known to Lightworkers to protect the basement and keep the Wisdom safely guarded."

Slowly the holographic images of her parents began to turn around, hand in hand.

"We have left many messages for you in here, Eyre. Live with courage and Light, my love," whispered her mother. Her mother's voice hitched, emotion overcoming her. Eyre looked at her beloved father as he spoke, his face sad.

"Be strong, my special girl, until the day we eventually see you in the Light!" The holograms faded and disappeared, leaving Eyre holding the old family book in her lap. Unable to believe they were gone again, Eyre cried and cried, her tears washing down over the cover of the book.

Eventually the tears did stop, and she rubbed her sore eyes. She examined the lock and key. When she tried, she realised that the silver barrel of the key was carved out in furrows that slotted perfectly into the grooves of the small lock. She turned it carefully; it made a soft click as the lock sprung open.

Eyre held her breath and opened the book. The front page was dedicated, in her mother's writing, to her.

"To our beloved daughter, Eyre," she read. "We will always love you. Fight the Darkness with whatever skills you have, whether Lit or Unlit. You are the most special soul. Live with courage and Light. Mum and Dad."

She loved seeing her mother's beautiful handwriting, and she passed her hand slowly over the words, wondering what 'Lit or Unlit' meant. Something else she would have to work out. But having the message there meant so much, and it helped greatly with the pain she had of never getting to say goodbye. She would cherish this one page forever.

But turning the page she was overcome with disappointment. It was blank. Desperately she riffled through the following pages, only to find they were all blank too. What help was a blank book? Eyre thought wildly. It was such a letdown, just when she finally thought she was going to get some answers. She stared at her mother's message as the familiar frustration began to rise from the pit of her stomach. Then suddenly more words began to appear underneath the message, materialising on the page. Squinting, she made out her mother's writing again.

"And your greatest power will come when you learn to control your temper ☺. Everything in good time." She started to laugh softly. Her mother knew her so well, her impetuousness and her need for things *fast*. Even from the grave she was anticipating Eyre's reaction. Feeling a bit ashamed, Eyre realised that the book was not something she could read in one sitting. She was going to have to learn patience, perhaps her biggest challenge in life, and the book would give her information as she was ready for it. It was comforting, in an odd way, to realise this, almost as if she had a mentor again, someone wiser and stronger than she, guiding her way. Resolving to be patient, she closed the Lightward-Tyson Wisdom carefully.

Suddenly she sensed a great peace and a feeling that she had not completely lost her family filled her heart.

Eyre sat for a long time in the muted blue glow of the basement, hoping that something else would happen. But she realised there was nothing more to come today. Eventually she heard a voice from the hallway above.

"Eyre? Eyre? Where are you?" Beatrice called from somewhere above.

"Down here, at the end of the hallway," Eyre shouted.

She heard Beatrice approaching the small doorway. "Come down the stairs, Beatrice. I'm in the basement!"

Beatrice stopped at the top of the stairs. "I can't!" she called down. "The door has been warded! I need you to come up and let me in."

Eyre stood up slowly and walked up the stairs. "Why?" she said. "What do you mean?"

From the other side of the doorway Beatrice looked at her. "If the doorway has been warded, it's been locked by energy vibrations. In this house, only you or a relative of yours can get through this ward—your aura is in sync with the vibrations, and it lets you through. The only way I can come through is if you pull me! Give me your hand, and I can get through—my energy waves will link with yours."

Eyre put her hand through the doorway, and Beatrice grasped it. Then Eyre pulled her through. Beatrice grimaced as she felt the icy blast from above. "That is so unpleasant," she said, shuddering.

"Come and look what I found," Eyre said, dragging Beatrice down the steps. "All my family's stuff is here—my chest, photos—I can't believe it! I thought they had all been destroyed in the fire. And the most amazing thing of all—wait till you see this!"

They came down the stairs, and Eyre looked at the floor in surprise. The book had disappeared, and the lid was now shut on the crystal box. Picking it up slowly she showed it to Beatrice, the little object glowing in the palm of her hand.

"This was in my old oak chest!"

Beatrice looked at it in amazement.

"BTL!" she whispered. "It's your Lightkeeper! It's so beautiful!" Gently she took it from Eyre's hand and looked at it in admiration as the crystal facets caught the light, sending beams of blue and violet in all directions. "What a masterpiece," she said in awe, holding it up. "The box is made of —" she squinted, "—ohhh, it's tanzanite! It's so beautiful! That's to help with spiritual perception. The vibrations from the crystals affect your aura. And that gold symbol on the lid is called an Inguz." She peered closer.

"Wow, those are diamonds in the middle!" She looked at Eyre in wonderment. "Isn't it *gorgeous*!"

She twirled it slowly around in the dim light, and it seemed to emit a violet-blue pulse, almost like it was alive. "What an incredible thing."

"It's what the Peragro told me to look for," said Eyre. "I didn't know what a Lightkeeper was. I thought it might be those crystals on the walls." She took it back from Beatrice, and they both watched as the little box seemed to glow with an inner light.

"When I opened it there was a hologram of my mum and dad in there. They told me how to get our family's book out of the crystal box. They called it the Lightward-Tyson Wisdom. Tyson was my mother's maiden name. But when you came down the book disappeared."

"That's because no one else is able see the contents of your Lightkeeper," explained Beatrice. "The Lightkeeper guards your Wisdom. Everyone gets a Wisdom, which records the genealogy of your family and other information about past generations. It's personal to your own family, and the information in a Wisdom is private. You normally get a Lightkeeper and your Wisdom when you turn twenty-one, unless your parents . . ."—she looked apologetically at Eyre, ". . . pass. My Wisdom is called the Edmunsun-Starr Wisdom, and I've never seen our Lightkeeper. There's a special ceremony, usually on your twenty-first birthday. Obviously your mother left you the Peragro so you could find your Wisdom if anything happened." She looked at Eyre's tear-stained face. "I'm so sorry something did happen, Eyre."

Eyre smiled crookedly. "Well, it's nice to know I can see them when I want to. That helps." It was true: to see the images of her parents, in whatever form, had somehow lifted the terrible darkness she had suffered since the news of their deaths.

Beatrice smiled back at her. "Well, I came to see if you wanted to come for a walk. I thought it might be nice to get outside for a while."

Eyre realised that she would love to get some fresh air—she had been down in the basement for quite some time. She went to follow Beatrice back up the stairs, but not before casting a last look at the precious belongings in the basement.

As they went up the stairs the crystal lights dimmed behind them. By the time they reached the top it was completely dark in the basement. Eyre pulled Beatrice through the doorway and then closed the door softly, her heart lighter than it had been for weeks.

CHAPTER NINE

EYRE AND BEATRICE crossed the small courtyard, past the Mantle Basin with its lattice of wood, and headed to the cabin opposite, where Eyre could see Nick sitting on the step. As they walked towards him, Abby came out the door of her cabin and clattered down the steps, singing at the top of her voice. Today she had tied coloured beads in her hair, and turquoise-coloured feather earrings dangled from her ears. Leather bracelets adorned both wrists, and a long necklace holding a Celtic rune swung side to side as she bounced across to them.

"Ah, I see you're ready for a bushwalk," Beatrice said, deadpan.

Abby chuckled good naturedly. "I know, I know. Can't help myself."

Beatrice and Abby began to discuss the best destination for a hike and Eyre sat beside Nick on the step. He was very pale, with cuts and scrapes all over his body, and the pallor of his skin showed bruising, in sickly green smudges. He had a large slash across his shoulder that had been patched with butterfly strips—a jagged wound that ran to his navel. She saw the old scars all over his body, too: round circular ones, long ones, others irregular, lumpy, and raised from the stitches that had repaired the wounds—a smorgasbord of awful mementos.

Eyre gave him a sympathetic look. "So I guess the hundred-yard dash is out of the question?"

Nick smiled. "Doubt I could do the two-yard dash today," he replied. He could obviously sense her curiosity about the scars all over him, and he added carelessly, "I've always had scars, I had an accident apparently when I was young. This can join them, a lifelong souvenir of my encounter with the dastardly Zyx." He looked down for a moment at his chest. "Goes well with the ones I got from dear old Dad and my old friend from school too. Nothing new here, but I'm a bit sore."

As Eyre wondered about dear old Dad and the unnamed 'friend', Abby and Beatrice walked over to them. Abby looked at Nick, concern showing on her pretty face as Beatrice patted him gently on the shoulder.

"Abby and I were talking, and we think that it's time for a trip to the Buyabarra Billabong. It will help you feel so much better. Come on!"

Nick stood up gingerly and followed as Beatrice led the way across the clearing towards a sandy track running through the gum trees. As they reached the edge of the clearing, Eyre experienced a strange sensation, like a small electrical shock. She jumped, looking around her.

Beatrice laughed. "It's the Mantle, Eyre. You can't see it during the daytime, but it's still there protecting our settlement. It gives you a buzz when you go through it. It's the energy waves. Doesn't it feel weird?" Eyre nodded, rubbing her arms. "You'll see it at nighttime," Beatrice continued. "It shimmers in the dark. The Mantle also hides our cabins from the sight of normal people flying over or travelling through—we're invisible when it's up." Eyre looked back as they continued walking, but she couldn't see any sign of the Mantle. It was good to know it was still there though. Anything that kept the Zyx away was worth a little zap—and it was also nice to know that the cabins were secure from prying eyes.

They followed the track as it meandered upwards, the heat of the day making the scent of eucalyptus very strong. Beatrice looked back at them as she led the way.

"So, Nick, I guess Abby has explained about Lightworkers and the Academy to you?" Nick nodded and flashed a look at Eyre, but said nothing. *What could he say?* thought Eyre, mentally shaking her own head. Beatrice smiled, understanding.

"You'll get used to it eventually. It's a lot to hear about all at once. We've grown up knowing these things, so it's no wonder you're finding it strange. One day is not much time to learn about it all. When we get to the Academy you'll get a lot more information about everything." She stopped suddenly and turned to face them.

"Eyre, you were probably going to apply to the Academy when you were old enough, even if you didn't know it," she explained. "It's where your mum and dad went. They were there with my parents, so you would have gone there, too, I'm sure. But Nick, apparently you're going to orientation as well, which is a really unusual thing. I don't think it's ever happened before to have a normal person there . . . I mean," she added apologetically, "one who isn't the child of a Lightworker. Dad said Whittaker Ray has organised for you to be considered, and I'm not sure why, but the school agreed. Maybe because you're his Ward and because of the respect they have for him."

Abby joined the conversation. "Next week we all leave for orientation at the Academy. Beatrice's dad is going to take us." She sighed. "Now *that* is going to be interesting."

At Nick's enquiring look, Beatrice explained. "Children of Lightworkers stay in a normal school until we are about fifteen. We don't know until we go to the Academy and go through training whether or not we will actually, what we call 'Elevate' or not. This is when our Light force—or Viq—ignites within us and gives us our Lightworking power. Before then, we have no special skills, and we can't tell who will Elevate, no matter who your parents are. Not all Lightworkers' children have the powers themselves. Some people stay Unlit."

Looking from Eyre to Nick, Beatrice realised that this was not actually making things any clearer and she tried again. "People who don't Elevate are still Lightworkers, but they are called the 'Unlit' and they stay in the Lightworking community. It's not at all dishonourable if you don't Elevate. In fact, many of the old families are quite proud of the Unlit in their family trees—many of them have been accomplished spies and couriers. It just means you serve the community in a different way. I guess that's where you'll go, Nick, to the Unlit Division, even though you're not a Lightworker. We don't know much about what they do in the Unlit Division—only members of the Lightworking Echelon know that. It's all kind of mysterious and secret—"

She broke off, laughing as she realised that Abby had slipped behind a tree and was stalking them as Beatrice spoke. Abby sprang dramatically from behind the next tree and Nick grinned. His face looked so different that Eyre realised it was the first time she had seen him smile since he had arrived. Beatrice carried on talking, obviously used to Abby's antics.

"Actually, families differ in how much they tell their children about Lightworking and the Academy before they Elevate. Because our families are together all the time, and part of the Echelon, we know more than other Lightworker kids." Here she looked uncomfortable, and her eyes glided away from Eyre. "But not all families are the same as we are—so you two won't be alone."

Eyre realised as Beatrice spoke that the secrets her parents had kept no longer bothered her. At least they had left her the Peragro, and probably they would have told her about everything if they had moved up to the Sunshine Coast with her. Right now Eyre was more interested in finding out as much as she could, and she was glad Beatrice and Abby seemed to know so much about the Lightworking world. But she was feeling rather disoriented. That a whole world could exist like this, be so closely aligned with her own family, and to have had no idea of it was very unsettling. It was going to take a while for it all to sink in.

It was getting hot standing on the track, so Beatrice suggested they keep moving, and they began to trek up the trail again.

Nick was very silent as they walked. Eyre turned the new term 'Unlit' over in her mind. Although Beatrice had said there was no shame if a Lightworker's child remained Unlit, something about it didn't sound so good. 'Un' anything didn't sound so wonderful to her; that some people might be able to have these fantastic skills and some might not. But she decided that she didn't know a lot about it and that obviously the Lightworkers held the Unlit in high esteem—no doubt it would become clearer as time went on. As she tossed all this information around in her mind, another thought came to her, and she wondered why Whittaker Ray had never let Nick know about any of this. After all, Beatrice had said Nick had been living with Mr Ray for two years, and he'd obviously never been here with Mr Ray. Another question with no answer. Her head hurt thinking about it all.

The track was getting steeper, and it was getting harder to move along. The flat track had given way to small rocks and boulders, and they had to clamber up them to keep going forward. It was becoming more like rock climbing than hiking, and Eyre was beginning to sweat a lot. It was so hot, and the arrival of the unrelenting blowflies was making the walk really unpleasant. She was beginning to wish they hadn't come after all when they finally crested the hill.

Eyre gasped. They stood on a cliff, and far below them was a beautiful water hole, deep green in colour and surrounded by trees that leaned over banks with tiers of sandstone rocks. It was quiet and peaceful, a mysterious oasis in the middle of the heat and dryness. Her body ached to slip into that cool water, and she wiped her brow.

"How do we get down there?" she asked Beatrice. Beatrice walked over to the edge and looked down. It was about ten metres down, and she contemplated the high rocky cliffs surrounding the water.

"We normally come from the other direction," she said, catching Abby's eye. "There's a flat area down the end where we can sit and relax. Somehow we've ended up taking the high road. It's been a while, and I missed a turn off, I think. So I guess we'll just have to climb down the sides. It'll be hot work—and hard."

Eyre and Nick groaned. They were already so sweaty and uncomfortable. Beatrice looked at them with a mischievous smile.

"Or," she said, holding out her arms, "you can get down like this!" Before Eyre and Nick's startled eyes, she leapt with a whoop off the cliff and plummeted into the water hole with a loud splash. After what seemed a long time, she rose to the surface laughing.

"By the Light," she yelled. "It's *gorgeous*! Come on, jump!" Abby laughed gleefully and leapt out into the air.

"Bombs awayyyyyyy. . . !" she shouted as she hurtled down into the water.

Looking carefully over the edge, Eyre tried to assess the likelihood of death or maiming by jumping from this height. Seeing both Abby and Beatrice treading water gave her a bit of confidence, so closing her eyes, she leapt as far out as she could. Her stomach dropped as she fell. After what seemed an eternity she splashed through the surface of the water. The sudden coolness felt blissful after the searing heat of the day, and she kicked upwards. As her head broke the surface she called to Nick, "It's wonderful Nick, come on!"

Nick needed no more encouragement, and he threw himself off the cliff with enthusiasm. "Geronimoooo!" he shouted as he plunged like a lead weight into the water. He surfaced spluttering and laughing, and the girls splashed him wildly. They swum around in the cool water, washing off the sweat and dirt of the walk, and they let their tired muscles recover from the long hike. Eyre turned over and floated on her back, looking up at the sky. It was exhilarating to be in this mystical place with the ancient sandstone cliffs above them and the beautiful old gum trees surrounding them. Whispers of spirits, of stories past, seemed to echo around the canyon; she could almost see their fingers ruffling the surface of the water. Only the wind, she thought . . . but lately, who would know?

They finally dragged themselves on to a large, flat sandstone rock and lay there as the sun dried them off. A wonderful lassitude had come over Eyre, and she closed her eyes. Before she knew it, she had fallen into a deep sleep.

CHAPTER TEN

SOME TIME LATER EYRE woke and realised that she'd slept for quite a while. Shadows now fell across the sandstone rock, and there was a coolness in the air. Sitting up, she yawned. She felt wonderful—rested and clear-headed, better than she had felt for a long time. Her muscles were free of pain, her whole body felt strong, and to her great surprise, even her bruises had disappeared. She stood up and stretched, savouring the feeling of energy that filled her body. She saw that Beatrice, Abby, and Nick had also dozed off—and they lay asleep on the rock beside her. She reached down and shook Beatrice gently.

"Beatrice," she whispered, "do you think we should go?"

Beatrice sighed and turned over, opening her eyes slowly. She sat up and looked around, smiling. "BTL, I love this place," she said. "Don't you feel fantastic?"

"It's getting a bit late, though," Eyre said. "It's four o'clock. We should get going, don't you think?"

Beatrice gave a start and jumped to her feet. "Four o'clock? We definitely have to go! We've got to be back before dusk, and it's going to take us an hour and a half, maybe an hour if we hurry." She reached over and shook Nick and Abby awake.

"Sorry guys, but it's time to leave. We *have* to get going!" She started to walk around the billabong to the side where the rock started to heighten leading up to the cliffs. Examining the rocks, she made a decision. "I think this is the quickest way up, come on!"

Nick leapt to his feet and took off at a trot after Beatrice, and as he passed her, Eyre saw that, like her, his dark bruises were gone and so were all the scratches and cuts on his body. His wound had healed completely, leaving just a smooth scar across his shoulder. There was definitely something wonderful in this water, she decided.

Eyre and Abby followed Beatrice and Nick around the base of the billabong and started the climb up the rim towards the top of the cliff. It was hard work, and Eyre was grateful that she was feeling so strong.

"What is that place?" she asked Abby. "It's healed us all! Can it fix anything?"

Abby looked at her and shook her head. Somehow those feathered earrings had survived the jump into the billabong, and they swung back and forth as she spoke. "It can't fix major injuries. It's more like a tonic for your body. It heals small things, but mostly it revitalizes your energy level. It's said that the billabong will keep you sleeping for as long as it takes to heal you." She chuckled, looking at the lengthening shadows. "Obviously we needed a lot of fixing!" Then she looked at her watch and a worried look skimmed across her face. "It's just as well. I think we're going to need all our energy to get back in time."

They finally reached the top of the cliff and turned inland down the track. The growing shadows galvanised them and they clambered fast down the rocks, panting with the effort. Eventually the boulders and rocks gave way to the sandy track, and they headed through the bush at a slow run, ducking under branches and jumping over tree roots. After a half hour they were feeling the effects of the heat and the constant running, and Eyre's feeling of well-being lessened the farther from the billabong they got. She looked into the depths of the bush and realised that the peace of the afternoon had given way to an ominous quiet. All the birds had stopped calling, and there was no sign of any wildlife. It was like the silence before a thunderstorm, but there were no clouds in the sky above, just a weighty stillness in the air.

"Hurry up, we've got to get home!" Beatrice urged, glancing around her wildly. Eyre nervously scanned the sky, fearful of seeing the dark shapes that would announce the Zyx were arriving.

Suddenly her hairs stood up at the back of her neck, and she stopped as she heard a deep growl emanating from the bushes about twenty metres behind them. Turning, she panicked as she saw a pair of widely-spaced red eyes peering balefully out from the bushes. A knife of fear sliced through her as Eyre realised that they were being stalked by something huge and definitely not well meaning.

"There's something back there!" she whispered, keeping her eyes on the bushes. The other three stopped and turned to see what it was. As they saw the bushes start to move, they walked backwards up the track, too fearful to take their eyes away from the trees. Then there was a savage snarl and the crashing of breaking branches as something monstrous charged towards them.

As it emerged from the foliage Eyre saw with horrified disbelief that the creature was as large as an ox but resembled a black panther with grotesquely deformed muscles. Gleaming teeth gnashed, and drool slavered down its face as its powerful muscles contracted, driving it towards them at immense speed.

"By the Light," Beatrice breathed. "It's a *Saevus!* Quickly, *run!*" She took off, and the others followed close behind. Fear ran like a bolt of energy through Eyre's blood and spurred her into a panicked dash down the path. Beatrice with her long legs, and Nick, who was a natural runner, covered the distance easily, but Abby and Eyre were slower and they struggled to keep up. They were falling behind, but then Eyre recognised the light from the compound, and she pumped her legs harder.

Gasping for breath, her feet flying over the sandy track as she followed her friends, Eyre finally saw the perimeter of the compound approaching, and in the darkening evening, the glimmer of the blessed Mantle shining outwards.

"Hurry, *hurry!*" Beatrice cried over her shoulder from up ahead. "We're almost there!"

Abby was breathing hard, her breath ragged, and as she started to slow down, Eyre realised in horror that she wasn't going to make it in time. A wild panic rose in her as she willed Abby to move faster; she could hear the Saevus slavering behind them, and she expected at any minute its huge, sharp teeth would sink into her. But then suddenly Abby appeared to launch through the air as if given a huge shove, flying three metres and through the safety of the Mantle. She landed in an ungainly way, flat on her face, and lay for a moment stunned in the dust.

The terrifying snarling behind Eyre gave her the impetus to put on an extra spurt of energy, and she dove through the silvery light just as the creature reached the perimeter behind her. Roaring in frustration, it circled just beyond the light, fearsome teeth snapping, tail flicking. It slunk back into the night just as the first swarms of the foul Zyx began to swirl through the skies above the treeline.

Abby stood up, wiping dust from her face and gasping for air. "Thanks Eyre," she said.

Eyre, who was bent over almost vomiting from the run, looked over at her, puzzled, but too winded to speak. "What for?" she asked when she could finally take a breath.

"You pushed me! I wouldn't have made it if you didn't."

"I didn't touch you," Eyre said, confused. "Are you sure you didn't trip?"

"No," Abby said, with a strange look on her face, "it was you. Can you do telekinesis?"

"I never knew telekinesis was a real thing," Eyre said in between gasps as they all staggered towards the cabins, "so how could I actually do it?"

The subject was abruptly forgotten when they encountered a very bad-tempered creature stomping towards them, almost, but not quite, as frightening as the creature they had just left behind.

"Are you completely mad?" shouted Jengles. "Well, I know you're stupid, but I would have at least given you credit for knowing when you should be back here!" He was frothing at the mouth with rage, and his red beard swayed back and forth as he gesticulated wildly at them.

"What would your parents say to me if I lost you? You know Saevus have been seen in the woods!" he screeched. "I oughtta use this foot of mine to give you a good kick up the—" Suddenly Jengles caught sight of Eyre, whose mouth was hanging open at his verbal onslaught. With a change of expression that was nothing short of miraculous, he raced towards her and fell to his knees, clasping his hands in front of him.

"Thank the Aura you're alright!" he cried. "St Ria be praised!" Eyre stood awkwardly as Beatrice rolled her eyes at Abby, and Nick just looked confused. Finally, Jengles got up, and, his brows forming a very angry line across his weatherbeaten face, he clomped off, muttering darkly as he looked back at her friends.

Eyre shrugged helplessly, and Beatrice shook her head in bewilderment as she watched the fiery-haired little curmudgeon disappear down his hole.

"Go figure," she said in a bemused voice.

Abby chuckled. "Well, his passion for you Eyre deflected his rage at us, so I think it's a good thing!"

"Oh my god," Eyre said in an awed tone, rubbing her forehead, "a Saevus? What *is* that? It was terrifying!"

"A Saevus," Beatrice said, shuddering, "is one of the Strigis. They've been sighted in the bush around here only this year. I've never seen one before, but there've been regular reports of them appearing around the rest of the country. They usually only come out at night, which is why we are, ahem, supposed to be back before dusk. They're only hunting for Lightworkers, normal people won't usually see them." A flicker of sadness crossed her face. "We're not the only ones ever to be out later than we should, but we are amongst the fortunate ones who made it back. Jengles was right, I should have been more careful." She shook her head. "We were lucky this time."

"Where do the Saevus and the Zyx go?" asked Eyre.

"We're not sure," Beatrice replied. "But we assume they go back to the Underworld—where the Gothak are—through a Seam. It's all so recent, these sightings of Strigis and the Gothak. Mum saw a Saevus earlier this year, and Jengles warned us they were out there, so we knew to watch out for them. But although the Zyx have been seen in other places we've never had them here at the cabins before."

Abby had been nodding solemnly as Beatrice spoke, but then she clapped her hands, her sunny smile back again. "Well, we survived the Saevus, good on us! We've got to celebrate! Come on, let's go and get changed, then I'll get some dinner for us. It's time for a barbecue and some music!"

Nick made noises of agreement, and each of them headed towards their own cabin.

"Dinner at six!" Abby called.

CHAPTER ELEVEN

AS DARKNESS APPROACHED THEY sat around the Mantle Basin, tucking into a barbeque that Abby had organised. Beatrice had set up some music in her cabin and it played softly in the background as they sat and talked. Everyone was sun-kissed and glowing; the trip to the billabong had energized them all and filled them with vigour, despite the pandemonium at the end of the hike. As Eyre remarked on this, Beatrice replied with her mouth full, "The Buyabarra Billabong is an ancient place. Somehow it resets the health zones and re-energizes your aura. It facilitates your body's healing and also rebalances your meridians. It has to do with biorhythms and energy fields—apparently the billabong sits above a famous ley line. Lightworkers travel there from far away to revitalise and heal themselves."

Eyre raised an eyebrow. "Well, I'm not sure if I understand all that, but it sounds like it's good for you, and I certainly feel fantastic."

Beatrice smiled. She took another large bite and continued, almost unintelligibly. "'Buyabarra' means quartz stone. And if you look at the rocky cliffs around the waterhole, you can see flashes of light from the quartz embedded in the sandstone rocks. We go down to the billabong all the time when we're here."

"Well, I'm definitely going again," Eyre said, "but I might aim to be back before dusk next time! I don't think my heart could survive another encounter with a Saevus!"

Nick suddenly spoke.

"So . . . the Academy?" he asked Beatrice and Abby. "Can you tell us about it?"

Beatrice laughed at him. "Warn you, more like it! It's hard work, that's for sure. The Academy is a school for the children of Lightworkers, both the Lit and Unlit. The Unlit students go into the Unlit Division—or the U.D. —where they study intensely with specialist tutors. Because the Unlit don't have energy or Light skills, they are trained in the use of their mind—sort of like intelligence and strategy. You're not a Lightworker, Nick, but I guess that's where you'll go if the Academy accepts you."

"Some of the smartest people in the community have been from the Unlit," Abby said. "There was even a Head of School once who was Unlit."

"All of us," Beatrice continued, "go into training as soon as we get there. It's always the beginning of December, and it goes for ten weeks. During the ten weeks we start to learn Lightworker skills, and we're given some basic training so that we can undertake the TEPs—that's Training, Evaluation, and Placement trials. The training is really hard apparently. Then, if you Elevate, you take the trial, which takes a day, and then you get your placement."

"So," Eyre said slowly, "how do you know if you Elevate or not?"

Beatrice and Abby looked at each other, and a trace of worry crossed their faces. Obviously, thought Eyre, they both want to Elevate. There might be no shame in being Unlit, but their faces made it evident that all students attending the Academy would probably want to Elevate.

"Well, what happens," answered Beatrice, "is that when you Elevate—which means you become eligible for the trials—an Inguz will appear on your skin at the top of your arm." She pointed at a spot just below her shoulder.

Nick looked curious.

"What's an Inguz?"

Beatrice picked up a stick and drew a symbol in the dirt.

Eyre recognised the symbol—it was the same as the one on the lid of her Lightkeeper.

"What does it mean?" she asked. Beatrice looked up at the sky for a moment and was silent, as if it was a big question. Finally, she replied. "Well, I guess you could say that the Inguz is the essence of the Lightworker. It's a word we say that sort of means 'blessings', but it's also the rune of connection with the earth—the harmonious relationship between us and the four elements: earth, air, fire and water. It reconnects our bodies, our minds, and our spirits as one entity, and it is the most sacred symbol to our people. It's a sign of great power."

As if the silver matrix could hear Beatrice, it burned more brightly for an instant, sending a silvery flare across the clearing. Eyre stared into the shining lattice, watching the lustrous lines of light as Beatrice continued speaking. "So if your Inguz doesn't appear before the TEPs you are not eligible to take the tests. At that point, you go home. The Dean of the Unlit Division will select students from those who have been involved in the training to join the U.D. at the Academy of Light next year. But, you know, it's as much an honour to become part of the U.D. as it is to be invited to join the Academy as a first year Lightworking student."

Nick spoke up. "How does it appear? The Inguz," he asked. "Is there a procedure?"

Abby shook her head. "No, it's just random. The symbol appears any time during the TEPs. Nobody really knows how it all happens really." She laughed and looked at Beatrice. "I guess it's a bit nervewracking waiting to see if you get one."

Beatrice nodded silently in agreement, her eyebrows creasing. *They desperately want to Elevate*, thought Eyre, *and, I do, too! I really want to have those skills!* She looked sideways at Nick, wondering how he was taking this and whether not being a Lightworker would bother him. But he seemed relaxed enough, sitting quietly with no expression on his face.

"What about the placement?" asked Eyre eventually. "What's that?"

Beatrice tossed her stick away.

"When you get your placement you are put into a Sector. The Sector indicates the Lightworking skills you are strongest at. Over the years the Academy will work to help you develop those skills."

"And we're at the Academy for three years," Abby said. "Four years if you undertake a graduate year. At the end of each year there is an assessment and exams, and you need to pass those to get into the next year. It's pretty hard," she added, "and sometimes even dangerous."

A silence descended upon the group as they contemplated this information. Eyre's head was spinning. Out of one new school and into the next! Only these classes would be a little different than maths and chemistry. Telekinesis and teleportation? Unbelievable.

Suddenly, as if someone had read her thoughts, there was a flash of light, and two people appeared in a white flare at the side of the cabin. As the brightness dimmed, Peter and Robyn Edmunsun strode out of the light. A second later another flash lit the area, and a man Eyre didn't know appeared. Then there was a third blaze of light, and Whittaker Ray stood by their side.

"Dad!" Abby raced over to the unknown man and gave him a hug, and Beatrice did the same with her parents. Nick went to greet Whittaker Ray, and Eyre stood a little awkwardly until Robyn came over and wrapped her arms around her tightly.

"Hi Eyre," she said softly. "I hope you're getting on okay." Eyre hugged her back, glad they had returned.

Jengles suddenly appeared from behind the cabins, bustling over importantly. "About time you got here!" he huffed in an irritated tone. He stood in front of them all, looking like a grumpy teacher facing an unruly class. Even Whittaker Ray looked chastened. Then before anyone could speak, Jengles spotted Eyre standing behind everyone. "Ah!" he cried, and shoved past the adults until he reached her and knelt on one knee in front of her. "How are you, my beauty?" he said as he bowed his head to the ground, hand extended. Peter Edmunsun blinked and then looked at Beatrice, who raised her eyebrows and shrugged as if to say, "I *know!*" Whittaker Ray looked hard at Eyre, and Abby's father smothered a laugh.

"You seem to have an admirer," he said. "But then, Jengles was always very fond of your mother." Eyre looked embarrassed and wrung her hands. It seemed to be the only thing she could do; how *should* one respond to such adoration? She felt totally ridiculous.

Fortunately, she was saved when Jengles stood again and strode over to the metal dish where the matrix lattice was shining brightly. He picked up pieces of wood and carefully placed them into the silver lattice of branches, muttering to himself importantly. Each branch flared in a bright line as it joined the matrix. There was silence as everyone watched him, and then Robyn motioned for them all to sit.

Whittaker Ray walked to the front.

"We heard that the Zyx attacked the night you came," he said. "We wanted to come back sooner, but Jengles assured us that everyone was safe and the Mantle was well lit, so we stayed away another night. The Echelon meetings were long. Lightworkers came from many countries, and we needed to discuss the way forward from here. The Gothak have breached Seams in many places and attacked a number of our people." He turned to Beatrice and Abby. "You saw a Saevus this afternoon?"

The girls looked slightly uncomfortable.

"Yes, it was our fault," said Beatrice, and Jengles harrumphed sourly.

"We were out too late," added Abby. "But Eyre saved me. She used telekinesis!"

Despite Eyre's protestations that she hadn't done anything, everyone turned towards her. The adults exchanged looks, but no one commented.

"She did!" Abby said stubbornly, looking around. "I know what it is, and she did it!"

After an awkward silence, Whittaker Ray spoke again, a grave look on his face. "We need to be very vigilant from now on. It is obvious that the Gothak are more active again. They have released the Strigis in many locations. For some reason, they do seem to breach more often at this time of the year. We have come back because we are expecting to see the Gothak tonight. They may try to attack the campsite. Their Dark energy is so powerful; they throw fire, and magma, and black soot called atra and it burns like the inside of hell." Eyre clenched her jaw: she knew all about *that*. She'd seen it first hand, but she kept silent.

Whittaker Ray continued. "However, they should be kept out by the Mantle, and the Mimir are at the ready. We've prepared for a quick exit should they get through." He paused and looked at the younger ones. "You must be ready to go with us at any moment. Stay close, and be prepared."

Eyre felt a dread creep into her stomach. The memory of those frightening creatures rose in her mind—that weird cracking as they walked, the greenish-white pallid skin, and those awful, dead black eyes. Whittaker Ray didn't have to tell her to be alert; she would forever be looking for sinister shapes in the shadows. But she realised suddenly that she also burned with a dark and ferocious determination; the fierce part of her that had often caused her trouble in her previous life had flared up within her, undeniable and powerful. She might be afraid of them, but she hated the Gothak to the depths of her soul, and she would always be searching for a chance for revenge. Abby seemed to think Eyre had done something back there . . . well, Eyre was equally convinced she hadn't, but she would relish the chance to shove the Gothak right back where they came from. If telekinesis or any of these other Lightworker skills could help her to do that, then the sooner she got those skills the better!

Silence descended, and everyone sat around the Mantle, each with his or her own thoughts. Despite the sombre mood, it was peaceful, and Eyre enjoyed the feeling of being with the group. Robyn organised mugs of hot chocolate, and everyone sipped at the steaming liquid as they stared out into the darkness, waiting.

They spoke quietly at random moments, watching the sky and the perimeter, and the tension rose as time went on. But after several hours no Zyx or Strigis had been sighted, and the Gothak were obviously not coming.

Whittaker Ray stared out into the impenetrable blackness, an unreadable look on his face. Almost to himself, he spoke softly. "I really had expected them to come. They know we're here. But they won't now. I wonder why. Where are they? And what are they doing?" But he spoke without expecting an answer, and indeed no one replied. Eventually he stood and took a last searching look outwards. "I might turn in," he said. "Come when you're ready, Nick."

But everyone was ready by now to finish up, and they all said goodnight. Eyre headed towards her cabin with a strange happiness. Despite the solemnity of the evening, she had a sense that she was heading *home*.

CHAPTER TWELVE

EYRE PICKED UP A slice of pineapple and took a bite. It was delicious—sweet and perfectly ripe, part of a platter of tropical fruits that had been prepared by Robyn Edmunsun. It was the day of the trip to the Academy, and in honour of that event, and to celebrate everyone being together again, a lunch buffet had been created in the clearing. A couple of long tables held a selection of fruit, cheeses and breads, and Peter was cooking sausages on the BBQ by their cabin. The smell wafted over to her, and her mouth watered.

The past two weeks had gone quickly. After a couple of uneventful days, the adults had headed away to rejoin the Echelon in strategic planning, leaving Beatrice, Abby, Eyre and Nick at the compound with Jergles as supervisor.

Eyre had finally sorted through all the boxes in her basement and spent some time looking through her cabin—and those of the others. The cabins of the Edmunsuns, the Wilsons (Abby's family), and Mr Ray were constructed in the same layout as her cabin. But they had none of the lights or elaborate woodwork of her family's; they were more functional in décor—still very comfortable and attractive, but she now understood why Beatrice said she had always been so keen to come and see Eyre's cabin. Eyre hadn't looked through the last cabin—the cabin that Beatrice had said was always unused. No one suggested she go there, and Eyre hadn't brought it up. It didn't seem right to go through someone's place when they weren't there.

Eyre had gotten to know Abby a little better and found that, despite being a chatterbox who loved to talk about everything, Abby was also a good listener. They'd had quite a few good conversations in Eyre's little cabin. Nick was more reticent, harder to know. She hadn't learnt much about him in the past couple of weeks, but it had been nice having someone there who was just as uninformed as she was about the

Lightworkers—there had been so many questions. She had spent quite a few days walking through the woods with Nick, Abby, and Beatrice, visiting the Buyabarra Billabong again and trying to recover after their dramatic arrival here. In the following two weeks the Gothak had not been seen again, and no Strigis had appeared, either. The Mantle had remained lit for the entire time, but even the ever-watchful Jengles had stopped his endless patrolling of the perimeter in the past couple of days. It seemed that for the moment the breach was over.

Eyre looked at her friends tucking into their final meal, and she suddenly felt quite nervous. So much lay ahead of her. Part of her wanted to stay in this lovely compound in her family's beautiful cabin with the magical billabong nearby and never leave. She'd had such a peaceful, happy time here in the past couple of weeks, and it had been a long while since she had felt so at ease. But part of her also wanted to go to the Academy and get started—to find out her destiny.

She had opened the Lightkeeper again quite a few times when she had been in the basement sorting through the boxes, and she had sat for some time with the Lightward-Tyson Wisdom in her lap. To her joy, she had discovered that on the first blank page of the Wisdom, a complete transcript had appeared of the words her mother and father had spoken to her. It was a permanent record that Eyre could read whenever she wanted, and something she had looked at often over the past couple of weeks. But there had been no new messages from the hologram, and the rest of the old book's pages remained blank. She was happy to see her mother's and father's images again, though; they were comforting in a strange way. She would happily watch that hologram over and over forever and read their words in the Wisdom—even if the Lightkeeper gave up no more messages.

Last night the adults had arrived back at the compound, giving nothing away as to what had happened during the Echelon meetings. But they seemed very tired—obviously the two weeks had been intense for them.

Whittaker Ray interrupted her thoughts when he came and sat beside her, regarding her with his enigmatic blue eyes. "So how are you doing, Eyre?" he asked. "I suppose you might be feeling a bit nervous today?"

Eyre nodded but didn't reply, unsure what to say.

Whittaker Ray smiled. "It's a lot to take in in just two weeks. But I wanted to let you know that I have complete confidence in you. Your parents were two of the most gifted Lightworkers in our history, and they would be very proud of you."

Eyre wasn't sure why they would be proud exactly; it wasn't as if she had done anything at all in the past couple of weeks other than run away from awful creatures as fast as possible, but she appreciated his kindness. "I'm looking forward to it," she said finally. "It will be good to know more about where I came from."

Whittaker Ray looked up at a screech of white cockatoos as they passed overhead. His eyes followed them as they flew with the morning sun on their wings, soaring over the tops of the eucalypts.

"Well, remember that I'm always around if you have questions," he said.

An hour later Eyre found her friends standing by the Mantle Basin, chattering in excitement as they waited, their bags tossed on the ground beside them. Eyre joined them and lobbed her coloured backpack and a duffel bag with her clothing on to the pile. Eyre had talked with her friends about what to pack, but Mrs Edmunsun had told them that everything would be provided by the Academy, and they wouldn't need very much, so she had just thrown in a few things.

"I hope I've got enough," Abby said, looking over at her bag with a frown. "It doesn't look like much." She made the others laugh when she added, "So glad I remembered my hair dye though."

"What to take is the least of our worries," a rather nervous-looking Beatrice said. The high achiever of the group, she was obviously thinking a lot about the coming challenge.

Finally, Mr Edmunsun arrived, striding across the clearing on his long legs.

"Everyone ready?" he asked, smiling at their obvious discomfort. "Don't worry, you're going to love it! Stand by me and hold hands." They crowded a bit closer, and Eyre took hold of Beatrice and Abby's hands. "Here we go then!"

Suddenly an intense beam of light radiated outwards and surrounded them and their bags in a blinding flash. She squeezed her eyes shut as everything whirled sickeningly around her in a vortex of dazzling brightness.

CHAPTER THIRTEEN

ONLY SECONDS LATER THE awful dizzying whirl stopped and Eyre cautiously opened her eyes. The bright light had gone as well and she was standing with Mr Edmunsun and her friends on a large flat oval of silvery metal the size of a swimming pool. Their bags were by their side in the same stack they had piled them.

Mr Edmunsun walked to the side of the metal oval and shaded his eyes, peering into the distance, then gave a satisfied huff. Eyre and her friends followed him, carrying their bags and looked over to where he indicated a vehicle coming towards them from the distance.

"Here it comes!" he said. "Won't be long."

As they waited, Eyre looked around her. Things looked pretty much the same as they had back at the cabins. They were obviously still in the Blue Mountains somewhere—the hills stretched as far as she could see, the familiar blue haze across the top of the eucalyptus trees a reassuring sight for her. In the distance, behind the vehicle that barrelled towards them and about a kilometre from the top of the clearing where she stood, she could see the irregular shapes of buildings that sparkled in the sunlight. Squinting, she tried to make out the details, but the buildings were too far away. She would have to be patient.

As the vehicle travelled back and forth across the dirt road that wound towards them, she could see that it was a strange silver-coloured bus with a large number 1 painted on each side. It had curved sides and reminded Eyre of a blimp, but one with circular windows like an aeroplane and huge wheels encased in rugged off-road tyres. It bumped along across the field and finally stopped in a haze of dust. The single door in the middle opened, and a staircase slowly descended to the ground. Practically holding her breath, Eyre waited to see what would happen next. After the events of the past couple of weeks, nothing would surprise her.

Suddenly a head stuck out the door. "Inguz! Welcome!" called the most outlandish looking individual Eyre had ever seen. Stepping down on to the ground, he came towards them and shook everyone's hand enthusiastically. "So glad to see you again Peter!" he said.

"Ranger Chrysanthe," Mr Edmunsun replied, "good to see you again too."

The Ranger was a man in his mid-thirties, wearing a long, vividly-coloured purple cape with golden runes all over it. A purple hat like something a Musketeer would wear sat atop a wild mop of hair that was bright green; and hanging from his hair were brilliantly coloured beetles, like the scarab beetles in Egyptian artworks. A couple of the beetles were attached by fine silken threads, and they flew lazily around his head like circling aircraft, occasionally alighting on the golden feather that adorned his hat.

The Ranger had strong eyebrows—coloured bright green—that arched over eyes of brilliant purple, and at that moment they seemed rather amused at the astonished looks he was receiving. Was *this* what a normal Lightworker looked like? Eyre wondered, speechless, taking in his gold and black pirate boots and the large black belt that held up green and purple striped pants. The buckle of the belt was gold and shaped like the Inguz that Beatrice had drawn in the ground. Finishing the vision of sartorial elegance was a pale green lace-up shirt from which peeked a deep green irregularly-shaped stone set in silver and hung on a leather thong. Looking at him almost gave Eyre a headache, he was so bright.

He smiled, revealing gleaming white teeth. "How was your trip?" he asked. "All two seconds of it?" Then he laughed uproariously and took Eyre's backpack from her. As he moved he jangled from the armful of gold bangles and bracelets that ran up and down both his arms, and Eyre noticed that each finger was adorned with a strange, heavy gold ring. Ranger Chrysanthe pulled a handle at the base of the bus, and a door opened upwards, revealing underneath storage.

"Chuck your bags in the Zepp," he said, waving towards the silver bus. "You're the fourth bunch to arrive. The others came this afternoon, and the rest are due shortly. There's a few Zepps out and about. Step aboard. I'll take you down to the Orientation Compound."

Beatrice looked at Eyre with raised eyebrows, and they got on board the bus, trying not to gawp at the strange-looking man. Inside there were about twenty seats that ran all around the walls, so that when they sat down and buckled up—in a strange harness-like contraption that fitted across both shoulders—everyone was facing each other. It was a bit like the inside of an aeroplane troop carrier. A circular raised platform about a metre across and half a metre high sat in the middle of the bus.

"Everyone buckled up?" Ranger Chrysanthe called from the driver's seat. "Off we go then!"

Peter Edmunsun chuckled at the dumbfounded looks everyone was giving him.

"You'll get used to him," he said. "He has a heart of gold, and he's actually one of the best scholars at the school."

Abby's jaw dropped. "He's a *teacher*?" she gasped.

"Yes," laughed Mr Edmunsun, greatly amused. "You haven't seen anything yet! There are some unusual educators for sure at this school! Don't underestimate them, though. They are some of the smartest and most talented people in the world."

There was a roar as the engine started up, and they were hurled back in their seats as the powerful wheels dug into the ground and the bus took off. Eyre strained to look outside, but it was difficult to see out the small windows. Ranger Chrysanthe waved a hand gaily from the front of the bus and gave a thumbs-up signal. Eyre noticed that he had a large gold ring with a beetle on it on his thumb.

Suddenly there was a whirring, and the walls of the bus started to vibrate wildly. As she watched the walls began to sort of—fade?—until eventually the sides were completely transparent and she could see outside as if the walls were glass. It was a weird feeling, seeing the countryside rushing by at high speed, and she had to stop herself from ducking as they went under trees and past rocks. Disappointingly, the bus turned away from the enticing, shimmering buildings in the distance and headed towards the edge of a rugged cliff.

"Up ahead we have Beggarman's Bluff," Ranger Chrysanthe announced, "which is part of the cliffs that surround the Orientation Compound and Lake Altum."

Looking out the front of the bus Eyre could see a wide expanse of air that indicated the ground fell away in a steep drop. In the far distance, the other side of the cliffs glowed with golden highlights as the lowering sun's rays hit the sheer rock face. Eyre settled back in anticipation; she would enjoy looking down at the Compound and the lake, and she hoped they would be allowed out to get a better view.

The Zepp changed gears, and Eyre held her breath. Weren't they going a bit fast? Her slight misgiving gave way to unrestrained panic as the Zepp went faster and faster. Suddenly she gasped in horror. They were heading straight for Beggarman's Bluff! She looked wildly at Beatrice, whose eyes were wide with fright.

"Dad?" Beatrice squeaked, but her father seemed unconcerned.

"Don't worry, it's fine," he said, but Beatrice grasped the arms of her seat desperately, petrified.

"Oh. My. God!" shrieked Abby as the Zepp accelerated towards the edge of the cliff. They all shouted in fear as it shot off the road out into the air. Eyre closed her eyes, waiting to fall to her death. But after a moment she realised that they weren't falling at all, and she opened her eyes cautiously. Through the transparent sides of the Zepp she could see that they were descending in a gentle spiral towards the ground, flying, it seemed somehow, through the air. Sucking in large lungfuls of air, speechless with shock, she gazed outwards—looking in the diminishing light at the tops of tall eucalyptus trees as the Zepp headed towards them. Ranger Chrysanthe brought the Zepp over the trees and landed smoothly, taxiing along the edge of a dark lake and towards a large flat area at the side of some buildings.

Four white faces turned towards Peter Edmunsun and glared at him accusingly. He had the grace to look sheepish.

"I might add," he said, choking back his laughter, "that Ranger Chrysanthe is also the best pilot on campus!"

CHAPTER FOURTEEN

AS RANGER CHRYSANTHE GOT their bags out of the storage compartment, Eyre studied the building in front of the Zepp. She could see that it was two storeys high, rectangular, and simply constructed out of pine logs, broken at intervals by small windows. The building looked like barracks, and as they walked through the Compound, Eyre realised that there were four of these buildings placed at angles, each forming the arm of a cross. At the centre was a square building, and Ranger Chrysanthe took them up towards it. Darkness was nearly complete, and crystals on tall poles had illuminated, lighting the pathways through the grounds.

"You're all going to wait in here for now," Ranger Chrysanthe informed them as he went up the steps of the central building. "This is the Common Room for the complex. It's the centre of the four lodges. When everyone gets here, you will be given a room allocation and instructed about orientation." He grinned in the dim light, looking like a well-meaning and brightly coloured clown. "I look forward to getting to know all of you," he said as he led them inside. "Please come and see me if you need help. No question is too trivial!"

There was a cluster of students already in the Common Room, sitting on stuffed couches and lounging around the walls with their bags. They looked up with keen interest as Eyre and her friends entered. Peter Edmunsun smiled at Beatrice.

"Time for me to go, darling," he said. "Good luck, and know that whatever happens, I'm proud of you." He gave her a hug and smiled at her friends. "Good luck to you all, too. I'll see you soon!"

He left with Ranger Chrysanthe, and they waved as he went down the stairs. There were about a dozen other students in the room, and Eyre looked at them curiously. She was casually running her eyes over the group, wondering who might be in her class next year, when suddenly she stopped at a vaguely familiar face. Disbelievingly, she looked again and turned to Beatrice, shocked.

"That awful guy from the markets is here?" she said in surprise.

Beatrice could do nothing but shrug awkwardly.

Nick was looking as incredulous as she was and sent Beatrice an angry look. "Ben Perrill is a *Lightworker*? But there's nothing light about him. His heart is as black as the ace of spades!" His voice revealed a surprising ferocity; it was the most emotion Eyre had heard from him in two weeks. Obviously there was some history between them, and obviously it wasn't good.

"Actually, Nick," Beatrice said apologetically, "the Perrills go back many generations. Their lineage can be traced to the time of Gordon the Third. In fact, they're a very honoured Lightworker family, believe it or not. His parents came here, too."

Looking over at Ben, who was standing in a group of boys that he clearly already knew, Eyre could see that he wasn't looking happy at all to see them there. In fact, it seemed to be *her* in particular he was focussing on; he was scowling so hard she thought his face might crack. Good! she thought with satisfaction. I'm glad he feels that way. The feeling is most definitely mutual! She had only encountered him once, and she had no idea why he had taken such an aversion to her, but she knew his type. Bullies were all the same.

A couple of Ben's cronies noticed him staring at her, and one of them snickered and whispered something in his ear. Furious, Ben shoved him hard, and the boy slammed against the wall before putting his hands up in defeat. Ben turned his back on Eyre and started to talk to one of the others in the group. Suits me, too, thought Eyre, I don't want to be looking at you either.

A sudden clatter diverted her attention and the door of the Common Room opened to a crowd of students bustling in, talking in excited voices. Obviously the later arrivals had been delivered. Eyre wondered how many were here; the Common Room was soon filled with bags and so many people it was getting hard to move. Finally, a loud voice stilled the chatter in authoritative tones.

"Silence!" One by one the students stopped talking until there was complete quiet in the room. A large form parted the crowd like a ship churning through Sydney Harbour and a huge woman walked up to the centre of the room. She was nearly two metres tall and built like a tank—all solid muscle, with a short hairdo that stopped an inch short of being a crewcut. Makeup-less and humourless, she scanned the crowd with a disapproving eye.

"Right! The last groups have been delivered, and we've been notified that all students are here. I am Sergeant Esmerelda Tottingham, and I am your trainer, your leader, and your *owner* for the next ten weeks. If I say jump, you say how high? If I say sit, you bark like a dog. And if I say fly off the cliff, you will, by the Aura, fly off that cliff like a god damned bird!" One of Ben's cronies snickered from the corner, and Sergeant Tottingham turned towards him with an icy glare. Then, faster than anyone could see, she shot her arm out. Suddenly he was halfway up the wall and kicking wildly, some unseen force holding him up in the air. Softly, Sergeant Tottingham spoke.

"I do find that every year some student who thinks he's clever tries to be a smartass. Looks like this year, it's you." The boy's face was turning bright red with embarrassment as he fought to get down. With a flick of her wrist, the Sergeant took the pressure off, and he dropped to the floor, landing heavily on his rump. Sergeant Tottingham walked over to him.

"I usually find that they've dropped their attitude within about the first five minutes." The boy scrambled to his feet, rubbing his rear end, and scuttled away to the back of the crowd. Sergeant Tottingham stalked back to the front of the room. Looking around the room, she scowled at them all.

"I hope that is the last time I have to deal with such insolence in the next few weeks. Listen up, babies." She put her hands on her considerable hips. "I am about to introduce you to the Dean of Curriculum. If anyone so much as opens their mouth while he is talking, they will be washing dishes for the next two months. Please welcome Mr Whittaker Ray. Mr Ray has been our Dean of Curriculum for twenty years but most recently was away on sabbatical for two years. We are very happy to have him back!"

As the students around her clapped, Eyre's eyebrows rose in surprise for the second time that night. Mr Ray was here? She wondered if the others had known. From the look on Abby and Beatrice's faces they were just as surprised as she was, but Nick's face was impassive—obviously he had been told. So Mr Ray had left St Jeffrey's and was here now. Eyre hadn't known that he'd ever been a teacher here, and neither, obviously, had Beatrice and Abby. Whittaker Ray looked around the crowd, and as his gaze settled on the four of them, he gave them a brief smile before starting to speak to the students.

"I would like to welcome you all to orientation," he said. "The Academy of Light is well known around Australia for its educational standards and the aptitude of the Lightworkers that we train. We pride ourselves on our elite student body, and it is only because of the effort that you, our students, put in, that we have such a great reputation. Accordingly, we would like to wish you well for the duration of your stay during the Training, Evaluation, and Placement weeks. As St Illuminado would say: 'May the Light Guide your Steps'! Good luck, and I hope to see you next year on campus." The students clapped again, and he acknowledged them all by dipping his head.

Sergeant Tottingham marched up to the front again. "Right!" she shouted. "Arrange yourselves in lines. And keep silent while you're doing it!"

The students moved quietly into an uneven line, and the front door opened again. In walked a scrawny man with pale ginger hair tied back into a ponytail. He had a wispy moustache and washed-out blue eyes that regarded the students with contempt. As if desperate to avoid touching anyone, he slid through the students and stood next to Sergeant Tottingham, surveying the crowd.

"This is Professor Mandig Vela," announced Sergeant Tottingham, "Orientation Supervisor and also Head of our Runes and Symbols Department. Together, he and I will be running the Training, Evaluation, and Placement trials—or TEPs—over the next ten weeks. Ten weeks of training and one week of trials. You are not to leave the campus under any circumstances during this time. Next year any of you who are worthy enough to make it through will have us as your Dorm Supervisors. So rest assured, you *will* be making an impression during your time here. Use it wisely."

She clicked her fingers, and the doors opened again. The students gaped as a group of eight small creatures bustled through the doors carrying plastic boxes. The troll-like creatures were about a metre high, dark-skinned with small eyes and high cheekbones, and they had small horns growing out of the rough black hair on the top of their heads. Tufts of black hair also grew from the sides of their faces like mutton-chop whiskers, and the same black hair grew thickly along their muscular forearms and down their stocky legs. They wore a rough-woven piece of clothing like a loincloth around their waist, and they were bare-chested, with strongly-defined pectoral muscles. Eyre watched curiously as the small creatures marched up to the front of the room and deposited the plastic boxes along the walls. Then they left out the front door again.

Sergeant Tottingham reached into the first box and brought out a clipboard. "We will be forming four groups, based on your surname, and those four groups will be labelled: Earth, Water, Air, and Fire, which are the groups for each lodge. The first group, Earth, is made up of those surnames beginning with A to F. Saskia Anderson, please step forward!"

A pretty blonde girl stepped forward, flicking her hair and smirking as if it was natural she should be called up first, and Eyre mentally rolled her eyes. Another "type" she was familiar with—the legacy of changing schools so often was that Eyre knew them all. The girl went up to Sergeant Tottingham who gave her a folded package from the box.

"This is your uniform for the duration of orientation, and if you're lucky, next year when you begin at the Academy of Light. You will wear it every day for training, and you *will* ensure it is clean at all times." Sergeant Tottingham pulled an article from the top of Saskia's pile and held it up, revealing it to be a vest with a number on it.

"You will also all be given a number. I am not going to be bothered learning everyone's names, so from now on you will be referred to only by your number, in your case," she indicated Saskia, "number one." As Saskia simpered at Sergeant Tottingham, Eyre confirmed to herself that, yep, she was definitely not going to like this girl. Sergeant Tottingham continued to call out the names of the Earth group and Beatrice went up to get her number—35.

Eyre was part of the Water group—surnames G to M—and she waited for her number to be called out.

"Number 88, Ire Lightward," Sergeant Tottingham shouted, and Eyre walked to the front of the crowd. "Ah, Sergeant, it's pronounced 'Air'," she said as she took her number, and the Sergeant nodded and made a note on her clipboard.

As Eyre walked over to join the Water group, she felt a strong hand grip her elbow tightly and turned in surprise to see Ben Perrill's spotty face shoved towards her.

"*Ire*, how nice to meet you," he mocked in a voice that definitely sounded like he didn't think it was nice.

"It's *Air*," Eyre said with gritted teeth as she wrenched her elbow away. She knew that Ben knew how to say her name, but she didn't want anyone overhearing and mispronouncing her name for the rest of the TEPs.

"Eyre. . . *Air*head," Ben said maliciously. "*So* perfect!" The henchman beside him snickered, and Eyre felt a sudden blast of adrenalin as her temper ignited. She smiled sweetly at Ben, then took a heavy step forward, stomping on his foot hard as she walked past him. He let go of her elbow and exhaled loudly; obviously it had hurt. Stepping back, he shot a venomous look at her.

Eyre continued on, her anger tempered with puzzlement. Why did he dislike her so much? But she set her jaw and breathed deeply. Often there was no logic as to why a bully chose his target, so if that's the way he wanted it then game on!

Sergeant Tottingham continued passing out the uniforms. Nick, Number 134, was in the Air Group with surnames N to S, and Abby was part of the last group—Fire—Number 173 and surnames T to Z. Once they had received their uniforms they looked wistfully at each other. It would have been nice if at least one of them was in the same group as the other. But looking on the bright side, Eyre thought, at least they could get feedback from each other about every student in the orientation group. She surveyed some of the students in her own group numbered 52–104. Fifty-three students, girls and boys. One girl—number 56—stood out from the rest; she was athletic and tanned, with black hair cut very short. She had sharp cheekbones and amber eyes, and she looked around the room mistrustfully. She looked like she could handle herself; one to watch, Eyre thought. A tall Aboriginal boy—number 61—surveyed the crowd quietly. He gave off a calm air, and he seemed interesting. But then the crowd started to mingle, and it was hard to tell who else was in her group. She gave up trying to work it out, deciding it would be easier when they got to their lodge. Numbers weren't a bad idea, she agreed mentally, there were so many people here it would be difficult to remember all their names.

Eventually everyone had a folded uniform and Sergeant Tottingham shouted for quiet.

"Right! Earth and Water groups, you come with me. Air and Fire, follow Professor Vela. On your way out the back door you will pass a row of boots. Please select your size and carry them with you to your lodge. Make it snappy, time is wasting!"

She led with her considerable bulk out the back door, and the students filed after her, carrying their uniforms and the bags they had brought from home. By now they were quieting down, tired from the excitement of the day. At the bottom of the stairs each person picked up a pair of long black boots from the neat row along the side of the building and placed them on top of their uniform. They were made of supple leather, designed to protect the leg to the knee, and were surprisingly lightweight. Then Sergeant Tottingham took her groups one way, Professor Vela his groups the other.

Eyre's group walked to the first lodge—Earth Lodge—and followed Sergeant Tottingham a few steps up the external flight of wooden stairs and entered the door to the bottom floor, crowding inside the lodge. Sergeant Tottingham waved her hand around the room, indicating the bunk beds that were placed against the walls. There were fifteen in all, each with a double locker next to it, meaning the total capacity for each lodge was sixty students if both floors were fully occupied. Obviously the amount of beds used depended on the number of boys and girls with surnames in each group.

"Earth group—boys are downstairs, girls are upstairs. You will find your name and number on the locker beside the bed, which will be yours for the duration of your stay here. Top locker for top bunk, bottom locker for bottom bunk. Anything that doesn't fit in your locker, get rid of it, or put it somewhere I can't see it. Boots under the end of your bed. Showers are down the hall, laundry facilities as well. In your locker you will find boot polish, washing powder, and a sewing kit. You are responsible for your boots and uniform, which will be clean, tidy, and in good order at all times. Water group!" she barked, and Eyre, along with all the other Water students, jumped.

"Your facilities are set up the same as this lodge. The Water Lodge is the Southern branch of this complex. You will head out now and organise yourselves. Lights out at 2100 tonight!" she shouted. "And we will be rising tomorrow at 0500 sharp." Then, just as they were about to leave, she added, "Dinner will be provided in the Refectory at 1800 for anyone who would like it. The Refectory is located to the North-East of the complex." She indicated with her hand a general direction. "It's a rectangular building stained green for ease of identification. Questions?"

Everyone shuffled around and looked downwards, the floor of great interest all of a sudden. Eyre didn't want to admit that she had trouble with 24 hour time. Left or right were the most she'd had to deal with in her life so far. If she didn't focus, she'd probably be two hours late for everything.

"Right then. Off you go!" Sergeant Tottingham commanded.

With a rueful smile, Eyre waved goodbye to Beatrice and headed out the door of Earth Lodge with her group of students. Sergeant Tottingham left in the opposite direction, leaving the Water group to find their own way, and they headed down the pathway towards the next Lodge, about 200 metres away. It was constructed exactly the same as the Earth Lodge, and the bunk beds were a carbon copy of the setup in Earth Lodge, too. The boys walked in the bottom door and slung their gear on to bunk beds as they found their numbers.

Eyre walked upstairs to the next floor and was happy when she found her bed was at the end of the lodge, a top bunk against the wall, near the window. She liked the view from out the window here; she could see the lake and the hills stretching off into the distance. She put her boots at the end of her bed and started to unpack her things into the locker.

Eventually a large and jovial girl with brown curly hair and broad shoulders shambled over and dumped her stuff on the bunk below Eyre. She had a friendly face and she leant against the bunk bed smiling at Eyre

"Carly Henderson," she introduced herself, "or I guess it's Number 55, now that we're officially part of this cattle drive. I'm from Borabinga. That's near Wagga Wagga. Where are you from?"

Eyre was a bit nonplussed, not sure where she was from now. But she defaulted to the most recent place she'd lived. "Er, the Sunshine Coast," she said as she put the last things away and closed her locker door.

"Nice!" Carly said. "Beaches, sun . . . lucky you!"

Eyre shrugged noncommittally and watched as Carly put a brightly-coloured crocheted knee blanket on her bed.

Carly laughed, misinterpreting her look. "Mum made it," she said. "Made me bring it! She always thinks I'm going to be cold, even in the middle of summer!"

Eyre smiled, wishing like anything her mother was around to hassle her about a knee blanket, but she simply said, "Shall we go and get some dinner?"

"Sure," said Carly, "I could eat a bullock!"

Some of the other students had already begun to wander to the Refectory, and Eyre and Carly followed them over.

CHAPTER FIFTEEN

THE REFECTORY LAY AT the perimeter of the complex—a low green building devoid of architectural extravagance. Built for functionality only, it was a squat rectangle with two sets of stairs—one leading in, and one leading out. Students were filing up the steps, chattering to each other in casually-formed groups from their lodges.

Inside, Eyre saw that the Refectory was laid out with white laminate tables scattered around in a cafeteria-style arrangement. Each table was surrounded by six white plastic chairs, and each had at the centre a jug of water and glasses, salt and pepper shakers, and a container of napkins. Already some tables had been claimed by groups of students who sat leaning back in their chairs, talking to each other. Along the side of the room was a servery area, with separate buffet units for hot food, a salad bar, a bread-toasting station, and a cold unit holding a selection of desserts. Looking at it all, Eyre was surprised that it was so well catered. After the rather brusque welcome they had received from Sergeant Tottingham, she would not have been surprised if the students were served up bread and water for ten weeks. The hot meal that night was lasagne and she joined the queue of students. While she waited to be served she used the time to size up the other students in the room.

The athletic dark-haired girl from her lodge—who Eyre now knew was called Pheria Galloway, Number 56, thanks to the locker labels—was sitting with a group of people in the centre of the dining room. Eyre studied them, trying not to be obvious about it. One of them was a tall, well-built boy that Eyre knew was in her lodge, but she didn't know his name yet. He had dark wavy hair that just touched his collar, and he leaned in close to Pheria, laughing at something she was saying, flashing straight white teeth. Suddenly he looked up and caught Eyre examining him, and his cool green eyes ran up and down her body, appraising her, before he lifted an eyebrow as if to say, "Can I help you?" Eyre blushed to the roots of her hair at being caught out, and as she looked away awkwardly, she realised that the boy behind her was regarding her with an amused look on his thin face.

"Busted!" he chortled.

Eyre flushed and hesitated, then retorted, laughing hard. "I so am! God, wasn't that awkward!"

The thin boy shook his head. "That's Jax—real name Jack Jackson. Don't worry, everyone stares at him all the time, including probably himself!"

"Ha!" Eyre laughed. She realised that she had seen the slightly built boy in Nick's group; he wasn't someone you'd forget once you'd seen him. He was thin with freckles and skinny legs, long blond hair tied back in a ponytail, and a mouth that had a mischievous smile.

"I'm Eyre. I'm from Water Lodge. I think you're from Air Lodge, aren't you? A friend of mine is there also. What's your name?"

"Zanda Nixon, Numero 106, ready for action!" the boy answered and did a sudden pirouette. He looked so silly that Eyre chuckled. Zanda laughed too, as he dropped his arms.

"Who's your friend in Air?"

"Nick, Nick Richardson," she replied. "Have you met him yet?" When Zanda shook his head, Eyre smiled at him and, finally reaching the stack of crockery, she picked up a white dinner plate. "He'll be here shortly I'm sure," she said. "He's always on time for meals!"

Just then, Nick walked in the front door, chatting to a lanky boy who was quite tall. They looked quite comical, Nick so short and the other boy towering over him. Eyre waved at him, trying to get his attention.

Nick finally spotted her and waved back at her as he and his new friend joined the back of the queue.

"Come eat with me!" Eyre gestured to him, and he gave her the thumbs-up.

The line weaved its way past the hot servery units, and Eyre spooned lasagne onto her plate. Then she headed over to the salad bar. She decided to head for the drinks canteen next, but as she turned away from the salad bar her foot caught on the end of the metal trolley and she tripped, falling flat on her stomach, painfully knocking the wind out of her lungs and sending her plate skidding along the floor ahead of her like a clattering Frisbee. There was a sudden silence in the room, then a few muffled giggles. Obviously everyone found it absolutely hilarious, but didn't think they should laugh, and as Eyre lay with her chest in her lasagne she could hear strangled choking from the few with less self-control than the others. Someone walked up to her.

"I take it you're not that keen on lasagne?" Nick said, his eyes crinkling at her in sympathy. He put out his hand and hauled her up, lasagne and lettuce leaves falling from the front of her shirt to the floor with a noisy glop. Someone at the end of the room gave a loud guffaw and she flushed again, her face probably matching her hair nicely now, she thought in annoyance.

She gazed at the mess on the floor, unsure what to do, but fortunately two of the small dark-skinned horned creatures bustled out from the kitchen, obviously alerted by the noise, and within minutes they had cleaned it all away. If only they could clean me up too, thought Eyre in embarrassment as she rejoined the queue, feeling like part of the smorgasbord.

Suddenly, someone moved up behind her.

"Classy move, Airhead," said the now familiar and hateful voice of Ben Perrill. "If you move as well during the TEPs they'll be booting you out of here! Excellent form, just perfect!"

Before she could react, he had moved on with his cronies, who were smirking and leering at her. How do people like Perrill manage to get a posse together so quickly? Eyre wondered. Already flanked by weak-minded yes-men. It was unbelievable. One of them was from her lodge—Tec Langford, Number 87. She remembered him because he had gotten his number just before her. Tall and thin, he had a spotty face and glasses. There were two brothers, muscular twins who didn't look like each other, from Beatrice's group and a couple of other guys she didn't recognise. They walked through the cafeteria like they owned it. Rage burned through Eyre. If only he would leave her alone! *Why* did he seem to hate her so much? Mentally gnashing her teeth, she took a few breaths to calm down, and noticed Pheria watching her with amusement from the middle of the room. The rest of her table were also looking at Eyre—wonderful! How to make an impression in one easy fall. Clenching her jaw, she looked away from them and made her way to the table where Nick and his friend were sitting. As she sat down, Zanda took the seat next to her.

"This is Robeson Paul," Nick said. "He's in my lodge." Robeson was tall and good-looking in an intellectual way. He had straight brown hair, long on the top and short on the sides, and black-framed glasses. A bit Clark Kent-ish, Eyre decided, and definitely attractive.

"Zanda's in your lodge too," Eyre said and then added in an irritated voice, "how appropriate. Air Lodgers and the Airhead."

"Don't worry about Perrill," Zanda said. "He's a jerk. I've known his family since high school. Unfortunately, my family has taken many overseas holidays with Ben's. His stepmother is a great friend of my mother. He's always been a narcissistic bully." His eyes followed Ben through the cafeteria with such dislike that Eyre felt sorry for him. Obviously his family holidays had not been much fun.

A few minutes later, Abby and Beatrice turned up, talking madly as they carried their food trays.

"By the Light," Abby shrieked in excitement, speaking in exclamation marks. "Isn't this amazing? It's all so weird and thrilling! St Jeffrey's eat your heart out! My bunk-bed partner is Zoe, and she's really nice, and she said she's really panicking about the training. Her older sister told her it's really hard."

Beatrice snorted. "I wonder how we'll *all* go in training!" she said as she shovelled lasagne into her mouth. "I'm definitely getting a feeling it's not going to be easy!"

Everyone nodded in agreement. Sergeant Tottingham hardly gave one a warm, fuzzy feeling, thought Eyre. And as for Professor Vela, he was about as friendly as an ice cube. But sitting with her friends brightened her again, and she filled up her water glass.

Eyre began to eat, realising that she was *really* hungry, and she cleared her plate even faster than Beatrice, which was really saying something. When she finished, she decided to brave the long walk across the room to get a cup of tea, hoping that she could get there without everyone staring at her. A few people did look at her curiously as she passed with that large inkblot of lasagne decorating the front of her shirt, but mostly they were too busy talking to each other. The interest factor had obviously passed.

Fortunately, she managed to make her way back to her table without knocking over a buffet unit or smashing the crockery or demolishing any walls. Doing well! she thought as she sat down again.

The rest of the meal was spent talking about each other—filling each other in on where they came from and who they were. It turned out that Robeson was from Melbourne, and he was hoping that he might specialise in research, depending on his placement.

"I'm interested specifically in the reconstruction of the Aura. I'm hoping to contribute to the solution of that problem." Then he hesitated and added lightly, though by now Eyre knew that it was anything but a casual issue for any of the Lightworkers, "Of course, that does depend if I Elevate or not. If I don't, then I'll work in the Unlit Division. I'm pretty interested in intelligence and coding as well."

At the mention of Elevation, the mood changed a bit and became more sombre. Unconsciously Zanda rubbed his arm.

"God," he said quietly, "if I don't Elevate, I'll never hear the end of it. I may as well just leave town. I'm already a major disappointment to my dad."

Eyre looked at him but didn't say anything. Obviously this was a touchy subject.

Aiming to change the mood, she said to Abby, "You like your lodge? Sounds like some good people there."

Abby nodded. "Yes, pretty good, I think. A couple I'm not so sure about. That girl with the red hair, for instance," she indicated a girl sitting at Pheria's table. "Ambrosia. She wasn't so keen on giving me any help finding my lodge, so I'll rest my judgement on her. But Zoe and a girl called Jo are cool, and that guy Huck," she indicated a fit-looking boy with brown hair sitting with Ambrosia, "seemed nice. There're a few others who were friendly enough, so I think it will be fine. How about you, Nick?"

"I've got a great cabin," Nick answered. "It's pretty cool. Of course there're always a couple of difficult people," his mouth twitched as he indicated Robeson and Zanda, "but I think I'll get on just fine. Phillip Outray from St Jeffrey's is in my cabin. He's a good guy." Then he rolled his eyes and grimaced. "I did, however, draw the short straw. I got Perrill," he said, and he received murmurs of sympathy from the others.

"My cabin is mixed, too," Beatrice said. "Colton seems decent." She indicated a good-looking blond boy sitting at Carly's table. "And I met a couple of nice girls when I was unpacking. But those awful twins that were with Perrill are in my cabin, and that excruciating girl Saskia, so it could be interesting."

"A mixed bunch for me too, I think," Eyre said. "Pheria's that girl with dark hair sitting at the middle table, and I'm not sure about her, but Carly is nice, and that guy—" she indicated Warrigal, "is cool, too. Tec Langford is one of Perrill's mates, so he's definitely off the list. But I don't really know anyone properly yet, so I'll wait and see."

"Agreed," Zanda said. "But you've nailed the ones I know pretty well. Anyone in need of information or gossip please feel free to ask me anytime!"

"Well," said Beatrice, leaning back in her chair and yawning, "I think I'll call it a night. I'm so tired!"

"Me too," Eyre said. "Five o'clock start? Horrendous!"

They all got up and took their plates to a hole in the wall, where others had already stacked their dishes on a wide metal ledge. From the other side the small, dark, troll-like creatures were whisking them away for washing; loud clattering, sounds of machines, and the swishing of water announced what was going on in the kitchen.

Eyre said goodnight to her friends and headed back to her lodge. She climbed wearily up the stairs, very keen to find her bed.

There was a shower unit at the end of the lodge and Eyre showered quickly and brushed her teeth before clambering into her top bunk. Carly was there already, half asleep.

"Goodnight Carly." Eyre whispered.

Carly mumbled back at her and soon Eyre was fast asleep.

CHAPTER SIXTEEN

A PIERCING WHISTLE BURROWED its way into Eyre's dream, shocking her awake. She groggily opened her eyes and waited for her thoughts to unscramble. Not only unsure what day it was (her usual confusion in the morning) but also where she was, was anything *after* her, and if not, what should she be doing? Her thoughts crashed together as she tried to shake the sleep from her head. She struggled to a sitting position and then registered that Sergeant Tottingham was standing in the doorway, still blowing the whistle. She carried a heavy staff in her other hand, a sanded straight branch of polished eucalyptus with a clear prism of quartz crystal embedded in the top and lashed on with a leather strap and golden cord.

"Right, everyone!" shouted Sergeant Tottingham, finally putting away the whistle. "It's Monday morning and your ten weeks training starts today! You have exactly fifteen minutes to be standing at the training area by Lake Altum, dressed and ready to start. Beds are to be made and not one thing will be left out of place or lying around or you will never see it again!" She looked around the room disapprovingly at the dishevelled group of teenagers who were in various stages of stupor. None of them looked ready for anything. She thumped the wooden staff on the ground loudly several times. "I suggest you hurry up!" she shouted. "Anyone who is late will be swimming across the lake this morning!"

That seemed to work and instantly there was the thunder of many feet hitting the wooden floor. Locker doors slammed open and bed covers were pulled up as the students suddenly found top gear, the threat of an early morning swim proving a great incentive to get them moving. Eyre reached into her locker and grabbed her uniform out, then leaped off the bunk onto the floor.

"Morning," said Carly cheerily, whipping her bed into shape. "And so it begins! Good luck my friend, I think we're going to need it!" Eyre agreed.

There was no nice cup of tea in bed here to start the morning off, obviously. Straight into it. She quickly made her bed and then began to get dressed.

The uniform consisted of a pair of tight-fitting, long dark grey trousers made out of a lightweight fabric, and a silvery tank top that looked like it had been woven from metal thread. When Eyre pulled the top on it hung closely to her body, a cool smooth fabric that felt like a second skin. She looked at herself in the long mirror on the wall beside the bunks and gave the uniform a mental thumbs up. Far better than the St Jeffrey's monstrosity with its heavy fabric and old-fashioned collar, and far more practical too. She pulled on a pair of socks and padded quickly around to the back of the bunk to get her boots. The soft black leather slipped over her calves as she put them on and she found that they were incredibly comfortable, moulding to her legs as if they had been made specifically for her. A large silver hoop remained and Eyre looked at it, mystified. It was about thirty centimetres in diameter, a flattened ring of silver about one centimetre wide, and she turned it around in her hands, trying to figure out what it was.

"It's your Halo," Carly explained as she pulled on her boots. "Put it around your head."

Eyre, feeling slightly ridiculous, leaned towards the mirror and put the hoop over her head like she'd seen depictions of the halo of an angel. She moved it down around her forehead, but it was too big, and Eyre looked again at Carly, unsure what to do. Suddenly the Halo became warm and began to glow with white light. Then with a high-pitched *zing*! it snapped inwards until it sat closely around her forehead, a gleaming silver ring. Then the ring dimmed and disappeared.

"Where did it go?" Eyre asked Carly, looking in the mirror and feeling her forehead with her fingers. She couldn't see or feel anything.

"The Halo is to help with focussing energies, directing the chakras, and concentrating your Light forces," Carly added. "You don't take it off. You can't see it now, but if you Elevate it will turn silver. Then it changes colour with your placement. We only have a Halo while we're at the Academy, but if you get an Inguz, the Inguz is permanent."

"How do you know so much, Carly?" Eyre asked, still feeling her forehead and staring in the mirror.

"I had two older brothers go through the Academy," Carly laughed. "I'm used to the uniform. And they've also told me all about things to expect in training while we're here. They laughed really hard! The struggle is real."

Eyre chuckled, then pulled her number vest from the locker. It slid over the silver tank top, a white square with her black number 88 in the centre and Velcro tapes that fastened the vest securely at each side.

Finally, she got her brush out of her locker, and with rapid strokes brushed out the knots in her hair until it gleamed like fire. Then with practised hands she braided two plaits and fastened them tightly.

Carly was also ready, so Eyre took a last look at their area, ensuring it was all tidy, then she and Carly set off at a run, hearing the sound of slamming lockers and last-minute routines as the last students in the lodge raced to make it on time.

As it was the beginning of summer, the sun was up, but it hadn't been up long and there was still a coolness in the air. Flocks of birds flew overhead calling to each other, filling the air with a layer of sound that was almost textured, and early morning wisps of clouds drifted on the horizon. Despite the rush, Eyre felt a cheerful anticipation rising within her as she hurried along beside Carly. Whatever came next, she was excited to be a part of it.

Up ahead they could see a group of students gathered by the edge of the lake. About half the students were there already and Eyre could see a knot of students at the side talking excitedly and gesturing at a muscular blond boy who stood with them. Colton, Eyre remembered—he had been at the Refectory last night sitting with Carly. He was tall and athletic and had short, very fair hair and tanned skin. And he was extremely good-looking, she noticed as well.

Eyre slowed down as they approached the group, and she could hear wisps of conversation from the students gathered around Colton.

"... this morning ..."

"the first of us ..."

"... amazing!"

They were looking at his arm and, curious, she headed over to have a look too. The reason for the general excitement became clear—Colton had an Inguz on the top of his arm, obviously the first student to Elevate in this group. And a brilliant silver stripe crossed his forehead—his Halo had appeared as well. Already! thought Eyre. She hadn't realised Elevation could happen so quickly. Colton's friends were congratulating him and slapping him on the back and Eyre moved closer to see better. The Inguz was about eight centimetres long and ran sideways across the top of Colton's arm. It gleamed silver in the sunlight, almost as if glitter had been cast along the lines. It was quite spectacular and Eyre felt a longing in her rise—she wanted one of those so badly! Her feelings were echoed in the faces of those around Colton—a wistful admiration coloured most of them. To his credit, Colton was downplaying the event, careful of the feelings of others. He shrugged.

"Being first to Elevate doesn't count for much. How you do in the TEPs is what will matter."

"What does it feel like?" Saskia Anderson asked coyly, running her finger over the Inguz.

Colton rubbed his arm contemplatively. "My arm feels the same as normal," he answered. "The Inguz was just there this morning when I woke up. I don't know exactly when it arrived and I didn't feel it come up either. I can't tell you much really."

By now most of the students had filed over to have a look; for many of them it was the first time they had seen one. Professor Vela's voice suddenly sliced through the hubbub. "Silence!" He moved from the back of the crowd like a shark sensing blood, and the students parted before him, instinctively stepping back. Professor Vela walked to the front of the students and looked at them distastefully.

"Okay, that's enough chatter. You, 44, stop the preening! And all of you listen to Sergeant Tottingham for instructions!" Colton looked embarrassed, and Eyre thought that it was rather unfair of Professor Vela to say that. If anything, Colton had been modest about his Inguz. With a sigh Eyre realised that they were all in for a harrowing few weeks. Professor Vela evidently liked the idea of harsh training and was going to make it tough for the students. Or perhaps that was just his nature; unpleasant and hostile. She steeled herself and waited for Sergeant Tottingham to speak.

Sergeant Tottingham, a whistle around her neck, dressed in a khaki shirt and trousers and wearing large black combat boots, was standing on a rock next to a eucalyptus tree. Eyre could see that today she had two silver leather braces that crossed in front of her shirt, over her shoulders to the back of her belt. They seemed to hold two short weapons, Eyre could just see the end of the handles protruding from behind the Sergeant's shoulders. The Sergeant's staff leaned against the tree beside her as, hands on hips, she surveyed the crowd. She didn't seem impressed with what she saw.

"Right, students," she shouted, running her hand through her spiky hair, "step up here in front of me!

"Line up numerically, and be quick about it! Shortly you will be leaving for a five kilometre run through the hills, which is what you will be doing every morning before breakfast until the TEPs. No complaints and no stopping or you will go back to the beginning and start again." She picked up her staff and looked around.

"We will meet here every morning and line up in this manner. You are to be ready by 0515 exactly. Anyone who is a minute late will swim across the lake and back before they start the run—in their clothes." A boy, Number 38, standing next to Eyre, snorted softly and whispered to his friend, "Does that include the professor then?"

Eyre looked over and saw Mandig Vela walk up to join Sergeant Tottingham. To her horror his pale eyes looked through the crowd directly at her, then his gaze travelled over her like an icy hand until his eyes rested on the boy beside her. With an imperceptible flick of his wrist he shot out a thin beam of light, and 38 suddenly screeched and held his forehead, bending over in agony. Eyre looked at him fearfully. Mandig Vela walked slowly over to 38 like a predator stalking its prey, his eyes slitted. He hauled the boy to his feet and clenched 38's jaw in his hand, tipping his face upwards. A strange character was burned into 38's forehead and it glowed painfully red as the boy gritted his teeth, tears running down the side of his face. Mandig Vela turned towards the crowd, dragging the boy with him.

"This," he announced to the crowd, "is the Nemoris character for donkey —or *ass*." He looked into 38's eyes and the boy cringed. With an awful smile Mandig Vela raised his hands towards the cowering boy and an invisible force slammed 38 onto the ground. Hard. Mandig Vela leaned over him.

"You are fortunate that I did not burn it deeper into your skin," he hissed, "because if I had you would be wearing that sign for the rest of your life. The way it is, there is a small chance it might disappear in a few months." Leaving the crumpled boy behind he strode through the students, who drew away from him as they would from a venomous snake; he was a small man, but he had a terrifying presence. Mutters of shock and fear swirled through the students.

Reaching the front of the crowd Professor Vela surveyed the students, unapologetic, his face twisted in fury. "Let this be a reminder that *nothing* you do or say while you are here goes unnoticed. I suggest you remember that over the next ten weeks and use your energies wisely."

Sergeant Tottingham moved up beside him, her face furious. But her voice was soft. "Andrew will no doubt hear of this, Mandig. Perhaps you should step back a bit?" Her voice might be soft, but her staff raised slightly.

Professor Vela suddenly looked uncertain and stepped back. As the rat-faced lecturer retreated, Sergeant Tottingham thumped her wooden staff on the ground for attention.

"You will now complete a five kilometre run as fast as you are physically able. Anyone slacking will be made to start again, so put in a good effort, students. Your course is this: run up the path, around the fringe of the bush and along the ridge," she pointed out the direction, "then come around the tall Wollemi pine at the top and back down the other side of the hill. You will then head straight in for breakfast at the Refectory. After breakfast you will be expected in the Lecture Theatre at precisely 0800. Any questions?" No one spoke up; they all huddled quietly as if trying not to attract attention. Nodding slightly, Sergeant Tottingham blew a loud blast on her whistle and thumped her staff on the ground. "Right then, GO!" she boomed, and all the students broke into a wild run up the path.

Eyre ran along as fast as she could, aghast at the number of students who rapidly overtook her and were running up the track in front of her. There were some seriously fit students here and they were bounding up the path like it was a stroll through the library. Her breath catching in her throat, she struggled to keep up but was gradually falling to the back of the pack. Abby and Beatrice were with her, gasping for air as they raced up the steep path, and Number 38 was struggling too, stumbling along in the last group of students.

"St Illuminado save me," Beatrice gasped. "I can't believe we have to do this every day! I don't think I've run this far in my whole life!"

Abby, her fair skin flushed bright red from the effort, was unable to talk at all; chest heaving, she staggered towards the top of the path. Suddenly Eyre looked behind her and noticed that 38 was lying face down in the path. She hesitated, then waved her friends on.

"I'll check him," she said. "You keep going." She raced back to 38, a heavy boy with dark hair now black with sweat, and rolled him over. He was conscious, just completely exhausted, and the red scar on his forehead glistened like a brand, scorched like charcoal on the sides and seared red in the middle.

"Are you okay?" she whispered urgently. "You need to get up!"

The boy sat up but seemed completely disorientated. "I can't do it," he said brokenly. "I hurt so much."

Eyre looked behind him to see if either of the Supervisors were coming.

"Come on 38," she urged, "it's only the first day. Don't give them the satisfaction of seeing you give up. I'll help you. Come on, we'll do it together."

Number 38 looked at her, pain glazing his eyes, then he struggled to his feet awkwardly. "Okay," he said softly, "I'm coming." He set off again at a lumbering run and Eyre ran slowly beside him through the tortuous route.

Five kilometres was not a very long run, but it was a difficult course around the fringe of the bush, with rocks that rolled underfoot, sticks that stuck up to trip them and parts of the path that were incredibly steep. By the time they made it the complete way around the course—Eyre sometimes helping 38 over the difficult parts—there was no one left running with them. As they came through the final stretch of the run they could see Sergeant Tottingham and Mandig Vela up ahead waiting at the finish. Eyre gritted her teeth, and they ran the final steps past the Supervisors. Number 38 collapsed on the ground, gasping tortured lungfuls of air, and Eyre, feeling not much better, fell to her knees retching, fire burning her lungs.

Mandig Vela strolled over to them, delighting in their pain. "I forgot to mention," he said silkily as he stood over them, "that those who come last on the run are assigned cafeteria duty for the day. Cleaning up. I'm sure you'll love it!" The Supervisors walked off, leaving Eyre and 38 gasping on the ground. Eventually the wave of pain and sickness passed and Eyre struggled feebly to her feet. She helped 38 up and smiled at him ruefully.

"Well, I guess I should know your name if we're going to be kitchen hands together," she said.

Number 38 grimaced and gently felt the brand on his forehead, wincing as he touched it. He shook his head. "My dad always said I didn't know when to keep my mouth shut," he said regretfully. "Looks like Professor Vela is not going to forgive me. I'm sorry I dragged you into it. My name is Rigmar Essendon, at your service." He bowed low, a comical movement given his ungainly size, and they both dissolved into laughter. Rigmar stuck his hand out.

"Eyre Lightward," Eyre replied, shaking his hand. "Don't sweat it," she said and smiled in a self-deprecating way, "I usually manage to drag myself into trouble anyway! Let's go and get some breakfast—if there's any left."

They walked as fast as they could up to the Refectory and along the way Eyre found out that Rigmar was in Earth Lodge and that he came from Geraldton in Western Australia. His father had gone to the Academy of Light thirty years ago and Rigmar informed her that he, Rigmar Essendon, was here to continue the fine family tradition. "With a donkey symbol on my forehead," he finished. Eyre dissolved into peals of laughter and told him about her lasagne incident the night before, which made them laugh all the more.

"That was *you*?" he choked. "Oh my god, that was *so* funny!"

"Maybe I should have a donkey on my forehead, too!" she said as they walked into the Refectory.

Everyone looked up at them as they entered, and she supposed it must be interesting to note who was the last to finish the run. It takes some doing to be known already for *not* achieving, she thought. But suddenly she saw the lighter side and felt happy that she had made a new friend.

They got some breakfast and then walked down to join Beatrice and Abby, who were sitting down the back with their plates still nearly full; obviously they hadn't arrived much before Eyre and Rigmar.

"BTL," Beatrice said, "that *sucked* big time. How hard was it?" Abby, still red faced, could only nod and roll her eyes in horror. Zanda was sitting with them, and he chuckled.

"Best news of the day is that we get to do it all again tomorrow!" he said, shoving scrambled eggs into his mouth. Everyone groaned.

Eyre spread some vegemite on her toast and ate it quickly. Then she had a bowl of fruit, two bits of toast, and some eggs, sighing with happiness. One thing was for sure, the food here was *good!* Finally, everyone was finished and they took their trays up to the kitchen window where the small horned creatures, which Zanda had told her were called 'Jotnar,' whisked away their plates.

One of the Jotnar, a bossy, cranky-looking creature, bustled out officiously and gave Eyre a cloth and bucket of water, gesturing that she was to wipe the tables. Rigmar was given a broom to sweep the floor and Eyre surveyed the room, calculating the time it would take her to finish her job and how long she had until 8 o'clock. She realised with a start that she only had half an hour.

"Come on Rig," Eyre said, "we'd better hurry!" She worked swiftly, cleaning all the muck off the tables, moving from one table to the next. There were a few people still sitting at tables and as she neared the table in the corner down the back, with a groan Eyre realised that the couple sitting there was Pheria and her boyfriend with the unfathomable green eyes—Jax. But she smiled at them with as much grace as she could muster, and they leaned back helpfully so she could clean the table.

"Do you work here then?" Pheria asked curiously. Gritting her teeth, Eyre realised that Pheria had probably finished so far ahead she would have no idea why Eyre had been given this job. Jax was surveying her coolly, and she could feel the colour start to rise in her cheeks as she felt his gaze upon her. Just for *once*, she thought in annoyance, could my stupid face please *not* betray me? But she spoke lightly.

"Well, I have the dubious honour of coming in last on the run," she said to Pheria. "My prize is to wipe the tables down. With my running skills you could well be seeing me every morning!"

"That wouldn't be so bad," Jax said softly, and Eyre was mortified to feel the red in her cheeks getting brighter, if that indeed was possible. Completely taken aback and not sure if he was making fun of her, Eyre was lost for words, so she looked down at the surface of the table like it was the most interesting thing in the world, wiping hard enough to take the laminate off.

Pheria's tawny brown eyes narrowed as she studied Eyre, suddenly unfriendly. "I think it's clean," she said. "You can probably move on to the next one I'd say." Quite happy to move on, Eyre muttered goodbye and scrambled off, despairing about herself.

But she forgot about it quickly—realising that they had only ten minutes to get back to the lodge and make the Lecture Room in time. She tossed her cloth and bucket through to the Jotnar in the kitchen and scrambled out the Refectory entrance.

"See you at the Lecture Theatre, Rig!" she called, running down the path to Water Lodge.

CHAPTER SEVENTEEN

EYRE RACED IN THE door of the Lecture Theatre with a minute to spare. She had gone the wrong way and ended up at the First Aid building in error—then wasted time trying to work out where she should be. Fortunately, she had seen students in the distance heading the other way and had followed them. Now she looked around the Lecture Theatre, which was nearly full, trying to spot a vacant seat. She could see Ben Perrill up the back, sneering at her, and felt her blood begin to boil. There was a seat empty next to him, but she would rather walk back to the Sunshine Coast than sit beside him. The noise in the hall was deafening as students talked to each other, and finally she spotted Beatrice, Nick, and Abby at the side of the hall on the end of the row. Abby was waving wildly at Eyre, indicating that they'd saved her a seat, and Eyre raced up the side stairs to sit with them. Somehow, in amongst the scramble of the morning, Abby had managed to put silver tips on the ends of her hair—silver glitter and silver beads sparkled in the light. "In honour of the silver tank tops," she whispered to Eyre as she arrived. Eyre laughed and moved along to the seat they had saved her. Each seat in the lecture theatre had a flip-up lecture tablet to lean on, and on each tablet was a strange silver board about the size of a manila folder. The centre rectangle of the board was glassy and black, and a metal stylus was clipped at the side.

"It's a Felsic," Beatrice explained. "Watch this!" she continued, unclipping the stylus. With a flourish she signed her name on the black area of the board and her writing appeared on the black rectangle, illuminated brightly by light. Beatrice drew a silvery flower and a sun on the board beside her name, the doodles appearing brightly against the black background. "It's made from obsidian, infused with light energy," Beatrice explained, grinning as she finished a drawing of Ben Perrill being decapitated by a very large Saevus.

Curious, Eyre played with the board for a while. It was such a novel way to take notes. She realised that if she slid her finger upwards, the information she had written would spill off the edge of the black rectangular glass and disappear in little flashes of light. But if she wanted the information back, she just swiped downwards and the shining letters tumbled out of the air like hieroglyphics, and landed back on the board. Using the reverse end of the stylus made the writing disappear, much as an eraser would. It was mesmerising and fun, and much easier than a notebook.

After a while she stopped drawing on the black screen and looked around, spotting familiar faces in the crowd. Colton was sitting with Saskia a few rows below them. Both of them were practising with the black glass too, heads down. Then she saw Zanda, who was on his own, looking bored at the other side of the hall. Pheria and Jax were sitting in the middle and a few rows below them was Rigmar, talking animatedly to the friend he had been with that morning. His scar was obvious even from the distance Eyre was sitting and she wondered how he was feeling. She could feel herself stiffening up after the intense exercise that morning and she knew she was in for a world of pain tomorrow.

Rigmar turned slightly in his chair to point at something, and with a shock Eyre realised that he had Elevated already—his Inguz and Halo shone brightly under the theatre lighting. She wasn't sure what criteria determined when a Lightworker Elevated, but Rigmar seemed to her to be such an unlikely candidate. Deciding that she obviously knew nothing about it and happy for him, she looked around to see if anyone else had an Inguz on their arm. She checked through all the rows, but she could only see a couple more; one on a slightly built girl down the front who she didn't know, and another on a thin, smart-looking boy who also sat in the front row at the other end. Eyre felt relieved that there weren't many around yet; she was already starting to feel the pressure of whether she would Elevate, and she would be heartbroken if it didn't happen. It must be a great relief when your Inguz appeared, she thought.

Trying to get her mind off the subject, Eyre looked down at the front of the Lecture Theatre, wondering who would be coming to speak to them. A lectern made of grey crystal shards sat centrally at the front of the Lecture Theatre and a large pink crystal, irregularly shaped, was sitting on top of the lectern. Next to the lectern was a chrome and leather director's chair, and a large blackboard was over to one side, freshly cleaned. The arrangement was pretty much what Eyre had experienced at any of her previous schools, although none of the lecture rooms she had sat in before was large enough to fit 200 students in at once, and she'd never seen a blackboard in a classroom before, except in old television shows. A sudden hush fell as Sergeant Tottingham walked in the door and crossed to the front of the room.

"Well then, welcome to your first information session," Sergeant Tottingham said brightly. "Please look at your Felsic where you will find a copy of the programme for today's orientation, and a map of the Orientation Compound and surroundings." She indicated the silver board, and as Eyre looked down a typewritten schedule appeared on the black part of the board. When Eyre tapped the shining black screen, the silver words tumbled off the screen and disappeared in a sparkle of fairy dust. Following that, a map of the Compound appeared.

"As you will see on the programme I am going to talk to you about the schedule for the next few weeks, and then Professor Vela will take over to discuss briefly the History of Light—or HOL—and a brief summary of what you can expect in the TEPs. After a break for morning tea, I will come back to talk to you about Elevation." An excited hum buzzed through the lecture theatre; obviously everyone was as keen as Eyre to hear more about Elevation. Sergeant Tottingham continued.

"After that we will have a lunch break, and then you will have a free afternoon to do as you wish. This is the only free time you will have where there is nothing to work on, so I would enjoy it and make it count." Sergeant Tottingham tapped her Felsic and the students in the auditorium followed suit.

"Right then. The next list is the schedule for the rest of the orientation sessions. Orientation runs for ten weeks, after which there is a week for the Training, Evaluation and Placement examinations. Professor Vela will discuss that in more detail shortly."

There was a hum of murmuring, instantly silenced as Sergeant Tottingham cast her stern eye around the room. When all the whispering had died down, she continued.

"We have a staff of the finest academics in the world for Lightworking skills at the Academy of Light, and four of them will be lecturing to you this week about various skills you will need for the TEPs. They will also form part of the evaluating board when you undertake your TEPs and will decide who will be accepted into our first year intake next year. So I would listen carefully—and respectfully—to these lecturers as they have knowledge to share with you that could make the difference to whether you will be part of the Academy next year or not." She looked meaningfully around the lecture room, her gaze lingering on the boy she had held up against the wall the night before, then looked back at her Felsic as she began to read out the programme.

"Each day will have a similar format. You will rise for your morning run at precisely 0500. Back for breakfast at 0630, then ready for Meditation at 0800.

"Every morning I will be instructing you in the Lightworkers' form of Martial Arts—or 'Ferito'—in the Training Shed. Ferito consists of two parts: Tego, or Defence, and Aditus, or Attack, and it will form the core of your Physical Instruction at the Academy for the time you are here. That instruction will start at 0845 and go for an hour and a quarter each morning. Following that, each day for the first week there will be a specialist lecture beginning at 1030, which also goes for an hour and a quarter. Our specialist lecturers will cover a variety of topics this week.

"Lunch is at 1200 to 1245. After lunch you will find a partner, and in the first week you will practise for one hour and a quarter with that partner to try and improve the skills you have learned with our specialist lecturer for the day. Afternoon tea will be available for those who want it from 1415 to 1430 in the Common Room kitchen. You then have two hours for general training—from 1445 to 1645, which you may undertake either by the lake or in the shed, or anywhere on the Compound you choose. Dinner is at 1800 every night and lights out without fail at 2100."

Sergeant Tottingham swiped her Felsic again and kept reading.

"Right. Now about our specialist lecture topics. We have expert lecturers from our staff body who will instruct you in a variety of specialist subjects this week. Tuesday morning we have Lord Philius Clarembout, the Head of our Defence Department and our Fulminology Lecturer, who will instruct you on Lightning Skills and the Art of Pounding. Sir Philius is our longest-serving staff member at the Academy and I'm sure you will find his session very interesting.

"Wednesday morning's specialist session will be held by Dr Mahogany Botolfe from our Psionic Division, and she will be instructing you on Levitation and Telekinesis. Dr Botolfe is an expert in the use of Viq force and an ex-Academy student herself.

"Thursday morning's Specialist is Madame Cheska Overmantle, the Head of our Psionic Division, coming along to discuss Cognitive Energies and Tapping into the Psychic Forces. Madame Overmantle is consulted by many people around the world for her expertise in readings and prediction. She will speak in the Lecture Theatre with you that morning and you will go to the Meditation Hall for the afternoon's practise session.

"Our final specialist session will take place on Friday morning when UD1 from our Unlit Division will be coming in to talk about Thought Processes and Decoding. UD1 is the Dean of our Unlit Division and he is an international expert on espionage, cryptography and coding.

"From Friday afternoon onwards, up until the week of the TEPs, you are free to practise any of the disciplines you would like. You will soon realise where your strengths lie and I encourage you to work hard at those areas that come less easily to you as well as the ones that do. The ten weeks will be long and hard, but during that time, if you apply yourself, you will acquire the skills to undertake the TEPs successfully."

Sergeant Tottingham paused to look around the lecture theatre. The silence was resounding; students were fascinated and listening hard. Even Zanda, who Eyre had realised was fairly casual in general, was leaning forward in his chair and making notes on his Felsic as Sergeant Tottingham spoke. Then Sergeant Tottingham walked across to the pink crystal and touched her finger to it. A bright light emitted from the top of the crystal to the floor beside the Sergeant, and suddenly a life-sized holographic image of a student appeared in the centre of the stage, a long wooden stick in hand, raised as if to attack. The image was frozen in place, unmoving. A low murmur filled the auditorium.

"I am now going to show you a brief demonstration of previous students training to give you an idea of where we are heading with our instruction and what you are aiming for. You will see, although we have only ten weeks to practise these skills, some of these students have managed to reach quite a high level of proficiency during that time. However, before I begin, are there any questions?"

A hand shot up from the back. Ben Perrill. Eyre turned to hear what he had to say. "I've got two questions," Ben said. "Firstly, I was wondering why we need to hear from the Unlit Division. They are not Elevated and I don't understand what they have to offer us, especially during the TEPs. With all due respect,"—most *dis*respectfully, Eyre thought—"it doesn't seem relevant to those of us who will join the Academy as First Years next year. The second question is that I have heard that we have a person here who is not a Lightworker at all, and I was wondering why he is part of the evaluation process." Ben didn't name names, but he was looking at Nick as he spoke and everyone in the auditorium turned in Nick's direction, trying to figure out who Ben was alluding to. Ben continued in a tone that made Eyre want to race up and spit in his face. "It's just that I heard places are limited for next year, so I'm wondering why we are bothering to include someone who we know will not Elevate and is not even from our community? Why not place him directly in the U.D. next year so he doesn't waste a position in the orientation lodges?"

Sergeant Tottingham's brows drew together ferociously and she took a second to respond to this gross display of prejudice and discourtesy. Eyre was amazed at Perrill's gall, but then she had heard from Beatrice that his father was someone of note in the government, so maybe he felt he could get away with it. Certainly Sergeant Tottingham seemed to be tolerating behaviour that Eyre was sure another student would be executed for.

"The questions I'm prepared to answer, Number 119," she replied in a tightly controlled voice, "are those to do with the programme and curriculum. Management decisions are not your concern and I will thank you to not voice them in this arena. If you particularly wish to discuss something of importance, perhaps you could see me after class." The tone of her voice suggested that this might not be a wise thing to do. Sergeant Tottingham tapped her stylus loudly on the podium, unsettled and furious. But Ben seemed impervious to her rage and he sat back in his chair, content now that he had got the information he wanted out to all the students; Nick was an intruder, he didn't belong. Perrill was trying to make an outcast of him on the first day. Eyre clenched her jaw and stared intensely at the large boy. If pyrokinesis was to be a skill she would learn, perhaps she could make him spontaneously combust. Unfortunately, despite the loathing she sent his way, it seemed it wasn't going to happen, at least not today, and Eyre had to be content with the outraged look on Sergeant Tottingham's face. Ben Perrill might have protection from his father, but Eyre knew he was going to pay sometime for this insolence.

"Right then, here is the visual I wanted to show you," Sergeant Tottingham continued, her controlled voice at odds with the incensed expression on her face. "These are the students from last year's TEPs, and you will see that there are varying levels of skills amongst them. The secret to conquering the TEPs is recognising your strengths—and to use those skills accordingly—and to adjust your technique to compensate for your weaknesses." Sergeant Tottingham touched the top of the pink crystal again and sat down as the hologram began to move and was joined by other figures.

Eyre watched the fifteen-minute display in fascination as the holographic students performed a variety of tasks under instruction. They fought skilfully with wooden sticks, they made leaves rise up in the air with their hands, they set things on fire using their minds—an extraordinary array of skills that Eyre watched with absorbed wonder, hoping desperately she might be able to do them one day.

When the exhibition was finished Sergeant Tottingham touched the crystal and with a soft zap the images disappeared from the stage.

"Professor Vela will now give you an abridged version of the History of Light, followed by a brief description of what you can expect when you undertake the TEPs. We will then have a short morning tea break."

Sergeant Tottingham left the stage and Professor Vela walked to the podium. His pale eyes surveyed the students, flicking briefly over Rigmar, but he didn't say anything. Turning to the blackboard he seemed to focus and silver words appeared on the board: 'History of Light. HOL' The words were written in light and they shone brightly from the black background. Vela surveyed the audience and a supercilious look appeared on his face as he spoke.

"Many of you will already know most of what I am about to outline, I do realise that. But for the sake of those that don't, I will summarise briefly what HOL is about and how it will impact your future study here at the Academy.

"Lightworkers have been part of the population since people have been on the earth," he started. "We are a secret community focussed on doing good in the world to perpetuate the Light."

Like burning Rigmar's forehead? Eyre thought cynically, but didn't dare say it aloud. Obviously the Supervisors had better hearing than she could imagine after poor Rigmar's experience.

"Once we were a major force in the world," Professor Vela continued, "and the Overworld was at peace. The Aura stretched around the earth, a rainbow of light that protected the world from dark forces."

"What's the Overworld?" whispered a girl sitting in front of her to her neighbour, and Eyre sat resolutely still. The last thing she wanted was Professor Vela's eyes upon her.

"The Overworld," Professor Vela said, almost as if he had heard the girl, "consists of five sections: the normal world that you know, or what we call 'Entis,' and four alternate worlds called 'Terra,' 'Aqua,' 'Caelus' and 'Incendium,' or the 'Alterworlds,' which are accessible through a Seam. Each of those worlds has their own race of beings. For example, in Terra they are the Nemoris, and in Caelus there are the Caelites as well as a special race of beings called Clementis with unique powers of healing. Aqua and Incendium also have their own communities of intelligent creatures, all of whom you will study in detail at the Academy. Each year we have guest lecturers from the Alterworlds visit our students to share their world with us. At the end of each year you must pass an exam in one of these worlds in order to move on to your next year at the Academy. These exams are called the TACI tests, which of course is an acronym for Terra, Aqua, Caelus, and Incendium. You will need to work hard each year in order to pass your exam." There was complete silence in the auditorium as all the students listened carefully, and with his small eyes registering satisfaction, Professor Vela continued.

"Below the Overworld there is the Underworld, a place of pain and darkness which, as most of you know, is controlled by malign beings called the Gothak." Eyre nudged Beatrice and raised her eyebrows. "The Gothak are intent on bringing mayhem and chaos into the world. They are evil creatures with a heart of malevolence, and you will train to acquire the skills to fight them." He hesitated a moment then paced across the front of the stage, his long gingery ponytail swinging in agitation.

"In 1908, the 30th of June to be exact, the Lightworking community was betrayed by one of its members and the Aura around the Earth was destroyed by the Gothak. The people of Entis called this the Tunguska event. It is the largest impact event in recorded history and their scientists still debate what actually caused it. *We* call it The Proditio or the Betrayal. The Earth has always had influences from the Gothak. Evil acts have always been perpetuated by man. But since the Proditio history has darkened: the Earth has had two wars involving all its countries, terrible weapons manufactured, and people doing unspeakable deeds to each other, mass murders of millions of people. Terrorism on the rise. Pestilence. Famine. The balance is tipping badly towards the dark side. Nostradamus, in his famous prophecies, predicted that the world would be in crisis this century, and unfortunately we see evil escalating every year. Indeed, the loss of the Aura threatens the existence of the entire Overworld as there have been similar terrible events occurring in the Alterworlds.

"You can see the power of the Aura, which generated the Aurora Borealis up north, the Northern Lights of Aberdeen and the Naga Fireballs in Thailand. The Hessdalen Lights in Norway was also seeded by the Aura aeons ago, and there are a few others you will learn about in future years. Without the Aura the Gothak have risen in power, and of great concern to us is that recently they are increasingly able to breach Seams and enter the Overworld. Our purpose as Lightworkers now is to not only spread goodness and Light, but also to fight the Gothak and prevent their further ascendance in the Overworld." His thin face twisted and he added softly, "It is a dangerous time in our history and you must not underestimate the dire straits the Overworld is in. It is a time in which we need our Lightworkers more than ever."

He walked back to the centre of the stage. "You will find more about these worlds and the Gothak next year in HOL, which is a core subject for all Academy of Light students. Does anyone have any questions?" His eyes travelled across the students to a girl who had her hand up.

"Yes?"

"Can we fix the Aura?" she asked.

Professor Vela bent his head briefly then looked up with a fierce expression on his face. He put his hands on the podium and leaned forward intensely. "We have our best minds researching the problem," he answered. "It's crucial that we work out how to achieve that. But for now the best we can do is to try and prevent the Gothak from ascending."

Suddenly he turned and strode to the front of the stage, pointing at Rigmar. "You," he said sharply, "the donkey. You like to clown around, and perhaps you think I was too harsh on you? Well, let me ask you how you feel about your training when the Gothak have hold of you? This is life and death, students, and your training is not a joke! I expect you to focus and to train as if your life depends upon it. Because it will, trust me, it will."

A silence descended upon the theatre hall. No one else was game enough to put up a hand. Professor Vela waved his hands in the air at the blackboard and it shimmered, then the writing disappeared and it was blank again.

"Well then, we will break for morning tea and then meet back in here afterwards. You have twenty minutes."

An instant clamour arose as students stood up, talking to each other, and clumped down the stairs in a sudden horde. Eyre followed Beatrice, Nick, and Abby out of the Lecture Theatre.

There wasn't time to go back to the Refectory for morning tea, so the Jotnar had set up tables in the Lecture theatre hallway and the students helped themselves to sweet biscuits, fruit, cheese, crackers, and a cold drink or tea and coffee.

A girl nearby looked at Nick thoughtfully. "Someone doesn't like you much, does he? What's his problem?" she asked as she took an apple off the table. She was a slightly built Asian girl with long, black hair and strong-lensed glasses. Eyre couldn't remember seeing her before and her number, 110, meant that she was in Air Lodge. The girl walked over to join them and introduced herself. "I'm Tina. Tina Pang. What was that all about?"

"Ben Perrill is a twisted toad," Abby said hotly. "He picked on Nick for years at St Jeffrey's, and it looks like he's intending to continue. What a pig!"

Eyre realised with a start that the "old friend" from school Nick had mentioned at the cabins must have been Ben. *He* had caused some of those scars on Nick's body? They were remnants of terrible injuries, not some schoolyard tussle. Eyre felt a rage begin to rise in her that she knew would never leave.

"Not a pleasant sort, that's fairly evident," Tina agreed, taking a bite of her apple.

"That leaf thing we saw in the hologram," said Beatrice fiercely as she munched on cheese and crackers, "that's what I want to do! I want to twirl Perrill around like that!" They all laughed at the image but with an undercurrent of anger. No one found Ben Perrill much of a joke. Eyre noticed him in a group of his cronies, smirking at them from across the crowd.

Nick shrugged off the conversation. "Ah, don't worry about it. To be honest, he does have a point. I really shouldn't be here. And I guess it isn't fair that I've taken a position someone else could have had. Whittaker Ray said that it wouldn't be common knowledge I wasn't a Lightworker. But Perrill knew me at St Jeffrey's so he obviously couldn't help himself."

As Eyre looked around she could see that many of the students were looking at Nick curiously, some even with disapproval. It was obviously a major break from tradition to have a non-Lightworker there. She felt a flame of anger.

"Whittaker Ray had good reasons to bring you here Nick," she said. "Ben Perrill is an insecure jerk. He'll get what's coming to him, that's for sure."

Beatrice snorted. "I'll say," she laughed. "Did you see the look on Sergeant Tottingham's face? God, Perrill has stirred up a hornet's nest there!"

Somewhat mollified at the image of the ferocious Sergeant Tottingham going after Ben, they laughed. Rigmar came over with his friend from the run that morning. Rigmar was moving slowly and Eyre could see that the burn on his forehead intercepted his new Halo like a cattle brand. It looked painful, but he smiled as he joined them.

"Hi all," he said. "I'd like to introduce you to my friend, Number 124, aka Thomas Peterson. Thomas and I are both from Geraldton, er, that's in Western Australia for some of you Eastern Seaboarders."

Thomas was an average height boy with straight brown hair and grey eyes. He had a quick smile. "Nice to meet you. Is anyone else as sore as I am?" They all groaned in agreement.

"How's your head?" Nick asked Rigmar. "That was a bit rough, what Professor Vela did. It looks like it hurts."

"Ah, it's fine," Rigmar replied dismissively, but Eyre could see he looked unwell and he had a fine sheen of sweat across his brow.

"You really should go and get it attended to," she said with concern.

"I thought I'd go at lunch time," Rigmar said. "There hasn't been time yet."

"Well, congratulations on your Inguz!" Beatrice said. "It's fantastic that you've Elevated."

Rigmar waved his hand regally. "Goes well with the ass symbol don't you think?"

They all laughed. Just then there was a strange sound and a blue flashing light sent circles spinning across the walls. Looking for the source of the sound, Eyre spotted a blue crystal set high against the wall that flicked on and off as it emitted a high-toned ping.

"That's the signal for the next session," Thomas said. "Now this I'm looking forward to!" They all made sounds of agreement and filed through the door to the Lecture Theatre.

Sergeant Tottingham was already at the front of the theatre, waiting patiently until everyone was seated.

"Elevation is the thing most on students' minds, we have found. You'll have a lot of questions about it. So I'll do my best to explain it to you now," she began.

"The Inguz is a grounding rune. It represents the balance between the physical, the spiritual, and the mental," Sergeant Tottingham said, writing on the blackboard with her fingertip. "It is the essence of Lightworker philosophy, that equilibrium.

"When a student Elevates, the sign of the Inguz appears at the top of your left arm in silver light and you will be able to see your Halo, which will also be silver. Once the Inguz appears it is with you for life. The Inguz can appear at any time during the weeks leading up to the TEPs, but most of those who are going to will have Elevated by the third week. It generally happens quite quickly once our candidates arrive at the Compound. Your Halo is part of your issued uniform, a mechanical device to help focus your mental energies. You will wear it for your undergraduate years at the Academy, after which it is removed. Hopefully you will have enough mental acuity of your own by then."

Sergeant Tottingham waited for the soft chuckles to subside, then continued.

"Elevating is a natural metabolic process of Lightworkers' bodies, and we still do not know how exactly it works. There is no obvious pattern to it. If it's going to happen, it will happen when your own body decides, and about ten per cent of Lightworkers remain Unlit.

"I want to pause here and be clear about one thing." Turning to the students, she surveyed them pointedly. "If you are Unlit, you should not feel wanting in any way. Members of our Unlit Division are an integral part of the Lightworking community and should be respected for the contribution they have made to our history. Amongst the Unlit are some of the most courageous, moral, and intelligent people you will ever meet. So there is to be no criticism or disappointment shown by or towards a student who is Unlit. Anyone who expresses those sentiments is ignorant of how our community works." She looked coldly at Ben Perrill. "Number 119, you might do well to remember that. It takes many individuals to make up a community, and we all have essential skills." She held his gaze until he looked away, then she continued.

"Those students who are Unlit on the morning of the first TEPs—that's Monday of the final week—will leave to go home that day. And those who are selected by our Assessment Team may rejoin us next year as part of our Unlit Division."

Sergeant Tottingham walked back to the lectern and tapped her Felsic.

"Please look at your Felsic, which will now show you a summary of the Lightworking Sectors. Some of you may know about the Sectors, others may not, so here they are."

She turned and listed seven names on the blackboard in glowing writing: Sappir, Flava, Rufa, Virens, Arant, Tyros, and Hese. Then she drew the sign of the Inguz underneath the names. Eyre looked at her Felsic and saw the same information appear on her screen.

Sergeant Tottingham continued.

"The Sectors represent an area of strength in the Lightworking world, an area that we will develop at the Academy over the years.

"After the TEPs we have a ceremony where your placement is decided by the Aura, and your Sector colour will appear in the centre of your Inguz. Your Halo will also permanently change to the colour of your Sector."

She picked up a laser pointer and aimed the red dot on the first shining word written on the blackboard, Sappir.

"As you will see on your Felsic, Sappir is a blue Sector." Eyre looked down at her board and saw it now showed a diagram of three intersecting circles. Each section of the circles was a different colour and labelled. The larger parts of the three circles were coloured blue, yellow, and red, and the intersecting parts between them were coloured also—green, orange and purple—the colours you would get if you mixed the two larger colours together. The central section was brown. Sergeant Tottingham touched the pink crystal on the lectern, which hummed and sent out a hologram of the coloured circles, suspended in midair above the stage, a reproduction of the diagram on the students' Felsics. She picked up a pointer and indicated the top section of the outer left circle.

"Sappir is a strongly spiritual and creative Sector, and we find that our healers, our faceters—those who cut the crystals into the many objects we need—and our artists are part of this Sector. People who can communicate cross-species also are part of this Sector. The talisman of the Sappir Sector is, unsurprisingly, a sapphire."

Sergeant Tottingham moved the pointer to the outer section of the right-hand circle, which was coloured yellow.

"Flava is the Sector of mental acuity. People in this Sector are our strategists, our researchers, and our academics, our brightest minds. Those with holographic programming skills often come from this Sector also. If you are in this Sector your talisman is a citrine."

The pointer moved to the outer section of the bottom circle, which was coloured red.

"Rufa Lightworkers have strong physical skills. They are our fighters, our lightsmiths, and our weapons experts. They are often the strongest physically of us all. Their talisman is a ruby."

Now the pointer indicated the section between the blue and the yellow Sectors, which was coloured green.

"Virens have a mixture of spiritual and mental skills. People here often work in the area of psionics—telepathy, cognitive forces (sometimes called fortune-telling by those not in the Lightworking community), and aura reading. Many of our agricultural workers have Virens as their Sector, and they sometimes have the ability to commune with plants. The talisman for this Sector is an emerald.

"It is important to note that these Sectors are not discrete or exclusionary. Many students of one Sector will exhibit traits or skills from another Sector. For example, a Rufa might exhibit strong telepathic skills, or a Virens can be accomplished at weaponry. The Sector is just a general indication of the set of skills that a student has."

Sergeant Tottingham looked around the auditorium at the intent faces.

"I know this is a lot to take in at once," she said. "But you'll have the information on your Felsic, and you are welcome to come to us anytime to ask us questions.

"Moving along to the intersection of Flava and Rufa, you get Arant." She indicated the section between the yellow and red circles, which was coloured orange.

"The Arant Sector is characterised by mental and physical strengths. This Sector works closely with the Unlit Division in intelligence work and the defence force, and light bending—or illusion—skills. Their talisman is a carnelian."

The pointer moved to the intersection of the blue and red circles, which was coloured purple.

"Tyros Lightworkers have physical and spiritual strengths. Their fields of specialty are also in the area of psionics—levitation, telekinesis, and pyrokinesis. Tyros students are often gifted at astral travel, one of the most difficult of Lightworking skills. Tyros has as its talisman an amethyst."

Sergeant Tottingham pointed to the intersection of all the circles, which was coloured brown.

"The central Sector, Hese, is bronze. These people show equal strengths in all areas. Their talisman is golden quartz. Many of our leaders, administrators, and managers have come from the Hese Sector. Many members of the Echelon are from the Hese Sector.

"I might note here," she said, "that equal strength does not mean a person is gifted at all the skills. It just means that no skill has appeared stronger than the others." She paused and continued. "Likewise, just because you are placed in a Sector does not mean that you won't show skill in another Sector's area. The placement is an indication of your general strengths and does not exclude the other skills. And sometimes a skill will evolve more strongly as time goes on." She looked around the room. "Are there any questions?"

A girl down the front, Number 28, raised her hand.

"Yes?"

"How will we hide the Inguz and the Halo from the normal world, er, the er . . . Endus?" the girl asked. "Most of my friends will know nothing about Lightworkers. They'll think the Inguz and Halo are weird, and they'll ask lots of questions."

Sergeant Tottingham walked across the podium towards her. "Only Lightworkers can see the Inguz and the Halo, so people who are not Lightworkers will be none the wiser when you get home. They won't be able to see anything on your skin. By the way, it's not Endus, the word for the normal world is Entis."

Zanda snickered. "The Gothak are trying to *end us*, that's for sure!" His wit wasn't appreciated by the Sergeant, however, who silenced him with a ferocious look.

The girl who had asked the question made a rapid note on her Felsic, head down.

Sergeant Tottingham looked around the room. "Any other questions?"

A boy sitting to the side called out. "So all the teachers are in a Sector?"

Sergeant Tottingham nodded. "I am Rufa. Professor Vela is Flava." She rolled up the sleeve of her shirt, revealing a huge muscular arm with a sparkling Inguz on it. The centre of her Inguz glowed brightly red.

"The centre of Professor Vela's Inguz is yellow. Similarly, your teachers' and your family members' Sectors will now be visible to you. The Halo you are wearing is a mechanical device that enables you to focus your energy so you can see the Inguz. This is why you have not seen the symbol on your family members before. After your graduation in third year, or fourth year, if you go on to take the graduate year, you will not wear a Halo, as your Lightworker force will be developed enough that you will be able to see the Inguz and the Sectors of Lightworkers without it." She rolled down her sleeve and looked around. "Any more questions?"

A boy at the end of Eyre's row put up his hand. "I thought the Aura was broken," he said. "How can it determine our placement?"

"Good question," Sergeant Tottingham replied. "As we outlined in the lecture, in past history, the Aura seeded many phenomena around various parts of the world, which show up as rainbow colours in the sky. But there are also some ancient pieces gifted from the Aura that have been held by various Light Academies for centuries, and they are considered to be amongst the most priceless treasures of the Lightworking world. These pieces of the Aura were taken before the Proditio, and they are used for the Placement Ceremonies of the schools that hold them. Our piece of the Aura is in the vaults under the school and securely guarded by the Mimir. It is our greatest asset, and irreplaceable, because now the Aura is gone, we can never obtain another—unless, By the Light, the Aura is somehow reinstated." She gave a sad smile, as if that was not something she considered likely.

"When the Placement Ceremony occurs, the Mimir will bring the Academy's piece of the Aura out, and it will determine your Sector, at which time your Inguz is charged with the appropriate colour.

"Many of you will already know where your general skills lie, and your placement, if it happens, will be no surprise to you. But sometimes the placement is not what you anticipated, and for some people with expectations, it can be a disappointment. But I urge you to embrace the results of your TEPs, whatever they may be, and accept that this is the greater purpose of your journey in this life."

She leaned over and touched the pink crystal so the image of the Sectors disappeared.

"I think we've talked enough for one morning, so unless there are any questions, I will leave it there, and we will take a break for lunch. You are free after lunch to do as you wish for the afternoon until dinner at 1800 sharp. Please feel free to come and see me should you need any assistance."

Eyre packed up her Felsic and followed her friends out of the Lecture Theatre, her mind spinning from all the information.

CHAPTER EIGHTEEN

IN THE REFECTORY THERE was an excited buzz as students discussed the information from the morning session. Eyre put her lunch tray on the table as she joined Beatrice, Nick, and Abby.

"Wasn't that amazing?" Abby said in excitement. She was looking at her Felsic as she ate, swiping through the information. "What Sector do you want to be in? I like the sound of Sappir. Art and music—bliss!" She tossed her silver-tipped hair with mock vanity. "And I really love the colour blue!"

Beatrice was more pragmatic. "Personally, I'll take anything as long as I Elevate," she answered. Everyone made sounds of agreement. Rigmar came up to join them, but he sat without a tray.

"You not eating, mate?" asked Nick, and Rigmar shook his head.

"I'm not that hungry," he answered. Eyre looked at the perspiration dotting his forehead and thought he seemed more unwell than he did before. He looked like a person who normally enjoyed his food, so he must be feeling sick to avoid lunch.

"I'll take you to First Aid after lunch if you like," she said. "I know where it is. I was trying to attend Lectures there this morning." Nick chuckled and grinned at her. Rigmar looked grateful and sank into his chair, apparently exhausted.

Soon they were joined by Carly and the Aboriginal boy, Number 61, from Eyre's cabin. Eyre introduced everyone to him, and the boy told them his name: Warrigal Guncungurra. He was a tall, good-looking boy with very white teeth and a calm manner that gave off a quiet self-assuredness.

Warrigal told them that he was from the Blue Mountains and that he lived in Katoomba with his family, some of whom were Lightworkers. With self-deprecating humour, he made them all laugh when he said, "Mum said if I don't make it into the Academy, don't bother coming home! Someone from the Gundungurra has been at this school for a long time. It's part of our history. And like you, people in our own community don't realise that some of us are different."

Eyre was caught up in the conversation, but suddenly she looked over at Rigmar and realised with a shock that he was going grey. His eyes were glazing over, and he barely seemed conscious. Whatever was wrong with him was obviously serious, and he was getting worse quickly. She thought if he didn't go now, they would have to carry him to First Aid.

"I should take Rigmar to the First Aid building. He's not well," she said, her face troubled.

Nick jumped to his feet. "I'll help you," he said.

Together they half-carried Rigmar out of the hall. He was not a small boy, and it was hard work, painful even, as Eyre was starting to suffer badly from stiffness. She and Nick struggled down the stairs and dragged Rigmar to the First Aid building. By the time they got there Eyre's arms were shaking from the effort, and she was covered in sweat. They knocked on the door and a young woman with a long blonde braid and pale blue eyes answered. She was dressed in the Lightworker uniform, and she had an Inguz on her arm with a bright blue centre. Two white leather straps ran over her shoulders and down to her belt, crossing each other. The young woman looked at Rigmar in concern.

"Bring him in here. Quickly."

Eyre and Nick heaved Rigmar inside. He was barely conscious now and was muttering as they lay him on a stretcher bed. The young woman looked closely at the brand on his forehead, examining the inflamed edges of the wound where tiny blue spots were starting to form. She put her hand across his forehead and frowned.

"He's burning up," she said in a worried tone. "I think he has Soil Sickness." She pulled back his eyelids and muttered in concern. Rigmar suddenly began to thrash around and then went into a sudden stiff rigor. The girl jumped up.

"My name is Leema. I'm a graduate student," she said to Eyre and Nick, "and I'm here voluntarily for experience during orientation. I hope to be a Medic one day." She looked down at Rigmar, who was throwing what seemed to be a fit. "But this is beyond my skills. I think we need to get a Clementis in." She looked desperately over at Nick and said urgently, "Can you go and find Sergeant Tottingham and get her here quickly, please? I need help. I'm not sure what to do."

Nick was out the door in a flash and the girl moved quickly over to Rigmar and turned him on his side. "Can you help me, please," she asked Eyre. "We need to keep him on his side and make sure he doesn't choke.

I've seen one case of Soil Sickness before. It's a rare bacterium that gets into open wounds, and it's deadly. It comes from Terra, and we have it here around the campus because of the first year TACI expeditions. The patient I saw unfortunately didn't make it."

Aghast, Eyre looked down at Rigmar, who was so pale he already looked like a corpse. He might not make it? It was that serious? He might die? She couldn't imagine it. He was a good friend already, and her stomach clenched in fear. Together she and Leema held Rigmar tightly, keeping him on his side. Despite the fact he was so unwell, he had great strength, and they struggled to hold him still as his muscles shuddered and locked together. Leema's face was stricken, and she looked desperately to the door, waiting for help.

"Can you hold him for a second?" Leema asked. "I'll get some cold towels to try to bring his temperature down." She jumped up and ran into the other room, and Eyre could hear a fridge door opening and closing, the sound of ice being thrown into a bucket. Eyre leaned on Rigmar to hold him still. He moaned in pain.

"Hang in there, Rigmar," Eyre said softly. "We're going to help you." She put her hand over the wound on his forehead and felt the heat searing through her hand. But as she held her hand there a strange feeling ran up her arm, a mixture between a static shock and a vibration. The heat under her palm dissipated, and in a few seconds Rigmar's forehead felt normal again. Surprised, she took her hand away and gasped. The Nemoris symbol on his forehead had completely disappeared, and as she looked in astonishment at him, Rigmar's eyes opened. He sat up slowly. Eyre was so surprised she jumped back.

"Where am I?" Rigmar asked in a confused voice. Eyre was speechless, unable to answer, her mouth gaping open. Just then Leema raced back in with an armful of wet towels. She stopped in amazement as she saw Rigmar.

"What happened?" Leema gasped. "How can he be sitting up?" She looked closer and dropped the towels.

"His forehead. . . ? Where's the . . . wound?" She looked over at Eyre, who was standing there in confusion. "What did you do? Are you a healer?"

Eyre raised her hands. "I just felt his forehead," she said lamely. "And then he sat up."

Sergeant Tottingham burst through the door of the First Aid building, Nick close behind her. She looked confused and then vaguely irritated when she saw Rigmar sitting up.

"I thought there was an emergency here," Sergeant Tottingham said in an annoyed voice.

"She healed him," was all Leema could say. Eyre could only stand there, not knowing what she had done. Sergeant Tottingham walked over and examined Rigmar's forehead and then looked at Eyre.

"Astounding," she said softly. "Normally only the Clementis could effect a cure like this. What did you do?"

Eyre could only shrug and look at Nick helplessly. "I really don't know. I'm not sure it was even me really. He just seemed to get better."

Sergeant Tottingham stared at Eyre's bare arm and shook her head. "Well, let's get him back to his bunk, and he can sleep this afternoon. Hopefully he'll get his strength back. How do you feel, 38?"

Rigmar stood up, the colour coming back into his face.

"I feel . . . better," he said slowly. "My headache is gone. The pain from my joints disappeared. I think I can walk by myself." He took a few steps and looked at Eyre.

"It's amazing," he said. "I don't know how you did it, but thank you!"

Nick and Eyre helped Rigmar back to Earth Lodge and left him there to rest. He was walking normally by the time they got there, but said he felt very tired and was happy to lie down and sleep. Eyre felt a great sense of relief: it looked like he was going to be okay. She realised that she was tense from the stress of the emergency, and now that the crisis had passed, she felt drained. She contemplated having a rest herself this afternoon, but the thought of the free afternoon was too enticing.

"Let's have a swim," she suggested to Nick. "Lake Altum looks gorgeous. It would be great to relax our sore muscles!"

Nick nodded. "Great idea," he agreed. "I'll go get the others."

He disappeared down the path, and Eyre headed back to find her swimming gear.

CHAPTER NINETEEN

EYRE ENTERED WATER LODGE to find many of her group already there. Some were busying themselves with various tasks around their bunks —tidying lockers, straightening bedclothes, cleaning boots—whilst others lounged up against their bunks chatting. Just before Eyre headed for the stairs up to the second floor, she saw Warrigal standing alone by his bunk

"We're going for a swim, Warrigal. Want to come?" she called, and he smiled.

"Awesome, I'll grab my stuff."

Other students looked up. Pheria, who had been talking to a boy Eyre didn't know, turned around. Her tawny eyes considered Eyre. "I think it's a great idea, Scrubber," she said, obviously referring to Eyre's cleaning task that morning.

Eyre gritted her teeth but refrained from biting. "Good then, see you there," she said. As she turned to go, Pheria added, "You might want to head to the Refectory first. Professor Vela was livid that you and that fat boy weren't there wiping tables after lunch."

Eyre clenched her jaw. Okay, the jury was definitely in. Pheria was categorically a cow.

"His name is Ragmar," she replied tightly. "And I think Sergeant Tottingham will let us off this time!" She thundered up the stairs, letting her feet expel the fury she felt. What an absolute slimeball that girl was!

"Swimming at the lake for anyone interested," she called as she walked through the top floor, and Carly, who was sitting on her bed reading, tossed her book aside.

"Cool!" she exclaimed. "I'm in!"

Word spread, and soon there was a crowd of students from all four halls heading along the gravel path down to the lake, wearing swimsuits and thongs, and carrying a jumble of brightly coloured towels that swung against their legs as they walked. It was a really hot day, and the sun beat down, creating a shimmering haze across the top of the eucalyptus trees that circled the lake. The lake itself was a deep mysterious blue, changing to black at the centre, and the surface of the water was glasslike, as lustrous as a highly polished gem.

Eyre walked down the path with Zanda and Carly and met up with Beatrice, Nick, and Abby. They tossed their towels on the grass before heading down the muddy banks to the water. With their swimsuits on it was evident that quite a few more of the students had an Inguz already. Lucky them, thought Eyre, but put it out of her mind as the lake enticed her in. Despite the heat of the day, the water was cool, and as Eyre ventured further in, the water got colder. It felt freezing against her hot skin. Other students came in, too, and some were splashing each other madly in the shallows, squeals of laughter dancing in the air.

Deciding not to prolong the agony, Eyre dove into the cold water and swum out and away from the edge of the lake. It felt wonderful to swim again, and her body rapidly adjusted to the temperature of the water. When she stopped about ten metres out and trod water, looking back at the shore, her skin burned with a buzzing warmth. It was blissful, and she leaned back and floated on her back, idly watching as a flock of pink and grey galahs screeched across the brilliant blue sky above her. With relief she realised that the soreness in her muscles was easing. This was such a good idea! Soon she was joined by a crowd of other students, and they bobbed around in the deep water, chatting and enjoying the heat on their faces and the coolness of the water.

As she drifted along with her eyes closed, Eyre bumped into someone and straightened up, apologising. When she saw who it was, the words died in her mouth. Jack Jackson, or Jax as Zanda had called him, that friend of Pheria's with the enigmatic stare.

"Sorry," she said briefly and went to swim away.

"S'okay," Jax replied, eyeing her with those cool green eyes. "My fault entirely. What's your name?"

Eyre hesitated then stopped, kicking her legs to stay afloat. "Eyre," Eyre replied guardedly. "I know your name is Jax. Zanda told me."

Jax's gaze flickered a little at the mention of Zanda, and then he pulled gently at one of Eyre's plaits. "Are you Irish?" he asked. "Your red hair looks Irish."

"My father's grandfather was, apparently," Eyre said. "My family has been here for a while, though."

"I was waiting for you to clean my table today," Jax said, his eyes teasing. Eyre's stomach flipped. Playful eyes were definitely a positive in her book. He certainly was handsome, with his black hair slicked back by the water. Probably thought a lot of himself too, she decided, and resolved to proceed with extreme caution.

"So was your girlfriend, apparently," she said pointedly. "She wondered where the 'scrubber,' I think she called me, was this afternoon."

Jax looked confused. "Girlfriend?" he repeated. Then understanding dawned. "You mean Pheria?" At the confirmation in Eyre's face, he laughed. "She's not my girlfriend. We knew each other in Sydney. We both went to the same school. So did Zanda. Pheria and I are just friends, that's all. She called you a scrubber?"

Eyre raised her eyebrows to confirm it. Jax laughed, then his eyes ran over her face again. "Well, I can assure you, you're anything but that, Eyre," he said. "Don't worry about Pheria. She has a sharp tongue sometimes, but she's a good person."

Eyre felt awkward at his nearness, and she felt he wasn't quite on track about Pheria. Either about her supposed goodness or her designs on Jax. Pheria might not be his girlfriend, but from the proprietary way she behaved around Jax, it was obvious she would like to be. Even now, Eyre could see Pheria's sleek dark head turned in their direction, no doubt those tawny eyes afire with jealousy. Eyre decided it was all a bit much for her, and she reversed slightly.

"I'm going to lie on the bank for a while," she said.

Jax's eyes showed disappointment, but he smiled lightly. "Catch you then . . . Eyre," he said.

Eyre struck out for shore with strong strokes and headed up the bank to lie on her towel beside her friends. Jax swam lazily over to join Pheria's group, and Eyre could see him watching her from out in the water. She shivered. Too good looking for his own good—and definitely too good looking for her.

She lay sleepily in the hot sun and dozed off to the dim sounds of students enjoying the water. Time passed until suddenly she was jolted into consciousness by a scream. Sitting up in fright she held her hand above her eyes to see what was going on. There was a group of students out in the deep water, shouting and screaming and pointing to something not far from them. The screaming caused instant panic, and students in the shallows splashed out of the lake as the ones farther out started swimming frantically for the shore. Eyre stood up, trying to see what the problem was. Warrigal had been sitting on his towel, and he ran over to join her.

"What is it?" he asked.

"I don't know," Eyre replied. "I can't see anything, can you?"

They both ran down to the water's edge and helped the stumbling swimmers out of the water.

"What's the matter?" Eyre asked them. "Why is everyone panicking?"

"There's something out there!" a girl cried in horror as she staggered out. "It attacked Jensen!" Eyre didn't know who Jensen was, but her stomach crawled in fear. She ran farther in to the water, helping people out and straining to see what was out there. Pheria made back it to the shallows, dragging someone behind her.

"Help!" she screamed. "Get over here, someone! And someone get Sergeant Tottingham! *Hurry up!*" A student took off and sprinted wildly up the path towards the Compound. Eyre and Warrigal raced over and took the person from Pheria, who was exhausted and crawled on her hands and knees from the water, gasping. It was a boy, Jensen, Eyre guessed as she lifted him out of the water. He was unconscious, his face drained pale. As they pulled him onto the bank Eyre realised that one of his legs was missing, completely gone from beneath the knee. A ragged nub of bone was left, and blood was pumping fearfully from his leg.

"Quickly!" she yelled, putting pressure above his knee. "Get me something to tie around his leg!"

A tall, fit-looking girl with short brown hair didn't hesitate. She whipped the belt out of her shorts and passed it over to Eyre. "Here, use this!" The girl knelt down to help apply pressure as Eyre wound the belt around the boy's leg and looped it through the buckle, pulling hard to tighten it. Warrigal also knelt down, and he and the girl applied pressure while Eyre tightened until the blood stopped pumping out. Eyre leaned over, feeling Jensen's carotid artery for a pulse and was relieved to feel a shallow beat. She could see his eyes fluttering, and she felt a shock of relief that at least for now he was alive. There was so much blood everywhere it was hard to see what was happening to the wound, but she turned him so that his legs were up the hill, above his head and then leaned heavily on his leg, hoping to stop the blood flow. Her wild eyes scanned the Compound, desperate for someone to come and help.

She had been so desperately working on stopping the haemorrhaging she had forgotten about the disturbance in the water. But suddenly she heard a fearsome, deep-throated growl behind her that made her hair stand on end. Slowly she turned back to see what it was.

"Oh. My. God," she whispered. Warrigal stood up beside her.

"Bunyip," he said softly. "Bunjil help us."

A huge creature, about ten metres long, rose from the water, towering above the students. Its head was leathery with a smashed-in face like a gargoyle's, and the huge triangular teeth that lined its mouth gnashed together viciously as the Bunyip looked around with a myopic, baleful stare. The roaring it made was so loud that Eyre couldn't hear anything; she could only see the mouths of the panicking students moving as they tried to call to one another in the deafening noise. And then everyone watched in horror as the massive creature began to move towards the shore. A reptilian tail with strange protuberances smacked the surface of the lake as the Bunyip walked into the shallower water, heading towards the students. A small group of people was still in the water after swimming in from the deep, and Eyre watched, her hand to her mouth, as they swam past the great beast to the shore.

Four people finally reached the shallows, and Eyre realised that one of them was Jax, helping a girl who was obviously exhausted. They looked like they were going to get out of the water safely, but as they staggered on to the shore, the Bunyip swung around suddenly and hit Jax hard with its tail. Jax flew through the air and landed heavily, lying unmoving on the bank. Then, reaching its long neck down, the huge scaled beast grabbed the girl that Jax had been helping, tossing her violently into the air. The small red eyes surveyed the girl as she smashed back into the shallows, bleeding, and the creature let out an ear-splitting roar as it opened its mouth and leaned down towards her.

Eyre was rooted to the spot in shock, unable to move, but Warrigal let out a ferocious war cry and dashed into the water, screaming and waving his arms to divert the Bunyip's attention. He stood beneath it as the creature, distracted from the girl, towered above him. Nick splashed through the water and stood beside Warrigal in the knee-deep water. The scars on his body gleamed as he leaned over the girl, protecting her.

Suddenly a blinding beam of light shot from behind Eyre and struck the creature in the neck. It screeched in pain and twisted back and forth wildly, trying to see what was attacking it. Warrigal and Nick grabbed the girl and half-carried her from the water on to the bank as the creature thrashed in the shallows, bellowing loudly.

Looking behind her, Eyre saw Sergeant Tottingham striding down the bank, her arm held straight out in front of her, a beam of light emitting steadily from her palm. It held like a bright burning laser, searing into the creature's neck in red lines of flame. She strode forwards, fearlessly walking towards the creature.

"Get out of the way!" she shouted. "Go up the bank!" The Bunyip's shortsighted eyes finally realised where the pain was coming from, and it reared up again, snapping its teeth wildly. Sergeant Tottingham stopped the beam of light and reached over her shoulders, pulling the two short weapons from the silver leather straps behind her back. As she pulled them out Eyre could see the weapons clearly for the first time. They were cut from clear sparkling crystal that reflected light in all directions, and along the edge of the blade was a silvery streak of metal. Eyre recognised them as the same weapons that Peter Edmunsun had used to fight the Gothak: dual shining, fearsome blades that seemed to emit shards of light. Sergeant Tottingham wielded them in front of her like double machetes, twirling them around her wrists as the Bunyip snarled and coiled to strike.

Another beam of light flew from nearby and Eyre watched as Professor Vela, eyes blazing, marched down the bank and stood to the other side of the creature, burning the side of its head. It screamed in agony and reared up in the air then came back down with a loud splash, sending waves of water flooding onto the shore. Its grotesque head snaked down, teeth slashing at Sergeant Tottingham. Moving with amazing speed for a big person, Sergeant Tottingham raised the crystal machetes and struck at the thick neck. The blades sliced effortlessly through the muscle, and in an instant the head was completely severed, falling to the muddy bank with a loud thud. The blades of the weapons ended up crossed in Sergeant Tottingham's hands, and a high *zing* reverberated in the air as she stepped away from the creature. The rest of the body hung for a second and then crashed into the water, lying in the shallows as huge waves of water crashed over it. Spurts of black blood poured from the neck and into the lake waters, forming a crimson oilslick.

Eyre dropped back down to the bank to check on Jensen, every muscle shaking as she did so. Fortunately, Jensen was still breathing, although he was unconscious. Beatrice and Abby knelt beside Eyre, their faces pale, and Abby put a towel under Jensen's head. There didn't seem to be anything else to do as they waited for Sergeant Tottingham to give them some direction.

"Clear the bank!" she shouted, waving her hands at the students crowding the slope. "Make room!"

As the crowd parted, the graduate student from First Aid, Leema, raced down the bank, a stretcher under her arm, and she skidded to a stop beside Jensen. Eyre helped her roll him onto the stretcher, and then Leema placed her hand on the stretcher. With a blinding flash, it disappeared. Then Leema put her arm around the girl who had been tossed up in the air by the creature. Her ankle was obviously broken, and she had some deep cuts from the sharp teeth, but fortunately nothing worse had happened to her. Eyre squinted as Leema and the girl disappeared in a white zap of light. There was a deadly silence in the air; the only sound was the slapping of the waves settling down.

Sergeant Tottingham was surveying the dead creature, concern on her face. Almost as if to herself, she was muttering. "Impossible, surely. . . ." But when she saw the students approaching, she turned around. "Filthy beast. Not the way I'd prefer to show you, but nonetheless, a good demonstration of the power of Ferito."

"Will Jensen be alright?" a girl said in a wavering voice.

Sergeant Tottingham's face gave nothing away. "Yes," she said softly, after a pause. "He is going to the Clementis, and they will look after him. He'll be okay."

Professor Vela walked over and nudged the huge head distastefully with his foot.

"Foul creature," he said in disgust. "Didn't realise there were any still around."

"Not for hundreds of years," Sergeant Tottingham said. "More evidence the Seams are weakening." She looked around at the stricken students, many of whom were holding each other and still shaking in fear.

"Who knows where the therapeutic pools are?" Many students nodded and a couple raised their hands. "Right then," Sergeant Tottingham continued, "I want every single student who was here this afternoon to head to the pools straight away. Help each other get there, and remain there for an hour before dinner. I will get rid of this abomination with the help of the Jotnar."

Slowly everyone picked up their gaily-patterned towels, the colours so ironically cheerful. In subdued voices they talked amongst themselves as they headed back up the path.

Eyre walked in silence with Beatrice and Abby. Jax was fortunately okay, and she could see him up ahead, walking slowly beside Pheria. As she watched them, she felt conflicting emotions: a begrudging admiration at Pheria's courage in bringing Jensen to shore and a sense of shame that she herself had been unable to move when the creature was about to attack that poor girl in the shallows. Eyre's lack of action hung over her like a dark cloud, and she trudged up the path. The pain that had eased this afternoon in the water was back in her body with a vengeance. Suddenly Jax looked back at her and smiled, and her spirits lifted a little. She might not have reacted very quickly—or at all—when the beast had attacked, but at least she had helped Jensen to a degree. She turned to Warrigal and Nick, who had been walking silently in the crowd behind her.

"That was incredibly brave," she said. "You both saved that girl's life. I was so terrified I couldn't even move." Other students murmured their agreement and echoed her comments, slapping Warrigal and Nick on the back.

Nick shrugged like it was no big deal. Eyre was coming to realise he was a person of few words. Yet again she contemplated the source of his terrible scars and wondered if his quick reaction to danger was a result of whatever had caused those scars—that he was used to thinking and moving fast in order to survive.

Warrigal gave a small smile, and Eyre noticed that sometime during the afternoon his Inguz had come in. Well deserved, she thought, feeling glad he had Elevated.

The therapeutic pools were located at the southern end of the Compound, a series of hot pools that simmered permanently at a temperature of about 37 degrees Celsius. They had been created out of huge crystals of different colours, and flat layers of the formations ran around the edges of the pools to make ledges to sit on in the water. There were about twenty pools of differing shapes, capable of holding up to fifteen students each, and they were situated at different levels so that the water ran between them, cascading down from one to the other.

The first pool was made out of large emeralds, and the water ran from it into a second pool formed from deep purple crystals, amethysts, Eyre could see. There were so many crystal pools of various colours—red, blue, pink, yellow—that the air was lit by a reflected rainbow glow that was mesmerising and calming. There was more than enough room for all the students in the intake to be there at once, but not all had been down at the lake, so only about half the pools were filled by the time all the students got in. Eyre headed for the beautiful clear aquamarine pool, and minerals dissolved in the water from surrounding rocks made the water feel almost silky as Eyre slipped in.

Her body felt instantly encompassed with a soothing heat, and she settled against the smooth aquamarine formations, leaning her head back and closing her eyes. The chunky crystals seemed to vibrate, and they massaged her back and muscles until a sense of well being began to glow through her. No one spoke. The afternoon had been too overwhelming, and it seemed no one had a desire to talk about it at all.

Eventually people started to leave, their stress now greatly alleviated from just being in the water. Feeling much better, Eyre grabbed her towel and headed back to Water Lodge to get ready for dinner.

CHAPTER TWENTY

THERE WAS A LOT of noise in the Refectory as Eyre waited in line to get her food. Two hundred voices had a lot to talk about this evening, but the voices were subdued—students were shocked about the day's events.

On the way to her table she passed Pheria and Jax sitting with their friends. She hesitated and then stopped and turned back to their table.

"Good job, Pheria," Eyre said. "Jensen was lucky you were there. You were really brave."

Pheria eyed her coolly. "He was lucky you were there too, scrubber. The tourniquet saved his life, I heard."

Eyre put her tray down on the table, sitting at an empty chair across from Pheria. "You know," she said, "could you *not* call me that? Scrubber? I really don't like it. My name is Eyre."

Pheria raised her eyebrows and put her hands up, palms outwards in a sign of peace. "No worries, Eyre," she said. "Didn't mean anything by that. I thought it was pretty funny."

Eyre's eyes narrowed, but she didn't respond. She looked across the room and saw that Number 182, the girl Jax had helped to shore, Edith Worth, was sitting at a far table. She had crutches, and her arms were bandaged, but she was obviously doing okay after her ordeal.

"Edith was lucky, too, Jax," Eyre said. "She wouldn't have made it if you hadn't been there. How are *you* feeling?"

Jax rubbed a lump on his head and shrugged. "Better than Jensen, I imagine, the poor guy."

Eyre looked around. "Have any of you heard how he's doing?"

"He's apparently with the Clementis in their Healing Centre at Caelus," a boy, Number 179, across the table answered. "He has lost a leg, and they can't do anything about that. But I heard he is going to make it."

"Well, that's a relief I guess, but how terrible for him." Eyre said, and 179 nodded. Then seeing Beatrice waving at her Eyre stood up to go and join her friends' table. "I'll see you all later," she said, picking up her tray.

As Eyre sat down with her friends, Abby looked around the room. "Where's Rigmar? Is he feeling better?" They knew he had gone to First Aid, but not the details. As far as they knew, he was resting in the lodge after feeling unwell. Not really wanting to go into it and still confused herself as to what really *had* happened, Eyre simply said that he was recovering and would hopefully join the group in the morning for the first training session.

Phillip Outray came in and joined their table and so did Warrigal and Nick, deep in conversation as they walked over. It became obvious they were talking about Sergeant Tottingham.

Nick said in an admiring voice, "Did you see her kill that beast? I'll never forget it."

Eyre agreed. "She was so ferocious. And so fast! No wonder she's in Rufa." Suddenly the Sergeant was no longer an annoying disciplinarian. Seeing her fight the Bunyip so fearlessly had permanently changed how Eyre regarded the TEP supervisor, and she was sure the others felt the same way.

Abby gave a short laugh. "I hope Ben Perrill was there to see. He may regret taking her on after watching her in action! Perhaps she could demonstrate those weapons on him?"

As if on cue, Sergeant Tottingham walked into the Refectory. A wave of applause echoed around the hall as well as a few whistles and cheers. She looked a little taken aback then held up her hands for silence as she walked to the front of the room.

"Thank you, students, you are very kind. Fortunately Jensen is with the Clementis and doing as well as could be expected." A low murmur greeted these words.

"I wanted to talk about what happened," Sergeant Tottingham continued. "A message has been sent home to your parents as we knew there will be concerns about the event, and whether there is any further danger to you students. Bunyips are rare creatures that have not been seen for centuries. Reports from settlements in the area historically have mentioned sightings of the creatures, but in actual fact, no confirmed encounters have been recorded since the 1600s. Until now it was believed they were confined to the Underworld.

"Recently, Lightworker leaders have become aware that Seams are being breached with concerning frequency, of Strigis and the Gothak being encountered regularly, when once their appearances were very rare. And they are causing devastating havoc throughout the world. Creatures that have until now been locked in the Underworld, such as the Bunyip, have been venturing into all parts of the Entis. We have had reports of Chupacabras becoming active in Puerto Rico again. And Yaoguai have been encountered on the Daxue Mountain in China. These are malignant creatures that are becoming more active in our world. The Alterworlds are similarly reporting frequent breaches and intrusions from the Strigis and the Gothak, and their communities are also suffering terrible losses. So the event this afternoon is very concerning, an ominous sign. And one we do not take lightly.

"However, as we have explained in our correspondence to your families, our most expert warders have reinforced our Runic Protections, and we have established a second Mantle above the first. We are confident that this will provide the extra security to ensure the school and its students stay safe."

Sergeant Tottingham looked around at the students. They were all listening with interest, but an overarching sombre mood filled the room. It was obvious that most of them were still in shock over Jensen's terrible situation.

"If anyone would like to look at the Bunyip before it is removed and dissected for research, we have pulled it up onto the bank at the western end of the Compound where we will leave it for one day. I would encourage you to go and look at it. It is a rare creature and one you may never see again. I will be available if anyone would like to discuss what happened this afternoon—any time. Are there any questions?"

Jax put up his hand. "Those swords that you used, what are they?" he asked. "Whatever they are, I want one!" Everyone chuckled softly; the light relief was welcome after the sobering afternoon. Eyre was glad he'd asked the question—she wanted to know, too.

Sergeant Tottingham reached over her back and removed one of the short swords. It had been sheathed in the silver, leather-crossed braces behind her back, with one sword in a scabbard on each side of the straps. As she held it up, it sparkled like diamonds, sending rays of light shooting across the room. Along the edge of the blade a bright silver strip of metal shone like a laser beam. Sergeant Tottingham held the weapon reverently.

"This is an Antarak, a form of seax that is cut from a single crystal of diamond. In your third year you will be presented with your Arms Endowment, and in it you will receive two of these. The Antarak is kept in pairs in the scabbard at the back of your leather baldrics"—she turned and indicated a pocket in the silver crossed braces that ran up from her belt —"and you must look after them vigilantly. You will not be given another one if anything happens to them. You will receive your baldrics when your Arms Endowment is presented to you. Third years have black baldrics, graduate students have white, and staff have silver."

The students studied the Sergeant's baldrics as she continued.

"These weapons are of the finest workmanship, crafted by the foremost faceters in the world and edged with a titanium/molybdenum alloy. They are irreplaceable. No two are the same." She swished the blade through the air. "The blade is so sharp that to even touch it will cut you, and you don't use them until your third year. So handle them with care if you ever pick one up. I will be talking about these and other weapons more in tomorrow morning's lecture." She re-sheathed the Antarak and paused. "If there are no further questions I would like everyone to head off and get a good night's sleep."

Students picked up their trays and started to leave, talking intently but quietly. Eyre hesitated and looked at the tables. They certainly were in need of a clean. Was she supposed to go and do that? She was about to head to the window and grab a cloth when Sergeant Tottingham spoke.

"Eighty-eight, you can leave the cleaning tonight. It's been a hard day." Three Jotnar hurried from the kitchen, and two of them swiped at the tops of the tables while the third scurried around with a broom. Gratefully Eyre started to leave, realising she was exhausted and craving her bed. But to her surprise the Sergeant walked towards her.

"I heard from Leema that the wound was cauterised on Jensen's leg," she said abruptly to Eyre. "That's why he survived. A tourniquet alone wouldn't have saved him. Do you know anything about that?"

Eyre was confused. All she had seen was a lot of blood. She shook her head slowly. Sergeant Tottingham regarded Eyre for a long moment then waved her hand for her to leave.

Eyre headed back to her lodge along the crystal-lit pathways, trying to shake the horrific images from that afternoon that filled her mind. Dark shadows gathered in between the blue lights, and she hurried to catch up with the students walking up ahead. Tonight was not a night to be walking alone in the gloom.

CHAPTER TWENTY-ONE

THE WHISTLE ROUSED EVERYONE early again on Tuesday morning, and Eyre went with her fellow students down to Lake Altum, moving as fast as she could. Her muscles still felt sore. She hadn't slept well and she was not looking forward to the run at all. As she stood trying to mentally prepare herself, Beatrice spotted her and raced over, showing Eyre her arm in excitement.

"Look!" she cried. "I've Elevated!" Eyre saw the silver symbol on Beatrice's arm. She gave her a warm hug and twirled with her around in a circle. The Halo across Beatrice's forehead caught the sun with a sudden flash of light.

"Good on you, Beatrice, congratulations! The first of us!"

Abby and Nick arrived shortly afterwards, and while they were waiting the last few minutes for the run to start, Eyre, Abby, and Nick closely examined the Inguz on Beatrice's arm. They hadn't known anyone who had an Inguz well enough to look at it so closely; now they had the chance to look carefully at it. They were fascinated.

It was a mark like a silver tattoo, smooth on the skin so you couldn't feel it if you touched it. The lines of the Inguz appeared to sparkle, like there was stardust sprinkled along them; and it lit up like a silver beam. It was really quite beautiful.

"I'm so glad you've Elevated, Beatrice. It's great news!" Nick congratulated her.

"Thanks, Nick," Beatrice said joyfully. Just then Ben Perrill walked past with Wyatt Rankins (Number 130, Eyre thought, committing it to memory) and the Curtis twins (26 and 27). Ben sneered at Nick.

"Have a good look, Mouse," he jeered, obviously using a familiar but, judging by the look on Nick's face, detested nickname. "It's the closest you'll get to one. You shouldn't even be going to the U.D., let alone be here. No doubt Whittaker Ray got you in somehow, making it easy for you. I suppose a little rat like you will do well scurrying around there, though."

Nick turned towards him angrily, clenching his fists, but before the moment could escalate Rigmar walked up to join them. He moved slowly, but Eyre was glad to see he had recovered enough to be there. Ben scowled at him.

"And that's just perfect, Essendon, too. Another one with contacts. Your father pull some strings, Rigmar? I don't know how you managed to Elevate. What are you good at? Weren't you last in the run yesterday and doing janitorial duties the last time I saw you?"

Rigmar flushed but shot back, "I don't see anything on your arm yet, Perrill, so perhaps you should keep your mouth shut!"

The tension was rising, and Perrill's cronies lined up behind him, their faces showing their joyful anticipation at the possibility of a fight. But Sergeant Tottingham's booming voice broke through the moment.

"Into numerical order, everyone! Make it quick! Tomorrow I don't want to tell you this, you should already be there!" As she shuffled tiredly in behind Number 87, Tec Langford, and in front of Number 89, Georgia Mahoney, Eyre noted the No Swimming sign newly erected in front of the lake. She mused that it was a rather unnecessary order; she doubted anyone would go near the water now. On the bright side she supposed that the threat of swimming across the lake for anyone turning up late was now probably void.

The blasting of the whistle cut through her thoughts, and Sergeant Tottingham thumped her staff on the ground. Everyone took off in a stampede, and Eyre followed along, legs pumping. Perrill and most of his mates were fast, and they soon disappeared out of view, up with the front-runners. Eyre still hurt, but she was determined to do better than yesterday. The thought of cafeteria duty spurred her along. The last thing she wanted was that "scrubber" nickname to stick!

Surprisingly, Rigmar was doing better today. Eyre realised that he must have been already sickening when he started the run yesterday. No wonder he ended up on his face, she thought; he had a life-threatening illness and didn't know it. Together she, Rigmar, Beatrice, and Abby puffed up the path through the bush. Nick had scampered off ahead. He was a good athlete and very fast at running—he would be amongst the first to finish no doubt. Beatrice and Abby eventually disappeared around the bend, too. They offered to run with Eyre, but she didn't want to hold them back and told them to keep going, so they said they'd catch up at breakfast. Eyre was struggling, unable to believe she was so unfit, but unlike yesterday there were still people behind her so she felt positive. At least she wasn't going to be last again.

Up the hill the last students went and around the top through the boulders and crevasses to the turning point at the Wollemi Pine. Rigmar was staggering along slightly ahead and Eyre followed behind determinedly, hoping both of them would avoid being last. She skinned a knee clambering over a large granite chunk, but she kept going, her lungs burning and a sharp pain stabbing her right side. Finally she was on the downhill path, and she raced towards the finish line where she could see Sergeant Tottingham waiting, Felsic in hand. Professor Vela was there too, and a little off to the side, Rigmar, who was bent over, hands on his knees, recovering from the run.

Suddenly a rock rolled under Eyre's foot, sending a sharp pain through her ankle, and she staggered off to the side. She bent over, breathing deeply to catch her breath against the pain. Jeremy Tucker, Number 160, a heavy boy who often sat with Ben Perrill, came lumbering down the path behind her, breathing heavily, and as he passed her he bumped her so hard she staggered farther off the side. The sandy soil crumbled underfoot, and she skidded down the side of the hill, landing in a sprawling stand of blackberry bushes. Wincing, she stood up, scratched all over by the thorny weeds and covered in blackberry juice from the dark berries. As she wiped at the stains futilely, she heard Jeremy Tucker laughing uproariously as he continued down the path. She felt rage rising up inside her. Seething, she clambered back up the unstable sides of the hill and back on to the path, running again as best she could with a sore ankle, trying to catch up. Everyone had long passed by so she crossed the finish line on her own.

Sergeant Tottingham marked her off the list as Professor Vela regarded her with those creepy eyes.

"Cafeteria duty again, 88," he said snidely as she hobbled along.

Abby and Beatrice had left the Refectory by the time Eyre eventually got there, so she quickly ate breakfast. Her arms were covered in blackberry stains; she'd managed to get most of the dark juice off, but a residual crimson stain marked her skin where the berries had squashed. She looked like she had a peculiar skin rash. Her damp shirt was uncomfortable. She had gone straight up to the lodge bathroom after the run and fortunately after rubbing maniacally for twenty minutes she had managed to rinse the stains out of her shirt. But that task had put her even further behind the rest of the students, and there were only a couple of stragglers finishing up breakfast by the time she got to the Refectory.

The clatter in the kitchen signalled the clean-up process was underway, so she put her dishes through the opening and filled a bowl with hot soapy water. Then she got a cloth and started working her way around the tables in the Refectory. Did anyone get anything in their mouth this morning? she wondered as she cleaned the messes off the white laminate.

Eyre scrubbed the tabletops fast, trying to finish as quickly as possible. As she stood up, her shoulders aching from leaning over the tables, she sighed in annoyance. Her shirt was dripping water down her back, she was covered in marks that made her look like she had an incurable skin disease, her ankle hurt, and she had twelve more tables to clean. This morning couldn't get any worse.

Or so she thought. Someone walked in the door at that moment. Ben Perrill, followed by Jeremy Tucker and the Curtis twins. Just wonderful, she thought. My personal fan club.

Putting down the cloth next to the bowl, she faced them as they walked over to her.

"Ah, Airhead the janitor at work again," Ben said gleefully. "Didn't take long for you to find your niche!"

"Well, give your bulldog a pat on the head then," Eyre snarled, indicating Jeremy Tucker. "Thanks a lot for knocking me off the path, you jerk." Jeremy at least had the grace to look slightly ashamed, but Ben Perrill was delighted. He laughed maliciously and moved in closer, looming above her. He was such a big guy, tall and solidly built, and his eyes burned with an insatiable anger. Despite herself, Eyre backed away. He made her skin crawl with that mad gaze.

"Not impressing anyone now, are we, Airhead?" Ben said softly and picked up the bowl of water. "Or perhaps I should say, Water Head. You are from Water Lodge, after all." And with that he dumped the bowl of dirty, soapy water over her head, leaving her gasping in shock. Before she could move, he had left swiftly with his pack, howling with laughter. Gritting her teeth in fury, she picked bits of food off her clothing, swearing to herself. She was close to tears. *Why* wouldn't he leave her alone?

Eventually she wiped her wet hair from her eyes and picked up the bowl. Wearily she mopped up the water off the floor with the cloth, and then went to fill the bowl up again so she could finish cleaning the tables.

She headed back to Water Lodge feeling tired to her bones, and she started to scrub herself off for the second time that morning. She put her head under the tap to rinse off the grimy, soapy water, and then brushed out her hair. Carly clattered into the bathroom to clean her teeth and stopped as she saw Eyre.

"Whoa, what happened?" she asked, looking at Eyre's shirt covered in food. "It looks like someone threw up on you!"

Eyre grimaced, leaning over the basin as she rinsed it under the flowing tapwater.

"Ben Perrill happened," she said and was horrified to feel tears threatening.

Carly's kind face softened sympathetically. "He sure is a jerk, that guy," she said. "I wish my brothers were here to sort him out. He really needs to pick on someone his own size. I'll look out for you, my friend. You're not alone here!"

Eyre smiled gratefully at Carly as she carried on trying to get the muck off her shirt. When she was finally clean again she headed out and found Beatrice and Abby. Both of them swore murder and mayhem upon Ben Perrill when they heard her story, and Beatrice suggested they look for another Bunyip to introduce him to. Feeling infinitely better with that image in her mind, Eyre walked with them to the Meditation Hall situated to the south of the Compound behind the Lecture Theatre and next to a single-storied log building.

A steady stream of students wandered down the paths towards the Hall, chatting to each other. Quite a few more had an Inguz now. Eyre supposed that about twenty per cent of them had now Elevated. Sighing, she hoped she would soon join them.

The hall itself was dug into the side of the cliff, the entrance a tall opening that was cut into the towering rock. The path to the Meditation Hall was made of black onyx pavement stones inlaid with polished opal. The opals formed patterns of various runic signs, symbols Eyre had never seen before, and they led all the way to the entrance. Inside, the floor changed to an aquamarine colour, the light blue crystal glowing and calming. A student Lightworker with a Tyros Inguz welcomed the students at the door, introducing himself as Simmons, and explaining that he was a graduate student who was there to help them. Eyre and Beatrice walked past him into the Hall, their eyes wide as they looked around.

"Wow, the whole floor is made of crystal," breathed Beatrice in awe.

Overwhelmed by the beauty of the room Eyre said nothing.

Tall, round, polished columns of moonstone towered to the ceiling at intervals through the hall, and stands of irregular quartz crystals of varying colours glowed in high clusters around the perimeter of the room. The roof was inlaid with sheets of white opal, flashes of coloured fire shooting from their depths. A magical water feature ran from a circular fountain cut from pale lavender amethyst blocks situated in the middle of the room. Eyre walked over to it, marvelling at the sight—the water seemingly moved in the air on its own, spiralling upwards and back down again from the pool in the fountain in a constant stream of coiling water. "How does the water get up there?" she asked, looking for a pump or some mechanical force.

"It's electromagnetic," Simmons explained, coming over to join them. He was tall and thin with a gentle face, and he moved with a grace that seemed effortless. He ran his hand through the spiralling water, breaking its fall.

"When the resonance in the water changes, the shape of the water changes, too, and follows the vibrational frequency of the sound. It makes a most beautiful display, constant and yet changing at the same time. Much like our lives."

Eyre smiled, mesmerized by the gentle flow. It was a beautiful room, glowing softly with colour and humming with a resonance that made her feel peaceful and rested, a place that had a hushed reverence about it.

Simmons waited until everyone was in the Hall, and then he asked them to sit down and cross their legs and shut their eyes. Eyre sat down as instructed and was amazed to find that the aquamarine crystal was warm to the touch; it seemed to hum with a low pleasing tone.

"We will be meditating every morning for half an hour," Simmons said. "We follow a variation of the Vipassana technique of meditation, which helps the follower to develop wisdom through silence. Meditation is an awakening of awareness through the stilling of thought processes. The aim of meditation is to focus your energies on well being and health and to clear your mind of toxic influences and negativity. There is to be no speaking during this time. When the half hour is up, please leave quietly."

He walked soundlessly around people as they sat, eyes shut, taking in the ambience. His voice was not intrusive as he asked them to let go of resentments and to focus on the joy of being, to focus on the present and the feeling of the energy of life flowing through them.

Eyre tried to concentrate on what he was saying and to embrace the ideology. The room certainly was beautiful and peaceful, but she had never meditated before and was unused to sitting still like this, so it felt strange and a bit ridiculous. She'd done plenty of exercise classes before, and the relaxation sessions she had done with her mother were similar, but nothing where you just . . . sat. It was going to take some practise—and she wasn't sure she would ever be able to take it seriously.

Intruding on her efforts at calming her mind were the thoughts of Jeremy Tucker and Ben Perrill; it was hard to feel "in the zone" when her soul was consumed with murderous rage.

But when she opened her eyes a bit she saw that everyone else was concentrating hard, so she decided to just pretend for the duration of the session and hope that no one would realise how disconnected she was. She supposed that after the run and the incident with Ben that today she could use all the peaceful moments she could get.

Finally, thankfully, the Meditation time was up, and she unwound herself from the floor. Simmons smiled at them beatifically as they left, and Eyre mentally shook her head. Perhaps *medication* rather than meditation might help her find the right vibe, she thought sourly.

The next session on the schedule was Ferito, the Lightworkers' Martial Arts Training with Sergeant Tottingham.

The shed for training was the log building next door to the Meditation Hall, and Eyre knew from looking at her map earlier that on the other side was the therapeutic pools where they had all recovered after the Bunyip attack. The Training Shed was a tall, single-storey rectangular structure like the lodges, similarly constructed from thick pine logs.

Eyre walked inside with her friends and looked around. The ceiling was very high, with large fans hanging from it, and the fans spun fast, moving the air to combat the heat that was already rising in the building. The floor was a large slab of cement covered with thick exercise mats. A bank of lockers lined the far left wall of the shed, and attached to the walls at the front of the room were a series of large charts with stick figure illustrations depicting various movements and positions. Down the back of the building several wooden targets hung at regular intervals on the walls; and black circles were painted about two metres apart on the floor in a grid-like pattern.

Sergeant Tottingham was standing at the front, already waiting for them, tapping her staff impatiently. In front of her and a little to the side a square platform was elevated slightly from the ground, covered in flooring made out of bamboo.

"Please find a spot and sit down, students," Sergeant Tottingham called, leaning her staff up against the wall and clapping her hands. "Hurry up! You don't need anything, just sit on the mats and keep quiet."

Nick came to sit with the girls, and they waited cross-legged in the middle of the floor. Zanda joined them shortly and Warrigal too, then a very short boy called Zac Travers came to sit beside Beatrice, his small squat shape looking out of place next to the tall, gangly girl, like a primary school kid had sneaked in somehow. When the last student was inside, Sergeant Tottingham closed the doors.

"Right then, silence!" Sergeant Tottingham called out. "Pay attention, students, this is possibly the most important subject you will learn at this school. You there, 58," she called to an attractive girl from Eyre's lodge who was still whispering to another girl—Ambrosia, Eyre thought—beside her, "anything you would like to share with the rest of us? Or perhaps you would like to conduct this session?" Number 58 stopped talking and flushed in embarrassment.

Sergeant Tottingham waited a moment then continued. "I thought not. Please be warned that anyone who talks in my classes will be sent outside immediately and will not be allowed back in for the day. I would suggest that this is not a good idea for anyone wishing to be accepted next year. You will need all the instruction and training you can fit in over the next few weeks if you are to perform adequately at the TEPs.

"Okay then. Ferito is a Martial Art form that has been used by Lightworkers for centuries. Its main purpose is defence, but we also teach attack as a basic skill that is sometimes necessary. The defence skills of Ferito are called Tego, and they cover things like shielding, masking, warding, and blocking.

"I might add here that one important form of defence that is often ignored or disparaged is retreat. Retreat is a necessary technique under certain circumstances, and sometimes it is the only sensible choice. So we will be learning about that, too. Retreat and regroup—very important tools in the strategies of conflict, and nothing you should be embarrassed about employing. Live to fight another fight? Well, the only thing you can say about that is that it's smart.

"The attack skills of Ferito are called Aditus, and you will learn several forms of attack with various weapons. Strategy and timing are important issues to learn alongside the use of weapons, and indeed it is those things that are often the more difficult to learn.

"Obviously in the short time we are here during orientation you will not be able to progress far with your skills. It takes years—sometimes decades— to master these techniques. But while you are here we will give you an introduction to the basics of Ferito, and we expect you to train hard so that you have progressed by the time you leave.

"We planned the programme so that you have undertaken Meditation before you come for your Ferito training. This is deliberate. You will need to focus in order to generate the energy for Ferito, and that means clearing your mind of extraneous thoughts and distractions. Right, I need a volunteer." Sergeant Tottingham looked around and saw Ben Perrill who most definitely had his hand down.

"As I thought, 119, our community-minded member, very keen to help out. Thank you 119, please come up here."

Ben scowled but lumbered to his feet and came to the middle of the room. Sergeant Tottingham looked at his arm as she led him onto the bamboo platform.

"Ferito is also practised by the Unlit, but they do not access Viq Energy when they perform it. Ferito without Viq is still a powerful skill, and those who go to the U.D. will continue to learn this martial art."

Ben looked irked at the reference to the Unlit, obviously not liking it that attention had been drawn to the fact that he hadn't Elevated yet. His neck suffused with colour and his jaw clenched.

"Okay, so what is Viq? Number 119 is going to help me demonstrate that to you."

Sergeant Tottingham turned towards Ben Perrill, and Eyre was gratified to see the uncertainty in his face. It was apparently dawning on him that perhaps it had not been a wise move to have spoken so brashly to the Sergeant yesterday.

"Viq energy," Sergeant Tottingham continued, "is the mind sourcing outside energy and converting it into a concentrated force that flows through and out the body, like so." She put her hand out towards Ben, shouting "Aditus!" and he flew as if struck across the bamboo platform, landing on his rear and skidding off the edge. His face darkened, and he got back up on the platform with his fists clenched. As if unaware of his rage, Sergeant Tottingham continued.

"We can also access Viq energy in this way. . . ." She pushed her palm outwards, and a bright beam of light shot from her palm and blasted across the room into a target on the far wall, which exploded into pieces.

"Another technique of Aditus is this . . ." she flicked her wrist sideways several times, and each time she did a disc of bright light flew from her hand. They zipped closely across the top of Ben's head, cutting a sharp path through his hair and leaving a wide bald stripe. He put his hand up in horror as the watching students guffawed.

Eyre felt a ray of satisfaction warm her soul. *That* wouldn't be as easy to clean up as soapy water. The shining discs continued across the room and smashed into the centre of another target, bright flashes shooting outwards in a sparkling shower. Once again, with a loud explosion the target was decimated, and murmurs of surprise could be heard in the hall.

"Oh, er sorry there 119, for that—uh . . . close shave. I must have misjudged," Sergeant Tottingham said most unapologetically, and the students tittered. She looked around the class and continued.

"Viq energy makes a force out of light and when directed competently is a dangerous weapon," Sergeant Tottingham said. "The use of Occ_do, or lethal force, is a Light tactic we try to avoid, and it is used in only the direst of situations. I hope none of you ever have cause to use it."

The door to the shed opened and three Jotnar came in carrying an array of weapons in their arms. Sergeant Tottingham unsheathed her Antaraks from behind her back and showed them to the students.

"Some of you saw the Antarak in action the other day, so you will know what powerful weapons they are. They are sharp enough to cut through rock, so they must be treated with the utmost respect. Our fourth-year students, those undertaking a graduate year, journey to Incendium each year to get the Zha'kara diamonds that these incredible weapons are made from.

"Zha'kara," she said, spelling out the word, "is the Armaturan word meaning 'unbreakable.'" A shadow crossed her face. "Normally we would have some Zha'kara diamonds to show you by now, but our graduate TACI expedition has been delayed this year and is yet to return. Hopefully before the time you leave the fourth years will be back with some of these crystals to show you. The strength and hardness of the Zha'kara diamonds are unparalleled in the Overworld."

She passed the Antaraks to Ben Perrill who was standing there in shock, feeling his bald stripe and shaking with rage. "I'd like you to take a swipe at me with those," she said. Ben took the weapons gingerly and looked at them uncertainly. He might be furious with his lecturer, but even he looked unsure about cutting her to pieces.

"Come on 119, attack!" Sergeant Tottingham bellowed, and Ben Perrill swished the blade at her.

"PUT SOME FORCE INTO IT!" the Sergeant roared, and Ben's face turned purple. He lifted the Antarak and sliced violently at her with it. With amazing speed, Sergeant Tottingham lifted her hands and performed two small circular movements at eye level, palm outwards, shouting "Tegc!" The blade stopped midair with a resounding thud, juddering the boy's arm up to the shoulder. A luminous sheet of light hung in the air between Sergeant Tottingham and the blade, and it stayed there while Sergeant Tottingham continued the hand movements. Eyre recognised the technique that Beatrice's mother had used with the Gothak. She knew how effective it was.

"This is called shielding," Sergeant Tottingham explained. "You need vast quantities of Viq energy to be able to stop an Antarak. It will take you many years before you have the strength to do this, but you will be able to shield against basic weapons fairly early in your training.

"Thank you, 119, you can return to your seat." She took the Antaraks from Ben Perrill and resheathed them in her baldrics. He left the platform glowering blackly, trying awkwardly to flick his hair over the bald stripe.

Stepping towards the Jotnar, Sergeant Tottingham took a weapon from one of the troll-like creatures. It was a golden dagger about thirty centimetres long with an obsidian handle, a lethal-looking but fascinating weapon.

"In third year you will be given your Arms Endowment, which you will keep forever. You will receive two Antaraks as part of that supply, as well as one of these, a Kulbeda, which you wear on your belt. What does it do?" She turned and threw it hard, and it flew across the room to embed in one of the targets on the wall.

"The dagger is guided by Viq energy. You use your mind to visualise where the knife will go, so that it can travel far beyond the range of a normal throw. The masters of this art can hit a target dead centre a half a kilometre away." She put her hand out in front of her and made a sideways turn, palm outwards. The Kulbeda jerked out of the target and spiralled back through the air until it landed gently back in her palm.

"You will want to practise that move carefully," Sergeant Tottingham said wryly. "Sometimes students aren't so accurate with the return journey, and it can hurt.

"Next we have the Flail," she said, taking an object from another of the Jotnar, a chain with a spiked ball on each end. As she whirled it around her head, it emitted a terrible, deafening screeching sound, and many of the students covered their ears in pain. Then Sergeant Tottingham let go of the weapon, and it flew through the air, smashing against the wall.

"How much Viq energy you employ will determine the power of the Flail. It is most commonly used for hand-to-hand combat, similar to the Japanese Nunchaku.

"Finally, your Arms Endowment will provide you with a Mnae." She took a long silver sword from the last Jotnar. The blade gleamed so brightly it was blinding, a long double-sided sword with engraving on both sides of the blade and an ornately crafted hilt. It was a thing of magnificence.

"The Mnae are crafted by the Mimir using precious metals extracted from the depths of Terra, and they are a remarkable weapon of outstanding craftsmanship. You cannot receive a Mnae unless you undertake a fourth year, and only if you have demonstrated that you have capably mastered the Clasis. It is a weapon of great power." Sergeant Tottingham swept the blade from side to side and rays of light flashed outwards from its side. Respectfully she placed it back in the Jotnar's arms. Then she said something briefly to the three Jotnar, and they went and placed the weapons carefully on the floor at the front of the hall before leaving.

"Okay," Sergeant Tottingham said, "finally, a quick word on the other forms of Tego. Warding is the use of Viq energy to bind and protect zones against unwanted entry. For example, we ward the school so that we control who or what can enter the grounds." Concern flickered across her face. She looked serious. "Recently not so successfully. Hopefully that has been rectified.

"Blocking is the use of defence techniques when someone or something is attacking with or without a weapon. We will train you to anticipate and deflect those moves and to turn them to your advantage, so that you can convert your defence into your own attacking move. You can block by creating a shield with light, by using outwards psychic force, or by physically using your body to deflect a blow. Practise is the secret to mastering blocking, knowing which technique is best to use at a given point, and we intend to give you a lot of that during your years at the Academy.

"Finally, masking is a defensive move to surprise and throw off your opponent. Viq energy can be employed to create panels of light that bend what your eye sees." The students gasped as before their eyes Sergeant Tottingham disappeared. Then they heard her voice from the place she had vanished.

"I am still here, but you cannot see me. The refraction of light using Viq energy has deceived your eyes into thinking I am not here. But as you can see," she suddenly reappeared, "I am indeed here. It takes many years to master masking, but it is a spectacular and extremely valuable skill." A low murmur swept through the watching students. It was indeed an impressive display.

"The final thing I want to mention is your staff." Sergeant Tottingham took her staff from against the wall and held it out. The wood glowed golden-red from the high buffing it had received, and the prismatic quartz crystal at the top sparkled in the light. "You will make your own staff next year. It is a multi-purpose article. You use it to walk with, to defend with," she whirled around and demonstrated several defensive moves, thumping the staff into the ground loudly as she did so, "and to attack with." She pointed the staff at the wall, and a ball of light blasted from the crystal at the top of the staff, shooting across the room in a fiery trail. It hit a target on the wall and incinerated the wooden board. "It is a most useful object, and one you will come to rely on and love."

Then Sergeant Tottingham indicated the weapons at the front of the room.

"Feel free to come up and examine all the weapons later. Pick them up if you like—carefully!—and have a good look. You will see that they are beautifully crafted. Our weapons are amongst the best in the country.

"Right, now we will try out some Ferito. These are the moves for Level 1 Ferito. We practise the moves in a suite of strikes and parries called a Clasis. Those of you who have Elevated can also try to raise Viq energy and use it as you practise your Clasis. It will take a while to learn to control your Viq, so be patient. Focus and inner stillness are the essence of Viq."

Sergeant Tottingham began demonstrating the various moves of elementary Ferito, counting out loud as she moved through the various positions that made up the Clasis. The students copied her awkwardly, trying to keep their balance as they repeated the unfamiliar movements. There were twenty different positions, some attacking, some retreating, and it was hard to remember them all. Eyre struggled to keep up. Just as she figured out one position, Sergeant Tottingham would move to the next, and she was constantly trying to follow what she was meant to be doing. Her muscles quivered with the effort of trying to balance in impossible positions, and several times she stumbled, on one occasion ending up sitting on the ground. The only consolation was that most of the other students— even the ones who were athletically gifted—all seemed to be having the same trouble. It wasn't just balancing; it was almost as if an outside force was required to prevent them from toppling over. Scaffolding, for instance, she thought in frustration.

"Use your mind," Sergeant Tottingham called as she balanced easily on one foot. "Focus on stillness. *Concentrate.* You will not be able to do this until you can centre your thoughts. Your Clasis should consist of a series of seamless transitions between the Ferito positions."

Huffing in frustration, Eyre tried harder to keep her muscles tight and balance the way she was supposed to. She failed dismally and overstepped, crashing into Beatrice.

Beatrice laughed. "God, this is hard!" she said. "How ridiculous do we look? I'm going to dislocate my hip trying to get this right!"

"Seventeen, eighteen . . ." continued Sergeant Tottingham.

Gritting her teeth, Eyre tried again, getting increasingly frustrated at her lack of skill. She couldn't even *stand* on her own two feet without falling over. She was getting hot, frustrated, and very discouraged.

"Look at Warrigal," Abby said, and Eyre turned around. Warrigal was balancing perfectly in the fifteenth position, his eyes closed. Shimmering in front of him was a translucent sheet of light, and when Sergeant Tottingham noticed it she cried out delightedly.

"Excellent, 61, you have employed Viq! That is wonderful for your first day. Students, look at 61. That is what you're trying to achieve."

Eyre put her foot down and shook her head. "How much longer till we finish?" she asked Abby.

"Ten minutes, thank god," said Abby, red-faced and wobbling with her arms in the air.

Finally Sergeant Tottingham called a halt, indicating the diagrams on the wall behind her. "There are a series of reference charts on the wall here for the various Level 1 Ferito Clasis: Basic Clasis, Clasis for Single-Blade Weapon, and Clasis for Two-Handed Fighting. Please study them carefully when you come back to practise so that you get the positions and movements right. Incorrect technique will result in your equilibrium being off, and you will overbalance, as many of you have found this afternoon. Only hours of practise will rectify that. Feel free to ask me for assistance if you need it. You may go now and I will see you here again tomorrow!"

The students left the shed, grabbed a quick drink at the Common Room, and then headed towards the Lecture Theatre. All of them were subdued, and Eyre trudged along gloomily with her friends. Ferito was not easy, she thought, and it seemed impossible she would ever manage to even balance on one leg, let alone summon Viq forces. That's if she ever Elevated, she added to herself despondently. And how on earth was she going to manage the TEPs, even if she did Elevate? It was so difficult. She was going to have to improve in the next few weeks or she'd be going nowhere but straight back to Highlight.

Still, she tried to brighten at the thought of another new topic. Lightning Skills and the Art of Pounding. I wonder what that is, she mused. Perhaps this would be an easier topic to get a handle on.

CHAPTER TWENTY-TWO

WALKING IN TO THE Lecture Theatre, Eyre wandered up the stairs and sat in the same seat as yesterday, near the end of the row in the middle of the theatre. Beatrice and Abby sat either side of her, and Nick was next to Abby, their two blond heads close together, talking and laughing about something. There was the ubiquitous sound of all classrooms in the hall—students chatting, bags being dropped, tapping on desks, the hum of the electrical equipment. Her friends were so happy and enjoying orientation so much, Eyre tried to dispel the feeling of gloom she was feeling. She hadn't expected to be brilliant here, but she didn't think she'd be doing so badly, either. If only she could do something halfway acceptably she would feel a bit better.

Suddenly there was a loud clomping of boots, and a giant walked into the room. Well, not a giant, Eyre thought, looking in awe at the huge form, but a very large person indeed. He was an old man, over two metres tall, and broad-shouldered, with big feet encased in huge red leather boots. He had long grey hair tied in a ponytail and a massive bushy grey beard with two forks at the ends. His eyes were almost hidden under fierce brows, and he had a large hooked nose with a pair of small round glasses perched on it. The glasses frames were metallic, and as he turned in the light, rainbows chased around them. He wore a red leather vest with chains strung across them and a black shirt and pants. Santa Claus the biker, Eyre decided in astonishment. So what was he like, the former or the latter?

"Welcome to Lightning Skills and the Art of Pounding," the mountain announced in a booming voice. "Lightning skills are an essential part of your training at the Academy, and they will take many years to perfect. I am Lord Philius Clarembout, and I am the Head of Defence at the Academy of Light. The Defence Division encompasses weaponry, fighting skills and tactics, and I am sure I will see many of you in my classrooms in the coming years.

"Right. First of all, I will introduce you to Lightning skills." A whirring sound came from the ceiling, and Eyre saw a short metal rod lower down and stop at the end of the stage. "This is what you will be trying to raise with your Viq," Lord Clarembout said, and facing the wall, pointed at the metal rod with his arm outstretched. Suddenly a jagged streak of lightning shot out of his finger and zapped into the metal rod. It made a loud zinging sound and crackles of energy travelled in visible waves up the rod, disappearing into the ceiling.

"Lightning rod," Lord Clarembout said with satisfaction. "Keeps everything safe." He turned to face the audience again. "There are many types of lightning skills, for example, the Corona. . . ." Suddenly a series of electric currents emitted from around his body, each one about a metre long, crackling and zapping around him like a noisy halo. "Great for protection against unwanted advances!" he chuckled. Might come in handy for Ben Perrill, Eyre thought with interest, leaning forward.

"We can do this—" he made a current appear between the palms of his two hands, then clapped his hands together, causing an explosion that hurt their eardrums, "and this—" he moved his palms in fast weaving movements in front of his chest—a sort of continuous figure eight. Lightning streaks shot out from his hands and whirred around, forming a sparking ball in front of his body, a crackling sphere of energy bolts. Lord Clarembout flicked his hands, and the flaming ball whirled like a tornado out the window, disappearing out of sight. A loud boom from outside suggested it had just blown up, and an acrid smoke streamed in through the window. Lord Clarembout made a sound of approval.

"That one is a useful weapon. Kills everything," he said matter of factly. "'Course, you can't sustain it for too long. It takes a lot of energy.

"Lightning skills are an invaluable tool for fighting, and they work in conjunction with your skills of Ferito in both Aditus and Tego. Creating lightning is not difficult, but as I said before, maintaining it for any helpful length of time and controlling it is, and that is what will take you years of practise to develop. Still, even in infancy these skills are useful.

"Until your Viq comes in, you will be unable to raise the lightning. But you can practise the moves of Ferito and the hand positions for each of the lightning skills so that when you do Elevate, you can start training your Viq to create lightning bolts."

He paused and picked up a Felsic from the podium. "Have a look at your Felsic. These are diagrams on the various methods used to raise lightning."

Eyre looked down at her Felsic to see a series of diagrams of stick figures displaying a confusing array of hand and body positions that were difficult to decipher. She focussed hard, but eventually gave up; it was way too tough for her at this point. She pursed her lips in frustration as Lord Clarembout surveyed the students.

"Now I'd like to pause here and explain the difference between lightning skills and light beams. It's in the shape of the hand and the focus of the mind. Watch. . . ."

Lord Clarembout went through a series of finely-tuned movements, demonstrating the different techniques that produced light beams and lightning bolts of varying sizes and shapes, but Eyre found her mind drifting. It was so much information all at once! She was feeling rather overloaded and not much was staying in her brain. When finally Lord Clarembout clapped his hands, creating a loud bang, Eyre jumped in her chair. Several other students did too and the lecturer grinned widely.

"I find it's rare that a student nods off in my classes," he stated. Some of the students were looking at their hands and surreptitiously moving them around, following the diagram on their Felsics. Lord Clarembout looked at the students. "We have lightning rods in the Training Shed," he said. "Best to try out any moves when you get there, and leave any practise to a safe area. Getting zapped by a lightning bolt is rather more serious than an electric fence. Once we had a student blow his ear off." The students who had been moving their hands paused mid-action and carefully put their hands in their laps.

"Okay then. Questions?" No one answered, including Ben Perrill, who seemed a little more reticent since his recent new hairdo, Eyre thought. "Please be aware that when you are practising lightning skills this afternoon, you must do so in an enclosed barrier, and wear a training suit to protect yourself and others. A graduate student will be at the shed this afternoon to help you locate and activate the safety equipment." Lord Clarembout walked to the podium and continued.

"A further technique in your Fighting skills set is pounding. This is another way we employ Viq force, and I guess it's best I demonstrate that also." He raised his voice and called offstage, "Can you come in here, please?" and a trio of Jotnar bustled in the door. They stood in a row at the front of the stage, unsmiling. Eyre studied the small horned forms—they certainly weren't the most attractive creatures she had ever seen, with their dark coarse hair and callused feet. But they were hard working and obviously invaluable to the Academy.

"My friends here have kindly offered to be part of this demonstration," Lord Clarembout informed them. "Would you step over here, please?" Moving them around, he made them stand in a triangle facing him. Then he raised his foot and stomped hard on the ground, making a deafening clap of sound like thunder. Instantly the three Jotnar were bowled over by an unseen force that sent them flying in all directions. But they were agile and landed on their feet before walking back to their positions.

"That is pounding," Lord Clarembout said, "a use of Viq to create sound waves that send out a powerful force. When you have mastered pounding you can knock your opponents over in a ten-metre radius. Very useful.

"We also teach you counter-pounding, which is sending out an opposing wave to negate the effect of pounding. The key to counter-pounding is timing, so we often find that students who are musically gifted can do this particularly well."

He walked to the far edge of the stage. "Finally, you will learn a technique called skimming. If someone sends a pound at you, and you miss the counter-pound, you need to ride over the sound wave so you keep your feet. This is called skimming. Once again our friends will demonstrate."

Lord Clarembout stomped his foot hard from the edge of the stage, and the loud clap came again. The Jotnar were hit by the force again, but this time they kept their feet and rode up and down on unseen waves, balancing with their arms out as if they were snowboarding or surfing. Eyre saw Nick lean forward, and he watched with great delight as the Jotnar moved up and down, expertly staying on their feet until the wave passed. She recalled that Abby had said he was a keen surfer back at the Sunshine Coast. The Jotnar rode the wave of energy and ended up standing on the floor again, still in their triangle formation.

"As you can see," Lord Clarembout continued, "this technique is not only a lot of fun," several of the students laughed softly in agreement, "but also a very valuable skill. If you are knocked over in the field, you are seriously disadvantaged in a fight and vulnerable to attack. However, if you 'skim the pound', as we call it, your opponent has exerted a lot of energy sending the pound, which leaves them significantly weaker, and you are still on your feet to counterattack. It puts you in a very strong position.

"Thank you, my friends. You may leave now," he said to the Jotnar, and they scurried out the door. Lord Clarembout walked back to the centre of the podium.

"In summary, lightning skills and pounding are further uses of Viq energy, which are invaluable in a fight," he said. "There are no forces that will automatically win a confrontation. What will make the difference is your skill in executing the various skills and your understanding of strategy —when to employ each of them in strike and counterstrike movements. As you gain more experience with all these skills, you will become more adept at knowing how to use them effectively to win the fight."

Number 28, who was again in the front row, put her hand up. Lord Clarembout strode over to the front.

"Yes, a question! Wonderful!" he exclaimed. "What is your name?"

Taken aback at being asked her name after being a number since she'd arrived, the girl was temporarily lost for words. Then she rallied. "It's Madeleine de Haven, sir, thank you. I was wondering how the use of force reconciled with being a Lightworker, a person who aims for truth and Light."

Lord Clarembout clapped his hands. "A philosophical question! Excellent, Miss de Haven," he said. "Exactly what I would expect from a girl in the front row! Well, the reality of Lightworking is that of course we aim to use our skills for the spreading of Lightness and good deeds in the world. But we also need to defend ourselves against evil forces, and we need powerful Light skills in order to do that. Unfortunately, as you have heard, in recent times the Gothak have found their way into Entis, so we must train hard and be prepared for any encounter. And I am sorry to say that you will undoubtedly use these skills in combat during your time at the Academy—the Dark Forces have been appearing all over the world. We know hard times are ahead.

"So you could call our study of the various Defence skills preparation, although we hope we might never need to employ those skills. Or to paraphrase a famous American president: '*Walk Lightly and carry a Big Stick*,' the motto of our Lightworker Defence forces."

"Teddy Roosevelt," the girl said, nodding sagely.

"Indeed!" Lord Clarembout beamed. "You are worthy of the front row, my dear!" His eyes twinkled, a strangely benevolent chord in such a massive and fearsome man. Madeleine de Haven looked pleased. Obviously she was the girl to sit next to in class next year, Eyre thought wryly.

"Well, if no one has any further questions, I think that will do for this morning. Please be at the Training Shed this afternoon for practise. Our graduate student, Terrigal Furnace, will be there to assist you with the equipment. I am available at any time for any questions you may have that he can't answer. Thank you all, and good luck in the TEPs."

He strode out of the Lecture Theatre noisily and everyone packed up their Felsics into backpacks. As Eyre headed dejectedly with her friends to the Refectory for lunch, she decided that the only thing she had right now was a 'pounding' headache.

CHAPTER TWENTY-THREE

SURPRISINGLY, LUNCH PASSED WITHOUT incident, and Beatrice and Abby and Nick helped Eyre wipe the tables afterwards.

"Please, Lord, let Ben Perrill come in here," Beatrice muttered fiercely. "I have the Viq, and I have the motivation. He'd make a great lightning rod!"

But the cafeteria cleared out quickly after lunch, students heading in various directions, and with the four of them doing the job, the tables were wiped clean in a short time.

"Thanks, guys, I appreciate that," Eyre said as they left. "I promise I'll run faster tomorrow to try to avoid this!"

"It wasn't your fault you encountered a snake on the track," Abby said. "Next time we'll stomp on its head!"

Their faces serious, Beatrice and Nick did a soft high five and nodded. Eyre brightened as she looked at her three friends. She'd never had a group of friends before because her family had moved around so much, and it was a new experience, an unexpected joy. Things might not be going so smoothly for her, but at least she had these good people with her.

They headed over to the Training Shed, where they met a stocky, muscular boy waiting at the entrance. Eyre figured it was Terrigal Furnace, the graduate student Lord Clarembout had mentioned in his lecture, as the boy had an Inguz with a glowing red centre, but no Halo, so he had obviously graduated from fourth year. And like Leema, the first aid graduate student, he had a pair of white baldrics crossing his chest. As the students approached, he confirmed her guess.

"Hi, I'm Terrigal, your tutor for today. Pick up a training suit from the locker on the left wall of the shed, then step on to one of the black circles on the floor at the back there, and wait for me to engage the barriers."

Walking to the locker they joined the queue of students selecting a suit. The training suits were made of a thick, shiny fabric that was rough to touch, and the suit itself was bulky and quite heavy with a hood that went right over the head and a plastic panel to look through. Eyre put hers on, feeling ridiculously like she was about to climb aboard a spaceship. The suits were awkward and difficult to move in, and she thought in annoyance that she didn't feel like she could walk, let alone defend herself in this sumo suit.

"I haven't Elevated," she said testily to Terrigal. "Why do I have to wear this?"

He looked at her calmly. "Sometimes students Elevate in the middle of training," he said as if speaking to a child. "If you are in the middle of a move, you can send out any form of Viq energy and blast someone's head off. Likewise, anyone can blast yours off. Or beams and bolts can rebound right back into you. Leave the suit on."

Chastened, Eyre went and stood on a black circle and waited. When all the students were standing on a black circle, Terrigal pushed a button on the wall and clear cylindrical tubes about two metres wide descended from the roof to the floor, surrounding each of them with a protective shield.

"You won't be able to raise your Viq strongly yet," Terrigal said. "But you should work through the movements that Lord Clarembout showed you this morning. The more you focus and coordinate your body and mind, the stronger your Viq and the more likely you will produce the light beams and lightning bolts upon demand. Feel free to try pounding as well this afternoon."

It was hot and sweaty in the suit, but Eyre decided she would run through the movements. Maybe she would Elevate, she thought without much hope. But after waving her hands futilely through the movements about ten times, she was getting sick of it. Flashes of light around the room showed that some people were having success in their practise, and it was making her more irritated. Occasionally a clap of sound announced that someone had managed to pound, and once it happened so close to her the wave knocked her off her feet. The big suit made it difficult to get up off the floor and gritting her teeth in frustration, she crawled up the side of the barrier. She started waving her hands around again, feeling like a kid in kindergarten playing pat-a-cake. It was so hot and so annoying. Nick was next to her, and he was also looking hot and bothered, and Abby had just sat down on the floor, waiting for the session to end. By the time the cylindrical barrier rose up again, Eyre was feeling despondent and defeated. The only thing she had managed to do in that session was badly dehydrate herself; she desperately needed a drink of water.

"I will be here this afternoon if anyone wishes to continue their practise," Terrigal announced. *I would rather swim across the lake with the Bunyip in it,* Eyre thought crossly. "Please hang your suits back up in the locker before you leave."

Dejectedly she joined her friends, and they walked to the Common Room for afternoon tea.

"I'm going to drink the lake dry," Eyre said. "I'm so thirsty!"

"Me, too," Abby gasped. "Wasn't that torture?" Beatrice didn't answer, and Eyre guessed that she had been one of the ones making flashes around the room. She tried to feel happy for Beatrice but found herself sinking further into the gloom. Yet another thing she couldn't do. *Why* was she here?

"Horrible," Nick agreed. "I might not be able to do any of these skills, but I can certainly feel the effects of them. A pound threw me in the air, and I fell flat on my face. Fun times."

Eyre sat in the Common Room and cooled down with her friends under a revolving fan, gulping down several glasses of water before she finally began to feel normal. Ben Perrill sauntered by smirking at her.

"Hey, Water Head—" but whatever he had been about to say was stopped when Beatrice pounded, sending a wave across the room that knocked him and others off their feet. He landed on his rear end with a loud "Oof!"

"Water Head might just have to start calling you Bouncing Butt," she shouted across to him, and the room erupted in laughter. Ben clambered to his feet, looking furious, but seeing the number of people watching, decided to leave without doing anything to retaliate. However, his evil look back at Beatrice told her quite clearly that he wasn't going to forget it.

"Wow, Beatrice, that was *amazing!*" Abby cried after he left. "Was that *you* doing the pounding during practise?"

Beatrice gave a small smile. "I was one of them, I guess. I've figured out how to focus to raise my Viq. Now it's just working out how to control it."

"That's awesome!" Eyre said, hugging her. She was genuinely happy for Beatrice, but was beginning to feel more and more like she wasn't actually going to Elevate. How could she bear it if she didn't? Glumly she headed behind her friends back to the Training Shed for their afternoon session.

CHAPTER TWENTY-FOUR

BEATRICE HEADED STRAIGHT BACK to the locker for a training suit
—determined to keep going with the progress she had made. Other students
were also decisive about what they were going to practise. Some headed for
the piles of Palum and chose either a single stick or picked up two shorter
ones. Nick went to find a quiet corner to meditate, winking at Eyre on his
way. Since he wasn't going to ever Elevate she figured he was just going to
chill out this afternoon. Why not? she thought. Meditation was obviously a
big part of mental strength so it was a valid choice for anyone training

Abby hovered around uncertainly, and then decided to run through her
Basic Clasis. She took up the stance in a corner and started to move through
the sequence of positions. Looking around, Eyre felt at a loss. She wasn't
making progress with anything, so no clear choice leapt out at her; in fact,
she didn't want to do any of them. She looked down at the faint crimson
marks still staining her skin, the scratch marks up and down her arms, the
stickiness in her hair where she hadn't properly washed out the soapy water
Ben Perrill had dumped on her. All in all it hadn't been a very successful
day.

Someone shouted "*Going up*! Whoop whoop!" 'Going up' was the slogan
the students had adopted when a friend suddenly Elevated. They would
shout it out loudly and throw the student in the air as a celebratory way to
mark the occasion. So obviously another person had joined the ranks. Eyre
sunk deeper into her depression. Surely she would Elevate soon, too? After
all, her parents were both apparently accomplished Lightworkers! But then
she thought of her mother's inscription in the Lightward-Tyson Wisdom:
'Whether Lit or Unlit' and realised that even her parents hadn't known
whether she would Elevate or not. The gloom inside her blossomed darkly.

She decided that she too would sit down the back and meditate. She
didn't have any hope of actually feeling the zone; she just wanted a way to

zone *out* for a while. So she sat down the back near the open door and shut her eyes, black thoughts crowding through her mind. Suddenly something furry crawled into her lap, and she nearly leapt out of her skin. Her thoughts turned to Bunyips and Zyx, and she raised her hand to clout the thing, whatever it was. A small placid face looked up at her; it sort of looked like a rabbit, but it had a long tail and was a pale lavender colour. Gentle green eyes regarded her raised hand, and shamefacedly she lowered it and reached down to stroke the creature on the top of its silky head. It snuggled up closer to her, so soft and fluffy, and then to her surprise, it curled up and went to sleep. Amazed, she kept stroking it, marvelling at the softness of its fur and the unusual colour. It was a gorgeous little thing, and she felt the stress leaving her body.

Suddenly she heard a panicking voice calling out, "Lenny! Lenny! Where are you?" Standing up she looked out the door to see Ranger Chrysanthe running wildly along the shores of the lake. She wandered over to him, still holding the soft little creature. Today the Ranger was wearing a red velvet smoking jacket, floral pants, and striped army boots. If she wasn't so concerned about him she might have laughed.

"Are you okay?" she asked him. He looked a wreck—his green hair was standing on end and the beetles were whirring around more madly than ever. He was sweating, and his eyes were wild, but when he saw what she was holding he exclaimed in relief. "Oh, Lumen be praised, you found her!" and raced over. Lenny yawned, showing small, even little teeth, totally unconcerned about the fuss she had caused. Eyre handed the creature over to Ranger Chrysanthe, and he cradled her. He stroked her fur with hands covered in gold rings, the many gold bracelets on his arms jangling.

"What a relief," he said, exhaling unevenly. "Lenny is short for Lenis. It means gentle. She got out of the Zepp. Normally she sits in the front with me, but when I delivered some supplies here this afternoon, I opened the door, and she bolted! She is far too delicate a creature to be roaming around here on her own. There's too many things that would eat her up in a flash!" He shuddered, sending the beetles spiralling back in the other direction. "Thank you for finding her."

"Well, she found me, really," Eyre said awkwardly. "She climbed into my lap."

Ranger Chrysanthe looked at Eyre, and his bright purple eyes looked concerned.

"Did she now," he mused, looking at her searchingly. "Well then, you must have needed her. She's a Hug, a type of chimera made up of a rabbit and a chat from Terra. Hugs are very loving creatures that are drawn to those who need succour. All they do is cuddle really. It soothes the soul. You must have had a bad day."

Eyre nodded, her throat tightening. Yep, that about summed it up. But she patted the lovely little Hug softly and turned to go.

"I'd better get back to practise," she said. "I'm glad you found her."

Ranger Chrysanthe headed back around the lake towards the launching pad, and Eyre went back inside the Training Shed where people were still practising their techniques over and over. Some of them were getting quite good at it; she saw a couple of people doing Ferito like they'd been learning it for years. And someone inside a barrier was producing jagged bolts of lightning with their Viq—quite impressive. There were plenty who were struggling, though, which made Eyre feel a little better, but she still felt disinclined to join in. It was getting late. There was only fifteen minutes to go in the session, so she decided to cut it short and head back to the lodge.

Georgia Mahoney and Iris Goff were sitting out the front of the lodge, having showered and changed into their very expensive brand name civilian clothes. Long tidy hair, bright complexions, healthy . . . *clean*, Eyre thought despondently, looking at her own filthy arms. They stopped talking and looked at her as she passed by. Eyre heard nothing until she reached the top of the staircase, then there was that telltale snicker that all girls understand, the one that says "Oh my god, did you see *that*?" Just one small sound spoke volumes. She headed into the shower, wanting to throw a bucket of soapy water on their perfect heads.

CHAPTER TWENTY-FIVE

EYRE WOKE WEDNESDAY MORNING feeling washed out and tired. Hearing Carly moving around, she kept her eyes shut and waited for her to leave. She couldn't bear to see that bright face this morning; the clouds of gloom had not dissipated in the night and were still firmly hovering overhead. When Carly had left, she slowly got up and dressed. It was hot again and steamy; it was going to be very humid, and her skin already had a sheen of sweat on it by the time she got across to the Lake. Students were standing around yawning; apparently the constant schedule of events was wearing them out, too. Eyre looked at the beginning of the run and gritted her teeth. She was *not* going to be last, and she was *not* going to be knocked off the path this time!

More students had Elevated overnight, and cries of "Going *up!*" filled the air followed by shrieks of congratulations. Eyre stood awkwardly with a smile on her face, happy for those that had Elevated, but beginning to feel more and more like this was a party she had not been invited to. Fortunately Abby, Nick, and Beatrice arrived at that point, and she was able to fill the time talking to them.

Sergeant Tottingham, looking immaculate, regarded the assembling students. As soon as they became aware of her stern eye focussing on them, there was a rapid move into a ragged numerical line. No one wanted to draw attention to themselves and risk unpleasant consequences.

The run eventually started, and Eyre took off as fast as she could. Her legs were stiff from the running, especially as, thanks to Jeremy Tucker, she'd done those acrobatics off the side of the track the day before. Her muscles were not used to so much activity, and they cried out at the torture. Her lungs weren't much better, burning in pain as she laboured up the hill. But she kept going and once again managed to avoid being completely at the back of the pack. As she passed Jeremy Tucker heading up the path, she swept her foot under his shins and tripped him into the bushes. He shouted in rage as he floundered around in the undergrowth, and students laughed as they passed by. Eyre smiled smugly as she puffed up the hill. Turning the other cheek was all very well, she thought with satisfaction, but sometimes an eye for an eye felt *so* much better.

She struggled determinedly up the hill, her muscles straining as she reached the top. She had just turned the corner to head back down the track when suddenly something dark and large caught her eye down the side of the canyon. What was that? She stopped and tried to look past the rocks and tree trunks that blocked her view, and her stomach lurched sickeningly when she thought she saw something move. It did not take much to wake up the dread that now permanently lurked at the back of her mind. She stared hard at the rocky hill, but despite scrutinising each bit of it, she couldn't see anything unusual. Still she lingered, convinced there was something out there.

"Move along, 88!" Sergeant Tottingham bellowed. "This is not a sightseeing trip!" Eyre jumped. She couldn't see Sergeant Tottingham from way up here. How could Sergeant Tottingham see her? She realised with a start that the Sergeant's voice was in her head. Obviously nothing was hidden from these instructors.

Eyre bounded back onto the track and raced down the hill, finishing ahead of the last few runners.

"Do it again," Professor Vela said, his pale eyes narrowing with spiteful glee. "Obviously you forgot the no stopping rule."

"But . . . I saw—"

"There's nothing out there but rocks and kangaroos, 88," Professor Vela snarled. "If you don't stop talking you will be running the track three times."

Seething with fury, Eyre started the run again and took the long journey around the path. She forced herself to keep running lest she be told to do it yet again, and by the time she arrived at the finish line she felt like she was going to vomit. She staggered over the line, retching.

"10 km, 88, outstanding," Sergeant Tottingham said, marking her off the list.

Eyre lay on the ground, unable to reply.

"Don't lie there too long," Professor Vela said as he stalked off. "The cafeteria tables need cleaning."

Both the instructors left, and Eyre smashed her fist in the ground. It was so totally unjust! This was such a nightmare. She wearily stood up and headed for the Refectory. Once again most people had left, but this time her friends were waiting to eat with her.

"It's really unfair, Eyre," Abby said hotly as Eyre stuffed down her cereal. "They shouldn't penalise you for that."

"Obviously people stop because they're finding it hard. Running a second time wouldn't help that at all," Beatrice, the logical one, pointed out.

"And the potential is there to be running all day if anyone couldn't do the whole thing," Abby added.

"I wasn't stopping because I was tired," Eyre protested. "I mean, I was tired, but that's not why I stopped. I thought I saw . . ." she trailed off. What had she seen? A shadow? A tree? Nothing? Certainly there was nothing there the second time she went around. ". . . nothing," she finished feebly.

Her friends looked at her with sympathy. Apart from the horror of having to run the track twice, it was awful to be singled out this way each day. They all grabbed a cloth and helped her to wipe down the tables.

"At least I'm going to be good at this," Eyre joked feebly. "Not too good at anything else so far!"

"You'll be right, Eyre," Nick said. "None of us are doing very well so far. Well, actually, you are, Beatrice. But Abby and I, we're definitely floundering. You're in good company, Eyre."

They finished the tables and headed back to their respective lodges, agreeing to meet in Meditation.

CHAPTER TWENTY-SIX

UNFORTUNATELY, MEDITATION DIDN'T GO any better than the session the day before. Eyre tried to focus on being calm, but thoughts kept crowding into her head, and if anything, she did worse than the first session. She couldn't even enjoy the beauty of the hall, her mind was churning so much. If there was any vibe surrounding her, she seethed, it was angry, cross, irate, furious. . . . Pick a word, any of those. Actually *all* of those. Wild thoughts crashed around her head, making it impossible to relax and find any sort of inner peace. Simmons walked around them, intoning in his gentle voice, but she could hardly hear him through the racket in her head, and she even felt annoyed with *him*. When she left she could feel his eyes, vaguely disappointed, following her out.

She walked with Abby, Nick, and Beatrice over to the Training Shed. Sergeant Tottingham was up the front of the shed, waiting for everyone to enter, Professor Vela by her side.

"Hurry up, don't dawdle," she called out to the students. "Get a move on! Hello 88, how are you doing after your stroll this morning?"

Eyre gnashed her teeth mentally, but acknowledged the lecturer with a nod as she walked past. She headed down the back of the shed, figuring she didn't need any more attention on her this morning. Lila Potts nudged Georgia Mahoney as she walked past them, and Eyre felt steam coming out her ears.

Sergeant Tottingham began the session, running them through the moves of Basic Clasis again. "We'll be doing this Clasis again this morning so that you have enough time to practise before we move on to our next Clasis," she thundered as she moved through the sequence of positions. "There is no point going on to the next Clasis until you have reached a measure of success with this one. Twelve, thirteen, fourteen. . . ." She counted as she smoothly changed from one move to the next. Eyre set her jaw in annoyance.

She wasn't doing any better this morning with Ferito, either. It was like her whole body had given up on her; she couldn't do anything. She stumbled over position eighteen and swiped the air as if searching for a handhold. Looking around the room she saw several people who had managed to find their balance in a variety of the positions, which made her feel worse. Warrigal was easily moving through the whole sequence like he'd been doing it since birth, she thought, feeling useless. He looked up and caught her eye, an inscrutable expression on his face. Then he looked away and continued the moves.

Nick had improved today, his natural athletic ability helping him to overcome his lack of Viq. He stumbled through some of the poses but otherwise seemed to manage quite well. Even Abby was doing better, thought Eyre. Is it only me that hasn't improved?

She tried over and over to do the sequence, getting increasingly annoyed as she failed again and again. Finally she gave up in frustration and watched other people doing their moves. Some people were even doing the moves together, moving in perfect coordination from position to position. Colton Ford and Phillip Outray had paired up, moving smoothly in a display that looked choreographed. Wonderful, Eyre thought. By the time we get to the TEPs they'll be teaching the class.

She moved to position eleven, wobbling dangerously, and noticed Jax performing his Clasis quite competently. Just then he looked over at her, perhaps sensing her gaze, and she stumbled gracelessly. She tried to stand up but hefted herself up too quickly, overbalanced and ended up on the floor again. Such a natural, she muttered under her breath. When she looked back at Jax he was studiously studying the front of the room. Eyre gritted her teeth. Things weren't going well in general. Congratulations; she was a study in mediocrity.

Eventually the session finished, and Eyre headed to the Common Room with Abby, Nick, and Beatrice. Sergeant Tottingham watched her as she went, no doubt sizing her up for cafeteria duty tomorrow, Eyre thought. Dismally she drank her cup of tea, wishing that the day were over already. No one was talking much in the Common Room; the students were all no doubt focussing on the training and the enormity of how much improvement they needed to make before the TEPs. No one with quite so much improvement needed as me though, Eyre thought grumpily.

Completely in a blue funk she entered the Lecture Theatre with her friends and walked up the stairs to the same seat she had sat in yesterday. Beatrice, Nick, and Abby sat next to her again, and everyone pulled up the lecture tablet on their chair. Eyre put her silver folder on the desk and leaned on her elbow miserably. Here we go, she thought, sunk in depression. Levitation and telekinesis? I can't even get up using my feet, how on earth will I do it with my mind? Rigmar dashed in at the last moment, grimacing as he took a seat on the other side of Eyre.

"Wish I could Teleport!" he said, pulling out his Felsic in a hurry.

Then the door opened. The lecturer entered the auditorium. . .

CHAPTER TWENTY-SEVEN

...FLOATING ON AIR! VERY tall and thin, she was a middle-aged woman with angular cheekbones and completely white hair that was tied in knots all over her head, resembling nothing so much as a World War II sea mine. Her skin was tanned brown, and she had sharply attractive features and piercing eyes. The whole auditorium murmured in surprise as she made her dramatic entrance, hovering a metre above the ground.

She floated smoothly across the stage, her long rainbow-coloured dress swirling around her ankles until she stopped, suspended in midair in front of the lectern. Her cold eyes peered at the students through cat-eye glasses, and she raised one of her pointed fingernails, instantly reducing the room to silence. Then she slowly descended to the floor.

"Levitation and telekinesis," the woman announced. "I am Dr Mahogany Botolfe, and by the end of this lecture I hope to impart enough knowledge that you can begin to develop your skills in this area. Some of you will remain Unlit, but this information is essential for you to know in your vocation as a Lightworker. How many of you have used this force already?" Two hands went up, Number 157, a boy up the back, and a slightly built Indian girl at the side of the room, Number 10.

Abby nudged Eyre fiercely, drawing Dr Botolfe's eyes to them.

"The Saevus," Abby hissed, and Eyre shook her head. But as Dr Botolfe continued to study her with an impatient look on her face, Abby held Eyre's hand up, elbow still resting on the table. Eyre pulled her arm down, but Dr Botolfe kept her eyes on Eyre and then looked across at the other two students. "What you have done is unusual for first week students," she said, "but not unheard of. Perhaps you three could come down to the front here, please?"

Shooting Abby a panicked look, Eyre walked down the stairs to the front and stood next to 157 and 10. She noticed in concern that both of them had a bright Inguz on their upper arm.

Dr Botolfe looked them up and down with her sharp eyes, her gaze stopping as she saw Eyre's bare upper arm. She looked at Eyre and raised her eyebrows, turning to one of the other students.

"Number 157, could you demonstrate to the class what you can do?'

Stepping forward, 157 screwed his eyes shut and concentrated. The hall was silent as the students watched in anticipation. Suddenly he rose above the floor about twenty centimetres, hovered for a second, and then thumped back down. Opening his eyes, obviously pleased with himself, he beamed at the audience who obligingly applauded.

"Very good, 157," Dr Botolfe purred. "You obviously have a talent in this area. Thank you. Step back. Number 10, could you show us what you can do also, please."

Number 10 stepped forward, her brows furrowed as she concentrated. She put her hand out in front of her and the Felsic of a student directly in front of her raised up into the air about five centimetres off the desk. Number 10 moved her hand sideways and, wobbling, the Felsic moved through the air over to the desk of the student next to her. It trembled up and down in its journey and 10's arm shook with the effort, until finally it slapped down on to the desktop. Once again students applauded, and 10 stepped back in place, smiling.

"Excellent, 10! I expect great things of you! Number 88, could you oblige us also, please, and share your talents with us?"

Oh my god, Eyre thought, this *can't* be happening! Sweating, she stepped forward, horrified to be standing in front of everyone like this and not having a clue how to do *anything!* She shut her eyes, mostly to avoid looking at the expectant faces in front of her, and concentrated hard, trying to breathe like Simmons had shown them that morning in Meditation. Come on, come on, Eyre pleaded to herself, do something! She focussed on energy coming out of her hand and thrust it forward. Nothing happened, and someone tittered. Gritting her teeth, she recited over and over in her head "Push, push, push. . . ." And then when nothing happened, in desperation she tried for pyrokinesis. "Fire, fire, *fire* . . ." she chanted frantically in her mind, but no conflagration appeared, no flames shot out of her hand or her head or her foot—although Eyre would have liked them to. She would have liked to have burnt up completely, her shame was so great. Or disappeared. Teleported, just like Rigmar wanted to—anywhere really. Anything but here, where the silence resounded more loudly as the time stretched on.

Finally she opened her eyes miserably, realising that nothing was going to happen. She looked out at the audience, mortified. She could see some faces snickering at her, some looked compassionate, some looked away. Pheria was sitting with Jax, and she was looking at Eyre with a mixture of boredom and vague amusement, which was bad enough, but by far the worst thing was that Jax was studying her with what seemed like pity. She wanted to melt into the floor seeing those green eyes looking at her with such a disappointed air.

Ben Perrill was loving the moment, chortling in delight up at the back with his cronies. She summoned all the rage she felt towards him, desperate for something that would demonstrate her ability. But it seemed even her hatred for Perrill today was not going to help her. She was a dud. Turning to Dr Botolfe, she spread her hands apologetically.

"I, er, it seems I can't do it," she said.

Dr Botolfe's eyes fixed on her brightly, lingering on her bare upper arm. "Stage fright, perhaps? Or maybe just an overinflated idea of your own abilities?" The sarcasm practically dripped off her words. "Never mind, perhaps you will learn to do what these students have demonstrated this morning with a bit of practise? Of course, that *is* if you *Elevate*. You *do* realise that is an essential part of generating Viq energy? I'm not fond of students either manufacturing stories *or* wasting my time, 88."

Eyre wanted to melt into the floor with embarrassment. She felt like the most awful, attention-seeking fraud. Nick suddenly stood up in his seat, and all heads swivelled to look at him.

"It's true," he said calmly. "Eyre does have special abilities. I've seen them!"

Beatrice stood up beside him. "Me, too," she declared. "Animals follow her."

"I've seen it," Abby cried. "She saved me from a Saevus."

"And she healed me," Rigmar said loudly, standing up so quickly his Felsic fell to the floor with a crash. Students gawped as they stared at them all.

Dr Botolfe's eyes widened in rage. "*Silence!*" she shouted. "That is *impossible* with an Unlit student. *No one* can raise their Viq when Unlit. This girl is obviously either delusional or a very good storyteller! If I hear one more word from any of you, you will be sent out of the class. *Sit down,* all of you!"

Nick, Beatrice, Abby, and Rigmar reluctantly sat back down, all eyes upon them. Dr Botolfe stabbed the screen of her Felsic angrily with her finger.

"Please go back to your seats, students. We'll start the lecture now. Thank you to those two students who were able to demonstrate their skills to us."

Eyre slunk back to her chair, feeling like she would never get over the embarrassment of this. She didn't mind so much that she was unable to use telekinesis—she hadn't expected to—she still didn't think she'd done anything that day with the Saevus. No, the most awful thing was that it looked like she had wanted to show off, that she was claiming skills she really didn't have. And when she thought about it, she wondered miserably whether she would actually ever get those skills. There hadn't been any evidence of her getting any ability in *anything* over the past few days, unless you counted wiping down cafeteria tables. Her friends patted her arm in support, but it didn't help much. After her dismal efforts in Ferito, and her singularly unspectacular abilities in the morning run, Eyre was beginning to wonder whether she really should be here. Were her parents really Lightworkers? Didn't they pass on any skills to her? Just being able to walk without falling on her face would be some comfort to her at the moment.

Dr Botolfe's sharp gaze returned contemptuously to Eyre a few times during the course of the lecture, and Eyre did her best to try and look like a good student as Dr Botolfe explained more about the process of focussing Viq and training it to work as a tool. But Eyre couldn't concentrate; her mind kept tightening in embarrassment. She couldn't wait for the lecture to finish, and as soon as it did, she was first out the door, and she kept walking.

"Eyre," called Beatrice, "where are you going? Wait for us!"

Eyre turned around. "I'm going to skip lunch," she said. "I'll catch you later, guys. Sorry, I'd just like some time alone."

She didn't know where she was going; she just knew that she had to get away from here. She walked and kept walking fast, past the lake, up the running track, and higher into the hills. Her mind was in a turmoil. It seemed that the events of the past few months had finally caught up with her, and she felt like she was imploding. Thoughts spun out of control through her head, she was breathing hard and half-sobbing as she climbed frantically, farther into the hills. Her parents, facing the Gothak and the Zyx, the Saevus, finding out about Lightworkers—so weird and unbelievable —the Lightkeeper, the cabin, the Bunyip—so many mind-blowing events in only a few short weeks. Her brain felt on fire and she could not stay in the school for one second longer. If one more person talked to her, she would self-immolate. Oh yeah, she thought angrily, I can't do that. I can't do anything; in my case, it would be more likely a wet fizz. An Unlit wet fizz.

Her muscles quivering, she attacked the pathway like a hated foe, her feet tearing into the sand, crashing over rocks, her hands pulling her up the steep slope like her life depended on it, which she felt it actually might. One more second in that place was going to make her explode into a million pieces.

Eventually she stopped, her lungs searing, her head aching, and her legs barely able to move. She had reached the summit of Beggarman's Bluff, and a soaring view of the Blue Mountains stretched before her. She sat on a rock cross-legged and stared out over the vast canyons, tears running in an unstoppable stream down her face. Everything was so goddamned hard, and frightening, and lonely. If only her parents were here. If only they had come with her to the Sunshine Coast. . . .

She put her head in her hands and wept, loud wrenching sounds of grief and tiredness and pain. This new world was too hard, too large, too implausible. Magic creatures and auras and powers that could kill—she wanted none of it; it was an unbearable load, and she was tired. She just wanted to lie down and sleep for about two decades. Finally the sobs stopped, and she rubbed her face in unutterable weariness.

Eventually she took a painful breath and sat up. She had exhausted herself mentally and physically, and in a strange way it had helped, a release of pressure that had been building up for a long time. She wiped her eyes and looked up out over the valley again and saw that the shadows were darkening, their smoky blue haze now turning inky as the sun lowered on the horizon. Uneasily she realised that her frantic scramble up the cliffs had taken hours rather than minutes and that she was rather a long way away from the Compound.

She stood up slowly, feeling like she had been run over by a large piece of machinery. She didn't want to go back, but she supposed she should. They would be looking for her if she wasn't back by dinner, and she didn't need any more attention drawn to her. They already obviously thought she was an attention-seeking drama queen; being out late like this wouldn't help that image at all. So she stretched her muscles gingerly and then began the tricky journey back down the rocky face of the cliffs.

It was slow going, a lot harder going down than coming up, and she struggled to find secure footholds and handholds. The sandstone rock was crumbly and dangerous, and she had to take her time getting to the bottom without falling. By the time she reached the base of the cliffs, the sun had almost disappeared, and she knew she was in trouble. It was going to be dark very shortly, and she was unsure of the way back. So she started to run through the bush, guessing at the path she had taken on the way up. She ran hard, her throat burning from the effort of sucking oxygen in, her chest as painful as if someone had hurled a pickaxe through it. And her legs were so sore and weak, her feet stumbled over rocks and logs; she was barely able to lift them high enough to get over the obstacles in front of her.

The sound, when it came, was almost expected. The terrifying snarl was chillingly familiar and her hair rose as she turned around slowly, gasping for breath.

The Saevus was crouched just behind her, so close to her that her heart nearly shuddered to a stop. The fearsome creature was so huge the deformed muscles on its shoulders rubbed up against the underside of the branch of a eucalyptus tree. Eyre stepped back slowly, her breath coming in short gasps. Was this how she was going to die? Eaten by this gross, misshapen creature? She took another step backwards, her hands up in front of her. Green foul-smelling slime dripped from its mouth down onto the track as it took a step towards her.

Desperately Eyre looked sideways. Could she climb a tree? Up a rock? But then the creature leapt at her, knocking her backwards onto the dirt as it tore at her with its razor talons. She screamed and hammered at its tough hide, trying to push it away, but the creature was so powerful she made no impression at all. Wounded badly and bleeding, she cried out in terror as the gruesome black creature opened its jaws, its red eyes focussing on her throat.

Suddenly there was a ferocious snarling from the bushes, and a huge pack of dingoes burst through the trees. Teeth slashing, they attacked the Saevus, which let out a savage growl and tossed its shoulders back and forth, heaving the wild dogs off. A few of them yelped as they were thrown into rocks and tree trunks, but the sound seemed to make the rest of the pack even more fierce, and they howled as they attacked the great beast, their teeth tearing into its thick hairless hide.

The Saevus twisted and screamed as the teeth of the wild dogs tore its skin away. They were so fast Eyre could hardly make out an individual form, and the eyes of the dingo pack glowed eerily silver in the dark. They were a ghostly battalion of twirling warriors, driving the Saevus back away from Eyre.

Suddenly with a roar the Saevus turned and smashed away through the bush, the snarling dogs charging after it. Eyre could hear the howls and crashing as the violent battle continued, diminishing as they got further away until there was only silence.

Shivering in shock, Eyre pulled herself to a sitting position. She couldn't see well, but she could feel that the Saevus had clawed her thigh badly, and blood was dripping down her leg. The pain was excruciating as she hauled herself upwards. She took a careful step and realised that she was fortunate: nothing seemed broken. She was in trouble though, the wound on her thigh was deep and she needed help quickly. In amongst the pain and fear was an underlying rage, as sharp as a knife, aimed only at herself. How stupid could she be? Was she indeed a drama queen looking for attention? Well, she had certainly got it, if that was the case. She was unbelievably lucky to have met the Saevus when a pack of dingoes was around; she would certainly be dead now if they hadn't been there. She shook her head, berating herself mentally for the predicament she was in.

She picked up a sturdy eucalyptus branch and staggered through the trees, taking a general downhill direction. She figured that the Compound was at the base of the cliffs, so she should be able to get there eventually if she kept going down. If she was lucky, she would bump into the lake, which would give her an idea where she was, and which way to go.

Her breath was shallow in her chest as she limped along as fast as she could, but the blood loss had made her weak, and she realised that she wasn't going to make it far. And lurking in the back of her mind was the terrible fear that at any moment the Saevus might return.

Sweat beaded her face as she struggled around a large rock, and then she gasped in terror: a dark form was standing motionless in front of her. She raised her stick at it, ready to defend herself.

"Eyre, it's me," the shape said. Eyre nearly burst into tears at the familiar voice. Warrigal. What was he doing out here? She put the stick down and tried to control her voice as he walked up the hill to her.

"Thank god," she whispered. "I'm a bit lost. Do you know where you are?"

"I can get you back," Warrigal said. He stopped talking as he noticed that she was covered in blood. "You're injured!" he said, kneeling down to look at her leg. When he saw the size of the wound, he took off his shirt and wrapped it tightly around her thigh.

"I met a Saevus," Eyre said, her voice wobbling. "But fortunately a pack of dingoes drove it away. I am so lucky they were there. It was a huge pack, and they chased it off into the bush."

"The Saevus is a hideous beast, one of many evil creatures of the dark," Warrigal said as he tied his belt around the shirt. "Grotesque aberrations that stalk the night. But there are also some creatures that fight for the light. Dingoes are ancient souls, and they undoubtedly were trying to help you. You are right, you were fortunate tonight they were there." He finished the dressing and stood up. "Do you think you can walk back? We're nearly at the lake."

"If we go slowly I can make it," Eyre said.

Eyre hobbled alongside Warrigal as he helped her down the track, relief washing over her in waves. But she was also curious.

"What are you doing out here?"

"I'm often out here," Warrigal replied. "I need to spend time on my own in the bush. It's my country. It's beautiful in the night, if you know where you're going. I find I need solitude in order to reset my equilibrium, kind of like the meditation we practised today." He stopped and looked at her. "I could ask you the same question."

There was a silence as Eyre felt embarrassment wash over her. All sorts of replies ran through her head, but when she answered she spoke frankly. "I am so stupid. I needed to clear my head. I haven't Elevated, the humiliating class this afternoon. . . ." Her voice caught. "I'm no good at anything and I'm so tired of it all. But I didn't mean to cause all this trouble. If only I could do those things. I so want to be part of the school next year."

Warrigal said nothing for a while as they continued in slow steps down the rocky slopes. Then he stopped. "You know," he said softly, "our northern people have a word, 'jangany'. It means always asking for things. Modern cultures have a problem with jangany. I want this, I want that. . . . It is not respectful. It is not good inside, either." He thumped his hand lightly on his chest, then kept walking.

Eyre heard his words, and they registered like whiplashes on her skin. He didn't say any more; he didn't have to. She got it. Jangany—it was a perfect word for the self-centred way she had behaved. Sure, she had reasons to be hurt and angry and tired. But then so did many other people; everyone had their own story and the Lightworking community had a long history of sad losses. Instead of focussing on her own problems all the time, she needed to accept circumstances for what they were, and deal with it. Shame burnt her skin. A long silence passed.

Finally she said quietly, "It's a good word, Warrigal. Thank you for helping me to find my way." She meant more than just getting her out of the bush, and he knew it.

They finally reached the lake and as they trudged towards the Compound, which was now in sight, the blue lights flickering in the distance, Eyre vowed that she would start tomorrow with a different attitude. She was going to accept whatever happened to her—even if that meant she was Unlit—and she was going to try as hard as she could to make the most of things, to be the best that she could be. Starting with her fitness. Once this leg was sorted, she was going to practise her running until she could run like a rabbit—at least that would give her half a chance when the next creature of the night tried to devour her.

She limped up the path towards the Compound and in to the First Aid hut. Warrigal kept going after she assured him she would be fine.

"I'll see you at the lodge, Warrigal, thank you again. You saved me. Not only my life, but a whole lot of trouble if the lecturers found out about this."

Warrigal smiled at her, his perfect white teeth flashing in the night. "I have a feeling they're going to know, Eyre, but the main thing is that you're alright. I'm glad I could help."

He left, and Eyre painfully walked up the steps into the First Aid hut. Leema was reading in a big comfy chair, and her eyes widened as Eyre entered, covered in blood. She threw her Felsic down and jumped off the chair.

"By the Light!" Leema cried. "What happened to you? Come over here, sit down!" She put Eyre's leg up on a stool and unwound Warrigal's shirt, examining the wound carefully, and tut-tutting at the sight of it. Then she bustled around, gathering the medical supplies she would need: swabs, disinfectant, needle and thread. *Needle and thread?* gasped Eyre mentally. But when she looked at her leg she could see that it needed stitches—the gouges from the Saevus' claws were deep and still oozing blood.

Leema worked away quickly, washing the wound to clean the sand and dirt out of it. When she heard the wound was from a Saevus, she added more antiseptic to the warm water and washed it again.

"They have bacteria in their talons that can make you very sick," Leema explained. "Not that many people have been sick from a Saevus's claws. Most of them are dead before infection has a chance to get them. You're amazingly lucky. I've never heard of anyone surviving once a Saevus got hold of them. And a Saevus in these parts? I can't believe it!" She gave Eyre some pain relief and then injected some local anaesthetic around the wound. Carefully, with small stitches, she sewed up the gaping wounds so that they were neat lines of black thread. There were about six stitches in each of the four deep gouges; Eyre supposed they would leave a scar. She decided to consider it a mark of wisdom. Something had happened out in the dark that she couldn't explain. She had changed in a fundamental way, but was unable to put it into words. A peace filled her, peace that had nothing to do with being safe. Every time she looked at that scar it would remind her of the lessons she had learned tonight.

"If a Clementis was here they would fix you differently. But this will do for now," Leema said, gently pulling the last stitch tight. "How are you feeling?"

"I feel okay," Eyre said. "I'll have a shower and go to bed. I'm sure I'll be right by the morning." Leema dabbed brown antiseptic wash over the stitches and then covered them with a white fabric square before wrapping a long bandage around it to protect it.

"You'll have to talk to Sergeant Tottingham," Leema said. "She'll need to know about this. A Saevus nearby is very bad." She shook her head in amazement. "This has been the most unbelievable start to the TEPs. I don't recall hearing about any other year having so many dramatic things happen. She's not going to be happy with you," she added confusingly until Eyre worked out what she meant.

Eyre shrugged philosophically. "I know that," she said. "It's my fault. I'll see her in the morning and—"

The door opened, and Sergeant Tottingham walked in, face like thunder. "In the morning? How about *now*!" she said tightly. "*What* happened here?" Leema raised her eyebrows sympathetically at Eyre and retired to the other room, taking all the used medical supplies with her.

"I want you to start from the beginning," Sergeant Tottingham said, a cyclone brewing between her eyebrows. "And explain to me *what* you were doing out in the middle of the night in the first place!"

Eyre explained how she had been walking and didn't realise the time had passed, then she'd got lost. She described the Saevus and how the dingoes had fought it off. She said she had come across the track back to the Compound by chance, leaving out Warrigal's part in it all—the last thing she wanted to do was to drag him into trouble also. By the time she finished, the cyclone had reached a force five, and Sergeant Tottingham pointed a furious finger.

"Your lack of forethought is beyond comprehension. I have not long ago explained to you students that the Seams are slipping. The Bunyip was clear evidence of that. Did you not understand the significance of that conversation? That *more* care is required under those circumstances rather than less? Breaches are becoming so common! I *can't* believe you thought a stroll through the bush on your own was a great idea *any* time of the day, let alone at night!" Her face was purple, and she had a look somewhere between rage and complete astonishment on her face.

"How you survived is beyond me. Pure dumb luck. You might have disappeared, and we would never have known what had happened if it wasn't for the dingoes. You have shown the most singular lack of judgement

I have ever encountered in a candidate. We have never sent a student home before, but that doesn't mean we won't. I am going to discuss with the rest of staff what we should do about your situation. Personally, I don't want the responsibility of someone as reckless as you on my shoulders. Perhaps another school might suit you better!" Sergeant Tottingham strode around the room, her voice getting louder and louder.

Eyre's stomach dropped. She knew she was going to be in trouble, but she hadn't anticipated it would be *this* much. Being sent home? Suddenly, desperately, she knew it was the last thing in the world she wanted.

Just then, Leema stuck her head around the corner. She looked tentative but determined. "Sergeant Tottingham?" Sergeant Tottingham looked at her fiercely. "I er—perhaps the student should rest now? It might be good to work these things out after she has had a decent sleep. Perhaps tomorrow? She will still be experiencing some shock I imagine."

Sergeant Tottingham scowled, then looked at Eyre's white face and softened a bit. "Right. Well, get to your lodge then, and we'll discuss this tomorrow once I've had a chance to confer with the rest of staff." She left, ferociously stomping down the First Aid hut stairs.

Eyre walked outside and found Beatrice, Abby, and Nick waiting at the bottom of the stairs. Abby, eyes wide, was watching Sergeant Tottingham marching off into the distance.

"By the Light, Eyre," she cried, turning back to Eyre and hugging her. "Are you alright? I feel so terrible! If I hadn't made you put your hand up in class this would never have happened! Sergeant Tottingham looked so angry!"

"We were waiting at the lodge," Nick explained. "Warrigal told us where you were, and we came over. We were so worried about you."

Seeing him so concerned made Eyre feel all the worse, and tears welled up in her eyes. Then it dawned on her that Abby had a silver Halo across her forehead, and she looked at Abby's arm.

"Oh my god, you've Elevated!" Eyre cried. "That's *so* wonderful, Abby! I'm so happy for you! Come on, walk me back to the lodge, and I'll fill you in on the whole sordid story. I'm so sorry. I've been a self-centred idiot. I'm really lucky to be here, and I know it. The Saevus did me a favour I think."

"Saevus?" Beatrice screeched. "Eyre, you saw a Saevus? That's terrible, you poor thing! And Sergeant Tottingham looked just as terrifying. What a night you've had!"

Eyre told them the whole story as they walked back to Water Lodge, asking them to keep quiet about Warrigal's involvement in it all. Abby gasped when Eyre talked about the dingoes.

"I've never heard of dingoes in such a large pack," Nick said contemplatively. "Lucky for you this time, I guess."

"Do you think you'll be in big trouble, Eyre?" Abby asked.

"Sergeant Tottingham is discussing with the other teachers whether I should stay here or not," Eyre replied ruefully. "If she talks to Dr Botolfs I'm sure I'll be leaving on the first Zepp!"

"Oh no," Beatrice exclaimed. "Surely not! You've only just got here. They've got to give you some leeway. I'm sure everyone makes mistakes some time. . . ."

"This was hardly a mistake, Beatrice," Eyre replied softly. "I made a decision, and now I've got to bear the consequences." Suddenly she yawned loudly, even the prospect of leaving the school not able to prevent the involuntary movement. Rather subdued, Nick and Abby hugged her hard and said goodbye at the lodge. Beatrice hugged her, too.

"You missed dinner," she said. "I'll get you a hot chocolate from the Common Room. I'll be back shortly." She left at a run, and Eyre slowly trudged up the stairs to Water Lodge. She tied a plastic bag around her wound and had a shower, keeping her leg out of the spray of water. Dirt and blood ran in a rusty swirl down the drain, but the hot water was welcome on her sore muscles, and she stood a long time under the powerful jets.

Finally she changed into her pyjamas, moving with difficulty. Every muscle, every bone, even the inside of her head hurt so much. She felt that she had been mashed flat, which she supposed she had, really.

Many of the lodge members were looking at her curiously. They had noticed she wasn't there for afternoon training and dinner, and questions were burning in their eyes. But Eyre said goodnight to them before they could ask, and somehow managed to climb into her bed without having to offer any explanations. By the time Beatrice arrived back with the hot chocolate, Eyre was sound asleep.

CHAPTER TWENTY-EIGHT

THURSDAY MORNING ARRIVED VERY quickly. The whistle woke Eyre at 5:00 a.m. and she sat up in a panic, disoriented for a second. Then the pain of her muscles hit her and she groaned. Carly was already up and dressing—she was obviously used to getting up early. She had told Eyre her family owned a sheep farm in Borabinga, and Eyre guessed it was a normal time to get up on a working farm; the past few mornings Carly had seemed as bright as a button. Carly spoke to Eyre from the end of her bed where she sat polishing her boots.

"Morning, mate," she said. "How are you doing? You had a bit of a rough time last night from what I heard."

Word gets around quickly, Eyre thought wryly. It's confirmed: Eyre Lightward, official Drama Queen of this year's TEPs. She rubbed her legs carefully, then swung them over the edge and jumped down. Surprisingly, her stitched leg felt pretty good, apart from the stiffness. She pulled her clothes out of the locker and started to dress, talking to Carly over her shoulder.

"Ah, well, I was really stupid, and I shouldn't have been out in the bush. I paid the price. Good lesson."

"You saw a Saevus out there someone said?"

"Yes, I'm lucky to be here," Eyre said briefly.

Carly spoke to the floor as she bent over, pulling on her boots. "Well I'm glad you're okay. It was really embarrassing for you in that class. I don't think Dr Botolfe should have put you on the spot like that. It's hard to perform in front of everyone. Not that I can actually do anything yet." She laughed.

Eyre felt better—what a nice person Carly was. She had a feeling that this sensible, calm girl would actually never miss a beat when called upon.

"Thanks Carly, I appreciate your sympathy!" Eyre laughed over her shoulder. "Hopefully I can do something eventually, or I'm going to look like the biggest fraud in history."

"Did you really use telekinesis?" Carly asked.

"I'm not sure," Eyre said awkwardly, finally turning and looking at Carly. "Abby thinks I did, but I'm not convinced. I think perhaps we just got lucky."

Then Eyre gave a gasp of delight as she realised Carly had a shining Inguz on her upper arm. She looked at Carly's forehead and saw a confirming silver stripe of light across it. "Wow, Carly, you've Elevated! Congratulations!" she said, and Carly looked happy and proud. But her eyes showed some uncertainty as she answered, obviously aware of Eyre's feelings.

"Thanks Eyre, I hope yours comes soon, too."

Determined not to overshadow Carly's joy, Eyre shoved any disappointment that her arm was still bare out of her head. "Whatever happens, I'll be happy," Eyre replied, and to her surprise, realised that she meant it. "I'm just glad to be here."

She pulled on her boots and stood up. Strapping on her number she was finally ready, so together she and Carly dashed over to the Lake, where many more students were waiting. Carly joined her friends from Wagga Wagga, and Eyre headed over to where Nick, Abby, and Beatrice were waiting. Eyre realised that despite the pounding her body had received yesterday, she was actually feeling quite good, and she stretched with relief, feeling the stiffness easing. The stitches in her leg didn't seem to be causing her any problem at all; she could walk normally and couldn't feel any pain. She thought she'd see how the running went and stop if she couldn't make it around the course.

Eyre saw Warrigal across the crowd, and she gave him a subtle salute, which he acknowledged by raising his eyebrows. He was a bit of an enigma, that one, Eyre thought, but she was definitely thankful for his nocturnal wanderings. Looking around the students, Eyre noticed that a few more of them now had an Inguz on their arm, and students milled around in an excited flutter, comparing the bright symbols and congratulating each other. Cheers of 'Going . . . up!' filled the air, mixing with the happy chatter of the students who had Elevated.

Some, obviously the ones who still didn't have an Inguz, were looking dismal but trying not to make it obvious. Eyre clenched her jaw and resolved to congratulate those students she knew who had Elevated and be happy for them. There was still time for her, and if she didn't Elevate, then she would make the most of being Unlit. It actually sounded quite cool being a spy and talking in codes, or whatever they did in their secret world.

Her thoughts were interrupted as Sergeant Tottingham marched up to the front of the crowd, and the students rapidly jumped into numerical order. As usual, she was dressed in crisply starched khaki clothes, and she walked with a strong, straight back, her muscular form right out of a Defence Force advertisement. She cast a hard eye over the waiting students. "Numbers 98, 23, and 106, come up here please!" Number 98 was an athletic boy from Eyre's lodge—Vaughn Michaelson. Number 23 was a girl from Beatrice's lodge who Eyre didn't know. She was average height with glasses and pale freckled skin, and she wore her black hair in two long plaits. Number 106 was Zanda, who jumped like something had bitten him when his name was called. Uneasily they went to the front of the crowd.

"Number 98—your boots are appalling. Number 23, your uniform needs a wash—you have black marks all over your shirt. And 106, your shirt is hanging out. We are not at a medieval festival, ladies and gentlemen, and our uniform must be kept neat and clean! Each of you three can do 50 push-ups and 100 situps this morning before starting your run. And if you haven't rectified the situation by tomorrow morning, that number will double." Zanda and the other two students, looking miserable, dropped to the ground and started the push-ups.

"Right, the rest of you it's time to run!" Sergeant Tottingham boomed, raising her staff. "Get ready! Go!" She thumped her staff on the ground, sending sparks flying from the crystal at the top, and the students took off like a great centipede along the track. Eyre was determined to improve today, and she forced her legs to run as hard as she could. There was no pain from the stitches, so she pushed herself as fast as she could go, which wasn't all that swift compared to the leaders up the front who were rapidly disappearing, but still better than her previous three efforts. Obviously attitude counted for something, she thought, forcing herself to keep up the pace.

Still, it was hard going, and the upwards section of the run was no easier than before. She staggered up the steep hill at the end of the pack of students, gasping for breath and struggling to keep moving.

She rounded the top of the track past the Wollemi Pine and pushed hard downhill, leaving a couple of students behind. When she finally crossed the line she was not last, and she felt elated. It felt good to improve even this much. She bent over, breathing hard, and stretched her legs out. The bandage was still snugly around her leg, and she had to admit that it felt fine. Obviously Leema had done a good repair job. She looked up as a pair of sturdy khaki-clad legs stopped in front of her.

"Make sure you head to First Aid before breakfast, 88," Sergeant Tottingham said, her eyes taking in Eyre's sweating form. "Get her to check that your stitches are intact after the run."

Eyre trotted over to First Aid, wanting to get it over with quickly so she'd have enough time to shower and make breakfast before Meditation. She knocked on the door and Leema opened it, smiling as she recognised Eyre.

"How are you today, Eyre?" Leema asked. "Come and sit over here, and I'll have a look at your leg."

Eyre sat with her leg up on a stool, and Leema started to unwind the bandage. She stopped about halfway and looked at Eyre in surprise. "That's strange," she said. "I would have expected quite a bit of bruising here. I can't see anything so far."

Intrigued, she kept unwinding and examining Eyre's leg. There was no bruising, no sign of injury at all, and when Leema took off the fabric pad covering the wound, she gasped out loud. Eyre leaned over, not sure what the problem was and saw with equal surprise that her leg had completely healed. The stitches were still there, showing the vague path of the Saevus' claws, but the wounds themselves had healed up, leaving only a slight white line.

Leema looked at Eyre in astonishment. "Did you see a Clementis last night?" she asked. Eyre still wasn't quite sure what a Clementis was, or what they looked like, but she knew she hadn't seen anything last night except the back of her eyelids. She shook her head.

"Well, this is amazing. I've never seen anyone heal so quickly," Leema said. She frowned in concentration and then got her small sharp scissors out. "Well, I don't know how that happened, but you certainly don't need the stitches any more. I'll take them out."

After showering, Eyre headed to breakfast and then joined Beatrice, Abby, and Nick as they headed to Meditation. She felt invigorated; she wasn't stiff, and her leg worked as if nothing had happened to her. She wasn't sure how she had healed so quickly, that had never happened to her before, but she felt really great. Maybe it's the endorphins from all the hiking, she thought, half-seriously.

"Eyre Lightward, you are such a puzzle!" Abby declared after scrutinizing Eyre's leg. "What magic is this?" Eyre shrugged, equally at a loss. But, she decided, whatever it was, she was very happy about it. It would have been very difficult to undertake the TEPs with a major injury.

"I may be a puzzle, but I'm a stupid puzzle," Eyre said after a moment. "What I did last night was dumb."

Abby's cornflower eyes were soft. "Eyre, my heart broke when my mother died," she said. "But I had time to say goodbye. It must be terrible to lose both your parents so suddenly, and you're still grieving. We understand." Eyre gave her a small smile as she left the table. As usual, her friends were forgiving, and she felt grateful for their kindness. It fell like a comforter around her shoulders, and a warmth grew within her.

Eyre sat in the glowing Meditation Hall and tried to focus on not focussing, to let her senses expand as Simmons had instructed. She put the negative thoughts she had previously had about Meditation aside, and tried to think of her body and mind becoming as one. The flowing sound of water was peaceful, and she felt herself relaxing as she sat cross-legged on the warm aquamarine crystal. She concentrated on breathing in and out slowly, and tried to clear her mind of any intrusive thoughts. Soon she found herself slipping into a dreamlike state, sitting in a zone of awareness of her senses, but not thinking.

When Simmons let them know it was time to go, she opened her eyes in surprise. The time had gone so quickly. She stood up and stretched, feeling clear-headed and full of energy. So *this* was what it was about, she thought. It was like washing the cotton wool out of her head, and she felt a lightness within herself. Not a bad way to start the morning after all, she decided.

She and her friends left the Meditation Hall and headed over to the Training Shed. It seemed a bit ironic to follow Meditation with martial arts training, Eyre thought, but then they were not unalike in some ways. The focus and the body control were similar in that they both required total mental commitment. Eyre supposed it would help her Ferito training to be so focussed after Meditation; it would probably help her concentrate, and her body certainly felt great.

Once again Sergeant Tottingham was waiting for them, but this time Mandig Vela was also there, two piles of stout wooden sticks at his side. His thin face was twisted into its usual look of distaste as he surveyed the students entering, and his eyes raked over Eyre as she walked by. Indicating the pile with longer sticks he shouted impatiently at all the students.

"Hurry up! Grab a Palum from this pile, find a place, and sit down. We have a lot to cover this morning, and I don't want to wait for you. Last ones in shut the shed door! Come on, move it!"

Finally everyone was in, and Mandig Vela picked up one of the sticks from the pile nearest him. "The Palum is a training aid for the weapons you will learn to fight with in the future. You will train with the Palum until the end of second year. Third year students practise only with the real weapons and continue to do so through their graduate year, if they elect to undertake one. We find we have a lot of third year students visiting our school nurse in the first few months of the year," he added drily.

"This Palum is a training tool for the Mnae. We will also use Palum from the other pile to practise Antarak techniques. I want you to watch while I demonstrate the basic Ferito Clasis of Aditus and Tego for the Mnae, which is called Clasis for Single-Blade Weapon. You will receive a Mnae in fourth year, but you are not permitted to use it until you have passed a special examination in this Clasis, which occurs at the beginning of your final year. Using a Mnae competently requires concentration of the highest order.'

Mandig Vela went through a graceful series of moves that led into each other continuously.

"Aditus, Tego, Aditus, Tego . . ." he repeated shortly as he demonstrated the moves. He was light on his feet, and the movements seemed almost like dancing, smooth transfers of muscle strength while balancing on either the front or back foot, depending on the action. After several minutes he stopped and turned to Sergeant Tottingham.

"Sergeant Tottingham and I will now demonstrate the way the actions of Aditus and Tego complement each other. Aditus can be a defence move just as much as Tego can be an attack move. It depends where in the sequence you place each action and how you play the next movement. Observe!"

Sergeant Tottingham and Mandig Vela saluted each other by holding their closed right hand, with the Palum in it, over their Inguz, and bowing to each other. Then they stepped their left foot forward, brought the right hand with the Palum up and back, and touched their left palms together. Then they shouted "Tollo!" stepped back and started to circle each other, Palum raised. The left hand balanced out to the side, hand open stiffly with the palm facing forwards. Their eyes studied each other fiercely, watching for the first movement. Mandig Vela struck first but Sergeant Tottingham was already gone. She parried with a smooth movement from behind her, whirled around, and thrust at Mandig Vela. His Palum clashed against hers with a loud thwack, and then they were fighting furiously, blow after blow being exchanged with the wooden weapons. The speed they were hitting the wooden sticks made a rapid-fire clattering in the air, and Eyre could hardly see what they were doing.

Then Mandig Vela sent a bright beam of light from his open left palm towards Sergeant Tottingham's Palum. She moved lightning quick, sending an opposing beam to meet it, and the light energy clashed in midair as they battled against each other to push the other beam back. Sergeant

Tottingham was too strong for Mandig Vela, and suddenly his beam disappeared, driven back by the force of Sergeant Tottingham's energy. Quick as a flash she turned the light beam on his Palum, and it incinerated instantly, causing Mandig Vela to shake his hand from the heat.

Eyre couldn't help herself. Ever since Mandig Vela had burnt Rigmar's forehead, she had disliked him intensely, so to see him lose in the demonstration was wonderful. She turned to Nick and made a victory sign, and he grinned back at her. But when Eyre turned back at the front, she saw with horror that Professor Vela had noticed their exchange, and he was looking at them furiously. Her stomach clenched, and she dropped her eyes. Already she had made an enemy—and an enemy on staff was something no one needed. Aghast at her own folly she gritted her teeth. Nick was looking equally abashed, and Eyre felt sorry she had dragged him into this.

"Right, students," Sergeant Tottingham said, well pleased with her win. "Now I will run through the Clasis for Two-Handed Fighting." She picked up two Palum from the second pile of wooden sticks. "These Palum are substitutes for the Antaraks you will receive in your Arms Endowment. The Antaraks are lethal weapons and it is imperative that you employ the weapons carefully and learn the correct way to handle them, which is why we practise with the Palum. Watch the Clasis as I go through the movements."

Once again the students watched a series of movements, this time with two weapons that smoothly transitioned from one position into another. It was similar to the Clasis for Single-Blade Weapon, but adapted to use both hands for Aditus and Tego. Sergeant Tottingham was a big woman, but she moved gracefully from movement to movement with faultless expertise. Finally, after running through the series of movements a few times, she stopped and put down the Palum.

"Okay, now it's your turn to practise your movements. Please pick up your single Palum and follow Professor Vela as he goes through the Ferito Clasis for Single-Blade Weapon. I will be back shortly to rejoin you."

Sergeant Tottingham left the shed. Mandig Vela picked up another long Palum and started in the beginning pose: head bowed, the fist of his right hand, which was holding his weapon, covering the Inguz. Then he brought the weapon up and strode his left foot forward as he began the Clasis. The students tried to follow as best they could through the movements. Eyre found it as challenging as the day before, but she was determined to do better today, and she forced herself to concentrate. Suddenly she felt an energy travel up her muscles and for three positions, she *got* it—smoothly transitioning between the movements. Then she stumbled and lost the momentum, but suddenly she understood what she was aiming for. Those three movements had felt strong and formidable, and she began to realise what the power of Ferito was about. She started again, focussing on keeping her muscles strong and centring her core as she transferred her balance between front and back feet. Again, she got it for a couple of moves, and pleased with herself, she looked up—only to see Mandig Vela glowering at her from the front of the room. He clapped his hands for attention, and all the students stopped moving.

"I see we have a student doing quite well here, so might I suggest a little competition?" His pale eyes locked on to Eyre's, and a slight smile curved his lips.

"Number 88, you seem to be quite pleased with your efforts, so I think it would be wonderful if you could give the other students a demonstration." He looked around the room as if trying to decide who to choose, but when he called out Ben Perrill's number, 119, Eyre was sure he had done it deliberately. Ben was the biggest and heaviest boy in the group. Smoothing his hair over the bald patch atop his head, he leered at her, looking gleeful at the prospect of taking her on. She lifted her chin and thought, Right then, let's go!

But then a voice beside her spoke up, and Nick stepped forward. "You can't do that, sir, Eyre was attacked by a Saevus last night."

Professor Vela's look was vicious, but he spoke in a slightly patronising voice. "Well, I actually think that as professor here, I can elect to do whatever I want. But since you've brought it up, I must say I'm intrigued. You say 88 was attacked by a Saevus, and yet, here she is, fighting fit. How can that be? I've heard they're quite ferocious beasts."

There was a murmur as the students in the hall looked over at Eyre, and she felt herself flushing. Just what she needed, more suggestions that she was showing off or making things up.

"You sure it wasn't a feral wombat you saw out there, 88?" Professor Vela said, in a bright, interested voice. "I hear they can inflict a nasty bite." The students started laughing but stopped when they realised he wasn't being funny. An uneasy silence hung in the air as Professor Vela fixed his eyes on Nick. His eyes travelled up and down Nick's slight form, and a spiteful look came across his face.

"Still," he said contemplatively, "perhaps we should give the poor girl a rest. I'm sure you would love to stand in for her, wouldn't you, 134? Would you head up on to the sparring arena, 134 and 119, and show us what you have learned so far?"

"Don't, Nick! I'll do it!" Eyre implored him, but Nick had a look in his eye that showed he was not going to be dissuaded. His face impassive, he walked up on to the bamboo mat and faced Ben Perrill as if they were about to play a game of chess. But the light caught on his scars, and they gleamed as if they were an omen. Eyre felt sick.

"Hello, Mouse." Ben smirked. "This is going to be fun."

"Did you get your hair done for the occasion?" Nick asked him and raised his eyebrows, and Ben's fair skin flushed vividly as his hand involuntarily touched his comb-over. His cheeks were beetroot red, large round circles of colour suffusing his skin. Then the huge boy twisted a horrible smile at Nick, and Eyre was terrified for him. Ben Perrill was going to smash Nick into the floor; that was clear enough.

There wasn't a breath of sound as the two boys performed the opening move of the Clasis and shouted "Tollo!" Then the whack of wooden sticks filled the air as they both attacked furiously. To be fair, Nick had learned a lot in a short time; he was a good athlete and had a quick mind, and he'd actually picked up some of the moves already. But he was hopelessly outweighed by Ben Perrill, who hacked away brutally with the Palum, driving Nick farther and farther back on the sparring mat. Several times the Palum connected with Nick's knuckles, drawing blood, but he didn't make a sound, fighting back bravely as best he could. But he was suffering badly; Ben smacked Nick's head a few times, and Nick had red welts across his face from where the Palum had struck. *Stop it!* Eyre thought desperately, looking at Professor Vela. *This is not sparring, it's calculated abuse!*

Suddenly Ben Perrill stepped in and hit Nick so hard across the head with the Palum that Nick crashed to his knees, his hand over his face. A horrified silence hung over the room as Nick struggled to get up. Ben towered above him, sneering at him. Eyre shut her eyes.

An exclamation from the door jolted her eyes open again and she saw Sergeant Tottingham standing there, her face like thunder. "That's enough!" Sergeant Tottingham strode up to the sparring mat and helped Nick to his feet. Shooting Professor Vela a look that could only be described as disgusted, Sergeant Tottingham lifted Ben Perrill's arm in the air.

"The winner," Sergeant Tottingham declared, her voice dripping with sarcasm. "Such a magnificent victory." Ben flushed with embarrassment. "You boys can head back to your places."

Nick stumbled out of the ring and walked slowly back to his place. He was going to have terrible bruises on his face, Eyre thought in distress, all because of me.

"Thanks, Nick," she whispered. Abby and Beatrice looked equally upset, although Beatrice had bolts of fire burning in her eyes. Professor Vela should not get offside with a clever brain like Beatrice's, Eyre thought with black humour. One day that smart head would figure out a way to get back at him. But for now all they could do was pat Nick on the arm in sympathy. He stood stolidly, not betraying that he was in any pain.

Sergeant Tottingham, a disturbed frown on her face, walked back to the front of the room. "Okay, I guess we will finish here now. Morning tea is available in the Common Room for those who want it. Then your specialist lecturer is Madame Cheska Overmantle in the Lecture Theatre at 1020. Please don't be late for Madame Overmantle. She can make your life miserable."

A couple of students laughed at this, but there was a very subdued vibe in the air. Most of the students were unsettled by the "demonstration", not knowing what to make of it, but realising that there was more to it than two students practising.

Professor Vela stood at the front of the shed, looking vastly annoyed at the way the fight had ended. As students started to leave, whispering to each other, Sergeant Tottingham marched out of the shed, her tight movements showing clearly what she thought of the incident. Professor Vela watched her go, then raised his voice.

"Students, don't forget that after specialist training this afternoon, you have the opportunity to come back here for sparring practise and to practise the Ferito Clasis you have learned over the past two days. There is a pile of shorter Palum here for Antarak practise, and you will find the Charts of Basic Clasis, and Clasis for both Single-Blade Weapon and Two-Handed Fighting on the wall here to refer to.

"Numbers 134 and 119, thank you for that exceptional demonstration. You have done so well this morning, I feel you should once again be paired this afternoon for your sparring practise. Please report back here at 1445 to continue your good work."

He exchanged a look with Ben Perrill, and Eyre realised in fury that Perrill had just been given a directive by Professor Vela: beat up that kid. And it was something that bully would be only too pleased to do. Where is the Light in *these* people? she asked herself desperately. How can such awful people be Lightworkers? Grinding her teeth in anger, she followed the wave of students out the door towards the Common Room.

CHAPTER TWENTY-NINE

AT THE COMMON ROOM they made a cup of tea and lounged in comfy overstuffed chairs placed around the room. Wooden coffee tables were centred in groups of chairs, and the students filled the room, talking and laughing as they discussed the training. Most of them were vastly amused at their failure to perform the Clasis with any competency, but Eyre felt wound as tightly as a spring. Nick was drinking a hot chocolate, gingerly feeling around his eye.

"Are you okay, Nick?" Eyre said. "I'm so sorry I got you into that!"

Nick shrugged. "Nah, not your fault, Eyre. Perrill was going to get me sooner or later. Better to get it over with, really."

Beatrice was not amused and still irate about the whole situation. She eyed Ben Perrill up from across the room like a voodoo queen taking measurements for her next doll.

"Just you just wait, Perrill," she said fiercely. "You and that rubbish lecturer. A couple of insecure bullies."

"Hear hear," Eyre said fervently. "Count me in. I'll do anything for the chance to wreak some havoc!"

Abby looked over at Ben, her face troubled. "You know, I remember that in Primary School he used to be okay."

Eyre registered her shock, speechless at this, but Zanda snorted in derision.

"Must have been a long time ago. I've only ever known him as a sadistic fiend." Once again Eyre felt sorry for Zanda. His eyes were hot as he watched Ben from over the rim of his cup. Being victimized was always hard to forget, or forgive.

When they had finished they set out for the Lecture Theatre for their next class.

"What's Cheska Overmantle teach again?" asked Abby.

"*Madame* Cheska Overmantle," Beatrice replied, "is with the Psionic Division and her topic is cognitive energies."

"Which is. . . ?" Nick asked.

"Well, I think it's telling people's fortunes. What's happened already to them. What will happen in the future. I think I've got some skill in that area already," Beatrice answered. "For instance, in Ben Perrill's future, I see a world of pain and suffering!"

Everyone laughed and headed into the Lecture Theatre.

Madame Overmantle came in quietly with none of the drama of Dr Botolfe from the previous day. She was a little woman aged about seventy, her grey hair a wild frizz about her very lined face, anchored by a multi-coloured woven headband. Her eyes were brown and bright with intelligence behind round purple-rimmed glasses, and she surveyed the whole class slowly.

When she got to Eyre her eyes hesitated and a small frown of puzzlement appeared, but she quickly kept going, so Eyre thought she must have imagined it. Unless of course, Madame Overmantle had been warned about the attention-seeking student in the class already, she thought drily, and was looking for her. Finally Madame Overmantle stopped her quiet perusal and started speaking.

"Well, I see we have a varied and talented bunch of students here this morning. Welcome to," she turned and looked at the board and words started appearing across it in bright light: "Cognitive Energies and Tapping into the Psychic Forces." She turned back to the sea of expectant faces.

"Some of you will have a special talent in this area, which I am looking forward to working with and developing. You will most probably be in the Sappir, Flava, or Virens Sector if so, but of course, you might be from any of the Sectors to have a gift in this area.

"As with many of the Lightworker talents, the Viq force is an essential part of developing your skill in cognitive energies. Once you have mastered tapping into that force, all the subjects will become easier for you. But even so, specifically reading the waves of the past and the future is a talent that takes practise and fostering. Charlatans have been *performing*—and I use that word deliberately— 'fortune telling' for centuries, using their skill at reading body language to pass themselves off as psychics. They have done a lot of damage to the reputation of our profession. But of course there are the genuine readers, and they are a powerful force in our community and the world.

"So how to start? Let me perhaps do a demonstration for you to show you how it works. Could I have a volunteer?" Eyre didn't move a muscle.

perhaps she did have cognitive talents, because something within her had a horrible feeling about this, a premonition of doom. She tried to shrink down in her seat without moving. *Surely* Madame Overmantle wouldn't choose her? Surely the universe couldn't be that cruel. As Madame Overmantle turned her calm brown-eyed gaze towards her, Eyre sat like a deer in headlights, unblinking and *willing* her to choose someone else. But no, no, no—it seemed the stars above *were* having a rather hilarious game with her because: "Number 88, would you come down please? Let me read you, my dear."

Eyre groaned internally as she got up, and she was sure the rest of the students were, too. Not *her* again they must be thinking. She caught Jax looking at her with a raised eyebrow, his green eyes perplexed. What was it about her? she wondered. Two hundred students, and you'd think someone else could have a go at being humiliated. But she rallied her newfound determination to make the best of things and headed down to the front of class.

"You all must be getting sick of me," she said, and Madame Overmantle looked slightly nonplussed, but the rest of the class laughed. Eyre had certainly made herself known to everyone over the past couple of days.

"Sit down, dear, and I will go through some basics of the cognitives—retrocognition and precognition. That is, reading the past and telling the future. Let me tell you something about yourself."

Eyre dutifully sat down, sweating under the gaze of all her fellow students. She desperately wished that she would get a chance to fade into the background and become one of the mob again instead of constantly being dragged into the limelight. It wouldn't be so bad if she could actually *do* something. It was the pain of being such a washout that was so embarrassing.

Unfortunately, things weren't getting any better. Madame Overmantle put her hand on Eyre's head, shut her eyes, and concentrated, a serene smile on her face. But as Eyre anxiously watched concern furrowed Madame Overmantle's brow. If it was possible to throw thoughts out into the air, Eyre was doing it—*chucking* every personal detail she could think of at Madame Overmantle, trying to pass on something that she could tell the students. But obviously nothing was getting through, and when Madame Overmantle opened her eyes in perplexity, Eyre miserably waited for the inevitable.

"Well, 88," Madame Overmantle said brightly, "your name is Mary?" Eyre closed her eyes in dismay.

"Uh nearly," she replied awkwardly, not wanting to embarrass Madame Overmantle, "it's Eyre. Sorry."

Madame Overmantle's kind eyes softened. "No, no, that's alright, Eyre," she said softly. "I picked you because I sensed a barrier there, and I like a challenge. It's rare I can't read a student. The Unlit are very hard to read, and it's a gift to be proud of. I feel that you are unusually protected by some force. I would like to try to read you another day when I have a bit more time. Your defences are making it difficult for me to read you in such a short time, but I have techniques that would eventually get through. Don't worry about this, you will be able to communicate telepathically if you Elevate. Thank you, I will try another student. Number 164, would you come down please?"

Eyre, her head down and aware all eyes were upon her, walked uncomfortably up to her chair. Madame Overmantle had said it was a good thing to be unreadable, but being compared to the Unlit and not being able to send out thoughts seemed actually like a bad thing. She felt like Madame Overmantle had been kind to her in front of everyone to cover up a great deficiency in her. Miserably she sat down, trying to rally positive thoughts but failing dismally.

"Thick as two planks! No wonder she can't read you!" Ben Perrill called from the back of the class. Suddenly there was a flash, and a ball of fire exploded above Ben's desk. He shouted in fear and jumped up backwards out of the reach of the flames. It looked so ridiculous everyone in the class laughed. He put his jaw forward and looked around, slapping Slade Curtis, who was sitting beside him, across the back of the head because he was laughing, too.

"Amongst my talents," Madame Overmantle announced coolly to the class, "is pyrokinetics. Please be informed that I do not like interruptions in my class. Sit down, Ben Perrill!" Everyone gawped. How did she know his name? Ben, mouth agape, sat down without saying another word.

Ambrosia Vollick, Number 164, walked down the stairs and sat on the stage. She was the girl with the long, dyed red hair who had sat with Pheria on the first day. By now Eyre was learning people's names and who they were friends with. Ambrosia was best friends with Saskia, Number 3, and they seemed to spend a lot of time flicking their hair around. But Eyre didn't know her too well, and she leaned forward in her chair, interested in the process.

"Reading people is like an intense form of empathy in which you use Viq energy to access the waves of their most central being. What has happened to them in the past has made a mark on their energy patterns, and similarly, what could happen in the future is reaching back and sending images into their present energy field, which we can see. I say 'could' because the future is never set in stone. When you read someone, you are seeing the *most likely* outcome of time and circumstance. But is not a given, and it is important to realise that when you do your reading.

"Having a gift for reading means you are able to connect your Viq energy with the Viq energy of the other person, and you become almost as one. Their memories flow into your mind, and you can access those patterns of the future that are flowing back into their Viq. You must have a stillness of being. You must clear your mind of self and focus unilaterally on the person being read in order to make that connection.

"So, Ambrosia," Madame Overmantle began, and Ambrosia gave a start as she heard her name, "I can see that you are from somewhere in the south of Australia, no, not South Australia, further south than that . . . yes, it's Tasmania, is it not?" Ambrosia's surprised smile confirmed that Madame Overmantle had got it right. Madame Overmantle continued.

"You have a sister and a brother, and you have a pet with a name beginning with P . . . Pinkle, no, Prickle . . . ah, Pickles? It's a dog?" Ambrosia nodded, amazed.

Ben Perrill, obviously slow at learning his lesson, couldn't help himself. He let out a loud guffaw and called out, "Anyone could find out that information. You must know all our names before class. Even I could look up and find out that Ambrosia has a brother and sister."

Madame Overmantle looked with bright eyes at the smirking boy. "Yes, so true, Ben," she said softly. "But could I have looked up the fact that when you were ten you were caught by your father painting graffiti on the school walls, and your father handed you in to the local police for a small chat? That, I believe, is something no one knew about except you, the Maroochydore constabulary, and your father. A bit of a family secret, I would imagine." Ben blushed bright red, and sat back in his chair, speechless.

"Some people are easier to read than others, Mr Perrill," Madame Overmantle said to him. "It's not necessarily a good trait."

Madame Overmantle continued to read Ambrosia, demonstrating the techniques while revealing some of Ambrosia's past.

"When your Viq connects with the person's you are reading, you get a tingle through your body not unlike static electricity," she said, focussing carefully on Ambrosia.

"I wouldn't mind linking with Ambrosia's Viq," Wyatt Rankins snickered to Tec Langford, and a blast of fire exploded above his desk, leaving his face blackened with soot. Madame Overmantle continued.

"This tells you that your energies are linked in, and at that point you will start to receive information about them. Once you have achieved this the first time, it gets easier until you are able to link your Viq without touching the person. Indeed, they can be anywhere, and you can get a read. A person's aura helps to give you information about them also, and when you connect your Viq, you will be able to see their aura. Ambrosia, I see that you have moved many times in your life, and you have lived in a country far away. I see exotic animals . . . South Africa?" Ambrosia nodded. "Well, what else can I see. . . . You are a people person, and you are good to your friends. The shades of pink and yellow in your aura confirm this."

"I'll be your friend," Saxon Curtis muttered and received a black face, too. Eyre shook her head in wonderment. They obviously couldn't help themselves.

Madame Overmantle sighed in an exasperated way and continued.

"The ring you thought you'd lost is in the bottom of your pink handbag. It fell through a hole in the lining, and you'll find it if you reach through. I know that ring has significance as it was your grandmother's. The citrine in it really is a most beautiful stone."

Ambrosia gasped and smiled with joy. "Thank you so much! I've been looking for that everywhere!"

"Why don't you head back to your place now, Ambrosia. Thank you for participating."

Madame Overmantle then touched the pink crystal on the lectern, and a hologram appeared hovering over the stage listing a range of colours from white to black, with a list of personality traits beside them.

"Now a bit more about auras. These are the colours of the auras and what they indicate generally. Please remember that there are shades of colours of auras, and the intensity of the colour can have meaning as well. In addition, one person's aura can influence the aura of another and colours will merge. Pretty much as being near one person can influence the behaviour of another," her gaze turned meaningfully to the group sitting with Ben Perrill, and they looked up at the ceiling, unable to meet her eyes.

"People rarely have one colour in their aura, just as we rarely have one defining characteristic about us. Most commonly there are about four different colours making up the mixture that is a person's individual aura, but sometimes there is even a rainbow of colours, usually associated with people who are healers. Each person's aura is unique, and in most cases a thing of great beauty.

"The shape of the aura also has meaning. A blurry shape indicates a person who might be influenced by others more, a lack of boundaries." Once again the group with Ben shuffled in their seats. "A ragged aura will indicate someone who often has been hurt in the past and is more likely to hurt others. Then there is an aura barrier, which is someone's attempt to block people out, to set defensive boundaries." Now it was Eyre's turn to squirm. Was that what *she* was doing?

Madame Overmantle finished, "And finally, the neutral shaped aura is found in people with a clear sense of self, those who have defined healthy boundaries with others, which I'm sure is most of you. You will become adept at reading auras after a while, and you will use all of those characteristics to understand the person you are looking at.

"This afternoon I will be pairing you up with a partner, and you will attempt both to read each other and to visualise an aura. It is a good opportunity to practise summoning Viq energy, too. As you leave I would like Earth Lodge members to pick a number, which will be a member from our Water group. That is your partner for the afternoon's session. Similarly, Air Lodge members please take a number from the Fire Lodge pile. I find this method a good way to randomly select partners and avoid the person knowing too much about their partner. Thank you for your time today, and I look forward to getting to know more of you soon."

The students jumped up and headed out the door, those Lodge members nominated selecting a white card from the appropriate pile. When they turned it over, there was a number on the back, and everyone lingered out in the hallway, working out who their partner was. Eyre looked around, trying to spot who from Earth Lodge had got her number, hoping desperately it wouldn't be one of the Curtis twins or that cheerleader-type Saskia. Despite Madame Overmantle's preferences, Eyre was really hoping it might be Beatrice who picked her number—that would be great. Finally she saw Colton Ford holding up 88, and she sighed in relief. Thank goodness— not Beatrice, but he seemed quite nice, and Eyre was sure he would be easy to practise with. They arranged to meet at the Meditation Hall at 13.00 and then went their separate ways.

Eyre walked along the path with her friends. Beatrice had chosen Carly, so she was really pleased. Nick got Jo Xavier, and Abby had been picked by Zanda, so they were all feeling fortunate.

"I was so worried I'd get Ben Perrill," Abby said. "I would have had to use Occido on him!"

They all chuckled, enjoying the image of Abby blasting the disliked boy with a beam of light. As they got to the turnoff to the Refectory, Eyre kept going.

"Aren't you coming to lunch?" Beatrice asked curiously.

"I'll come in a bit later and grab something," Eyre replied. "Madame Overmantle's reading of me—or should I say non-reading—made me think that I should accept the possibility that I might stay Unlit. So I'm going to put my lunch hours into practising Ferito. I'm hoping that if I do well in the basic training maybe it will help me be considered for the Academy's Unlit Division if I don't Elevate. More importantly, I still haven't heard," she added softly, "whether they are actually going to let me stay here after my nocturnal wanderings. I'm hoping if I practise hard and show that I want to be here, they will overlook my transgression."

"Good idea," Beatrice said. "BTL, you've *got* to stay here, that is non-negotiable! And you and Nick can be in the U.D. together! It sounds pretty cool."

Eyre nodded. "I don't mind if I'm Unlit, but I would be devastated if I don't come here next year."

She jogged along the path to the lake. A light breeze ruffled its surface, and coins of light skipped across the ripples. The lake was like a live creature the way it constantly moved and changed, Eyre thought. Mysterious and unfathomable.

Closing her eyes she tried to remember the Clasis for Basic Ferito and moved awkwardly through the twenty positions of Aditus and Tego. Some of them she couldn't remember properly, so she passed over them and went to the next move. After running through the moves she could remember ten times, the connections became smoother, and she could feel a strength running through her muscles.

Stopping briefly, she concentrated on Clasis for Single-Blade Weapon, trying to see the moves in her head. Then she started again, trying to translate what was in her head into movement, and she worked through the consecutive positions, stumbling and overbalancing as she tried to get it right. The first run through was awkward, but she did it again and again until the movements became easier. After ten repetitions of the Clasis, she moved on to Clasis for Two-Handed Fighting. Then she started again, repeating each of the three Clasis over and over. "Aditus-Tego-Aditus-Tego," she muttered under her breath, again and again.

Finally she felt she had begun to feel the goal of the Clasis: to train your body to move without thinking about it, to make each move as automatic as breathing, as smooth as gliding on water. She had a long way to go yet, but she was beginning to understand. She stopped, breathing heavily, and let the breeze that scampered across the lake cool her down.

She realised it was only ten minutes until the specialist session, so she grabbed a sandwich from the Refectory and ate it as she headed to the Meditation Hall. Colton was inside waiting for her, tall and fair and looking rather good, she thought, in his Lightworker uniform. He certainly was handsome, and Eyre decided she would have no trouble at all practising with him this afternoon. He smiled at her, and they went to the back of the hall and sat on the aquamarine floor, waiting for instructions. She soon found out that Colton was indeed as nice as he looked and funny as well, as he entertained her with tales of his family back home until Eyre was laughing so hard she couldn't breathe. She told some stories of her own, mostly based around her lack of grace and falling on her face, and Colton seemed greatly entertained by her revelations.

Feeling eyes upon her, Eyre looked up and saw Beatrice and Carly giving her the thumbs up from across the room. Blushing and horrified that Colton might notice them smirking at her, Eyre frowned at them crossly.

As she looked around, she noticed someone else looking at her, and she stopped in surprise. Jax was watching her, his eyes narrowed in annoyance, and she wondered what she had done. Perhaps he felt she was showing off again, she guessed, laughing so loudly in the Meditation Hall. Uncertain and unsettled by the intensity of his gaze, she looked away. Although people might be thinking she was a drama queen, in actual fact the last thing she wanted was drama; her means of survival as she moved from school to school had been to keep her head down and avoid attention. In fact, in the past it had been most unusual for people to even know her name. Unless they did something mean to her, in which case her explosive temper had always got her in trouble and left people even less inclined to get to know her. She had been working on learning to control that temper with her mother over the past couple of years. She clenched her jaw in annoyance and *breathed*. Jax could think what he liked. She was only here for a few weeks and she just wanted to make it through peacefully.

Madame Overmantle walked in and stood in front of the unusual water feature.

"There is no structure to this afternoon's session," she said. "Just work with your partner, and try to read them. Whether you have Elevated or not, if you focus hard you should find that it is possible to see the person's aura. The Unlit can see auras, although they can be unreadable themselves. Take your partner's hands in yours, and try to hear the story of that person's life in your mind by concentrating on their energy flow. I am not expecting amazing progress today. It's a process that takes a long time to perfect, even if you *do* have potential. Use the energy in this exceptional place to help you raise your consciousness."

Eyre looked into Colton's crystal blue eyes and thought that it wouldn't be hard to raise to another plane with him in front of her. He really was handsome with his blond, Nordic good looks. But she tried to concentrate on practising properly, so she shut her eyes and held his large hands. For a while nothing happened, and she willed her mind to relax and to flow clear of thoughts. Then suddenly, crashing into her mind came an image of a small boy with blond hair floating under the water with his eyes open. A feeling of terrible grief welled within her and she opened her eyes as tears dripped down her face.

"You had a brother," she whispered. "But not now?" Colton's eyes opened wide in shock, then clouded with a terrible pain that hit Eyre almost like a physical blow.

"I'm sorry, I'm sorry," Eyre said. "I shouldn't have said—" More images crowded into her brain: Colton, aged about nine or ten, diving into freezing water under the ice, nearly dying himself as he tried to reach his little brother. Then explosions, fire . . . The grief afterwards, shock and pain. . . .

Colton, stricken, was unmoving. "You were brave," Eyre whispered. "It wasn't your fault, and you tried so hard. . . ."

Colton rubbed his hand across his face as if trying to erase the memory. "We were hiking around Blue Lake, and he. . . uh. . . *fell* in under the ice. I . . . ah . . . I tried to get him, but it was so dark in that water . . . by the time my father got back to us we couldn't find him. My mother wasn't with us, and my father isn't a Lightworker. There was no way to find Iwan in time to save him. It took two hours once the search party arrived. Dad's never forgiven himself, and I can't forgive myself either. It was a terrible day, and it's still terrible. I miss him every day. . . ."

"I'm so sorry," Eyre whispered, pain and sadness overcoming her. "I didn't mean to intrude. . . ."

Colton held her small hands in his and shook his head slightly. "It's what we're here to do," he answered. "It's no secret about my brother, and my family has had to deal with it for many years. Don't worry, Eyre. I'm glad you can read me. As Madame Overmantle said, it's a gift."

Eyre looked at him and realised with shock that she could see a brilliant white aura around his head. Thinking back to the day before, she recalled that white was the colour of compassion, of goodness and purity. She realised that here was a very special person, kind and strong. She was almost speechless at the surprise of seeing all this, but she managed to suggest that Colton try to read her, too.

He shut his eyes and concentrated, but after a few minutes opened them in surrender. "Nope, no good," he said apologetically. "I've got nothing! Obviously I have no talent in this area whatsoever. You'll have to tell me all about yourself. I'm not going to find out through my cognitive skills, apparently."

They laughed and the sadness passed. For the rest of the hour as they talked, Eyre trained her gaze on people around the room, and to her surprise and delight realised she could see their auras! Carly—a mixture of orange, yellow, and green; Abby—definitely blue and pinks; Nick—red and brown and blue; Beatrice—purple and yellow. From what she could recall of the list yesterday, the colour of their auras made complete sense. Carly's aura confirmed that she was a physical person who cared about others; Abby's showed that she was indeed a kind friend, artistic and a verbal communicator; Nick's was full of energy and creativity; and Beatrice's aura showed clearly that she was wise, matriarchal, and mentally alert. It was fascinating to see the display of auras, a visual confirmation of the wonderful things about her friends. She was also happy that at least if she hadn't Elevated she was showing some Lightworking skills. Perhaps there was hope for her yet.

Eventually the hour passed, and Eyre said goodbye somewhat regretfully to Colton. She and her friends went for afternoon tea before heading over to the Training Shed together. The euphoria of the past hour left Eyre with a jolt, and a stone settled in her stomach when she saw Mandig Vela standing at the front of the room. She remembered that Nick was going to be paired with Ben Perrill again, and a dark dread crashed down on her. Seeing Mandig Vela's mean little smirk, Eyre knew that poor Nick was once again in for a thrashing.

She clenched her fists and vowed that he would not face Perrill alone this time. As soon as Ben started to hurt Nick, she was going to jump in, Professor Vela or not. She started the Clasis routine again and ran through it several times until the room hushed, and Ben Perrill walked in. Obviously everyone was anticipating a fight, as all eyes watched Ben stroll over to Nick.

"Ah Mouse, there you are," the huge boy sneered. "Time for some lessons, I imagine?"

Nick looked at Ben Perrill, resignation in his eyes, but a fire also. "Bring it on, Ben, I'm looking forward to it."

They walked on to the bamboo platform. Everyone stopped what they were doing to watch. Nick and Ben performed the opening greeting for the Clasis then shouted "Tollo!" and began circling each other. This time there were no weapons, so they performed a few Aditus and Tego moves of Basic

Ferito, moving around the mat in sync with each other. Nick was holding his own quite well until suddenly Ben punched him hard in the nose, knocking Nick flat on his back.

Stunned, blood pouring from his nose, Nick lay there as the hall erupted in sound.

Eyre moved through the crowd towards the platform. "Cheat!" she shouted. "Stop the fight, that's not fair!!"

Professor Vela looked unconcerned. "You will find, students, that when you are facing an opponent who wishes to do you harm, they will not be playing by any rule book. The Gothak are not going to consult page five of the training manual to consider whether the move they are about to perform is fair or not. Accordingly, any blow landed is acceptable in our training bouts. Continue!"

The noise in the hall rose as students shouted and called out, encouraging Nick to get up. He seemed dazed, and Eyre knew that one more blow would knock him out, and the fight would be over as quick as that. She felt a slow burn in her head and moved to the edge of the stage. She was going to go in there and smash Perrill herself.

But suddenly Nick sat up, seemingly recovered. He stood up easily and stretched his arms. A stunned gasp moved through the crowd like a Mexican wave, and hushed whispers rose like fluttering birds in the hall as every eye was on Nick's arm. A bright shining Inguz stood out, sparkling under the shed lights and a silver Halo shone across his forehead. Eyre gasped in confusion. Nick had an Inguz? He had *Elevated*? How?

Beatrice and Abby gaped at him, too, their eyes wide in surprise. Speechlessly they all turned to look at each other, but all Eyre could do was shrug back at them in bewilderment.

Nick faced Ben Perrill with a stillness that was powerful. Ben was also unmoving, staring in shock at Nick's Inguz. Slowly Nick assumed the Third Aditus position of Ferito. Before Ben could move, Nick had knocked him across the mat and out of the ring with such a force that Ben slid along the ground on his rear end.

Furious, the larger boy charged back into the ring like an enraged bull, his huge arms reaching out to seize Nick in a bear hug. Nick stepped back calmly, and a beam of light shot from his palm, blasting half of what was left of Ben Perrill's hair completely away. He stood up, looking ridiculous with half his head bald and singed, the other half with his hair intact.

Mandig Vela was watching in astonishment, and he suddenly collected himself. Parents would not be happy if their students came home with third degree burns, so he raised his hands.

"Halt! The fight is over! Number 119 wins due to illegal use of Light by 134. Everyone go back to practising now. Number 134, I'm disappointed that you chose to use a lethal weapon unfairly in this fight. You will clear the dishes in the cafeteria tonight."

Unable to help herself, Eyre shouted in rage. "What happened to 'anything is acceptable'?" She looked at Professor Vela furiously, and his cold gaze raked her up and down. "Use of Light is a skill that is not permitted in a contest until first year and only then under careful supervision," he said venomously. "You can join 134 on table duty tonight for your impertinence."

He strode out of the shed, his mouth in a thin line, leaving the students frozen in shock. Ben Perrill, mortified and furious, stumbled off the mat.

"You're not even supposed to be a Lightworker!" he screamed. "This is Dark Energy! I'm going to speak to my father about this!" He raced out the door, hands clenched tightly, his face contorted in rage.

Everyone looked at Nick, equally astonished. How could this boy who wasn't supposed to be a Lightworker not only Elevate, but also use Viq with such competency? It was astounding.

Despite the blow he had received, Nick stepped lightly off the mat, wiping at his nose, and came down to join Beatrice, Abby, and Eyre. He was shaking his head in amazement, rubbing at his Inguz as if afraid it might disappear.

"How can you be Elevated?" Beatrice shrieked in wonderment. "I thought you weren't able to? I thought you weren't even a *Lightworker*!"

"Me either," Nick replied, obviously hardly believing it. He looked at his Inguz closely, and then a fierce joy filled his face. "But I don't care why! It means I can stay with you guys next year . . . well, I guess that is if they choose me. But I'm in the running!"

Feeling elated for him, Eyre hugged him hard. "You deserve it, Nick," she said. "Congratulations!"

Eyre resolutely shook off feelings of sadness that she alone had not Elevated and focussed on being happy for Nick. She used the rest of the training afternoon to practise the Ferito Clasis over and over. More than ever she was determined to make it into the Unlit Division so that she could stay at the school. At least she could still see her friends if she was accepted into the U.D. When the session finished and everyone headed off to get ready for dinner, Eyre kept going, practising the three Clasis until she could do them without hesitating.

Finally she stopped, sweat dripping from her body, all her muscles quivering from the exertion.

Finding a fierce focus within herself she headed back to Water Lodge for a shower. As she hung her uniform in the lockers and got her clothes and towel ready, she made up her mind. Tonight she was going to talk to Sergeant Tottingham and find out what they had decided about her, and she was going to make sure that they would consider her for the U.D.

CHAPTER THIRTY

AFTER DINNER, EYRE AND Nick cleaned the tables with rags and a bucket of water. She was beginning to make a career of this, she decided wryly. During the meal many students had been gazing at Nick surreptitiously not only because the supposed non-Lightworker student had suddenly Elevated, but also because he had managed to summon his Viq so dramatically. It had been an awesome spectacle, and many of them congratulated Nick as he walked through the Refectory. Eyre was happy for him. He had suffered for so many years at the hands of bullies—first his father and then the ever-present Ben Perrill. Somehow Eyre understood that Nick was never going to be pushed around again. Nick's face was terribly bruised and battered but he would recover from the bashing he'd received. And Eyre doubted Ben would ever call Nick 'Mouse' again.

Ben had appeared for dinner, his hair now completely shaved off. He sat with his cronies, his face daring anyone to comment. No one did. Even in the short time they'd been at the Compound all the students realised there was a perpetual rage simmering within him, just waiting for a reason to erupt.

After Eyre finished wiping the tables, she summoned her courage and headed over to the Staff Quarters located at the northern end of the Compound behind the Refectory. Lights were on in each of the rooms, but her indecision about where to find Sergeant Tottingham ended when she heard her voice singing a ballad loudly from behind the farthest door on the veranda. Eyre grimaced. Whoa, Sergeant Tottingham had an appalling voice; it sounded like a tone-deaf bullfrog honking in the marsh.

Hesitantly she went up the steps and approached the door, knocking softly when she got there. The honking sounds stopped, and heavy footsteps approached the door. Eyre stepped back as the door was flung open, and then she had to stop herself from falling over in fright.

Sergeant Tottingham stood there with a green clay facemask on, resembling nothing so much as the bullfrog she had been imitating. She was wearing a huge pair of green trackpants and a green sweatshirt bearing the motto: *Walk Lightly and carry a big stick* with the picture of a crystal-topped staff on it. Her eyes studied Eyre fiercely, and then she gestured for Eyre to enter and sit down. Eyre sat in a well-used striped couch and took a breath, unsure how to begin. Her eyes were round as she studied Sergeant Tottingham.

"Don't mind me, I'm camouflaged," Sergeant Tottingham said, and Eyre relaxed a little. It seemed that the rage Sergeant Tottingham had displayed towards her the night before might have abated a bit. Mentally strengthening her backbone, she decided to leap in while the signs were good.

"I, ah, was wondering if you'd made a decision about me," Eyre began. "I want to apologise for leaving the Compound yesterday. I realise it was an unwise thing to do, and I accept full responsibility for that. But I was hoping that I might be able to stay and finish out the training."

Sergeant Tottingham looked at Eyre silently for a long while. Finally she spoke. "I spent part of today looking into you, 88," she said. "And I know your background now. I understand now that there may be extenuating circumstances concerning the way you behaved yesterday, so I've decided that you may finish out the orientation."

Eyre felt a wave of relief wash over her. She had been so tense her muscles almost collapsed from the reprieve.

"Thank you so much, Sergeant Tottingham," she said. "I promise I'll adhere to the rules from now on. I appreciate your consideration, and I won't cause trouble again."

"Make sure you don't," Sergeant Tottingham said gruffly "My benevolence does have limits." She studied Eyre's arm, and Eyre felt failure twist her solar plexus. "You haven't Elevated yet?" Eyre shook her head. "Well, there's still time, about ten percent Elevate in the later weeks," Sergeant Tottingham mused "You did something to that boy's head—38?"

"Well, I took Rigmar to the First Aid station, and he seemed to get better. But I really didn't do anything," Eyre confessed, although she wished she could claim to have actively cured him. "It seemed that he just healed suddenly."

"You helped the boy when the Bunyip got him," Sergeant Tottingham added.

Eyre shrugged. "I just tied a tourniquet," she said. "Others did far more."

"Well, you showed courage, 88, it was a terrifying encounter, so you should be proud." Eyre nodded and Sergeant Tottingham looked at Eyre's strained face with understanding. "Whether you Elevate or not, 88, we can use good people in the U.D., so make sure you train well over the next few weeks."

"I will," vowed Eyre. "Thank you so much for giving me a chance!"

As she stood to leave the room Sergeant Tottingham said, "I knew your mother, Eyre. She was a person of Light. I expect better things of you."

Eyre felt the flicker of shame again but just nodded. As she walked away along the veranda, one of the doors opened. Professor Vela stood there looking at her with a dark and unfathomable expression. Eyre left feeling like an icy claw had just clenched her heart.

✕✕

She headed back to the lodge along the path, relieved from talking to Sergeant Tottingham and curious about the woman's connection with her mother. But she also had a crawling feeling down the back of her neck from her encounter with Professor Vela. He really gave her the creeps.

She soon forgot about that as she focussed on the joy of realising she was not going to be sent away. Remembering the unfortunate students at the run that morning, she decided that she would wash her uniform and shine her boots to avoid incurring any further wrath from Sergeant Tottingham. Eyre's uniform was looking woeful after her long trek through the bush and the encounter with the Saevus, and her boots were scuffed and dirty. She really should have done the situps also this morning, she thought—obviously Sergeant Tottingham had given her a break. She got the boot polish out of her locker, and sitting on a chair at the end of the hallway rubbed in the oily dark polish and buffed the boots until they shone like a mirror. She decided with satisfaction that they looked a lot more respectable, and placed them at the end of the bunk bed. Then she headed to the laundry.

Someone was already in there and Eyre realised to her discomfort that it was Pheria. Pheria hadn't been overtly hostile towards her, but Eyre felt uncomfortable around her, like she was being perpetually evaluated by the tall, confident girl—*and* found wanting, she added to herself. But she summoned up a smile and casually said hello to Pheria as she entered. There were two washing machines in the room, one of which was already rotating loudly with Pheria's uniform in it. Eyre tossed in her uniform and washing powder into the other. Standing back up, she saw Pheria looking at her coolly. But the other girl smiled in a friendly enough manner and asked her how the week was going.

"Wel . . ." Eyre said, unsure really *how* to sum up the week so far. One adjective wasn't going to do it, really. But she decided just to be honest about it. "Actually, not so good so far," she answered. "I've had some mixed days, that's for sure. But I'm really happy to be here, and I'm hoping I'll improve if I practise. How about you?"

"First of the girls in the run," Pheria answered. "And I've Elevated," (of course, Eyre thought, trying not to be sour) "but some things aren't coming easily. I can't get any sort of force from my mind, and Ferito isn't as easy as I thought it would be. But I'm sure if I practise over the next few weeks I'll do well enough in the TEPs to get in."

"You're from Sydney?" Eyre asked. "Jax said you went to school together. Where was that?" She saw a flutter of annoyance cross Pheria's sculptured face, but then it disappeared.

"East side," she answered. "Watsons Bay. My family have lived there for a long time. Here, I've got a photo," she said, picking up her wallet. She pulled out a photo of her family—an attractive family of five. They had Pheria's dark hair and strong features, all of them tall and fit. She had two brothers, one older and one younger, Pheria informed her. Eyre smiled and passed the photo back to Pheria.

"Will your brothers come here, too—or are they here already?"

"Will's doing his Caelus TACI next year, so he's third year. Stratton— Stratt—is starting a year behind me. My family has been coming to the Academy for generations."

Pheria put the photograph back in her wallet, but as she did so, she fumbled, and another photograph dropped out of the wallet. Eyre picked it up and passed it to her, and as she looked at it she tried not to register her surprise. It was a picture of Pheria and Jax locked in a decidedly more-than-friends embrace. Eyre averted her eyes, feeling she was prying, but Pheria didn't seem to mind, and suddenly Eyre wondered whether perhaps Pheria had dropped the photo on purpose.

"Jax and I have been together for a while," she said. "I'm glad he's coming to the Academy too."

Pheria's comment confirmed it: obviously Pheria was staking her claim. Eyre registered irritation on *three* levels: firstly, that Pheria would assume Eyre could be so easily played; secondly, that Pheria obviously took it for granted that she and Jax both would be selected for first year—there was no self-doubt or uncertainty in her vocabulary. Wouldn't it be nice to be so sure about life? And thirdly, it was galling that Jax had misled her about his and Pheria's relationship. What on earth—*or Entis*—for? she thought testily. He could easily have told her they were together. What did it matter? He was obviously one of those good-looking types who like to fool with people's feelings. He hadn't been fair to Pheria and not to her, either—although it had been only a casual conversation. She vowed to keep a wide berth from him; the last thing she needed was complications in her life.

She spent the rest of the time chatting generally to Pheria, not giving any indication of her chagrin while the washing churned. Pheria's machine eventually finished, and Pheria hung her uniform on a hanger to swing it from a drying line. The material was lightweight and would dry by the morning. She said goodbye to Eyre and headed off, leaving Eyre alone with her irritated thoughts.

CHAPTER THIRTY-ONE

FRIDAY MORNING DAWNED, AND Eyre got dressed quickly after her run and breakfast, contemplating the fact that today was the last morning of structured lectures. A few more people had Elevated overnight, but not many. There were about forty students left who hadn't Elevated, and Eyre knew, based on the usual percentages, that roughly half of them would become the Unlit.

This lecturer—UD1—might be her most important teacher if she was one of those who ended up in the Unlit. So she headed with a great deal of anticipation towards the Lecture Theatre for the final Specialist Lecture of the week. Many students seemed equally curious as they settled in their seats, and a hum filled the room as people talked to each other.

"Would everyone quiet down, please?" called a voice from the centre of the seating tier, and a slightly built, middle-aged man rose from one of the seats. There was a gasp of surprise—no one had noticed him sitting there, even the ones sitting beside him. How had they not noticed him, Eyre wondered? Weird.

The man manoeuvred his way across the row and headed down to the front of the theatre. He was average in height and wore a brown shirt and brown tie, brown long pants and a pair of brown leather shoes; he was completely unremarkable in appearance. Straight short brown hair, a pair of brown-framed rectangular glasses, and even features, none of which stood out. Ordinary and average; nothing notable about him at all.

"I am UD1, the Dean of the Unlit Division," the man began, "and I would like to welcome you to Thought Processes and Decoding, one of the core subjects in the Unlit Division. Today I will explain to you a bit about those thought processes and also a little about how the U.D. operates. Some of you will be joining our Unlit Division, and I'm sure you're very curious to hear what that will entail for you."

"Airhead!" a loud voice shouted from the back, and Eyre didn't need to look to know who it was. UD1 looked up calmly at the interruption and then continued.

"Our role in the U.D. is one of security and protection for the Lightworker community by being the eyes and ears out in the normal world. As we are Unlit, we are unable to be read by the Gothak or other creatures of the dark, and this gives us a power that those who are Elevated don't have. We are able to blend in and go unnoticed, which enables us to source information and effect important strategies that protect our people.

"Our greatest strength is being average. The thing that stands out about our Division the most is that we don't stand out. As such, we are a force to be reckoned with. We are experts in coding and decoding, at intercepting data, at blending in to a crowd so that we can find out crucial information. Do not underestimate the U.D. It plays a vital role in our world. Central to our ability to blend in is examining the basic thought processes of people and understanding their motivations. It's like an expertise in psychology, so that we can anticipate what people are going to do and use that knowledge to our advantage."

"When does this lecture end?" the same voice said loudly from the back, yawning in an exaggerated manner, and Eyre shook with rage at Ben Perrill's rudeness. Even common courtesy seemed to be missing from his makeup. She could only hope that his appalling behaviour would ensure that he would not be selected for the Academy. It would be unbelievably joyful news to hear he had gone to another school. As she looked back at him she saw, with immense irritation, that sometime overnight he had Elevated, his Inguz shining brightly on his arm. It seemed out of place to have such a beautiful symbol on someone so dark-hearted.

UD1 ignored the outburst and indicated his Felsic.

"On your Felsic you will see a series of symbols. This is a message in code and I'd like you to attempt to work it out. You have half an hour to put your brain to the test, then I will reveal the solution to you. Your clue is that the symbol ⊠ is S."

Eyre looked at the screen, which displayed a string of symbols in groups that obviously composed a sentence:

She wasn't sure how to start, but she picked up her stylus to try. She could see that there were common symbols, and working on the premise that every word should have a vowel, and that the most common vowel should be E she began to try various combinations of letters to see if she could crack the code. The double symbol for S in the middle of the message gave her a clue that it was probably a vowel following, so, following her reasoning, she substituted E for the next symbol and tried to see if that made sense. Still, she hadn't made much progress by the time the half hour was up, and she put her stylus down in frustration. Beatrice was annoyed, too; she had made several notes crossing out possibilities on her Felsic, reducing the options, and, loving a mental challenge, she had really wanted to work it out, but she didn't have enough time.

"It's a hard message to begin with," UD1 consoled them. "It's a short message, and it has some unusual words. And ones that contain letters that are hard to crack. But basically, you try combinations and permutations of known common letters. As an Unlit student you will be taught the patterns and the techniques that will help you decipher codes such as this. If you manage to crack this code, you get this message:

congratulations for passing your first ud test

"By the time you have finished your first semester with us, you will be able to decipher a code like that in ten minutes. I want to say to those of you who might be joining our division next year that we are a united and dedicated group of Lightworkers who work very hard. You will enjoy being part of our division, I know that, and I look forward to meeting you individually. If you have any questions, I am available any time."

There was a loud noise outside the window of the Lecture Theatre as something large appeared to crash to the ground. The students looked at the window curiously, wondering what was going on. When they looked back at the front of the hall, UD1 was gone.

A murmur of surprise went through the hall, and students began packing up their notes. Ben Perrill's cronies jumped up and headed fast down the stairs, keen to get out and off to lunch. Ben attempted to follow them, then stopped in surprise as he felt his leg stop. Muttering an oath, he looked under the lecture desk to see what he'd caught his leg on. He swore out loud when he saw a pair of large cuffs locking his ankle firmly to the metal row of chairs. Looking at the commotion up the back as he tried to get loose, students realised what had happened, and soon the whole lecture theatre was exploding with laughter. Eyre laughed so hard she had tears running down her face. Note to self, she thought as she left: Don't annoy UD1!

Ben Perrill's screeches of rage could be heard all the way down the hallway.

"Oh my god, that is so hilarious!" Eyre gasped as they hurried along.

Nick grinned. "Hopefully they won't let him out until it's time to go home. Do everyone a favour!"

As they walked out of the building, Eyre saw with surprise that Whittaker Ray was waiting there. He said hello to them all and then turned to Nick.

"I'd like a word, Nick. Come for a walk?"

They left and headed down the pathway together.

Beatrice studied their receding forms. "Wish I could mask! Would love to hear what *that* conversation's about!"

They headed down the path towards the Training Shed. Abby left at the Meditation Hall, saying that she was going "to work on what she was good at," in Sergeant Tottingham's words.

Beatrice looked at Eyre ruefully. "I think I'll practise what I'm *not* good at! Want to have a go at Ferito?"

Eyre laughed, and they walked into the Training Shed. Most of the students were already there, practising a range of disciplines. Some were trying to levitate, some were going through Clasis with a Single-Blade Weapon, others were sitting on the ground trying to use Viq to move objects. There were even a few trying to meditate in the midst of all the chaos; Eyre thought if they could manage that, then they were doing really well. Beatrice picked up two of the shorter Palum and tossed them to Eyre.

"Clasis for Two-Handed Fighting?" she asked, picking up two for herself. Eyre nodded, happy to have a go; since she hadn't Elevated, it wasn't worth trying levitation and telekinesis, or any of the other psionic forces.

Beatrice pointed out the far door of the shed, her eyebrows raised. Eyre turned to look and could see Whittaker Ray and Nick walking by the side of the lake, deep in conversation. They moved out of sight, heading around the edge of the water. She wondered what they were talking about, but she was pretty sure it must have something to do with the fact that Nick had Elevated. That would require some explanation!

Eyre raised her Palum and assumed Position 1 of the Clasis. "Tolla!" she shouted, and they began to spar. Beatrice was hesitant, so they stopped and started again. Eyre was familiar with the positions; she just needed practise doing them, whereas Beatrice still had to learn them all. So they moved through the exercises slowly: first the two-handed fighting Clasis, then Clasis for Single-Blade Weapon, and finally Basic Clasis. After an hour of sparring they were tired, but Beatrice was looking happy; she had finally learned all the positions. Eyre was also feeling positive—although she was awkward, each time she practised the positions became more natural, and she thought that at least by the end of the ten weeks she should be able to do this competently.

She looked around and realised there was mayhem in the Training Shed. Some of the students had managed to levitate half a metre in the air, which was a disconcerting sight, and some of those were even trying to practise their Clasis from up in the air. Not many managed it, though, and there was the constant thump of students falling back to the ground. She saw Warrigal fall on his back with a loud groan of frustration, and another boy thud down beside him, face down and swearing. Objects were rolling across the floor of the Training Shed as some people managed to get their telekinesis underway but not completely under control. She saw Carly chasing a block of wood out the door, trying to get it to stop, and Zanda had accidentally started a fire in the corner employing pyrokinesis by accident instead of telekinesis. As he ran around in a complete flap, trying to put it out, Eyre couldn't help herself and laughed out loud. Just your normal school day, she thought.

Robeson Paul, wearing a bulky training suit in the barrier, was sending lightning strikes out that suddenly rebounded and zapped him in the rear, and he rubbed the sizzled patch ruefully, looking embarrassed. Brilliant of mind, but not so accomplished yet at lightning skills, Eyre thought. Enjoying the spectacle, she watched as someone else across the room tried a pound, only to have the sound waves reverse and knock his feet from under him. The unlucky student shot up in the air, spun a complete 360 circle, then landed flat on his back with a loud thump. As he sat up groggily Eyre realised, with a small measure of satisfaction, that it was Jax. So even the accomplished students weren't finding it easy!

Suddenly the room erupted in hilarity, and she turned to see someone floating up to the roof. It was Rigmar, holding his hands out helplessly. "I can get up here," he said in frustration, "but I can't get down!" He was trying to pull himself back down the wall when suddenly his Viq evaporated, gravity intervened, and he plummeted downwards, shrieking. Crashing onto the floor he made an exasperated face.

"Well, now, as you can see, I'm ready for the TEPs," he said as people roared with laughter.

Eyre decided that despite the varied levels of accomplishment, she could actually learn something by watching the students practise. So she sat in the shed all afternoon, watching and trying to remember the techniques of the successful students. If nothing else, it was a very entertaining afternoon.

CHAPTER THIRTY-TWO

AT BREAKFAST ON SATURDAY, Eyre grabbed her tray and went to sit with Abby, Beatrice, and Zanda, who already had their food. Eyre looked around curiously.

"Where's Nick?" she asked. "He wasn't here last night, either."

Beatrice's brow furrowed. "I must admit we've been wondering that, too. I hope he's okay. Let's go and check on him after breakfast."

They started to chat about the day when the metal door to the Refectory opened, and Sergeant Tottingham strode in. She was positively beaming, a sight that was so unusual that Beatrice and Abby dug each other in the ribs, eyebrows raised. Silence fell instantly in the room.

"I have good news!" the Sergeant began. "We have had notice that the fourth year TACI expedition may be returning sometime tomorrow from Incendium. They are overdue from their trials due to encountering an Extraterrestrial Cyclone, a most dangerous and wild sand storm, and it meant they had to bunker down for a week. This is an unusual event, but fortunately they are on their way back, and we should see them tomorrow sometime.

"Accordingly, you may see members of the Mimir around today. The Mimir manage our crystal vaults and our energy sources. Amongst other things, they organise our Armament Stores and the manufacture and care of all our weapons, and they usually remain underground, attending to a multitude of responsibilities. But they will be getting ready to process the gazae—which is the treasure that the TACI teams have harvested from Incendium—to be stored in the vaults and collection bays underneath the school in the Gazae Depot. So you may see some of the Mimir around the campus. Please treat them with respect. The Mimir are an integral part of our Lightworking community. You may find them a little—standoffish, I guess is one way to put it—" Beatrice harrumphed a trifle loudly, and

Sergeant Tottingham looked at her with a slight frown, but continued without comment, "—as they are not social creatures except within their own community. But they are always willing to help us in our endeavours. You probably won't see much of them today, but you will see them tomorrow when the TACI team arrives back.

"Okay. On to other things. Lake Altum is officially clear and safe now, so you are welcome to swim or train in the water as you wish. The International Lightworking Division of Warding has tested the wards and examined the Seam to ensure the area is clear and protected. All other areas in the Compound are open at all hours for students to train, and I would encourage you to make use of them. We will get you up for your run every morning, but beyond that, the rest of the ten weeks is for you to train however you see fit."

The Sergeant looked around the quiet room and then stared towards the window. "Ah! I see the first of our Mimir has appeared. Some of you will not have met a Mimir before. They are quite remarkable." Heads turned as one to look outside, where they could see a small figure with a fiery red beard stomping along the perimeter. Sergeant Tottingham peered hard. "General Gel Lithium Silica, if I'm not mistaken. He's a bit reticent, so you won't see much of him, but he is a fearsome fighter and a legend amongst his people. No doubt he'll be heading underground now." Students stood up and crowded towards the window, craning to see the small form.

Instead of going underground, the little man strode towards the Refectory, and Sergeant Tottingham looked puzzled. "That's strange," she said. "I think he's coming here—" she broke off, speechless as the general clomped up the steps and marched through the front door. Everyone turned towards him.

"Ah—what? it's Jengles," Eyre managed to blurt out before the stocky little Mimir she had met at the cabins stomped across the floor and knelt down on one leg, in front of her, bowing deeply. Students moved away, gasping in astonishment. Sergeant Tottingham's eyebrows were so far up her face in surprise they almost disappeared off the top of her head.

"By St Ria, beauteous one," Jengles said in his gravelly voice as he stood up, "it is an honour to see you again!"

Eyre smiled awkwardly, wishing she could melt through the floor. "You, too, Jengles," she said. "I'm glad you're here." Although she would have preferred to meet him again in a far less public arena . . . she thought wildly. Sergeant Tottingham looked like she was going to faint with the shock of it. Jengles looked up at Eyre, his eyes glinting.

"Gel Lithium Silica is a stone of tranquillity and harmony. It is representative of my mission in life, which is to achieve peace in the Overworld. I have dedicated my existence to that goal, and I now publicly extend that commitment to you." He put his open fingers threaded together and rested his chin in them and bowed, a strange gesture that Eyre had never seen before.

Abby and Beatrice smothered their laughter as they looked at the students' dumbstruck expressions.

Jengles took a step backwards. "I must be going," he said importantly. "There is much to do! Gazae incoming and treasures to process. But I will see your wondrous self later!" He bowed low to the ground, his knotted beard touching his toes, and he backed away three steps with his arm outstretched towards her. "Inguz!" he said, then stood up and strode out of the Refectory, across to the rocky boundary before disappearing down a hole in the ground.

Everyone looked at Eyre. "I . . . er . . ." she said, into the clamouring silence, but stopped. What *could* she say about that? She stood uncomfortably until Sergeant Tottingham, finally recovering from the surprise, thumped her staff on the ground.

"Right, everyone, show's over," she said. "Finish up, clear your dishes, and get going. You have a lot of practising to do today!"

The students dispersed back to their tables to finish their breakfast, and Eyre and her friends sat back down. The sounds of voices and utensils clattering filled the air again as everyone went back to eating, but a number of people were looking over at Eyre, and she was sure she was the topic of many conversations right at this point.

Sergeant Tottingham, rubbing her brow in bewilderment, glanced back at Eyre and then left the room without comment. Eyre looked at her friends, not sure what to say.

Beatrice tittered. "*Your wondrous self*? What is it with you, Eyre? I've never heard him say so much at once—ever! That little fellow has been haranguing us for years, grumpy, cranky little crab apple that he is. When we were kids we used to run away fast if we saw him coming. I can't believe the way he is with you, but I have to say what a hoot that was!"

"Yes," Zanda said with glee, "right after Sergeant Tottingham's speech about how aloof the Mimir are, in marches General Gel Lithium Silica to declare his eternal loyalty to Eyre. Did you see the Sergeant's face? Priceless!" They all exploded with laughter.

Eyre looked at Beatrice curiously. "He's a general?" she asked Beatrice. "I thought he was a maintenance man?"

Blue-tipped Abby answered her. "Apparently when we were younger we couldn't say General Gel Lithium Silica. It was too much of a mouthful. So we all called him Jengles."

"And he's not a maintenance man," Beatrice added. "He just lives there and considers it his duty to look after the area for us. Underneath that crusty exterior he has a heart of gold, I guess. It's just that he doesn't share it with anyone but you apparently!" They all burst out laughing again.

Just then Nick arrived through the door. He looked around, and when he spotted them he came over to join them.

"BTL, Nick, did you just miss a show!" Beatrice said, laughing. Then she peered closer at his pale face and her smile dimmed. "Where were you? We were a bit worried about you."

"Aren't you going to eat something?" Abby asked as Nick poured himself a glass of water. Eyre looked at him and agreed he looked very peaked, as if he had had a terrible night's sleep.

"I'm not hungry," he said. "But thought I should catch up with you guys."

"Are you okay, Nick?" Eyre said.

He looked away for a moment then shrugged. "Well, I guess I may as well tell you now. It'll come out eventually I suppose. My talk with Mr Ray? Wasn't great news." He stopped and then continued again slowly, his eyes not meeting theirs. "He wanted to talk to me to explain how I had managed to Elevate. Seems my father *and* my mother were Lightworkers." At Abby's gasp, he nodded. "I know. Whittaker Ray didn't tell me because my mother died. Killed by the Gothak. She was part of the Unlit, working undercover when they got her. And my father. . . ." He drew a breath. "My father is an Ex."

This time Beatrice exclaimed, hand on her mouth. "Oh no!"

Eyre was confused. She didn't know what an Ex was but obviously it wasn't good. Nick looked at her, understanding. "I didn't know what an Ex was, either. It's an abbreviation for 'Exile'—apparently someone who has been stripped of their powers because they have done something unspeakable. Mr Ray didn't tell me what my dad did." He hesitated and added softly, "I guess I don't want to know."

Abby was trying to follow him. "So Mr Ray knew you were a Lightworker when he was at St Jeffrey's?"

Nick nodded. "Mr Ray recognised Dad for what he was, which is why he started to look out for me. When Dad disappeared shortly afterwards, Mr Ray took me on. He said he was sorry he sent me here without telling me I was a Lightworker—because of the breach at the cabins, he had to go back to the Echelon and there wasn't time to talk to me properly. He thought I might be Unlit because of Mum, and he decided that if I didn't Elevate then he would wait and explain my family history after the TEPs. He didn't want to embarrass me about my dad."

Eyre nodded. She could just imagine what Ben Perrill would do with this information if he found out. And unfortunately he would find out eventually; there was no way to keep a secret like that, especially now Nick had Elevated.

Nick looked pensively at his Inguz. "I always knew Dad was violent, but this is even more shameful. I feel like I've been given something special only to find out that it's tainted."

Beatrice spoke up. "No, Nick! Just because your dad was bad, that's not your fault. And what about your mother? Whittaker Ray said she sacrificed her life fighting against the Gothak, so she was a true Lightworker. We can find out more about her. You'll have a family history somewhere. Maybe even a Lightkeeper!"

Nick shrugged. He looked so conflicted Eyre felt sorry for him. She knew what it felt like to have secrets sprung upon you. But some of the tension had left his face—Beatrice's words had obviously helped.

Abby gathered up her tray. "Come on, Nick, let's go show everyone what a great Lightworker you are! I can use some Ferito practise."

The two of them left, and Beatrice watched them walk across the room. She shook her head and said softly, "An Ex. Poor Nick."

Eyre was curious. "How do they decide if you're going to lose your Inguz? It must be a huge decision to make."

Beatrice nodded. "There's a part of the Echelon called The Governance of Laws and Regulations. When Lightworkers do the wrong thing, a judge and jury decide what will happen to them. Like going to court in Entis. Sometimes when a Lightworker does something *really* bad, they have their Inguz removed permanently. Those are the Exiles—or Exes. Those people live in their own communities elsewhere. They are not good people."

Eyre mulled this over. Imagine *getting* an Inguz only to have it taken away! That would be so terrible. She wondered what would be a severe enough crime to have that happen. Poor Nick indeed; he would be wondering, too. Personally she thought it would have been easier for Nick to know the truth two years ago, but she decided that Whittaker Ray must have his reasons for the way he'd handled it.

Beatrice looked at her watch. "We'd better get going to training, too! Let's meet at the shed in fifteen minutes and find those two." Eyre agreed, and they chatted as they headed towards the kitchen, dumping their trays on the towering pile already stacked at the window.

Beatrice left in the opposite direction and Eyre walked towards the doors, feeling rather pleased that she was leaving this morning without having to clean the tables.

CHAPTER THIRTY-THREE

EYRE WALKED INTO THE Refectory after her run on Sunday morning, her face still flushed despite the fact she had showered. She hadn't finished last, thank goodness, but she was still way behind most of the students. As she walked to the table with her tray, she looked around curiously at the buzz of excitement. Obviously she had missed something.

"What's going on?" she asked as she sat down.

Beatrice looked at her excitedly. "There's word going around that the graduate TACI students are arriving back from Incendium this morning."

Eyre raised her eyebrows. She wondered if they would get the opportunity to talk to the fourth years—it would be good to hear about their expedition.

The door to the Refectory opened, and Sergeant Tottingham entered, followed by the as usual sour-looking Professor Vela. The Sergeant strode to the front of the room, and all conversation halted. Only background noises from the kitchen could be heard as the students looked at Sergeant Tottingham.

"I trust you enjoyed your run this morning," Sergeant Tottingham said, and a few people rolled their eyes. "I have some good news," she continued. "Some of you may already have heard that our Graduate TACI students are expected to return this morning. It is customary that the Academy student body welcomes the fourth years when they return, which is normally during the school year, the last week of term.

"However, since the expedition has been delayed this year, we have decided that you all will come up to the main campus and welcome the Graduate students back this morning. It will only take an hour out of your day, and it will be good for the fourth years to have a welcoming gathering after their arduous trip. They will have harvested the Zha'kara diamonds for your Antaraks, so that is another great reason to support them as they return.

"After breakfast the staff here at the Compound will pilot Zepps to ferry you all up to the Receiving Stone, where the Mimir have already gathered to receive the diamonds. Each Zepp will carry twenty students at once, so it will only take us two trips to get you all there. I would like you to be ready in half an hour, waiting at the arrival/departure pad. That is all. Please clear your dishes and get moving."

Students leapt to their feet and cleared out of the Refectory, talking madly to each other. All the students were keen to hear anything they could about the TEPs.

Twenty minutes later Eyre and Carly hurried to the arrival/departure pad, where seven Zepps were lined up spectacularly along the runway, facing outwards towards the lake. A large number painted on the side of each vehicle, numbered one to seven, identified them.

"Line up numerically," Sergeant Tottingham called out, "and board the Zepps in groups of twenty. If you don't make the first flight you will be brought up on the second."

Eyre was in the fifth group of twenty students—numbers 81 to 100, which was made up of all Water Lodge students. They climbed aboard Zepp 5 and Eyre sat next to Carly and Georgia in one of the seats around the wall. Disconcertingly, she was sitting opposite Jax but she avoided the awkwardness by turning and watching out the window behind her as the other students boarded the Zepps.

"All buckled up then?" came a cheery voice from the front of the bus as the engine started, and Eyre saw that their pilot was Madame Overmantle. When everyone was safely fastened, Madame Overmantle tooted the horn, and the Zepp slowly rolled forward, following behind Zepp 4, which took off smoothly ahead of them. Once it had cleared the area, Madame Overmantle engaged the gears with a loud crunch, and the motor roared; then the Zepp surged forward at a terrific speed before soaring into the air. It was rather a bumpy ride, and Eyre realised that not all pilots had the skills of Ranger Chrysanthe.

"A slight patch of turbulence. Nothing to worry about," Madame Overmantle called as they suddenly dropped ten metres. She corrected the Zepp, and it started to head straight up into the air, a loud whistling coming from outside as the air rushed over its fins. Eyre held on tightly, trying not to look nervous, but she didn't feel very comfortable as the Zepp bucked and heaved its way up to the top of Beggarman's Bluff. Fortunately it was only a short ride, and the Zepp finally landed, veering back and forth over the ground as Madame Overmantle trod on the brake too strongly and crashed the gears. She drove far too fast along the dirt road, causing the Zepp to swerve wildly as they travelled towards the shining buildings in the distance. Someone coughed into his hand, hiding his face, and all the students looked at each other, wide-eyed with the effort of trying not to laugh. Finally the excruciating trip was over, and Madame Overmantle pulled up unevenly next to Zepp 4.

"There we go!" she said brightly. "Out you get. Join the other students over by the pathway there. We will be going together as a group to the Receiving Stone." She leaned over and looked at Tec Langford. "You are quite correct, Number 87," she said matter-of-factly. "I do fly like a complete beginner. Piloting was never one of my better skills. Unlike telepathy," she added, looking at his mortified face.

They filed out and waited with the other students who had already arrived, and then Zepps 1, 2, and 3 (with Ranger Chrysanthe, Sergeant Tottingham and UD1 at the helm) took off again for a second load of students.

While they waited, Eyre, along with the other students, looked up at the towering buildings beside the landing pad, so high she had to crane her neck to see the top of them. The structures were magnificent, completely crafted from massive shards of shining quartz crystal about fifty metres high, and the morning sun sent sparkles of light shooting out from every edge of the buildings. A set of gleaming bronze doors was set into the smooth façade of the entrance, and fastened by two handles, circlets of twisted bronze.

Wiping wisps of hair from her eyes, Madame Overmantle beamed with pride as she walked up to the huge bronze doors. "This is the Central Administration building for the Academy," she said, running her hand over the doors. The bronze was wrought with intricate designs of leaves and trees, flowers and runes twisting in the polished metal around the edges. In the centre of the door, the figure of a Lightworker was fashioned in the bronze, battling a Saevus in the Sixth position of Ferito with a shining Mnae upraised. At the top of the doors stained glass panels had been inlaid in a diamond shape, like the one at her cabin, Eyre thought. The glass moved as figures fought, ran and danced through a series of continuous actions. It was mesmerising.

Madame Overmantle studied the doors, looking as proud as if she herself had crafted them. "The scene depicts Sir Lonegan Burnish fighting in the twelfth battle for the Aura. It's a famous story—you'll learn about it in the

History of Light next year. Our school has many beautiful art installations throughout the campus. We are truly blessed."

As she finished speaking, a roar announced that the Zepps were back again, and the students waited for everyone to get out and join the group. Ranger Chrysanthe was first to join them, resplendent in a gold tuxedo and top hat, no doubt in honour of the return of the Graduate students, Eyre thought. He sparkled almost as much as the building he stood next to. Sergeant Tottingham jumped out of Zepp 2 and strode to the front of the group, staff in hand. She thumped the ground for attention.

"Follow me, please," she bellowed and started walking along a path that bordered the huge school buildings.

They walked through to an open clearing where a large square of stone, a deep forest green in colour and about ten metres square, was set into the ground like a huge floor tile. The stone was partly translucent, and its surface was polished to a high sheen. Next to the stone and also set into the ground, was a set of large bronze doors. The doors were decorated with images of the Mimir, digging with spades, breaking rock with axes, carrying loads of rock on their backs, while a huge fire burned in the background as more Mimir prodded it with iron tools. The doors were beautifully crafted, although Eyre thought they looked somewhat incongruous, set in the ground like that. She wondered what they were for.

Almost immediately her question was answered when the doors were flung open from under the ground. The doors opened in the middle and flattened back to lie on the ground, creating an opening about five metres square. Eyre could see a winding staircase going down into the darkness beneath the ground.

Suddenly a fiery red head appeared and one of the Mimir, large-nosed and scowling, trudged up the stairs and out into the light. He strode to the edge of the green stone set in the ground and waited, saying nothing. More Mimir followed him out, and each of them went and stood next to the other, until the stone floor was completely surrounded by the red-haired creatures. Eyre was greatly interested, wondering what they were up to, when out came Jengles, stomping into position. Suddenly his head whipped around as he saw her. Oh no, she thought, here we go.

And indeed, it was the beginning of a very embarrassing five minutes, as each of the Mimir left their positions around the green stone and came over to bow deeply before her. Eyre could feel all the students' eyes upon her, and she sighed. *What* was this about? she wondered, really wishing the Mimir could walk past her for once without causing a ruckus. Perhaps it was the red hair—maybe if she dyed it they would lose interest in her? She gritted her teeth and studied her toes until finally they had all bowed before her and returned to their positions surrounding the green stone. A final Mimir appeared from the depths and walked over to stand with the members of the staff.

He was taller than the other Mimir and more solidly built. His face was not scowling, but not smiling, either. He stood, unspeaking, with an authority that exuded strength and quiet fortitude as he waited by Sergeant Tottingham. He had a long red beard that was plaited into a single braid, and a very long red moustache, also braided. This Mimir had a single braid down his back, and he had a large gold medallion on a very heavy gold chain around his neck. And unlike the rest of the Mimir, who were dressed in leather and coarse cloth, he wore a forest green robe, and his clothes were made of a dark-blue satin-like fabric.

Turning towards Eyre, he bowed deeply, putting the final touch to her embarrassment. Weakly she nodded back, avoiding Beatrice's eyes.

But by far the most astounded were the staff, apart from Sergeant Tottingham, because they had never seen the Mimir behave this way before; and it was all the more astonishing to see it done to an *Unlit* student. Dr Botolfe in particular had her mouth wide open, flabbergasted. She swivelled her head from Eyre to the Mimir and back again, completely unable to work it out. Fortunately the arrival of someone else saved Eyre from any further awkwardness: Whittaker Ray, who walked through the crowd of students and up to the Mimir who wore the dark green robe.

"President Zircon, thank you for coming," he said, putting his hand out to shake the president's big, rough hand. "It is good to see you again And I thank the Mimir for joining us on this celebratory day. Today we have with us our student candidates who do not know about the traditions of the TACI tests, so please bear with me as I explain to them some of what is about to happen.

"First of all, students, you should know that President Zircon and his people live in the Mimir's Domain, below ground. They are responsible for our Armament Stores, our Mineral Supplies, and our Weapons Manufacture here at the Academy. Underneath the school is a series of holding areas, forges, and technical rooms run by the Mimir, and you will be visiting the area in first year if you join the Academy. Today the Mimir are here to receive the gazae from the TACI—and in the case of the fourth-year expedition, the gazae is Zha'kara Diamonds, the most valuable gazae of all the TACI expeditions, and also, I might add, the hardest to find.

"The Mimir will take the gazae down into the Domain and deliver it safely to the Gazae Depot,"—he indicated the open brass doors in the ground—"where it will be stored appropriately until it is processed."

Whittaker Ray then walked over to the flat green square. "This is the Receiving Stone, which is a large square of moldavite, a type of tektite which is known for its extremely intense energy properties. When students leave for and return from their TACI expeditions, this is where the Seam opens to let them through. We had notice last night that the Graduate students were almost at the departure zone, so they should be arriving any moment. Please stay here while we wait for them. And when they arrive, applause is appropriate. They have accomplished a great feat by successfully sourcing the gazae from Incendium."

Students looked with new interest at the green stone on the ground. The respect in Whittaker Ray's voice had communicated to them that this was a very special substance. It was certainly beautiful, Eyre thought, with its gleaming, polished green finish.

Suddenly there was a high-pitched noise, and a thin, brilliant strip of light about three metres high appeared, situated exactly in the middle of the moldavite square.

"The Seam has opened, watch carefully!" Sergeant Tottingham instructed the students. After a few seconds, a strange-looking object appeared from the Seam, a rounded metallic capsule about a metre and a half long, which launched out of the bright light and slid across the Receiving Stone. Shortly afterwards, another one appeared, skidding across the polished stone until it came to rest at the edge. More and more of the shining capsules appeared until there were over twenty of the objects spread randomly across the moldavite. Then there was a flare of light, and the Seam zapped and disappeared.

CHAPTER THIRTY-FOUR

EYRE LOOKED CURIOUSLY AT the objects on the ground, which President Zircon was now organising the Mimir to sort into neat rows. The silver capsules were large and obviously heavy, as it took two of the Mimir to manoeuvre them into position by pushing them across the stone. When the capsules were all arranged at the edge of the moldavite square, the regiment of Mimir stood at attention on each side of them, unmoving and clearly on guard. Sergeant Tottingham also stood closely by the capsules, her hand firmly on her staff as she waited.

The students shuffled around, waiting as the teachers talked quietly to each other; from the way the staff were looking at the metal capsules, they were obviously discussing the gazae. Someone moved up beside Eyre and as she turned she saw to her irritation that it was Ben Perrill. What now, she thought, instantly on guard.

"See that those red-haired freaks have taken a shine to you, Airhead," he said nastily in a soft voice. "Maybe you can go and set up house with one of them since you don't have a family any more?" The sheer viciousness of the comment left Eyre at a loss for words, and tears glistened in her eyes. Ben chuckled, enjoying her shock, and moved away through the crowd.

Eyre rubbed her forehead, pain coursing through her as if a sharp knife had sliced her. How could words hurt so much? Suddenly she saw a tall form stride through the students towards Ben Perrill. She realised it was Jax, who had been standing behind her and must have heard Ben's comments. Eyre was astounded to see Jax grab Ben roughly by the shoulder, spin him around, and punch him hard on the nose, laying him out flat on the ground. Ben sat up groggily, wiping blood from his mouth, a dark expression on his face. But Jax's face was just as furious as he stood fiercely over him.

"You have got to be the biggest jerk I've ever met, Perrill," he said tightly, clenching his fists. "That was *so* not cool. What is it with you?"

Ben stood up slowly and spat on the ground.

"Fine by me, Cover Boy," he said, a strange smile crossing his face. "Bring it on." The two boys slammed into each other, fighting fiercely, exchanging blow for blow. Ben Perrill was a big, muscular boy, but Jax was athletic, light on his feet, and very quick. It was a fairly even match, and the other students stood around, silent and aghast until suddenly there was an explosion of light that blew the boys apart. Dr Botolfe strode in between them as they lay on the ground, stunned.

"*What* do you think you are doing?" she cried angrily. "There is *no* place in this institution for behaviour of this kind! I've a good mind to—" but whatever she had been about to say was lost as a thin beam of light appeared in the middle of the Receiving Stone.

The Seam was opening again!

"Get up," Dr Botolfe spat. "I'll deal with you later!"

The fight forgotten, everyone crowded around the Receiving Stone and watched the Seam in anticipation, ready to applaud.

There was a sudden movement from behind the light, and the students gasped in surprise as a strange creature launched out of the Seam onto the Receiving Stone. It was a round ball of brown fluff, about a metre high, with a snub nose, eight jointed legs, and big bulbous eyes on stalks. It was making a loud snuffling sound, and as it hit the moldavite, it skittered around, trying to get traction on the polished stone. Immediately, twenty Graduate students emerged from the beam behind it, laughing and tumbling over each other as they tried to grab the creature.

"Quick! Get a hold of it!" a boy cried as he launched across the Receiving Stone and dived for it. The creature shuffled sideways and scrabbled around, getting closer to the edge of the stone, and the boy shot past it, crashing off the side of the moldavite square. Ten other students came out of the Seam, and, laughing loudly, careered around the edge of the stone trying to grab the fluffy creature. One of them tripped clumsily over the boy on the ground, causing a pile up as others fell on top of them. They lay on the ground, gasping with laughter. The waiting students stood in shock, mouths open, their hands stopped halfway to clapping, not sure what to do. This certainly didn't look like the formal event they were expecting.

Suddenly another woolly creature, less lively than the previous one, slipped out of the Seam and plodded around on the stone, its large eyes swivelling around, taking in everything. But a movement from behind it as more students emerged from the light startled it into flight, and it shot off the side of the Receiving Stone, eight legs clawing at the ground in panic.

"Capture the Desert Hirtus immediately!" roared Sergeant Tottingham, still standing by her post at the Receiving Stone beside the regiment of Mimir, but obviously getting very annoyed at the pandemonium.

Four more of the creatures emerged, and Sergeant Tottingham threw her hands up in frustration.

"*Hurry up*! Send them back to Incendium!" she roared. "They breed like rabbits, and they'll overrun the place if we don't capture them all!"

The uproar increased as everyone chased the hapless creatures. The Hirtus clattered around the edge of the Receiving Stone, then took off across the grass with the fourth-year students, who had by now all arrived back through the Seam, after them. The TEP students, finally over their stunned inaction, joined in the chase with gusto, so there were over four hundred students running around madly trying to catch the nimble creatures. One Hirtus ran up a tree, another shot underneath Zepp 2, and one climbed the side of the building where it sat surveying the ruckus below with its protruding eyes, like a rotund fuzzy spider.

Even the staff started to join in the chase, trying to capture the creatures before they disappeared into the bush and became public enemy number one on Australia's biosecurity list. Lord Clarembout, brows drawn in agitation at this ridiculous scene, strode around giving orders, while Madame Overmantle, her hair in complete disarray, tried to cajole the creature out from underneath Zepp 2.

Dr Botolfe had levitated up the side of the building and was facing the Desert Hirtus on the wall, not sure how to grapple with the creature. Students were running everywhere after the other three Hirtus, which were very quick and very panicked. Whittaker Ray stood at the front of the metal capsules on the moldavite square, running his hands through his hair in bemusement. Things weren't exactly going to plan.

Eyre stood off to one side, not sure how she could contribute to helping. She had been running around with the rest of the students, but she couldn't even get near the creatures; there were so many people crowding up ahead of her, so she just decided to wait and see what happened. There were shrieks of laughter, shouts of frustration, people going everywhere, and long-legged creatures scuttling along at amazing speeds all over the place. Eyre thought this was probably better exercise for the students than the morning run.

Suddenly she felt something behind her, and turning around, she nearly leapt ten metres in the air in fright. The closest I've come to levitating, she thought, as her heart slowed down again. One of the creatures had come up behind her and was watching her with its bulging eyes. They twitched in opposite directions, taking her all in, before the creature settled down to sit beside her, folding its eight legs up underneath itself. Hesitantly she put her hand out to touch it and found it to have a rough coat the texture of rope. It seemed to like being touched, so she stroked it tentatively, trying to keep it calm so someone could come and grab it.

A couple of seconds later the Hirtus on the wall sprung past Dr Botolfe and landed lightly on its feet before skittering along and sitting down beside the Hirtus next to Eyre. The Hirtus under the Zepp timidly came out and scuttled over to join them, and eventually the other three Hirtus ran over to join them as well. Eyre stood there, completely bemused, surrounded by the strange-looking creatures as they snuffled at her and edged closer. Everyone stopped mid-movement, like someone had pressed the pause button. The silence was resounding.

"See if you can entice them back to the Seam," Whittaker Ray said quietly, and Eyre, feeling like the Pied Piper, coaxed the creatures by calling them and patting her leg gently. Their eyes rotated nervously from side to side, looking at the horde of ferocious people who had been chasing them, but they hesitantly clicked across the moldavite square until they stood in front of the Seam. Then, obviously sensing something familiar on the other side, they leapt through the light on their long legs and disappeared.

Cheers and applause interspersed with loud bursts of laughter erupted as the last one departed. Students picked themselves off the floor, the staff straightened their clothing, and everyone tried to get back into some sort of order. Lord Clarembout stood with mud all over his knees, and Madame Overmantle had a wide streak of grease from the underside of the Zepp across her cheek. All the students were covered in twigs and grass and dirt, and Eyre could see that Ranger Chrysanthe was desperately trying not to smile.

Whittaker Ray looked wry as he faced the unkempt group. "Well, one thing we have definitely learned to expect from the TACI expeditions is the unexpected," he began, and everyone laughed. He looked over at President Zircon and the scowling Mimir, who lowered their weapons. Eyre suspected that the Mimir's way of dealing with the problem would have been to chop the creatures up and roast them for dinner. And she was also fairly certain that Sergeant Tottingham might have agreed with that approach.

"Thank you for your patience, President Zircon," Whittaker Ray said, trying to settle down the circus and restore the solemnity of the occasion. "Would you exhibit the gazae?"

President Zircon, an inscrutable look on his face, left the ranks of the Mimir and walked slowly across the moldavite square and over to the precisely lined-up capsules. He approached the one nearest Whittaker Ray and unclasped the locks on the capsule, ceremoniously lifting open the lid.

There was a sound like gas exhaling, and a strange-smelling vapour escaped. All the students leaned forward, keen to get a good look at the contents. Eyre could see there were huge crystals stacked inside, and President Zircon took one out and handed it to Whittaker Ray.

It was a clear, sparkling crystal about a metre long and thirty centimetres wide, an astonishing prism that caught the light and sent it charging back out again in a riot of rainbows. All the students gasped when Whittaker Ray held the crystal up in the light to examine it.

"The fourth-year students are to be congratulated," he said respectfully, handing the crystal back to President Zircon. "The quality is superb."

President Zircon placed the crystal back in the metallic capsule carefully and then re-latched the case. "The Mimir congratulate the TACI expedition also," he said formally, interlacing his fingers with the thumbs up and bowing to the fourth-year students. All the Mimir performed the same action, holding their bow for a couple of seconds.

Then President Zircon clicked his fingers, and the Mimir jumped into action. It took four of them on each capsule to pick up the heavy containers and carry them through the brass doors in the ground and down the staircase that led to the Mimir's Domain. Where the capsules went from there, Eyre couldn't see, but she guessed that they were destined for the weapons section, somewhere in the vaults below the ground.

When the last capsule had been taken, President Zircon bowed to Whittaker Ray, then to the staff, and finally the students.

"Inguz!" he said, and disappeared down the hole as well, slamming the brass doors shut after him. Eyre could hear a loud slow clanking like gears turning.

"That is the lock to the Mimir's Domain engaging," Whittaker Ray explained to the curious students. "It is a massive mechanism made of the strongest titanium." Then he turned and faced all the students. "Turnby Williams, where are you?" An older boy with wavy blond hair put up his hand and started to move forwards, tucking in his shirt and smoothing down his hair. As he walked up to Whittaker Ray, the man put out his hand and shook the boy's hand.

"Turnby was our Graduate Leader on the TACI Expedition to Incendium. It has been a most successful mission, and we congratulate you also, Turnby. We are sorry that the Extraterrestrial Cyclone has meant the rest of the school is not here to acknowledge your efforts, but would the

TEP students please show your appreciation to Turnby and to our Graduate students for their outstanding achievement."

Everyone applauded enthusiastically, and the fourth-year students beamed with pride. It was obviously a moment of significance for them, because some students were wiping tears from their eyes and hugging each other. Eyre realised that this was the final event for them in their schooling years at the Academy and therefore a very memorable moment.

"Fourth years, you may head back to your quarters at the Academy. We will all look forward to celebrating with you again at the Lifting of the Halo next year.

"Students," Whittaker Ray continued, "you are to head back by Zepp to the Compound, and the rest of your day is free for you to use for practise wherever you see fit. Sergeant Tottingham will now issue instructions about boarding the Zepps."

The students clapped politely, and Whittaker Ray left, heading towards the Administration Building. Sergeant Tottingham walked across the Receiving Stone to the front of the crowd.

"I trust you have found this morning's proceedings informative," she said. "We don't normally deal with overexcited creatures from the Alterworld, but I guess at least you could say it was an interesting experience. The Zha'kara Diamonds you just saw will be milled by the Mimir to make the Antaraks, a process that takes significant time and exceptional skill. Those of you who join us at the Academy next year will eventually receive the Antaraks cut from this gazae in your third year. It is an interesting process, and first year students will go down to the Armaments Section to see them being crafted.

"Okay, well, we will leave now via the Zepps in the manner that we came up here. Board numerically and wait for the second flight if you don't make the first."

Students started to shuffle into place. Madame Overmantle, her hair still sticking out in all directions after her scramble under the Zepp, welcomed them aboard brightly, and Eyre noticed that this time, everyone was hanging on tightly to the handrail as the Zepp took off over the edge. The Zepp dipped, accelerated, and spiralled around as it descended and finally landed on the arrival pad with a violent thud and a screech of tyres.

All the students looked down at their feet as they arrived, trying not to smile—aware that if they looked at each other they would completely lose it.

CHAPTER THIRTY-FIVE

EYRE FINISHED UP HER breakfast the next morning and stacked her plates on her tray, thinking about the run. She had tried hard again today, and her lungs still burned from the exertion. She thought she was improving marginally, but she wondered if she'd ever manage to do the course without feeling like a horse had kicked her.

Suddenly someone with a bucket and a cloth began cleaning the end of the table. Eyre looked across and realised it was Jax, who raised his eyebrows at her.

"My turn this morning," he said. "Courtesy of Dr Botolfe." Eyre swung around and could see Ben Perrill down the other end of the Refectory, scowling and also carrying a bucket. He had a swollen red nose, and he looked rather peculiar with his bald head. He wiped the tables as if he'd like to smash them into the ground.

"Well, er . . . thank you for . . . yesterday," she said awkwardly. "It was good of you to stick up for me like that."

"Perrill's a jerk," Jax said, leaning on the table and looking at her with those piercing green eyes. "He deserved it. I'm sorry to hear about your family, Eyre."

He continued wiping his way across the room as Eyre put her tray at the window of the kitchen, feeling a strange lightness inside her. When she left the room, she could feel Jax's eyes on her.

She walked down the paths, looking for her friends, past the Meditation Hall, and into the Training Shed. They weren't there, but she spotted Nick and Abby by the side of the lake, and she walked out to join them.

"Watch this, Eyre," Abby said with glee.

Abby and Nick slowly rose into the air. Nick was more steady; Abby wobbled up and down, but she managed to stay above the ground. Then they started to skip bright discs of energy like flat stones across the top of the lake. Sometimes the discs disappeared beneath the water, and sometimes they ricocheted straight up into the air. But when they got it right, the discs skipped a series of times across the surface, then whizzed off into the distance out of sight. A loud boom at the other end of the lake indicated that they had hit something with great force. Eyre hoped it was uninhabited down there.

"That does look like fun," she said wistfully, and Abby descended to the ground, coming down a little too fast and ending up sprawled on the grass.

"Damn," she said, "still can't do that very well." Her eyes were sympathetic as she looked at Eyre.

"I wish you had Elevated, too, Eyre," she said. "But there's still nine weeks to go. And if you don't, I'm sure you'll be chosen for the U.D. They do a lot of cool things there, too."

Eyre nodded. "I know. And I'm sure I'll like it there if I get in. Keep practising," she said. "I like seeing what you can do. If I eventually do Elevate, it will help me if I've watched you do it." Abby wobbled back up in the air and sent a beam of light from her palm across the surface of the lake. It went for about fifteen metres then faded off into nothing.

"You're doing so well," Eyre said admiringly.

Abby rotated in the air awkwardly, then landed heavily, although on her feet this time. "It's hard," she said. "But Nick is really good. Do that thing on the water, Nick!"

Nick was still up in the air, and he moved forwards towards the lake. Eyre watched as he walked over the surface of the lake out about five metres. His feet dipped down towards the surface of the lake, and then he wavered as he rose again. It was obviously very difficult, and Eyre could see him concentrating hard with the effort. Finally he turned and slowly made his way back to them, rising and falling as he tried to maintain a steady pace. Abby looked at him admiringly as they both hovered above the ground.

"I can't do that," she said. "As soon as I try to move off one spot I fall down. If I went out there I'd end up in the lake. But hopefully I'll get the hang of it."

Both of them descended to the ground, Nick landing gracefully on his feet and Abby on her rear-end again, laughing.

"Now show Eyre the bubbles, Nick!" Abby said, waving her hands around, palms upwards.

Nick looked apologetic. "I'm not really good at it yet," he said, but Abby harrumphed.

"Yes, you are! Go on!"

Nick waved his hands in the air with his palms facing the sky, similar to what Abby had done, but when he did it spheres of light emerged from his palms and floated up into the air. Then Nick flicked his fingers, and masses of spheres erupted from his fingertips and drifted upwards like glowing soap bubbles. They were beautiful, silently moving up in the air, all different sizes and turning slightly in the wind. Eventually they disappeared as the breeze or the altitude snuffed them out.

"It's called bullic," Abby said, watching more bubbles rise. "Isn't it lovely?"

"Wow," Eyre breathed, "that's really something. You've both learned an awful lot in a short time." When the final glowing sphere had disappeared, Abby suggested that they go and find Beatrice.

They walked to the Training Shed, but Beatrice still wasn't there. Then they checked the Meditation Hall again, and the therapeutic pools, not really expecting to find her in either of those. She wasn't in the Lecture Theatre, either. After some discussion, Abby surmised that perhaps she had gone to ask a lecturer a question, so they trooped over to the staff room. A very icy Professor Vela answered their knock and informed them that she wasn't there, nor had she been there, and hadn't they best be off *practising*?

Stumped, they tried Beatrice's lodge, then each of their own lodges with no success. Finally Nick said, "What about the Common Room?" at which they all burst out laughing. The idea of Beatrice, the A+ student, lounging around the Common Room was ridiculous. But they walked up the stairs of the Common Room anyway, passing by a few students who were hanging out on the outside veranda. The students were just chatting: Saskia was there, and Tec Langford, laughing and gossiping—obviously not concerned about practising for anything at all. Not really expecting to find Beatrice inside amongst this unstudious lot, they checked it anyway, and to their immense surprise, there she was.

She was sitting opposite someone at one of the tables, both their heads down, working intensely at something. As Eyre, Abby, and Nick entered, Beatrice shouted, "Done!" and as she threw her stylus down, the other person exclaimed in defeat.

"You win this time," he said. "Again?"

"Sure," Beatrice said, tapping her Felsic.

They both looked up as Eyre, Abby, and Nick walked up to them. Eyre recognised Beatrice's opponent: it was Robeson Paul, the Clark-Kentish intellectual boy, Number 114.

"What are you doing?" Eyre asked as they sat around the table.

"We're practising codes," Beatrice replied. "I was so annoyed that I couldn't crack that code the other day, I went and asked UD1 if he had some practise questions I could work on. Robeson's doing it, too. It's actually quite fun. Want to join us?"

"Sure!" said Eyre, thinking this was probably a good idea, especially if she was going to be in the Unlit Division. She took out her Felsic and Beatrice sent the questions over. Frowning, Eyre studied the first line of code, which just looked like a bunch of gobbledygook. She had no idea and looked across the table as Beatrice and Robeson scribbled furiously. Robeson won this time, just beating Beatrice, while the rest of them were still scratching their heads. But they practised for an hour, and slowly Eyre began to understand the system of working out the code. The practise questions they had were very basic, there were no tricks involved, just a logical system, so she worked through them all until she understood the basics of solving a straightforward code. Beatrice was right, it was fun and a challenge to see how fast she could do it. She'd never be as quick as Beatrice and Robeson, but she was glad that she'd spent the time with them.

"We've got time to practise in the shed before lunch," Beatrice said when they'd finished the last code. "Does anyone want to come over?"

Robeson said he was going to meditate, but Nick and Abby were quick to say yes, as they hadn't practised their Ferito that day. Eyre decided to join them—at least she could do that.

They walked along the path to the Training Shed and Beatrice, Abby, and Nick headed inside. Eyre went to follow them when suddenly the unwelcome, hulking form of Ben Perrill blocked her way. His face was twisted with malice as he stood across the doorway. Eyre tried to act unworried, but she found the sight of his battered nose and the hatred in his eyes disconcerting. Determinedly she refused to show her fear.

"Love the nose job, Perrill," she said in a flippant tone. "Don't think it improves your looks though."

In a flash the huge boy grabbed her shoulder hard, bringing his face down towards her. "I had to do cafeteria duty because of you, Lightward," he said through gritted teeth. "You're going to pay for that!"

Eyre struggled to get away, but he was too strong, and a sharp pain stabbed through her shoulder. She could see Beatrice, Abby, and Nick still walking away, oblivious to what was going on behind them.

"Let me go!" she shouted, pushing against Ben Perrill's chest.

Suddenly there was a commotion behind her, and something slammed into Ben, releasing his grip on her. As Eyre stood back in surprise, rubbing her shoulder, three more red-haired forms hurtled past her and leapt on to the large boy, shoving him backwards into the shed. With a shout of surprise he landed on his back with four angry Mimir on top of him. They growled in fury, and Eyre's eyes widened as Jengles strode forward from the back of the Mimir and up the steps past her, his weapon drawn.

He leaned over Ben Perrill, a fierce look on his face. "*By St Ria*. You will never touch Erin," he said softly, his lips bared as he drew the Crescent Blade across Ben Perrill's neck. It didn't cut Ben's neck, but it did leave a mark, and he lay with a petrified look on his face as Jengles leaned over him.

"Allowances have been made," he said. "But this is not acceptable. Touch her again and I will put the blade through your neck."

He stood up and the four Mimir rolled Ben aside, clearing the way for Eyre to enter. She could see her friends walking quickly back towards her.

Jengles bowed low. "I trust you are unharmed," he said to Eyre. "You should not have any more trouble from this mali."

"Thank you, Jengles, er, General," Eyre said, her voice shaking slightly. She entered the shed, walking past Ben Perrill, who clambered to his feet and ran outside with hot, angry eyes. The Mimir left, too, marching off in geometrical formation down the path.

There was a silence in the shed—the fracas had caught the attention of everyone, and they had stopped what they were doing to watch the spectacle. Eyre was aware many people were looking at her curiously, but she was preoccupied with the thoughts tumbling over in her mind. Jengles had called her Erin. What was that? A memory lapse? Could the Mimir suffer forgetfulness as they aged, like people? He seemed to *revere* her, so how could he get her name wrong? And what "allowances" had been made? What did that mean?

As she turned the puzzle over in her head, her three friends arrived, and Beatrice exclaimed at the marks on Eyre's shoulder, her face worried.

"Are you okay, Eyre? Perrill is a beast! Thank goodness Jengles was there. He called Ben Perrill a mali, a demon. So true! I couldn't put it better myself!"

"I'm fine," Eyre said, brushing off her concern. Obviously Beatrice hadn't heard Jengles' mistake with her name, and Eyre decided that she herself must have misheard him. And as the trembling in her body started to lessen, she realised Beatrice was right: thank goodness Jengles had appeared. Ben had seemed intent on doing some damage, and from the scars on Nick, she knew what he was capable of. But as Eyre looked back at the receding forms of the Mimir, she felt a warmth surge inside her. Somehow she doubted Ben Perrill would bother her again.

"Let's practise!" Eyre said, heading for the pile of Palum. The other students in the shed relaxed, and a hum rose in the air as they got back to what they had been doing before the excitement. Eyre picked up her Palum and faced Beatrice fiercely.

"I don't think Perrill will try it again," Eyre said. "But I'm going to be ready if he does!"

Beatrice laughed and picked up a Palum, too.

"That makes two of us!" she said and assumed the starting position.

"Tollo!" they cried together, and the clatter of their Palum rose in the shed as they moved slowly through the positions.

CHAPTER THIRTY-SIX

THE WEEKS PASSED QUICKLY, and the days merged into one another as the students prepared for the TEPs. There was something reassuring in the familiarity of the routine, and Eyre liked being a part of the group. She wasn't used to knowing people so well, and she had discovered that it was a nice feeling to be so settled.

Ben Perrill had indeed left her alone after that day at the Training Shed, to her great relief, and so, it seemed, had the Mimir. Obviously engaged with other duties, they had not been out again. Eyre had to admit she was secretly relieved about that too as her previous encounters with them had been rather awkward.

When the alarm went off, the first day of week seven, she sat up and quickly looked at her upper arm, as she had done every morning since she'd arrived at the camp, but saw that it still remained bare. Sighing, she climbed down and started to dress, a rock in her stomach. It looked like she wasn't getting an Inguz. Although she had tried to have a positive attitude about joining the Unlit, she still felt the pain of not Elevating, and she had secretly believed that it might take a while, but she would eventually get one. She had wanted so desperately to be a student Lightworker and to be able to do the Lightworking skills.

But her pragmatic side kicked in, and setting her jaw, she thought about the Unlit division and focussed on UD1. He was an enigma, so nondescript and quiet, yet emanating an aura of serenity and wisdom. He hadn't given a lot away in the lecture that first week, but she was sure she could learn a lot from him. And undoubtedly the Unlit Division would be interesting—she just had to concentrate on getting in.

She thought of her parents every day, and the pain of their deaths hadn't lessened, but she was getting more able to deal with the fact that they were gone. The thought of them motivated her and drove her to try harder, determined to bring honour to the name of Lightward. Sometimes she had needed to walk alone for a while when the memories became too difficult, but she was learning to accept her new reality, and to focus on the happy times they had had together as a family. She was greatly helped by the knowledge that the lovely cabin and the Lightkeeper would always be there for her to help preserve those memories.

As she climbed down from the top bunk to get her uniform, she suddenly realised that there were feet floating half a metre above the ground. Eyre looked up and saw Carly hovering in the air, her shoulders level with Eyre's bunk bed.

"I got dressed up here," Carly said to Eyre proudly.

Eyre clapped her hands and congratulated her, and Carly floated backwards through the cabin and out the door, wobbling up and down but not touching the floor. She waved as she disappeared through the doorway. Laughing, Eyre quickly got dressed herself and raced down the stairs. She opened the door fast, and it hit someone on the other side.

"Oops, sorry!" she exclaimed as she walked outside, and then she saw it was Jax, looking at her with an amused expression.

He leaned against the wall and raised his eyebrows as she closed the door awkwardly. "That keen to get to the run?"

Eyre smiled back at him, feeling once again the strange unsettled feeling he seemed to cause within her.

"Sorry," she said, trying to be casual, but it was a bit of a task to be cool with those green eyes looking at her; that dark hair and engaging grin were very distracting.

"So how are you going?" he asked, walking beside her. There was a brief silence as Eyre looked around uncomfortably for Pheria, but then she relaxed. Jax might have a girlfriend, but there was nothing wrong with just talking to him, after all.

"I'm doing okay, thanks. How about you?"

Jax shrugged. "I Elevated in the first week, but I definitely haven't shown any signs of brilliance yet. How about you?"

Eyre smiled. He was being modest—from what she had seen, he was pretty good at everything he did. "Well, definitely no brilliance for me either, *and* I haven't Elevated, so you're doing better than I am." She indicated her bare arm; then her mouth twitched. "But at least I've avoided cafeteria duty for a while."

Jax laughed. "Yes, I hope I don't have to do that again, not fun at all!"

He looked at Eyre, his green eyes inscrutable. "I hope you're here next year, Eyre."

Eyre was silent for a moment, unable to come up with a response as she processed the possible meanings of that comment. Then as they arrived at the lake, she finally replied. "You, too. Good luck."

Jax walked over to join his friends, and Eyre looked around for Beatrice and Abby, a bit baffled as to why she felt so confused. After all, Jax was probably just being friendly; it wasn't as if he meant anything by it.

But she forgot about it as she spotted Abby and Beatrice over by the lake, and as she headed towards them, a tall fair-haired form detached itself from the crowd and sauntered over. Colton grinned down at her.

"Care to practise some Two today? Since we've already mastered the Single," he asked. The names for the various Clasis were a mouthful, so the students had begun to shorten them to make it easier: "Two" was they called Clasis with Two-Handed Fighting, similarly, Clasis for Single-Blade Weapon, was called "Single," and Basic Clasis was just called "Basic."

Eyre laughed. She had improved quite a bit in the past couple of weeks, and the last time she had sparred with Colton she had actually managed to land a couple of blows. It had both disconcerted and amused him, and since then he had taken to asking her to practise with him.

"Sure!" she replied, her mood lightening. "I'll meet you after breakfast if you like." Beatrice was flapping her eyebrows at Eyre from behind Colton, as intensely as a ship sending out Morse code. The meaning was clear, but Eyre tried to ignore her.

Fortunately Sergeant Tottingham walked through the crowd at that moment, distracting them, and as Eyre turned she saw Jax watching her from across the crowd. It was quite discomfiting; he seemed to do that a lot. She wondered what Pheria would think knowing Jax had told her that he and Pheria were just friends. Eyre had a feeling that Pheria wouldn't be too impressed. Anyone who carried around a photograph of her boyfriend definitely *was* serious about the relationship. Still, it wasn't Eyre's business; and she sure as anything was going to keep away from that potential minefield.

She looked away from him deliberately, examining the crowd. No one had Elevated last week, and already about 90 per cent of the students had received an Inguz. The normal percentages meant that probably no more students would Elevate, herself included. Now that she had faced that disappointment, her focus was making sure that she was chosen for the Unlit division. She scanned people's arms, trying to see who was in the competition for places in the U.D. Number 110, Tina Pang, who had spoken to them after the information session on the first day, still hadn't Elevated, Eyre noticed. Physically, she would probably be good in the U.D. She was nice, Eyre remembered, so perhaps they could study together if they both got in.

Sergeant Tottingham thumped her staff for attention, and Eyre joined the students as they shuffled into numerical order. It didn't take long—everyone was used to it now and knew who to look out for to stand next to.

"Well, time is passing quickly, and from what I can see, you are all working hard at your practise. But it is important that you don't let the momentum fail until the day you begin your examination. Round about now students can start to get jaded with the process and feel they have done enough. But I exhort you to keep working hard. Every minute you spend training will affect your outcome, and it is well worth spending the time available to try and increase your skills. "Right then, off you go!" She thumped her staff on the ground, and the body of students started running up the track.

Eyre ran along as hard as she could, trying to keep her breathing even. Her legs felt good today, and mercifully, the awful burning in her lungs hadn't appeared—yet, anyway. She felt fairly strong as she ran along. Soon she saw Abby and Beatrice up ahead, and giving them a wink, dashed past. Her legs were handling the run well, and her familiarity with the path now meant that she knew when the obstacles were coming that might trip her up—the log across the path, the huge boulder at the top of the trail, the area of slippery pebbles. She rounded the top of the trail past the Wollemi Pine and headed at a fast pace down the track so that she had made her way in to the middle of the pack by the time she crossed the line.

"Well done, 88!" Sergeant Tottingham exclaimed, causing Professor Vela to scowl even more darkly than usual.

Eyre ran past them and then, as their heads swivelled to follow her, she kept running and started round the track again. She had decided that for the next three weeks she was going to run the track twice. Since she probably wasn't going to get the opportunity to demonstrate any skills in the TEPs, she wanted to make sure she was remembered for something other than coming last in the run and doing cafeteria duty.

As she raced up the track she was aware of Sergeant Tottingham and Professor Vela watching her, surprised looks on their faces as they followed her progress.

The second time around the track, instead of finding it harder, she was amazed to find that her feet flew, and she charged up the hill without the usual struggle. She could feel the strength in her muscles, and an energy that filled her with joy as she raced over rocks and sticks and headed for the top of the track. She'd never been fit enough to experience anything other than pain while exercising, so it was a new and exhilarating feeling. Breathing hard, she flew around the top of the track and sprinted down to the finish line.

Sergeant Tottingham looked as close to beaming as her stolid face could manage, but "a nice improvement, 88," was all she said as she marked off Eyre's name. Whether she was referring to Eyre's running or her attitude, Eyre couldn't be sure, but she was happy for the rare note of approval from the usually impassive Sergeant.

Professor Vela pursed his mouth as if he had had just taken a bite out of a large lemon. Eyre walked past them, trying not to puff, and headed for the Refectory. Despite the fact she was last to leave the field, she wasn't assigned cafeteria duty, which she took as a tacit sign of approbation from the Sergeant.

When she arrived Beatrice waved at her to join them. Eyre got her breakfast and then weaved her way through the crowded tables.

"*What* were you doing? Twice around by *choice*? I think your brain's going, my friend!" Beatrice exclaimed as Eyre sat down at the table.

"Nice work," Nick said with a smile. "Run with me from now on!"

Abby, who this morning was sporting bright green tips on her hair, laughed out loud. "Just as well we're not at St Jeffrey's any more. You'd be signed up for the track team!"

Eyre smiled at her friends' ribbing and started to eat, enjoying the hubbub that surrounded her, but it was a bittersweet feeling. With only three more weeks to go, she was already starting to feel sad at the prospect of leaving. Her lack of an Inguz meant that she was probably not going to be eligible for the TEPs, and it was hard to see so many students walking past who had Elevated, the Inguz gleaming like quicksilver on their arms. But it reinforced her determination: she was going to work harder than ever for the next three weeks and give herself the best chance possible. And that started with getting her head in the right place—after her weeks at the Compound she had realised how important the mental side was to training: focus, concentration, and positivity. Once she had understood that, her Ferito had improved greatly. And she was absolutely convinced it was her change in attitude that had made all the difference in the run this morning. Something other than endorphins had fuelled the energy that had filled her body as she raced up the hill.

So when she finished her breakfast, she headed straight to the Meditation Hall, determined that in addition to working hard physically, she was also going to focus on improving that powerful mind force in the remaining few weeks.

CHAPTER THIRTY-SEVEN

THE LAST DAY OF free training arrived soon enough. After her run with Nick and breakfast Eyre walked along the path to Water Lodge, feeling a thread of sadness begin to wind through her. She had only been here ten weeks, but already it felt so much like home and so familiar. She hoped that she would be selected for the Unlit Division, so at least she wouldn't be leaving the Academy permanently. But even so, this phase of her schooling was almost over—and the TEP training had been a memorable and mostly wonderful experience.

She headed upstairs to her locker and pulled her bag from under the bunk. At the lake this morning Sergeant Tottingham had instructed the Unlit students to pack their bags after breakfast to be ready for their departure tomorrow. As Eyre started packing her belongings, Carly walked in, carrying something in her hand. She held it out, and Eyre saw that it was a soft, hand-crocheted knee blanket.

"I wanted to give you a going away present," Carly explained. "And I don't have anything to give you. So I asked Mum to make you this. She sent it this morning."

Eyre hugged Carly, touched by her thoughtfulness. She folded the blanket carefully, knowing she would take it with her wherever she ended up.

Carly left to go and practise her Ferito while Eyre finished packing. It didn't take long; Eyre hadn't brought much, the only things she left out were the clothes she would wear home the next day. She looked down at her Lightworking uniform. Today was the last day she would be wearing it— even if she made the Unlit Division, they wore their own inconspicuous brown uniform, so she would be giving this back tomorrow. It felt like part of her now, and although she was trying to be philosophical about it, she felt a pang of sadness stab through her.

She decided that to fill in the afternoon she would run the course again, then practise some Ferito in the shed for the last time, and finish with meditation. She thought it would be nice to visit all the places that held so many memories for her.

She ran the course, feeling like she was flying, her feet barely touching the ground as she strode up the slope and around the top of the track. It was a wonderful feeling, exhilarating, and she felt fantastic as she crossed the end point at the bottom of the hill. So different from how she felt the first time she had run the track; if nothing else, she was glad that she had gained a love of running during the ten weeks training.

When she entered the Training Shed just about all the students were there, practising hard. Even the Unlit were going through their Ferito, realising that this was their last opportunity to be noticed and considered for selection next year. Sergeant Tottingham and Professor Vela watched from the sidelines, occasionally calling out adjustments and corrections to students' techniques. The mood was a lot more intense today than it had been in the past weeks; it was the last day of training and everyone wanted to be part of the Academy. They were practising as if these last minutes would count. And who knew? Maybe they would.

Eyre could see that a few of the students were excelling in their skills. Colton, of course, was outstanding in everything; he was a natural athlete and had picked up all the techniques quickly this week. But others were surprising—Rigmar, for instance, who didn't look athletic at all, had a remarkable eye and his aim was incredible. He was practising with a Falum for the Kulbeda—the small dagger that would be part of their Arms Endowment—and he could hit the bullseye from across the shed. Accuracy with throwing, Eyre recalled, was part of using your Viq energy, and she realised that Rigmar, for all his joking around, was undeniably a Lightworker with a strong force already.

Warrigal was another one who could do any of the Lightworking skills easily; his aptitude was so high it was almost as if he had already been at the Academy for some time. The small girl, Advika Bhaduri, Number 10—the one who had done so well in Dr Botolfe's levitation lecture—was also surprisingly good at all the skills. She was so slight it was hard to imagine that she could fight well, but she could handle Ferito as well as she could levitate. And Jax and Pheria—of course—shone at everything. They had no problem with any of the skills, and Eyre had to admit it was a foregone conclusion that they would be at the Academy next year.

Nick was accomplished also; he had natural ability and had been performing all the disciplines solidly for some weeks now. Eyre expected that he would do really well in the TEPs. Beatrice, with her smart brain and determination, had managed to improve over the ten weeks until she was reasonable in most of the areas, and Abby had proven a natural at the psychic forces, so Eyre imagined they both had a good chance, too. As she looked around the room, it was hard to figure out who was going to be selected—everyone had improved so much over the training weeks. She imagined the pressure would be quite intense during the examinations.

Eyre ran through her Ferito a couple of times, but then had an overwhelming sense of being finished. She knew the moves, she felt confident with them, and she realised that it was time for her to call it a day. There was nothing more she could do; and it wasn't helping her to watch the other students excel at skills she was unable to even perform, let alone show any prowess at. So she decided her final task would be to do some meditation in the glowing crystal hall next door, a sort of farewell to the Compound.

She wandered over, met Simmons at the door, and walked along the translucent aquamarine floor past the magical water fountain to the far corner of the hall. She sat quietly, absorbing the peaceful vibrations of the vast space, then shut her eyes and tried to clear her mind of any intruding negative thoughts. She felt rested and at peace, sensing that whatever the outcome was from these past weeks, she had tried her hardest and given her best effort. Overwhelmingly she had a sense of gratitude that she had been part of the whole process. Finally she left, thanking Simmons for his guidance, and he smiled gently at her.

"I think you, of all the students, have made the most progress over the weeks," he said. "Wherever you end up, this will be the essence of your strength, Eyre. Good luck."

Eyre left and headed back to her lodge, a sense of finality overcoming her. She showered and then searched out Beatrice, Abby, and Nick, who were heading over to dinner. They were obviously uncomfortable, realising how difficult this must be for her. Abby took Eyre's arm as they walked into the Refectory.

"Well, we are going to miss you tomorrow, Eyre. But you can relax at the cabins and sort out your stuff. We'll be back in a week."

"Yes," said Beatrice, "you can laugh at the thought of us falling flat on our faces in the TEPs!"

They were eating dinner—a lamb roast, in honour of the last night for some of them—when Sergeant Tottingham and Whittaker Ray walked in and stood at the front of the cafeteria. The Sergeant thumped her staff, and everyone looked up.

"Please be silent while Whittaker Ray speaks," she said.

Whittaker Ray looked at the students from under his bristling eyebrows, his blue eyes kind. "So the end of the ten weeks is here. I'm sure it went faster than you thought, but also slower than you thought at times!" The students chuckled and watched him expectantly. He continued. "Let me congratulate *all* of you on your efforts. We have been very pleased with your attitude over the weeks and your willingness to learn. It bodes well for you as students next year, no matter which Academy you end up joining." His eyes travelled around the students.

"Those of you who are not selected for the Academy next year, we want you to know that this is mainly just because we have a limited capacity for new students. Each and every one of you would be a worthy student to come here, and I hope to hear of your successes in coming years.

"Those who have Elevated and are accepted by the College will be receiving official notification, but will also have their names listed on the blackboard in the Common Room after the Placement Ceremony on Sunday, the official ceremony where you receive your Sector. Sergeant Tottingham will now issue instructions on the structure for the coming week."

Sergeant Tottingham stepped forward. "Tomorrow is a significant day for you all," she began. "Please pay attention, and I will outline what will be happening. I won't be repeating myself.

"Okay. Those students Numbers 1 to 40 who have Elevated, please be at the lake at 0930 sharp. The first challenge will begin exactly at 1000, but you will be receiving your instructions at 0945, so don't be late. We will not repeat instructions, and if you miss them, you will be heading off on the challenge, trying to catch up with the others, not knowing what you are supposed to be doing. Therefore, I would strongly suggest you are on time. This information and a list of the groups for the week will be posted on the board in the Common Room if anyone needs to refresh their memory."

She paused briefly and looked around the room. "Students who are Unlit, please come up to the front of the room now." A group of about twenty students, Eyre amongst them, walked up to join Sergeant Tottingham, and they stood awkwardly at the front beside her. Eyre recognised most of the students standing with her, but only knew a few of them by name. 53, 72 and 94 were from her Lodge—Julia, Doc and Andrew—but she hadn't really talked to them much over the past ten weeks. Thomas Peterson, Rigmar's friend, was in the group standing beside Tina Pang, the girl Eyre had met outside Lectures on the first day. And Edith Worth, the girl who had been attacked by the Bunyip, was also there. Eyre felt happy to know at least a few people who might be in the U.D. next year.

Sergeant Tottingham indicated the group of students.

"I would like you to congratulate these students for the effort they have put in these past ten weeks. Some of them will be joining our Unlit Division next year and providing invaluable services to our Lightworking community. If you are to be offered a place, you will receive official notification by Peragro within the week. We are sorry to say goodbye to you all but look forward to seeing some of you next year."

Sergeant Tottingham started to clap, and the students all joined in the applause, cheering and stomping feet, a noisy tribute that made the Unlit students smile. Sergeant Tottingham indicated that they could go and sit down again, and she continued. "You Unlit students, please be waiting in the Common Room tomorrow morning at 0800 with all your gear. You will be travelling back from there to your homes or your nominated destination. Please do us the courtesy of being on time as we have a lot to accomplish tomorrow. Ranger Chrysanthe will be helping you to travel, so please look for him when you arrive in the morning."

Sergeant Tottingham looked around the crowded room and smiled a rare smile.

"It's time to leave now. Thank you all again and good night."

And then, to Eyre's surprise, Sergeant Tottingham and Whittaker Ray stood by the doorway and shook the hand of every last student as they headed back to their lodges.

CHAPTER THIRTY-EIGHT

EYRE WOKE EARLY THE next morning, accustomed to the five o'clock whistle. This morning, everyone was still quiet in their bunks, tired from the intense buildup to the TEPs. She sat up quietly and looked out the window at the lake as the early morning sun rose. The water was millpond still, glassy and dark, but the waking sun had started to decorate the surface with streaks of orange. She drank in the peace of the scene, savouring the last moments in this place she had begun to think of as home.

Soon others stirred in their beds, and it wasn't long before people were up and getting dressed in a frenzy of activity. None of the Water Lodge students had their TEPs today, but there was a sense of significance about the morning: the day the first challenges started.

Eyre made her bed and put on her shorts, T-shirt, and runners. She folded her Lightworker uniform and put it on the end of her bunk, smoothing it neatly, her heart sore. Carly was bustling around putting on her uniform, and she stopped for a moment, understanding Eyre's difficulty.

"Sorry, Eyre," she said quietly. "But I know we'll see you in the U.D. next year, so this is just a temporary goodbye." She hugged Eyre hard then headed off to run the track despite the fact it wasn't required.

Eventually it was breakfast time, and Eyre walked over to have her last meal. The Refectory was noisy with the clattering of plates and chatter of students. She grabbed a tray and sat with Beatrice, Abby, and Nick and tried to stay upbeat as they all discussed the TEPs. Beatrice was white and picking at her food; obviously the stress of the upcoming exam was getting to her.

"By the Light, I'm going to fail. I just know it," Beatrice said gloomily. "What will I tell my parents?"

"Oh, stop it!" Abby said, laughing. "If *you* fail, then the rest of us may as well just head home now! When have you ever failed an exam?"

"Yes, but this has such a physical side to it," Beatrice said, determined to be glum. "Nick has far better a chance at doing well with this than I do."

Eyre had to agree she had a point. There were so many skills in the Lightworking world that were physically oriented. But she understood something else after her time here these past weeks.

"Beatrice, the physical skills are only as good as your mind makes them," she said. "Athleticism is only half the way to success. You have to concentrate your Viq to be able to do any of those skills, and that takes mental ability. With your brain, you'll be fine!"

Beatrice looked at Eyre gratefully. "You're such a good friend, Eyre. Thank you. I wish you were going to be here."

"Me, too," Eyre said with a wry smile. "But I'll be sending you all support telepathically! Make sure you pick up on it!"

"Wish I could pick up on what's going to be in the test," Abby said, frowning. "If only they would give us some idea. I don't know what to practise. I'm not particularly good at any of it!"

"I don't think we can make much of a difference now," Nick said. "Go hard at it, then at least you'll know you couldn't have done anything else to get in."

They all nodded, finished their breakfast, and started packing their dishes on their trays to take them to the kitchen window.

Suddenly Abby nudged Eyre and whispered, "Check it out, twelve o'clock!"

Eyre looked up in the designated direction and was a bit disconcerted to see Jax walking over. He stopped by Eyre's seat and looked at her.

"You heading home today?"

"Yes," Eyre said. "I'm packed. Heading to the Common Room after the Remembrance Day silence." Today was November 11, a day when the Commonwealth paused at 11am for one minute to honour those in the armed forces who had died in battle. It was also Eyre's 14th birthday, but she hadn't mentioned that to anyone.

Jax's eyes softened, and he bowed low to her, mimicking the Mimir. "Seems to be the thing to do around you," he said sombrely, then laughed. "Take care, Eyre. I hope you're back here next year." He left before she could answer. Abby rolled her eyes.

She smirked at Eyre. "Well, he seems to like you, despite your lack of encouragement!" Eyre laughed, but her eyes followed Jax (as did those of most of the girls in the Refectory) as he walked towards the exit. She couldn't work him out; he did seem rather nice. But a glance at Pheria waiting in the doorway for him, made her shake her head. Way too hard, and anyway, she was on her way. Let someone else figure out the complexities of Jack Jackson.

They wandered out of the Refectory, and when Eyre reached her lodge she turned to her friends. "I might say goodbye now," she said. "I'll see you in a week, so there's no need for prolonged farewells. Good luck, you three, show 'em how good the Sunshine Coasters are!" She hugged her friends fiercely and tried not to show how sad she felt. Beatrice left at a run to go and get organised for the TEPs, and Nick and Abby headed off in the opposite direction. Watching them leave was a physical pain in her chest.

Eyre headed upstairs to her lodge and did the last of her packing. Then she picked up her bags and looked around for the last time. Her boots were neatly under the bed and her locker empty, still with her name and number on it. She picked up her backpack and duffel bag and headed down the stairs. Then she walked down and sat on the shores of Lake Altum, enjoying the beautiful view, the breeze and the silence as the next couple of hours passed. She thought back over her time at the Academy and realised that she didn't regret any of it. It had been an incredible time in her life. And then, when 11am arrived, she paused and remembered those many souls who had died to allow her and the country to live in peace.

After the minute of reflection had passed she sighed and stood up. She may as well get on with it. So she slung her backpack over her shoulder, picked up her duffel bag and headed towards the Common Room. On the way, she met up with Julia, Doc and Andrew walking silently along the path. It was ironic that she was just getting to know them as they were leaving, but no doubt next year if any of them were back, she would get to know them well. There was a subdued air as they trudged over to the Common Room; they seemed equally down about leaving.

"What will you do if you're not accepted here?" Eyre asked Julia.

"Well, my mother went to an academy in Melbourne," she answered. "So I've put my name down there, as well as at one in Adelaide. But I really wanted to come here," she said wistfully.

"I'll be going to the Brisbane Academy of Light," Doc said. "It's in Fortitude Valley, disguised as a nightclub. Should be fun, I guess." But he sounded like he didn't think it would be fun at all.

Andrew shrugged. "Not sure," he said. "Hopefully somewhere will take me. My uncle was Unlit, so I'll probably talk to him about it. I don't think my parents imagined I would actually be Unlit, so it's something I'm going to have to sort out when I get home."

They entered the Common Room where a number of other Unlit students had already gathered, looking at Ranger Chrysanthe, who was sitting at a table with a list of names written in light on a Felsic. He was wearing long black robes today, obviously part of the formal school process, Eyre thought gloomily. The Ranger was studying his Felsic and occasionally looking up as he checked the students' names off the list. Eyre and the other students from Water Lodge put their bags along the wall and waited for Ranger Chrysanthe to finish.

Finally he checked the last name and put the Felsic down as he stood up. He smiled understandingly at the unhappy faces before him.

"This is a difficult day for some of you," he said. "But it's the beginning of the next phase of your life, and the world of the Unlit is a joy and a mystery that only a few people will ever experience. So embrace your gift, for that is what it is, and you will find that you are on as amazing a journey as the rest of the students."

He winced as one of the whirling beetles struck him in the eye, and he brushed it away, his gold bangles jangling as he flicked his wrist. One of the bangles caught on the corner of the Felsic as he lifted his arm, sending it flying.

"Whoops," he said, trying to grab it, but overbalancing and knocking the table so that it began to teeter.

"Oh dear . . ." he continued as the table crashed sideways and his chair tipped over. Ranger Chrysanthe stepped backwards and tumbled over it onto the ground, his green hair flopping completely over his face and his feet sticking up in the air, revealing that he was wearing an enormous pair of yellow fluffy slippers.

Several of the students burst out laughing. Ranger Chrysanthe looked delighted as he picked himself up off the ground, straightening his robes, tucking the irregular green stone he always wore around his neck back into his shirt, and brushing back his hair.

"Aha!" he beamed, lifting the table off the floor. "That's a much better way to start the journey!"

Eyre smiled, struck with the sneaking suspicion that perhaps he wasn't as much of a buffoon as he appeared.

Ranger Chrysanthe picked up his Felsic again. "Well, I have you in alphabetical order here on my list, so could you please step up, with your luggage, as I call your name, and stand on this spot here."

He clicked his fingers and a picture of a kangaroo and an emu waltzing appeared on the floor. The image was completely made out of light, and it twirled around and around on the same spot.

"Now, stand on the kangaroo or the emu, whichever you prefer, and I'll send you home to your family," Ranger Chrysanthe said, calling up the first student to leave. As Noah Bentley stood on the whirling picture, Ranger Chrysanthe put his palm on Noah's forehead and a silver Halo suddenly appeared in the Ranger's hand. The Ranger put the Halo on the table and then tapped Noah on the shoulder. "Good bye and good luck!" he said. With a flash and a zap, Noah disappeared.

"Okay, could Christopher Fingleton step up now, please?" Christopher grabbed his bag and stood on the light, and Ranger Chrysanthe retrieved his Halo and sent him home, too. Slowly the students were marked off and sent home, and Eyre felt an overwhelming sadness as the stack of Halos grew and her turn approached. Several of the students had tears in their eyes, and she struggled to keep herself calm. After all, she had the beautiful cabin to return to, with all her possessions, her chest, and the Lightward-Tyson Wisdom to investigate some more. Perhaps there might be some more messages from her parents, too. She started to cheer up a bit as she thought of these things, when suddenly Julia gasped, and all eyes turned towards her.

"Eyre!" she cried in amazement, causing Eyre to jump in fright. "Look at your arm!" Eyre, completely confused, looked at her right arm, expecting to see blood or something; Julia had seemed so shocked.

"No, the other one!" Julia exclaimed, "Look! It's an Inguz!"

Eyre looked at her other arm and nearly fell over in surprise, because sure enough, an Inguz had appeared faintly at the top of her arm. Weirdly, it was very indistinct, and unlike all the other Inguzes she had seen, it wasn't sparkling silver but a faint black and formed from incomplete lines. She looked up in bewilderment. *Was* this an Inguz? It didn't seem very impressive, and it was so hard to see, perhaps it was something else completely? Ranger Chrysanthe stopped writing on the Felsic and walked over to her, looking perplexed.

"Well," he said slowly, peering at her arm, "it certainly looks like an Inguz, but I've never seen anything like it before. It's hard to see. I'm not sure what it is." He looked closely at her forehead, and Eyre felt her forehead hopefully.

"Do I have a Halo, too?"

The Ranger nodded slowly, then stepped back, frowning, deep in thought.

Everyone was examining their own arms, hoping they might see something appear also, but Eyre was the only one who had the strange symbol.

"Eyre, would you wait over at the table?" Ranger Chrysanthe said eventually. "I'll confer with the rest of the staff once these students have headed home." Eyre wandered off awkwardly to sit at the table, wanting to scrutinize the symbol on her arm but aware that the other students might feel bad if she did. She waved at the students she knew as they left—Thomas, Tina, Edith, and the ones from her lodge. It was strange to see them disappear; it was symbolic of the ending of this significant time. But at the same time she was trying to suppress the vague breath of hope that was sighing through her mind. Perhaps now she might be able to stay? Was the Inguz on her arm—more like a charcoal sketch than anything else—enough to allow her to participate in the TEPs? She desperately hoped that it might mean she was eligible to become part of the students undertaking the trials. She sat anxiously, agonising over the possibility until the last student disappeared.

Ranger Chrysanthe came back to her, his brow furrowed in bafflement as he again studied her arm. "I must say, Eyre Lightward," he said, shaking his head, "you've been a mystery ever since you arrived here, and once again you have dealt us a new puzzle to deal with. Healing people, bowing Mimir, attracting Hirtus—and now this." He pursed his lips.

"Would you wait here while I go and consult with the staff? I'm not actually sure what to do." He disappeared in a flash of light, and Eyre sat apprehensively at the table. She scrutinized the Inguz, willing it to turn sparkling and silver, but it remained indistinct and black, almost as if it had barely managed to make it onto her arm and had run out of steam. Eyre grimaced in irritation. So was she Elevated or not? She had made peace with the fact she was going to be part of the Unlit, *now* what was she? Something in between or something completely different? Maybe now she wouldn't even be permitted to join the Unlit, would have to go back to a normal school. Her thoughts raced around in ever-gloomy circles, no answers available, and she tapped her foot nervously on the floor as the minutes stretched out silently, and Ranger Chrysanthe didn't return.

A large flash of light zapped in the centre of the room, and Eyre jumped in surprise as she saw some of the staff members standing there. Lord Clarembout, Dr Botolfe, Madame Overmantle, and UD1 headed over to her, their expressions perplexed, and looked at her arm curiously, turning it this way and that to try and see the strange symbol better. Then they studied her forehead, frowning in concentration.

"Intriguing," muttered Lord Clarembout, peering closer. Dr Botolfe rubbed at the mark on Eyre's arm as if she suspected it might be a muddy smudge of some kind. Madame Overmantle didn't look at the symbol at all; she studied Eyre's face with an intensity that was unsettling. Hopefully she couldn't read Eyre's mind, Eyre thought, because at this point she was thinking that Lord Clarembout had obviously eaten far too much garlic for dinner the night before.

Then the door flung open and a very annoyed-looking Professor Vela whirled in the door. He took in Ranger Chrysanthe's unconventional footwear with a disdainful sneer, then stalked towards Eyre, irritation choreographing every step.

"I don't have time for this," he said acidly. "I'm *trying* to get organised for the TEPs!" He looked dismissively at Eyre's arm, obviously expecting it to be nothing of significance, then did a double take and leaned over closely.

"What is this?" he said slowly. "A black Inguz? I've never seen that before." Sergeant Tottingham also clumped in through the door and joined the intrigued staff, bending over to examine the mark on Eyre's arm.

"Oh, By St Ria," she said, echoing Professor Vela's exasperation, "this is the last thing I need on the first morning of the TEPs."

Another flash in the room signified the arrival of Whittaker Ray, who marched over to Eyre, an intent look on his face. He studied the faint black mark on Eyre's arm and the indistinct Halo across her forehead carefully. Then he turned to the staff, who obviously didn't know what to make of it.

"This is unprecedented in the Academy's history," Whittaker Ray said. "So I'm not sure what the protocol should be in in this instance. But I think that as there is definitely the outline of an Inguz there, we should consider Eyre to have Elevated, therefore eligible for the TEPs."

Eyre's stomach did a somersault, and she tried not to show her elation as she waited for the rest of the staff to reply.

Lord Clarembout spread his hands. "Why not?" he said. "If she can't do well at the TEPs, she won't be accepted to the Academy and then becomes someone else's problem." Eyre winced. Support of a kind, but a little too frank for comfort.

"I'm for her doing the TEPs," Madame Overmantle said. "She has demonstrated some inexplicable skills these past weeks that could be related to Viq. Let's give her the chance."

Dr Botolfe looked at Eyre coldly. "Well, personally, I haven't seen any evidence of any skills whatsoever," she said, "other than rather good self-promotion skills. But I'm prepared to give her a chance to show she can actually do something."

Sergeant Tottingham was pragmatic. "I just want to get back to the TEPs," she said. "One more student in the mix won't make a difference, but waiting around here for hours will. Let her join in."

Professor Vela looked at Eyre with the dislike she had become accustomed to. "Fine by me," he said shortly, and Eyre realised that he thought she was going to fail spectacularly and therefore was not worth worrying about.

"Ranger Chrysanthe?" Whittaker Ray asked, and Eyre was surprised he was being consulted. She knew he was on the staff at the Academy, but she had become more used to him being a pilot and a general administrator than anything else. He turned his strange purple eyes towards Eyre, his wild hair with the metallic whirring beetles shining bright green under the light.

"She absolutely has to join the TEPs," he said with conviction. "It's incontrovertible."

While Eyre tried to figure out what *incontrovertible* meant, the final member of staff, UDi, studied Eyre with an unreadable look in his eye. "We'll be sorry you won't be joining us, Eyre," was all he said, and Eyre felt an unexpected wistfulness as she looked into his kind brown eyes.

Did this mean she was *in*? Her heart leaping, scarcely daring to hope, she waited for confirmation.

Whittaker Ray looked at the rest of the staff and then back at Eyre. "Take your bags back up to your lodge," he said quietly. "You have a lot to think about and prepare for. If you have any questions I'm sure the staff members will be happy to help you."

Eyre felt a joy rise within her, an unbelievable sense of relief coursing through her, and she picked up her bag quickly, before they could change their minds. She wasn't leaving after all! She was staying! And doing the TEPs! A fierce determination to do well seized her.

"Thank you so much!" she said to the staff. "I will try to make the most of this opportunity."

She headed out the door with as much restraint as she could muster, but once she was outside she careered wildly along the path to Water Lodge, happiness soaring through her. She thundered up the stairs and threw her bag down, unpacking it into her locker in milliseconds. Then she changed into her Lightworker uniform as quickly as she could.

When she looked up, she could see the few students who were still on the top floor of the Lodge looking at her with their mouths open. Iris Goff, one of Saskia Anderson's friends, and obviously just out of the shower, towelled her hair as she wandered over. She looked at Eyre, bewildered.

"I thought you were going home?" she said. "Why are you still here?"

Eyre felt a momentary awkwardness. She had an Inguz, but it wasn't exactly a real one, or at least one like everyone else's. What should she say? That she'd Elevated after all?

"Well, I got an Inguz this morning," she eventually said. "So the staff have decided I can stay." She tried not to show her Inguz to Iris, but Iris came around, looking at it in bafflement.

"That is such a strange looking Inguz," she said bluntly. "I can hardly see it." She looked at Eyre's forehead, squinting. "Or your Halo, for that matter. I'm surprised the staff let you stay, actually."

Other students came over, too, bending closer to examine the symbol, and Eyre let them, realising she would have to get used to this. It was a small price to pay for being allowed to stay, she decided. As they crowded around, Eyre laughed. "It's my birthday present I guess."

Carly looked at her. "Today's your birthday? Remembrance Day?"

"Yep, November 11th," Eyre replied. It had always been a mixed day: a day of reflection and poignancy, but also a day she celebrated her birthday. Despite the sombreness, she was proud to be born on such a significant day. The end of hostilities in World War I, way back in 1918.

"Well, Happy Birthday, and congratulations," the good-natured Vaughn Michaelson said, smiling. "Goooooing . . . .up!" The few students around her applauded—Iris somewhat reluctantly—and Eyre felt better. She would be happy whichever way she got into the Academy, even if was via a dodgy Inguz.

Beaming, Eyre raced out of the lodge to try and catch Beatrice before she started the TEP exam.

CHAPTER THIRTY-NINE

EYRE DASHED UP THE stairs of Earth Lodge, past students who looked at her curiously as she headed in such a rush towards Beatrice's bunk. Beatrice had a lower bunk, and Eyre found her, head inside the bottom locker as she put a few things away.

"Beatrice!" she cried, and Beatrice jumped, bumping her head on the shelf inside the locker. She emerged, and Eyre could see the glint of Beatrice's lucky diamond stud in her nose.

"Geez, girl, you didn't need to screech!" she said crossly, rubbing her head. Then it dawned on her that Eyre was still there and wearing the Lightworker uniform.

"You're still here!" she shrieked, stating the obvious, and enveloped Eyre in a huge hug. "What happened? Did Whittaker Ray organise it?"

Eyre showed her the Inguz. "Well, I sort of Elevated," she said. "It's not exactly a normal one, but the staff decided I can stay."

Beatrice smiled widely, looking at Eyre's faintly outlined Inguz and Halo and waving them into insignificance. "I don't care why you're here," she said. "I'm just *so* happy you *are* here! Let's go and find the others. This is fantastic!"

She slammed the locker door shut, and they headed off to find Nick and Abby. They were at the Training Shed, running through some Ferito, Abby's weak point. There were a lot of other students in the shed, too—those that weren't doing their TEPs today—practising a wide range of techniques that required Viq. Eyre was quite glad about this—the sooner everyone found out about her staying and her odd Inguz, the better. Then she wouldn't have to explain it every time she came across someone who had expected her to leave that morning.

Nick and Abby were as happy as Beatrice to see Eyre there, and they raced over to hug her.

"Brilliant!" Abby exclaimed. "You *should* be here. You're so good at Ferito! And I think the Mimir would vacate the premises if you didn't stay!" Everyone chuckled.

Nick looked at her. "What's this I hear about your birthday?" Eyre looked surprised. "Vaughn told me," Nick grinned. "News travels fast around here!"

"Eyre!" Beatrice exclaimed. "You are in for a serious hot chocolate tonight, and a belated celebration when we get back to Highlight!"

Eyre chuckled and indicated her Inguz. "*This* is all I need, I can assure you!"

Other students stopped what they were doing to come and see Eyre. Many of them were peering at the Inguz with mystified looks on their faces, but eventually Nick cried out "Goooing . . . *up!*" and most of the students in the shed applauded enthusiastically. She was part of the group now, and they accepted the staff's decision. A couple of people abstained from the congratulations, Eyre noticed. Unsurprisingly, Ben Perrill stood at the other end of the shed, glowering as he watched her. And a couple of other students ignored her, continuing with their practise. They were obviously the competitive students who were determined to let nothing get in the way of their success.

Beatrice gave her a final hug. "I've got to head to the Lake," she said. "It's almost nine-thirty, oops, sorry, I meant 0930!" Everyone laughed. "Wish me luck!"

A chorus of comments and good wishes followed her as she headed out the shed door towards the lake. Students went back to their practising, and Eyre looked at Nick and Abby.

"I have a little bit to cover in two days," she said, her tone conveying that this was somewhat of an understatement. "Any suggestions where I should start? I don't even know if my Viq works or not. And it's going to be impossible for me to catch up. Some of the students have ten weeks' headstart on me."

Nick looked around the room, thinking. "You know," he said eventually, "none of us know what's going to be in the TEPs, but if I was you, I'd try to at least get a handle on the physical skills. Levitation. Pounding. Lightning. You're already good at Ferito, and you're fit after all that running, so if you can get some of those Viq skills underway, you'll probably be able to manage in the TEPs. It's going to be hard to learn them in such a short time, but if it was me, that's what I'd go for."

Eyre nodded at the sense of this, and Abby added, "After the day training, maybe you can go to the Meditation Hall and see if you can find your telepathy." She beamed, and Nick smiled.

"Abby's really good at it," he said. "She's able to read people from a long way now. For instance, she read Sergeant Tottingham thinking Ben Perrill is a spoiled brat, and that she was glad she zapped his hair off." They all laughed at the memory of Ben with half his hair. So even the staff found him to be a pain, Eyre thought. Hopefully that would mean he wouldn't be back next year.

Nick and Abby left to go and practise. Nick had decided to work on his pounding, and Abby headed off to the Meditation Hall.

Still smarting from Dr Botolfe's suggestion that she was an attention-seeking fraud, Eyre decided to try to levitate. She soon became aware that many eyes were upon her, wondering how she would do, so she decided to go to a more private place to try it out.

She left the Training Shed and decided that she would head to the source of one of her life's most humiliating moments: the Lecture Theatre where Dr Botolfe had called her down to the stage for that outstandingly unspectacular demonstration of Viq. She wasn't sure if the Lecture Theatre would be open or if she was even supposed to be in there, but it would be a good place for privacy, and the front stage had a good-sized area to practise on. She walked along the paths, hardly seeing a soul. The first group of about forty students was out by the lake being instructed on the requirements before they undertook the exam. Many of the remaining students had been in the Training Hall, and a few were in the Common Room as she passed by. There were probably some students in the lodges, too, but there was no one wandering around. The week was too important and every minute was significant, she thought—especially for her.

Eventually she got to the Lecture Theatre and found that fortunately it was unlocked. She entered through the outer door and made her way through the hallway to the empty lecture room. Her feet echoed as she walked across to the centre of the stage, no bodies in the seats to muffle the sound of her footsteps. Standing with her feet slightly apart she had no idea how to begin.

She focussed furiously, looking hard at her feet, but unfortunately remained solidly on the ground. So she concentrated harder, her face scrunching with the effort of trying to generate the levitation force. Again, nothing happened. Then she thought she might try to jump to give it a bit of a head start, so she leaped into the air at the same time as she stared at her feet. She didn't jump particularly high, and she certainly didn't keep going. She thumped heavily back down on the floor, the sound echoing through the room as if the lecture hall was laughing at her. The only thing she was close to achieving was a migraine, she thought, discouraged.

She decided to skip levitation for a while and try some telekinesis. She took off her boot and put it on the ground a little way from her. She sat down and focussed hard on the boot, trying to make it move across the floor. Suddenly to her horror a wisp of smoke started to rise from the leather, and she jumped up, stamping it out ferociously. Just what she needed, setting the fire alarms off! she thought, waving her hands wildly to dispel the smoke. But she was elated that she had managed to perform pyrokinesis – her first ever Viq force! Encouraged, she sat back down and tried to focus her mind in a different way, in less of a fine point, trying to widen the spectrum of her focus and she pushed *hard.* The boot moved a millimetre along the ground, and she clapped her hands in startled delight. Instantly a beam of light shot out from between her palms, ricocheted across the room, and rebounded towards her. She ducked, and it hit the metal stand of the blackboard before slicing upwards and hitting the pink crystal on the podium. A bright light streamed from the top of the crystal, and the hologram of the students performing telekinesis and levitation started to display above the stage, the sound blaring loudly through the auditorium.

Argh! thought Eyre, jumping up and racing over to the podium. *This* was not keeping a low profile at all! She prodded and pushed the pink crystal until suddenly, thankfully, there was a quiet zap and the hologram disappeared again. Eyre's heart was racing. Not exactly the way to remain under the radar.

Suddenly she heard footsteps and quiet voices outside the hallway. In a panic, she jumped behind the podium, concealing herself in the storage gap underneath it. She sat there hoping the people were going to continue on down the hall, but with a start of alarm she saw two things simultaneously: the door starting to open and her boot sitting in the middle of the stage. Without thinking, she sent a wave of force outwards towards the boot, *pulling* it back towards her, and it shot backwards across the stage into her lap. She was so shocked it was all she could do to not shout out in surprise. She scrunched herself into a ball and tried to remain as still as possible as she heard the footsteps of two people walk inside and sit down in seats in the front row.

"Do you have it?" came a voice, and Eyre realised in great surprise that it was Professor Vela. Wasn't he supposed to be down by the Lake? If she had been worried before, now she was terrified. If he found her here, he would send her home with a snap of his fingers.

Someone else replied. "Here," he said, as obviously something exchanged hands, and Eyre realised with a start of shocked horror that it was Ben

Perrill speaking. Then there was a shuffling and the slap of something metallic on a desk.

"Right," Mandig Vela said. "Read this. You get five minutes, then I'm out of here. And I never saw you."

Realising that she was in a very precarious position Eyre sat stone still. Whatever Professor Vela and Perrill were up to, it was obviously not good, and if they discovered her here she knew she would be in terrible trouble—if not danger. Suddenly she heard feet hit the ground as someone stood up. Professor Vela spoke, his voice alert.

"Wait!" he said curtly. "There's someone here." Eyre's stomach dropped sickeningly, and she considered running out of the Hall, but knew she wouldn't get two paces before either of them stopped her in her tracks. She heard Professor Vela walking deliberately up the stairs to the top of the Lecture Theatre, searching for the hidden intruder, and Eyre closed her eyes and started to concentrate as hard as she ever had in her life. She forced her mind to close down her senses and put up mental barriers to any thoughts intruding—inwardly or outwardly. As if it was a matter of life or death, her body responded, falling into a mesmerising quietness, her breathing slow, a wall of energy surrounding her body.

It seemed from a far distance that she could hear Professor Vela thundering down the stairs and towards the stage. Holding her courage and her will, she continued to focus, breathing out, breathing in, eyes shut and clearing her mind of anything but blocking the outside world. She felt rather than heard Professor Vela cross the stage and come to the back of the podium, examining it intently, then he moved on to the other side of the stage, looking behind the blackboard for the concealed trespasser. Finally, seeing that no one was there, he walked slowly back to join Ben Perrill in the front row.

"I must have imagined it," Professor Vela said, sounding unconvinced. "Perhaps it was the remnants of Viq from the last lecture. Anyway, you've had long enough to look at that." Eyre could hear him pick something up, and the soft jangle of buckles as it was presumably put away in a bag. Then, without another word, both people exited the Lecture Theatre.

Eyre remained unmoving, still concentrating, maintaining her pose, which was just as well, because a couple of minutes later the door opened again. She was aware of someone standing there for a long moment, then the door closed again, and whoever it was—Professor Vela, no doubt—walked away down the hallway.

Only then did Eyre relax her mental control, exhaling as if in pain. She felt like she was putting down a huge weight, and her body crumpled into a heap on the floor as she lay there, unmoving, trying to recover from the huge amount of energy she had expelled. In amongst her aching recovery she felt an incredible amazement. Professor Vela had not been able to see her! She had used her Viq to disappear somehow; he hadn't been able to detect her underneath the podium. Something within her knew that this had saved her from a terrible disaster. Whatever Professor Vela and Ben Ferrill had been up to it was definitely no good to be hiding here while they were transacting their business. She shuddered to think what might have happened if she'd been discovered.

Eventually she managed to stand up, the fear dissipating, and she felt a growing jubilation begin to take over. She had used pyrokinesis *and* telekinesis! As well as—what was the term for disappearing?—masking? It was meant to take a long time to master that skill; no doubt her desire to stay alive had helped with her motivation, she thought wryly as she pulled her boot back on. Her success gave her new determination, and she began anew trying to levitate.

After about half an hour, she realised that she had been raising enough energy in her previous trials, but she hadn't been sending it in the right direction, so it had dissipated outwards, achieving nothing. When she trained her mind to focus the energy in the right place, that was when Viq was able to achieve something. So with levitation she had to send the energy beneath her feet in a strong force, so it would rebound back upwards, effectively *pushing* her up into the air. The difficulty with it was maintaining a steady force; if her aim was off, it would shoot Eyre off sideways in the wrong direction or flip her completely over.

Now that she knew she was actually able to accomplish something and wouldn't just be standing there in the middle of the room like a useless ornament, she decided that the Training Shed, with its soft mats to land on, would be a better place to practise. Picking herself up off the ground, she decided to head in to lunch and go to the Training Shed afterwards.

She left the Lecture Theatre, closing the door quietly behind her and heading down the hallway. As she rounded the corner, her heart nearly stopped, because standing out the front of the building, waiting intently like a Rottweiler, was Professor Vela. Eyre could see him through the small side window, pacing back and forward, watching the exit door with his mean little eyes. Fortunately he hadn't seen her yet. She stopped and flattened against the wall, not sure what to do, but knowing that she would wait here for two days if she had to, to avoid being seen by him.

Suddenly Professor Vela turned towards the Lake and appeared to make a decision. He took a last look at the exit door then strode off down the path.

leading to the Lake. Eyre exhaled, her heart pounding, and after a moment left the building.

She found Nick and Abby already at the Refectory, sitting at their usual table down the back of the room. The Refectory was buzzing; the knowledge that the first group of them were in the trials was the topic of everyone's conversation. How were they doing? What were they doing? When would they be back? The last question was answered when the door opened and the first of Beatrice's group, Rigmar, came through, dishevelled and weary, wiping his face. All conversation stopped as everyone looked at him, and he smiled wryly at the expectant group.

"All I can tell you is that line dancing with the Gothak was a real hoot," he said in a serious tone. Everyone erupted in laughter, and he smiled. Other students from the examination group crowded in behind him, and they all headed to the food line, hurrying before the next session of their trial began. Beatrice eventually appeared, too, and once she selected her lunch, she raced down to sit with them.

"*B... T... L...* guys!" she said, rolling her eyes. "That is all I can say." She ate fast, cramming the food in. "Professor Vela apparently takes the next session, the mental challenge. Two more hours of hell," she added gloomily. Eyre realised that that was why Professor Vela had not been at the Lake that morning—he wasn't required until the afternoon session. Obviously Sergeant Tottingham was the supervisor for the morning physical test.

"Well, I hope you did well, Beatrice," Eyre said. "And at least in a short while it will be all over for you, one way or another."

"Yes," Abby said. "I've got to wait all week. It's going to be hell!"

"Are we allowed to talk about the tests between us after we've all taken them?" asked Nick.

"Yes," said Beatrice, "but only after everyone has finished. It's the same rule for the TACIs in the coming years. And logically, why would you anyway? If you talk about it with other people, it gives them an advantage and will affect your own chances. Or it might help someone get a place who doesn't deserve it. They're very strict about it, and if you get caught you're automatically expelled."

Her explanation was interrupted when the door suddenly opened, and Professor Vela entered the Refectory. There was instant silence as everyone looked at him.

"Those students doing their TEPs today, please be ready at the Lake this afternoon at 1300 for the instructions on the mental challenge, which will begin at exactly 1330. I will not be repeating instructions for anyone who is late." He turned to go but suddenly he raised his head as if sniffing the air, then slowly turned around to stare at Eyre. He stopped in his tracks and an instant of recognition and understanding crossed his face, followed by a blinding anger. But it was over so quickly, Eyre realised that no one other than herself would have noticed it. How could he tell it had been her in the Hall? she wondered. Perhaps there were traces of Viq that gave her away. Whatever it was, she realised that she was going to have to be very careful around Professor Vela from now on.

They all finished lunch and wished Beatrice luck as she headed off to the second half of the TEPs. She seemed nervous, and Eyre understood completely. So much rested on this one day.

Nick and Abby decided to head to the Meditation Halls so Nick could practise telepathy with Abby, and Eyre walked to the Training Shed on her own. She felt a bit awkward entering the shed as she knew students would be watching her, wondering how she would go. She had realised at lunch that a lot of them were taking surreptitious looks at her arm and her forehead and there was a lot of curiosity about her. Eyre knew some were even discussing whether she should actually be here. Pretending she didn't notice their gazes, she headed to the far corner of the shed, and to calm her nerves went through the three Clasis of Ferito to warm up. She decided to get a training suit out of the locker and practise lightning skills, as she hadn't tried that yet. The last time she had been in the barrier in her heavy training suit, she had been sweating it out like a stout, reluctant participant at a health spa. She put the suit on, lowered the barrier, and tried to use her Viq to send out a lightning bolt. It took some practise. Once again it was a case of channelling the energy in the right way. Too wide a focus and the energy just fanned out in a soft cloud of light; too narrow and it cut like a laser through the air—lethal, but too fine, which made it difficult to be effective.

Then there was the delivery. To make a good lightning bolt, the energy had to be sent out like a pulse rather than a steady stream. A constant force of Viq created a light beam; pulsating the energy in a strong blast followed by a tapering off caused a zap and an explosion that resulted in a lightning bolt. It was fascinating; now that Eyre understood the use of the mind to focus the direction and the force of Viq and how that would change the outcome, she tried to switch back and forth from light beam to lightning bolt, but it was difficult and she couldn't do it very well. The magnitude of the lightning bolt was the amount of energy it contained, and the intensity was the speed at which it struck—so a higher intensity meant more strikes per minute. The way she held her hand mattered, too, as did the direction the hand was pointing. She could see that learning to control these aspects of the skill would take years to perfect. But despite the fact she wasn't doing amazingly well at it, after being able to do *nothing* for weeks she was happy enough sending off wild bolts of lightning in all directions—at least she knew she could create them.

She realised that now the other students could see her performing Viq skills, even if not particularly well, their interest died off, and they returned to their own practising. It was a relief not to be the focus of so much attention. She decided that she would practise pounding next, and was just about to raise the barrier, when a zap of lightning skimmed past her face. Surprised, she looked at her hands. She hadn't done that; she didn't think so, anyway. Where had it come from? Just then, there was another flash, and this time the lightning bolt actually hit her hard on the arm. If it wasn't for the suit, her arm would have been burned to a crisp, but even so, it hurt quite a bit, and she knew she would have a bruise there the following day. She looked around wildly, trying to figure out what was going on, when another lightning bolt, and another, filled the barrier, bouncing off the shield and back onto her.

Eyre tried desperately to raise the barrier, but it seemed that it was stuck, and she was trapped inside the protective shield while searing bolts of energy struck again and again at her suit, knocking her to the floor. She was screaming in panic, but no one could hear her through the barrier, and the bolts increased in magnitude and intensity. Some of them were so strong they seared the suit she was in, despite the fact it was meant to protect students from the lightning strikes, and smoke started to fill the barrier as her suit caught fire. She stood up and started pounding on the barrier, coughing as the smoke filled her lungs.

Finally, the student next to her noticed the smoke coming out of the barrier and raised the alarm. As he shouted out for help, everyone came rushing over. Eyre could see their mouths open as they saw the sheets of lightning bolts raining down on her.

"Out of my way!" roared Sergeant Tottingham, and she charged through the crowd of students with one of her Antaraks raised. In one strong blow she cut the barrier down the side, splitting it open so Eyre could tumble out. The strong smell of smoke filled the air, and the lightning bolts sparked off in all directions, whizzing around the room and rebounding off metal objects in lethal tangents. Students ducked for cover and swore as they raced in all directions, trying to avoid the violent energy. Sergeant Tottingham raised her hands, performing shielding manoeuvres until all the students were safely under a protective light shield as the lightning bolts zapped and bounced above them.

Finally the lightning bolts stopped as suddenly as they had begun. Sergeant Tottingham knelt down to look at Eyre. She was face down, with her hands covering her head protectively, but once she realised the strikes had stopped, she sat up slowly. Her face was black with soot, and her suit was burnt badly, with several holes right through to her skin.

"You were lucky," Sergeant Tottingham said, although Eyre didn't feel particularly lucky. She just felt incredibly sore. "That was a lightning sheet. They are uncommon, and it's unusual for a student to create one." I didn't, Eyre thought, without a doubt in her mind. Sergeant Tottingham continued, "Once they get going, it's very hard to stop them. They can be lethal." She helped Eyre to her feet, and Eyre took off her training suit, which was almost completely burnt. She felt like she had been in a ring with a heavyweight boxer, every muscle bashed and bruised. Eyre moved her arms around painfully, trying to gauge the damage.

"Do you want to go across and see Leema?" Sergeant Tottingham asked, and Eyre shook her head. "No," she answered, "I might go and hang out in the therapeutic pools for a bit. I'm sure that will help."

She headed slowly towards the exit as the other students went back to practising. There was a subdued feel in the room; that had been a fearsome event. As Eyre left the Training Shed, she saw Ben Perrill looking over at her triumphantly, wearing a loathsome smirk. Somehow Eyre knew that he had something to do with it or knew something about it; his hateful face was too knowing and too exultant. She lifted her chin and looked him in the eye, raising her hand suddenly. She had the satisfaction of seeing him duck, even though in reality she knew she couldn't raise another bit of Viq if her life depended on it.

Eyre sat in an emerald green pool with her eyes closed, savouring the feel of the warm water bubbling around her. The crystals at her back vibrated, massaging her tender muscles, and she felt her body loosening up. It had been a violent episode, and she was still shaky from it. She had feared for her life, and the feeling of being trapped in the barrier had been terrifying. One thing was certain: she had not caused that lightning sheet herself. Someone with much greater skills than a student had generated the force that caused the wild storm of energy. Ben Perrill obviously knew something about it, but she doubted he had the skills to create something like that. It was unsettling and frightening to think that someone out there obviously wanted her dead.

A few other students joined her as time went on, and eventually the whole contingent from the Monday TEPs was in the pools, groaning in ecstasy as they entered the water. It was very evident that the test was extremely difficult both physically and mentally. All the students from the examinations looked exhausted and sore. At least they were finished, though, Eyre thought enviously. It would be great to be done with it all and have the pressure over with.

Beatrice arrived after a while and joined her, too, sighing blissfully as she entered the water. "This has got to be the best feeling I have ever had in my life," she said, lying back in the sparkling green water. "By the Light, that feels good." She rested against the gleaming crystal formations lining the pond. "How are you, Eyre?" she said. "I heard there was some drama at the shed this afternoon."

Eyre nodded slowly. "I had a first-hand demonstration of the potency of Viq energy," she said. "It was pretty frightening."

"I think the idea of using Viq is that you aim it at your foes, not yourself." Beatrice laughed.

Exactly, Eyre thought. So who is regarding me as their foe? She certainly had two people in mind. But she laughed with Beatrice; for some reason she had decided to keep her experience in the Lecture Theatre to herself.

Thankfully the water flowing around her calmed her intense thoughts and eventually she relaxed, enjoying the feeling of the warmth on her muscles. The green water seemed to pull the pain and fear from her body and she sat on the emerald ledge for a long time, letting the therapeutic pools do what they were designed to do.

CHAPTER FORTY

THE NEXT MORNING EYRE awoke feeling refreshed and more positive. Whatever had happened the day before, it was over with, and she stretched her limbs, working through the stiffness. She ran the track twice, flying around the course with little difficulty, feeling better with every step as she breathed in the fresh morning air. The effects of the lightning sheet had gone, no doubt helped by the long soak in the therapeutic pools, and she headed to breakfast with her friends, feeling a new determination to learn as much as she could in this final day before her TEPs.

Beatrice was in joyous spirits, elated to be finished with it all.

"I'm going to read in the Common Room for the next four days!" she announced happily. "What a relief to be finished! Sorry, guys," she added as she saw their wistful faces.

"Ah, it's not long for us, either," Abby said. "You've earned your time off. Enjoy it!"

They cleared away their dishes and headed outside. Eyre hadn't managed to work on her pounding yet, and Nick agreed to meet her at the Training Shed in half an hour to try to help her learn the basics of the technique. But thirty of the Water Lodge students—Carly, Warrigal, and Fheria amongst them—were doing their TEPs today with the remaining ten students from Earth Lodge, and Eyre wanted to see them off, so she hurried along the path to her lodge. The TEP contenders were all gathered on the bottom floor, talking in a hubbub of nervous energy, and Eyre wished them luck before she headed over to the Training Shed. She felt very glad she was in the group tomorrow; she could use every bit of time available to her today to try and work through some of the skills she was going to need.

Nick had learned to pound quite effectively over the ten weeks, and they stood down the back of the Training Shed so he could demonstrate the technique, stomping his foot hard and creating a strong wave of energy that radiated outwards. Eyre watched his movements carefully, trying to follow what he was doing.

Now that she better understood Viq, she knew that she had to aim a blast of force downwards as she stamped on the ground, and she tried to copy Nick's technique. Unfortunately she wasn't able to generate much energy at all, and it barely caused a ripple. Nick was patient and showed her again, creating such a wave of force that he knocked her over. Apologising, he helped her up.

"No, don't apologise!" Eyre said. "Do it again! I need to learn how to do it, and also how to skim it."

Nick stomped again, hard, and a huge wave hit Eyre in the ankles, unbalancing her again. This time she did a complete somersault, landing on her front, winded. Gasping like a fish, she struggled to breathe.

"That is so difficult!" she gasped, standing up again.

"You try," Nick said, and Eyre tried again to pound enough energy across to him. Focussing as hard as she could, she sent a wave downwards as she stomped. This time she managed to send a small force of energy, a wavelet really, she thought in embarrassment, which Nick skimmed easily, only a few centimetres off the ground.

"Sorry, Nick," she said, "this isn't much of a challenge for you."

Nick smiled. "No, keep trying," he said. "It's good practise for me, too. Every bit helps." So Eyre pounded and pounded and eventually got a stronger wave to travel across to Nick. He counter-pounded and sent it crashing back towards Eyre, and once again she landed on her rear end. Ruefully she got up.

"I'm very glad there are mats on the ground," she said. "Saves my body a bit of pain!"

They practised for an hour, and Eyre managed to get the rudiments of the three techniques—pounding, skimming (she only managed a few seconds before she fell off), and counter-pounding. But she hadn't expected to master the technique, and by lunchtime she was happy that at least she understood the concept and was able to perform it in a basic way. She felt quite satisfied with how she'd done as they walked to the Refectory.

The rest of the day was spent practising all the Viq techniques and running through Ferito again and again. Eventually Eyre was happy enough to take a break, so she wandered over to the Common Room to see how Beatrice was doing. Beatrice was curled up on a soft old couch reading something on her Felsic, a cup of tea by her side. That will be me in one day's time, Eyre comforted herself as she sat down.

"How's the training going?" Beatrice asked her, sitting up.

"Not too bad," Eyre replied. "I'm about as ready as I can be. There's not too much point in trying anything else now, I think. I need approximately five years to improve, so one more hour isn't really going to do it! I thought I'd finish today by meditating in the Hall. How's your reading going?"

Beatrice turned her Felsic around so Eyre could read the title: *A Beginner's Guide to Aura Physics and Forces*.

"Just a bit of light reading?" Eyre said, and Beatrice smiled.

"I found it on the recommended reading list. It looked interesting, and it is, actually. I'm learning quite a bit."

"Well, I'm heading off to meditate," Eyre said. "I'll try not to let thoughts of Aura Physics intrude on my focus!"

Eyre found Abby at the Meditation Hall—it was obviously a place where Abby felt at peace. Eyre was startled to see her sitting facing Simmons, about six metres apart, but obviously involved in some sort of communication. As Abby noticed Eyre, she turned and looked at her, and suddenly Eyre could hear her in her head.

"We're communicating telepathically," Abby explained in her weird telepathic voice. "I'm getting better at it with Simmons' help!"

"Good for you," Eyre sent back, more as a joke really, not actually expecting Abby to "hear" her. But Abby put her thumb up, and Eyre realised that she had indeed got the message. It was very impressive, she thought, for Abby to be this good so quickly. Obviously one of her talents.

Eyre sat alone and closed her eyes. She was here really just to relax and to finish off what had been a very intense week. She felt herself slip easily into the zone—it was getting easier each time she did it. Clearing her mind of all thoughts, she felt the familiar peace and strength course through her, a zinging of energy that was at the same time relaxing and energizing.

Suddenly she heard Abby gasp—jarring into Eyre's mind. She opened her eyes and realised that she was floating a metre off the floor. As she looked around in surprise, her concentration was broken, and she fell with a resounding thump back on the floor, wincing as it jarred every bone in her body.

"Wow, Eyre," Abby whispered mentally, "that was pretty cool!"

Eyre rubbed her back but gave Abby a telepathic smile, and sat again in the cross-legged position. She focussed again on relaxing and once again slipped into the serene zone of meditation. This time she kept her mind on staying down on the ground and was relieved to find that she could relax and stay at a normal altitude. It was relaxing and refreshing, and when she opened her eyes after half an hour, she felt wonderful.

Abby walked with her out of the Meditation Hall, and they agreed to meet for dinner, heading off to their individual lodges. Eyre was feeling anxious for Wednesday to arrive. She wanted to get the examinations over with—whatever the outcome.

That night she lay in bed, finding it hard to go to sleep as she contemplated the challenges that lay ahead of her the next day. But a sudden thought intruded.

"Go to sleep, Eyre," Abby said from a long way away in her own bunk. "Count some sheep or something. You'll need your energy tomorrow!"

"I'm going to have to work on those mental barriers," Eyre replied telepathically, chuckling out loud. Then she transmitted, "You're getting too good at this!"

Despite Abby's advice, Eyre lay awake for a long time, unable to stop worrying about the exam in the morning. She'd only had two days of practise with her Viq force, and she knew it was going to matter tomorrow.

CHAPTER FORTY-ONE

THE MORNING OF THE TEPs dawned sluggishly. Thin streaks of clouds veined the sky, sending shadows across the morning and indicating a change was coming. The air was cool, and Eyre could see gusts of wind chopping the water on the lake. It was a surprise to see the weather changing. It had been so clear and perfect for most of the weeks since they had arrived, and Eyre had gotten used to it.

She dressed quickly and headed down to the Refectory, eating her breakfast in record time.

Nick smiled at her as she stood up to go. "Good luck, Eyre," he said. "I hope you get through it okay."

"Me, too," Abby said in Eyre's head, and Eyre slapped her softly on the arm.

"*Would* you stop doing that?" she exclaimed, laughing.

"Well, you've got to be telepathic to receive the message, too, Eyre, so consider it a form of practise." Abby chuckled.

Beatrice was looking rested and happy—obviously feeling okay about how she did in her examination on Monday. Eyre wasn't so sure of her own chances. But putting a bright, confident smile on her face, she said farewell to them and left early.

Rather than run the course this morning—Eyre figured she'd be getting enough exercise in a couple of hours—she had decided to go to the Meditation Hall and try to get her mind in the right place. She realised that the mind was the key to all the skills; controlling Viq well was a result of focussing your thoughts in the right way, and she wanted to make sure her head was clear.

Eyre soaked up the serenity of the translucent blue hall for half an hour, then decided to head over to the Lake. There was no point putting it off any longer; she might as well go and have a look. When she got there she realised that others had the same idea—there were about twenty people already there, milling around, looking out over the water and up the running track, wondering what the physical challenge would entail. Sergeant Tottingham was also there already, of course, waiting in her stolid way for everyone else to arrive.

Eyre mingled with the other nervous students, when she suddenly became aware of a presence beside her. Ben Perrill smirked at her, looking at her indistinct Inguz with a look of derision.

"Surprised you're here, Lightward," he said. "What did you do, draw that on with a pencil?" Eyre opened her mouth to retort, but he had already moved on, snickering. Determined not to let him bother her, Eyre kept her meditation lesson in mind and focussed on keeping calm in preparation for the TEPs.

At a quarter to ten precisely, Sergeant Tottingham stepped forward and asked everyone to get into lines numerically, and then she went along and divided the students into four groups. Four people had ended up as Unlit in the students numbered 81 to 120, so there were thirty-six students eligible to undertake the TEPs that day. Eyre was in the first group of nine and she stood beside Jax, Tec Langford, and Georgia Mahoney as they waited for instructions.

Sergeant Tottingham thumped her staff on the ground. "Right, here we go!" she said. "I'm only going to say this once, so listen carefully. No one is to speak until the TEPs start, unless you have a question, in which case you will raise your hand. No muttering under your breath or gossiping with your neighbour," she added, looking pointedly at Ben Perrill. Surprisingly, he looked back at her belligerently, obviously not too concerned about upsetting her. Some people were slow learners, Eyre thought.

A movement from behind caught her attention, and she turned around, only to be faced with a most unusual sight. Ranger Chrysanthe sailed merrily in, two metres above the ground, sitting cross-legged at the front of a faded black and gold striped carpet. The carpet was quite large, but Ranger Chrysanthe weaved it through the air as smoothly as a manta ray through water. A little disconcertingly, today he wore an oilskin coat and hat— obviously prepared for inclement weather, Eyre thought dismally.

Most bizarre of all, however, were the four incongruous-looking chairs, which were placed two on each side of the carpet. One was a battered old leather easy chair; one was a black and chrome director's chair; there was a floral linen stuffed wing chair; and the final chair had a red leather seat and was ornately carved and high-backed, resembling a throne. Eyre watched the odd collection of furniture, like escapees from a charity shop's warehouse, glide through the air under Ranger Chrysanthe's guidance until he settled the carpet gently on the ground beside the students. Silence thundered through the watching students. If a question mark could be visible, it would have been floating above their heads.

"Good morning, students!" boomed a familiar voice, as Lord Clarembout marched through the crowd with Dr Botolfe, Madame Overmantle, and UD1. The students, largely speechless, were slow to reply, so there were only a few return greetings as the four lecturers headed towards the carpet.

Dr Botolfe walked onto the carpet and sat in the director's chair; Madame Overmantle settled herself with a happy sigh into the floral wing chair; UD1 moved smoothly to take the leather easy chair; and Lord Clarembout, of course, sat on the wooden throne. Ranger Chrysanthe beamed at the students, and the carpet rose up into the air, hovering about a metre above their heads.

"The lecturers will be your examination panel today," Sergeant Tottingham explained. "They will be following you closely and grading you according to how you perform. Success at the individual tasks is not the only thing they will be marking. Teamwork is important. Speed and problem solving also count in your assessment. They will be close by you at all times, so please consider that when you are undertaking your exam."

Suddenly the floating carpet and all its occupants disappeared.

"So you are not distracted by their presence, however," Sergeant Tottingham added, "they will be masked the whole time."

"Now as to the logistics for today. When I give the signal—" she thumped her staff to demonstrate, "—you will perform a series of skills. The ultimate aim is to hit the bullseye, which signifies the end of your physical challenge. Finding where the bullseye is, and how you get there, is the basis of the challenge. I will give you some simple instructions, but it is up to you to work out how to complete the challenge. One word of caution: don't touch the wildlife.

"Your groups will be sent off at ten minute intervals, and you have two hours to complete the challenge. At the end of your two hours, the staff will send you back here whether you have finished the challenge or not.

"To start the physical challenge you are to cross the lake and climb the cliffs at the side. Once you reach the top, you will have to work it out on your own. Are there any questions?"

She looked around. Obviously everyone had a million questions, but none they could ask and expect to be answered, so the students were silent.

"In that case, we will begin. First group, off you go, and good luck!" She thumped her staff on the ground beside her.

Eyre looked dubiously at the lake. Cross the lake? She couldn't see a boat, so that left swimming, running around the edge or. . . . Her thoughts stopped as she saw one girl from her lodge, Number 83, a fit-looking intense girl with short brown hair—start to take tentative steps across the lake on top of the water. Yep, of course, Eyre thought drily. Why didn't *I* think of that? Levitation, the obvious choice.

Her name was Vicky, Eyre recalled as the girl made unsteady progress across the top of the water. Others, seeing her success, started to follow her out over the dark lake. Anders Johnson, Number 84, was wobbling along not far out from the shore when he suddenly plunged down into the cold water. Gasping, he splashed around on the surface, trying to pull himself up to walk above the water again. Eventually he was successful and continued his tentative steps across the surface. Eyre wasn't too confident about her levitation skills, but she could see that if she ran around the edge of the Lake, it would take her way too long to get to the cliffs. Already some of the students who were quite good at levitating were halfway there. So she stepped out, focussing her Viq so that her feet hovered about ten centimetres above the surface of the water. It was like walking on Jell-O, hard to keep her balance, but Eyre managed to start moving across the surface of the water. The choppy water was making it hard, interfering with the balance of her levitation energy. Her feet were moving up and down in sync with the surface of the water, and it was difficult to keep moving forward, like being on the deck of a rocking boat. A cockatoo swept past her with a raucous cry. Laughing at me, no doubt, Eyre thought wryly as she struggled across the water.

Despite the difficulty, she was making slow progress, not too far behind the rest of the group, when a sudden force—like a strong gust of wind—knocked her feet from under her, and she dropped like a stone into the blackness of Lake Altum. It was freezing cold in the deep waters, and for a moment she panicked as she realised she couldn't get free of something that was keeping her down under the surface. But then the water roiled and she broke free of the force, kicking upwards desperately. She gasped in shock as her head broke the surface and she took several shuddering breaths. Her nervousness about the lake hurtled like a wild beast through her mind, and she was on the verge of complete panic. But then she grabbed hold of herself mentally and shoved her fear aside, realising that she had to concentrate to get herself back above the water.

Focussing, she tried to *lean* her hands on the top of the water to pull herself up. But every time she did so and managed to get halfway back up, it was like an unseen force pushed her back down into the water, so she was unable, despite her best efforts, to get back out. It was exhausting, fighting the invisible force, so she eventually gave up and started to swim across the lake, following the other students who were walking on top of the water. Finally, gasping for breath after the huge swim, she staggered out of the water through the shallows and stood at the base of the cliffs, her chest heaving painfully.

"Nice technique, 88," Tec Langford said snidely and Eyre, embarrassed by her unimpressive display, flushed red.

"Still early days, Tec," Jax said. "Don't get too proud of yourself just yet." He stood on the bank, hands on his hips, completely dry. It had obviously been no problem for him to walk across the water; he looked like he'd just had a gentle stroll through the park.

Eyre was grateful for his comment. Even if she'd managed to think of a snappy comeback to Tec, at this point she still didn't have enough breath to deliver it. She looked upwards at the towering sandstone cliffs and contemplated how to get up there. She dismissed her first thought of climbing the rock—obviously the physical challenge was to demonstrate how well you could use your Viq to overcome obstacles, not how well you could climb—or, she thought with renewed discomfort, swim. Levitating seemed the obvious answer, but it was a long way up, and if your concentration failed, a long way to fall. Was there a safer way? Or an easier way?

All the students seemed engaged in the same problem-solving concentration, when suddenly Eyre, remembering her time in the Lecture Theatre, thought she had an idea. She looked up the top of the cliff, searching for a likely spot and saw a eucalyptus tree perched on the edge of a flat sandstone rock.

Picking up a branch from the ground, Eyre focussed hard on it and *threw* it with her mind up at the tree. The stick hurtled towards the tree, and holding tightly on to it, Eyre followed at great speed. She landed in an ungainly way on the sandstone rock and wrapped her arms tightly around the smooth white trunk of the tree. Taking a deep breath, she looked apprehensively back over the uneven edge of the cliff. She'd never been too keen on heights, and this was definitely a long way up.

"Telekinesis works!" she shouted down to the other students. "Pick up something and throw it up here—but hang on tight! I'll grab you when you get up!"

As the rest of students hesitated, Vicky, who was obviously a very sporty girl, made up her mind and searched around until she found a sizeable rock. Concentrating hard, she stared at the rock until it suddenly hurtled into the air, pulling the girl behind it rapidly in its trajectory towards the top of the cliff. As she neared the tree, she twisted in the air and landed neatly on her feet in front of Eyre, who pulled her back from the edge.

"Good work," Eyre said. "Let's help the others up." Vicky nodded and stood to the side of Eyre, and together they grabbed each student as they careered over the edge towards them. A couple of students didn't get high enough and had to climb the last few metres, clinging precariously to the rock face before someone could help them over the edge.

Eventually all nine of them had reached the top of the cliff. They dropped their telekinesis objects on the ground and looked around.

"Where to next then?" mused Lindi Jamieson, Number 82, a small girl with dark wavy hair and metal-rimmed glasses. Her telekinesis object had been a worn out sneaker she had obviously found on the banks of the lake, and Eyre gave her ten points for creativity. And she was impressed too: obviously this girl had strong Viq to be able to hurl a sneaker that far.

A sandy track led away from the cliff into the scrubby bush. Vicky shrugged as she considered it. "That way?" There were nods of assent, and feeling more like a team now than adversaries, the group started along the track.

They hadn't gone far when Vicky, who was leading the way, stopped suddenly, almost causing the students behind her to ram into each other. Looking around her, they could see why she had stopped: their way was barred by a huge, dark-grey granite boulder twenty metres wide and three metres high that stretched across the track and into the bush on either side.

Embedded into the granite were nine brass doors. They were all plain with no adornment and exactly the same to look at. Eyre studied the rock. It was obvious—nine doors, nine students—they each had to enter one. But what was on the other side? There was trepidation on quite a few faces, and Eyre laughed, feeling nervous herself.

"Well, here we go, then!" she said. "Pick a door, I guess, and good luck!" Without consultation, they automatically went in numerical order to the doors—81 picked the first door, 82 the second and so on—meaning that Eyre headed for the eighth brass door. It had a simple brass knob that turned easily, and she stepped inside, her heart beating furiously. The door slammed shut loudly behind her, making her jump, and she was instantly in complete darkness.

How to make light? Eyre thought frantically, racking her brains. If she could do bullio, like Nick, she could make light bubbles in the air, which would be perfect, but she hadn't managed to achieve that yet. Thinking hard, she bent down and felt along the ground tentatively (god knows what's on the ground here, she thought fearfully) until she found a few branches of wood. Then, concentrating furiously at the wood, she focussed her Viq in a thin beam, attempting pyrokinesis. At first nothing happened, and she was afraid it would never work. But then with a spark, a bit of the bark caught until finally the end of the branch was alight. She sighed with relief as the glow from the fire enabled her to see. The light didn't extend very far, but she could make out that she was in a long corridor that had been cut through the boulder. Holding the smoking branch before her, she walked slowly through the narrow passage, her eyes skittering backwards and forwards at the shadows.

Her apprehension was justified when suddenly a huge form stepped out in front of her. It had the body of a man, but six muscular arms, two from the shoulders and two below them on each side. His face was fully bearded, with chiselled features, and he wore a copper helmet on his head. He had a leather loincloth around his waist and leather sandals on his feet, and in each of his six massive hands was a weapon. It was a most fearsome sight. Eyre gasped in fear.

"What are you?" she said, stepping backwards, holding the branch in front of her like a pathetic weapon.

"I am Gegenees," thundered the man, grinning at her through his black beard with big strong white teeth. "You will fight me. Pick three weapons." He held out his six hands. Two of them held scythe-like swords, one held an object like a Flail, there was a broadsword similar to a Mnae, one had a Kulbeda-like dagger, and the last had a metal-studded club. Oh my god, thought Eyre. What happened to the lessons on Clasis for *Six*-Handed Fighting?

Eyre looked in bewilderment at the array of weapons in front of her. What would give her the best advantage? Looking at the monster, she thought that she might as well have a toothpick for all the good these were going to do her. Gegenees stood silently while she looked from weapon to weapon, trying to make up her mind. Finally she shrugged and spoke, trying to sound confident as she stuck the burning branch in a crack in the wall of granite. The fire was barely glowing now, but it still emitted enough light to see a little.

"Okay then, my friend, I will take the Flail, the Mnae, and the Kulbeda."

Gegenees passed the weapons to her, and she put the Kulbeda in the waistband of her pants, held the Flail in her right hand and the Mnae in her left. Oddly, Gegenees took up a stance similar to the Clasis and put his hand (his left top hand, that is) up facing her. Mentally rolling her eyes, if that was possible while she was quaking with fear, Eyre moved the Flail to her right hand, holding both the Mnae and Flail, then touched her left palm to his. They shouted out "Tollo!", she seized the Flail with her left hand, and they began.

The giant man circled her, his eyes focussed piercingly on her. She gazed back at him, waiting for any movement. It came soon enough when he drew the two scythe-like weapons and assumed Position 17 from the Clasis for Two-Handed Fighting. But Eyre was ready for this; she had known he would use the Two-Handed Ferito because of the matching weapons, and she was so familiar with the sequence that she automatically defended with Tego Position 4, causing the huge man to step back, unbalanced. He grinned ferociously, then suddenly struck with his club at her legs. But again she was too quick—her hours of practising Ferito were paying off— and she performed Basic Ferito, Tego Position 6, which spun her around past the club and behind Gegenees. Quickly she whirled her Flail around her head and striking fast, ripped the club from his middle left hand. It flew backwards behind her down the corridor, hitting the bronze door with a resounding "Gonggggg. . . ."

"Ha ha ha," boomed Gegenees in his deep voice. "Well struck." But in a second, he had sliced his two scythes together, and her Flail fell to the floor, cut in half and useless.

His big feet circling, he shifted sideways, the blades of the scythes gleaming orange in the fading light of the burning branch. Eyre was feeling desperate, but then suddenly she felt a shimmer of energy shoot from her toes to the top of her head and a burst of clarity in her mind. In one smooth movement she seized her Kulbeda and threw it unerringly at Gegenees's wrist. It hit hard, burrowed deeply into his flesh, and he roared in pain as he dropped one of the scythes on the floor. Instantly his good humour was gone, and he studied her ferociously, his eyes glinting in the light from the dying embers of the branch. As he circled around her, Eyre felt certain that he had until now been toying with her and that her life was about to end.

He moved suddenly. Position 12 from Clasis for Single-Blade Fighting. Eyre deflected the blow with her Mnae, defending herself desperately as he threw Aditus position after position at her. All she could do was block with Tego, being driven further and further backwards up the corridor until her back was against the bronze door. Feeling the club under her foot, she *threw* it at him with her mind, clouting him across the chin—hard.

Enraged, he grabbed the Mnae out of her hand in a movement so quick she didn't even see it coming, leaving her defenceless. Shaking with fear but determined not to go down without a fight, she raised her hands in Basic Ferito, Position Two, snarling at him.

"Come on, then! Fight me!" she shouted. He responded by throwing down his scythe, picking her up bodily with his six arms, and carting her like a sack of potatoes down the long dark corridor. Hammering at him with her fists and shouting loudly, she tried to get him to let her go, but he was so huge and powerful it was impossible to make any impression on him at all. Finally they got to the end of the corridor, and he stopped. It was too dark to see, but there was obviously another door, because she heard him turn the knob and open it. Suddenly her eyes were blinded by the bright light coming in from outside.

Without further comment he tossed her out the door onto the sandy track and disappeared back into the corridor, slamming the door shut. Astonished that she was still alive, Eyre stood up, brushing the sand off herself and looking around. Six grinning faces regarded her from the other bronze doors—obviously they had been thrown out like she had.

"Did you see a Gegenees, too?" she asked Georgia Mahoney, who was sitting on a rock outside the last bronze door next to Eyre's.

"Sure did," Georgia said, chuckling, "I got thrown out the door after about thirty seconds!"

Suddenly the door on the other side of Eyre crashed open, and Tec Langford came sailing out through the air. He landed flat on his face as the door slammed shut behind him. As everyone erupted in laughter, Tec got up, rubbing the sand off his face in annoyance.

Then the first bronze door also banged open, and out came Jax, flying backwards at top speed, two metres above the ground. He landed in a banksia bush on his back and lay there stunned for a moment as he caught his breath. Finally he stood up and gave a huge grin, assuming Position Four of Basic Ferito, balancing on one foot.

"Sure showed him!" he said as everyone laughed uproariously.

Now that the last one of their group had arrived—rather spectacularly, Eyre thought—they started to head down the sandy path again.

It was long and winding, and Eyre was starting to wonder if they should have gone another direction when suddenly something trundled across the path in front of her. Looking at it she realised it was an echidna, but remembering Sergeant Tottingham's advice to not touch the wildlife, she walked around it. It rattled its spikes at her, and someone behind her laughed.

"Scary!" he said, and everyone chuckled. But then another echidna crossed the path, and another, until suddenly there was a whole—what do you call a group of echidnas? Eyre wondered—*herd?* of them crowding through the bushes and lumbering along the track towards them. They all rattled their spikes, and Eyre began to feel a bit uneasy. She'd never seen such a large number of echidnas before—there must have been hundreds—and as one charged towards her ankle, she levitated awkwardly so that the creature passed underneath her. Number 85, a small boy with freckles, wasn't quick enough, and the creature spiked him with one of its spines. Instantly he fell to the ground. Panicking, Eyre moved over above him, trying to avoid the creatures and see what was wrong, but she was dangerously close to the ground. Other students hovered above the track, too, but they were managing better than she was. She moved up and down, unused to levitating, and finding it hard to maintain the height. Finally she found a large sandstone rock and stood on it, away from the crawling creatures on the track.

"God, what happened?" Anders said in a worried tone as he hovered in the air and called down to the immobile boy. "Todd! Are you alright?" He suddenly had his answer as Todd sighed and turned over, snoring loudly.

"By the Light," Georgia laughed nervously. "He's asleep!" A few of the echidnas trundled up the track and curled up next to the boy, snuggling into the warmth of his body.

"What will we do?" asked Lindi, peering down through her glasses.

Jax surveyed the prostrate form beneath him. "Let's pull him up and lie him on a rock. Then if he wakes up he can catch up."

It was a good idea, so gingerly Jax and Anders grabbed an end each, avoiding the spiky creatures. Bobbing up and down from the effort of carrying him while trying to maintain their levitation, they manoeuvred the sleeping boy over to the sandstone rock where Eyre stood.

"Hopefully he'll wake up," Anders said. "What bad luck!"

Glad to have had a rest, Eyre focussed her Viq again and followed the others as they levitated over the horde of echidnas. When the track was clear, they landed back on the sandy ground and continued down the trail as it meandered through the silvery-barked eucalyptus trees. Suddenly it opened out onto a wide expanse of white sand. Sand dunes in the Blue Mountains? Eyre looked at them curiously.

The dunes stretched in a gleaming expanse of drifting mounds, spurts of sand blowing off the edges in the gusts of wind. She could see across to the other side, but left and right the sand stretched out of sight. Too far to walk around in the time they had. Weird, thought Eyre. But then she hadn't exactly expected "normal" for the TEPs.

After the experience with the echidnas, everyone was a little less gung-ho about heading straight on to the stretching white desert. Eyre got a branch and poked gingerly at the gleaming sand, not sure what to expect. As she disturbed the surface, the sand started to move from underneath, and tiny mounds of sand began to poke up everywhere around the branch.

Suddenly she dropped the branch in shock as hundreds of small black forms erupted out of the sand, leaping about a metre in the air, hairy legs scrabbling.

"Oh my god, spiders!" breathed Georgia, appalled. The spiders landed on the sand and rushed over to the branch, winding silken threads around it in seconds, binding it tightly. Eyre stood rooted to the spot, not daring to move. Then the spiders jumped high in the air again and disappeared beneath the sand.

Everyone was looking at each other then back at the sand dunes, unsure how to proceed.

Number 86, a tall good-looking guy with chestnut wavy hair and strong shoulders, bowed deeply to Jax. "After you," he said grandly.

Everyone spluttered with laughter. *This* was an interesting challenge. The clouds had thickened overhead, and drifts of sand were starting to puff up along the edge.

A sudden sound behind them announced the arrival of the second group of students running along the track—obviously they had been quicker and had caught up with Eyre's group. Eyre didn't know any of them except Vaughn Michaelson, 98, but the expressions on the faces of some of the other approaching students showed that they meant business. Obviously competitive, those ones.

"Don't . . ." she exclaimed, beginning to warn them, but three students rushed past, obviously sensing an advantage. ". . . go on the sand," she finished lamely. The students made it ten metres across the dunes before the sand exploded around them. Thousands of black, hairy spiders sprang out of the sand, landing all over the hapless students who shrieked in horror. Unable to help, the other students hesitated on the edge of the track and watched, aghast, as the three students were wrapped up tightly in silken thread within five seconds. Unbalanced, they tipped over and lay on the ground, screeching as the spiders jumped in the air and disappeared under the sand again.

"Get us *out* of here!" shouted Number 95, a red-faced, tall girl.

"Okay," Vaughn called, "give us a sec to work it out."

Everyone looked at each other.

"How about we levitate across to them?" suggested one.

"No, that might not work," Anders replied. "We don't know how high those creatures can go. They still might end up on top of us."

Georgia shuddered.

Eyre thought hard. "Well, I might have an idea." Well, she hoped she did. She didn't want a repeat of Dr Botolfe's disastrous lecture, standing foolishly doing nothing.

Focussing intently, she reached out with her mind to one of the students on the ground and *pulled* him towards her, as she had done with her boot in the Lecture theatre. But this was a heavy load, and perspiration dripped down her face as the hefty boy inched towards her across the sand. As he slid over the dunes, clouds of leaping spiders, like a manic flea circus, jumped in the air around him, trying to find the source of the movement. He eventually ended up on the side of the trail, looking up at them with pathetic eyes.

"I . . . hate . . . spiders," he said feebly.

"Who's good at Light Viq?" Eyre asked, and Jax looked falsely humble.

"I've managed to do it adequately on occasion," he said, and Vaughn groaned, shoving him on the shoulder.

"Oh come on man, get on with it!"

Jax aimed his palm at the unfortunate boy on the ground, and a thin beam of bright light emitted from his hand. It struck the silken threads, and they parted instantly, like cutting open a cocoon. The boy—Number 96, Eyre could now see—tumbled out gratefully and stood up slowly.

"Whoa," he said. "Thank you. That was *not* pleasant!"

The other two students were calling out from the middle of the sand, urging the group to pull them in, too.

"How did you do that?" Jax asked Eyre.

She looked upwards, trying to think of the best way to explain it. "You just sort of *pull* with your mind," she said eventually. "Focus hard on the object and get your mind to *drag* it."

Jax stared intently out at the girl with the loud mouth, who was still issuing instructions from her trussed up position in the middle of the desert, and before long he had managed to start her moving towards him. Eyre wasn't surprised; he seemed to be so naturally good at everything.

"I wish she'd got some of that stuff around her mouth!" muttered Anders, and everyone snickered. Another student, 97—a girl from the second group with a riot of black curls on her head—fiercely concentrated on the third victim, and others joined in until between them they managed to pull him over to the edge, too. Soon all three were free and brushing themselves off.

"Thanks," said the loud girl—Number 95—grudgingly, obviously unused to thanking anyone for anything. She was tall and heavily built with a sour look around her mouth that had made Eyre reluctant to get to know her at the lodge over the past weeks. Appropriately enough, Eyre thought, her name was Belinda Meaney.

Just then there was a ruckus behind them as more students raced along the track. Eyre noticed that amongst them was the boy Todd, Number 85, who had been stuck by the echidna; obviously he had woken up and managed to make it along the trail. The delay at the sand dunes with the jumping spiders had meant that the groups from behind had caught up with them. Eyre was philosophical about it: more people meant more chances for good problem-solving ideas, in her experience. But some of the others were obviously uncomfortable about them all being together, their competitive natures coming out.

"We have to hurry!" Belinda said sharply, confirming Eyre's assessment of her. Obviously she had forgotten already that she had just held the group up for fifteen minutes. "How are we going to get across?"

"Well, I've got an idea," said Vaughn, thinking hard. "What if we divide into our four groups and half of us use their Viq to pound and shield. One group pounds and another shields underneath. The other two groups can then skim across to the other side on the pound waves, while the shielding below the waves stops the spiders from jumping up on to us. Then, when we get to the other side, we'll do it for the other two groups to come across."

"Good idea, but I'm going first," said Belinda unsurprisingly.

"Me, too," said a voice from the back of the group and Eyre saw, with her teeth gritted, that it was Ben Perrill.

"I'm going too," said Tec Langford. "You're not leaving me here while you go across."

"Fine," she said. "I don't think it matters now. We're all together, so let's just get everyone across. I'll stay and shield, I'm not so good at pounding." Or skimming, she thought to herself ruefully. She wasn't sure how *that* was going to go.

It ended up that the groups stayed roughly as they were originally numbered, except that Zanda, Phillip Outray and Robeson Paul stayed, letting Belinda, Tec and Ben go across in the first group.

The group sending the others across split into the areas they thought they were better at. So those who had mastered pounding got together, and the others stood together to do the shielding.

"Okay, on three—" said Vaughn. "One, two, *three!*"

As soon as the countdown finished, everyone focussed hard on his or her allotted task. The pounders created huge waves of energy across the top of the sand dunes, and instantly the shielders focussed, sending a sheet of energy flatly across underneath the pound so that the waves undulated above it. The force of the energy pitted the surface of the sand, causing thousands of the jumping spiders to leap upwards searching for the source of the disturbance. But the leaping spiders were unable to break through the barrier; they hurtled into the shield, bouncing backwards down into the sand and then springing upwards again.

Gritting their teeth in concentration, everyone tried to keep the energy focussed as the other group of students jumped up on top of the pound waves. Some of them—Belinda amongst them, and Perrill, Eyre thought in annoyance—easily skimmed across the waves, riding them smoothly across to the other side. Others—with a talent level similar to Eyre's, she imagined —bumped and slid their way across, skidding sideways, rolling and tumbling across the pound until they eventually landed on the other side, crashing on top of each other.

With relief, everyone released focus and the energy stopped. Agitated spiders were now leaping five metres into the air, thousands of them erupting from the sand in black swarms.

Jax yelled across to the group on the other side. "Okay, do the pound and shield, and bring us across!" The students across the desert, small figures in the distance, picked themselves up off the ground and waved back, grouping into two parts. But as Eyre's group watched, a few people across the sand detached themselves from the larger mass and started to head off.

Peering over, Eyre spluttered. "You've *got* to be kidding me!" she exclaimed. "Some of them are leaving!" Her group looked over and sure enough, about five students had disappeared from the group, taking the advantage and aiming for the lead.

"Well, I hope the magic carpet caught that on Grading-cam!" Zanda muttered in annoyance.

"Except that we don't really know how they mark this," Vicky said gloomily. Eyre had seen that she was competitive, so this was probably quite a blow to her to see the opposition disappearing into the distance. And she might be right: coming first might hold a lot of weight in the grading for the TEPs.

"Well, at least they all didn't go," said Anders in a positive voice. "We'll still get across."

Unfortunately, the group across the sand wasn't as strong as Eyre's group, and she could see that the waves from the pound were a lot weaker than the first group. The energy barely made a mark in the sand, and the shield also seemed to lack strength, as some of the spiders were jumping through it. Everyone looked at each other and grimaced.

"Better get onto it," Jax said grimly. "Their energy is only going to get weaker. This is as good as it's going to get!"

He leapt onto the pound and started to skim along the waves. His balance was effortless, and when Number 86, whose name Eyre had found out was Luke Jordan, joined him, the pair of them looked like a couple of professional surfers, sliding down the waves with easy grace.

Todd sighed enviously. "They make it look so easy!" he said. He clambered up onto the wave awkwardly, then the rest of the group jumped on the pound, and they all made their way across precariously, nobody else doing it with any style at all. They wobbled along, falling down and slipping from side to side. To make it more difficult, the energy surge was wavering, the wave getting closer to the ground, and the shield was losing efficiency, too—with some spiders making it through the barrier and skittering along the top of the pound. Eyre slid on her rear end down a wave perilously close to a spider, and when it jumped towards her she fried it with a huge blast of Viq from her palm. A bit excessive, she thought, but better than the horrid creature landing on top of her. She eventually got to the other side just as the pound lost power completely, and she slid ignominiously facedown as the wave died, skidding on her stomach to land at Jax's feet. She stood up, brushing herself off and laughed merrily, looking back at the swarm of jumping spiders with a wide smile.

"I don't care how I got here. I am just *so* glad I made it!"

The large group of students stood together, discussing their next direction and decided to follow the existing track again. Ahead of them the sand dunes gave way to a stretch of grass that eventually became a stand of twisted trees, getting denser and denser and heading back upwards to the exposed cliff edge. The wind was picking up, and the sky was now grey with towering clouds. Eyre could feel the change in pressure and the coolness of the wind that was whipping up from the lake. She felt a sudden chill as the sun disappeared behind a cloud for an instant.

The change in weather was also causing a change in mood. The laughter was giving way to a dark concentration, and Eyre realised that they had used up half their time. Her thoughts were echoed in the faces of the other students, and they hurried along, moving faster than they had before. Eyre didn't know how much of the challenge lay before them, but one thing was for certain: there wasn't a bullseye in sight yet. They obviously had a bit of ground still to cover.

Footsteps in the dirt on the track showed that the other students were ahead of them, and she ground her teeth in annoyance. They certainly had been played by that lot, she thought.

They walked through the gnarled forest at the top of the cliff as the wind began to howl through the branches, whipping the leaves wildly. No wonder the trees were bent and twisted, Eyre thought; they were obviously continually battered by the harsh weather. It was eerie and unnerving, and she hurried along, keen to get through it. She had a sense of being watched, which she probably was, and constantly jumped at shadows caused by the low scudding clouds.

As they headed back down the track, they heard a terrible ruckus coming from somewhere out of sight, loud shouting and explosions of sound. Instantly they began to run, tearing down the rocky path towards the commotion. They turned the corner, and Eyre screeched to a stop, her eyes round in surprise.

Up ahead was a flat expanse of rock, open and exposed to the elements with not a tree in sight. In the middle of the area was a shining metal pole about a metre thick and stretching upwards ten metres to a small, square platform. A dozen huge warriors wearing plated armour stood on guard around the metal pole, silent and unmoving, and as the students approached the warriors turned as one and stood silently facing them.

Adding to the strange scene, Eyre could see a cage made entirely of light beams shining brightly on the ground at the edge of the clearing. In it were five huddled forms—no doubt the students who had deserted them. With a sense of satisfaction, she remembered that Ben Perrill was amongst them, and she loved the thought of him being caged like the beast he was. Karma.

As the five students in the cage saw the approaching group, they stood up and called desperately for help, bashing sticks against the side of the energised bars. Each time they touched the bars the wood burnt and blew up with a loud clap of thunder. This obviously was the source of the disturbance the group had heard as they came down the track, but this time the cries of the imprisoned students were ignored. No one felt any guilt at all about leaving them in their cramped enclosure.

They approached the battalion of silent giants carefully. The creatures were huge of physique, with massive muscles, bright red leathery skin, and black dreadlocks that fell past their shoulders. They had big, wide, lipless mouths; each with a long black moustache that draped on either side of their face down to their chest. Their eyes were completely black, no pupil or white of the eye, and they had no eyebrows, giving them a strange, sightless look—though Eyre was quite certain they could see the students very well.

Protecting their body was a shining suit made out of small circles of metal linked together with metallic hoops. The armour covered their chest and was split down each side at the front of their legs like a skirt made out of metal; their feet were encased in heavy silver boots, which were laced with black rope to just below the knee. Brightly-coloured jewels were sunk at uneven intervals into the strange red skin of the massive creatures, and their arms and legs were covered in designs that appeared to be drawn in glittering golden ink. Scrolls and runes, spirals and geometric shapes covered every inch of their skin. Completing their fearsome image was a large gold bar through their nose, and a hollow gold ring set into each earlobe so that they were stretched into a huge hole.

And last but definitely not least, they each carried a huge club with studs on it and a long sharp sabre. Friendly looking sorts, Eyre decided.

Jax turned to Luke and bowed. "After *you*," he proffered, twirling his hand flamboyantly. Everyone laughed. At the sound, the unit of giants moved as one, stomping their feet and raising their sabres. The laughter stopped instantly, and everyone looked at each other.

"This, I guess," said Number 118, a boy with sandy hair and thin features, raising his eyebrows, "would be another test of our Ferito. But I'm wondering if we'll actually get out alive this time." Everyone nodded nervously. These creatures had none of the good humour exhibited by Gegenees.

"Well, before we charge in," Number 111, the short girl standing beside 118, said pragmatically, "what are we trying to achieve?"

They all looked around then up at the silver pole with the platform.

"I guess we're supposed to get up there somehow," Vicky mused. "But why?"

"You must be able to see the bullseye from there," said Robeson. "It's obviously the final challenge."

"Well, those five haven't done any good," Todd chuckled with satisfaction, but then his smile fell a bit. "I hate to admit it, but if they weren't able to fight these creatures, then I don't have a hope at all."

Everyone nodded. Robeson looked over at the massive warriors. "I guess we have to work as a team again. At least we know we can trust each other." He eyed the electrified cage meaningfully.

The wind started to moan through the open area, and a splatter of rain slapped sideways across the students. It was getting colder, and ominously, lightning flashed in the clouds above their heads. The crowd of students huddled together. An intelligent-looking boy from the third group, 105, spoke up.

"I think we should aim to get one person up the top first. They can help others to get up, and each person gets a chance to go for the bullseye while the rest of us try to fend off the . . . er. . . ."

"Armatura," Zanda supplied helpfully. "They're from Incendium. The greatest warriors in the Overworld."

"Wonderful," the boy said, shaking his head. "How encouraging. Still, it's a plan. Does anyone want to try it?" In the absence of a better idea, everyone nodded. Eyre knew that they were all conscious of the time passing, realising that their clock was ticking down. A jag of lightning seared down and struck a gnarled scribbly gum nearby. It exploded with a huge blast, and the students looked over at the smouldering stump fearfully.

"Whoever gets up there first has to create a shield against that," Robeson said. "Otherwise we'll all be smoked kebabs. That metal platform is about as perfect a lightning conductor as you can get. As far as the target," he continued, "let's just aim for as many bullseyes as we can manage. Help each other get up there, and go for it as fast as you can." He looked over at the silent warriors.

"Now, any ideas for getting near the pole? And please," he added, "don't suggest we take on the Armatura in hand-to-hand combat. I'm sure they'd be only too happy to throw us in the cage with those other five, which would probably take about six seconds." He rubbed his back, looking over at the huge warriors. "I think I've been thrown around enough for one day!"

A sudden thought struck him. He levitated a bit, and one of the Armatura levitated, too. He went higher, and the Armatura went higher, raising his sabre. Robeson descended to the ground, and the Armatura warrior followed.

"Okay, so levitation's only going to work if we can distract them," he said.

As the rain started to fall more heavily, faces scrunched in concentration, trying to work out what to do. The Armatura hadn't moved towards them since the group had stopped laughing. Experimentally, Eyre laughed, and one of the Armatura raised his sabre.

"Obviously doesn't like happy people," Eyre said. But that gave her the glimmer of an idea. She laughed again, and the Armatura took a step towards her.

"Something about laughing is threatening to them," she said, wiping rain off her face.

"*I* don't like being laughed at," Todd said in a plaintive voice, and everyone chuckled. The Armatura' glinting sabres raised high at the sound, and they thudded their clubs on the ground threateningly.

"Well, how about this . . ." Eyre said, thinking hard. "The fastest of us try to lead the Armatura back to the desert and into the sand. Hopefully the spiders will tie the Armatura up for long enough that the runners can get back here. While they're gone the others can levitate up the pole and shoot for the bullseye. If there's any Armatura that stay back, Robeson can use his Ferito on them." She laughed at Robeson's mock-pitiful look, and the Armatura reacted again. She shook her head, looking over at the massive red creatures.

"That's quite disconcerting. Rather unhappy sorts, aren't they?"

"Well, time's running out, and I think it's a good plan." Robeson said. "Given that we may have some hand-to-hand combat, I think Eyre should run, and Zanda, and Georgia."

Eyre looked worried. Until a few weeks ago she would have been laughed out of the room if anyone suggested she run anywhere. She had improved, but she didn't know if she was good enough for such a critical duty. Georgia was fast—she had been on the track team at St Jeffrey's—but Eyre wasn't sure if Georgia's nerve would hold out. Still, they had to try something, and Eyre knew neither of them was up to fighting one of those huge creatures. Eyre's ten-kilometre run each morning had improved her stamina greatly, and her Light skills were undoubtedly weaker than everyone else's, so it probably did make sense for her to run. And she knew Zanda was a great sprinter, so hopefully he would be the key to their success and lead the Armatura away, even if they caught her and Georgia.

No one else seemed eager to volunteer, so she shrugged. "Okay, let's give it a go."

Robeson nodded and continued. "If all the Armatura follow you, we'll levitate up the pole, then get ready to help you up when you come back. If there's some Armatura left here, we'll prepare to do battle and accept that some of us may join our comrades in the cage. Are you all happy to try that?"

No one dissented, and eyes turned expectantly towards Eyre, Georgia, and Zanda; it was time to begin. Eyre swallowed nervously. Her mouth was dry, and she was finding it hard to make any sound, let alone laugh. She couldn't find anything remotely funny when her whole future rested on this particular performance. It was decidedly un-funny. But she, Zanda and Georgia looked at each other and managed a nervous ha-ha. The Armatura's weapons twitched. The rest of the students walked back to the stunted trees and hid in amongst them, clearing the track for the runners. Eyre thought desperately for something to make them laugh. Her eyes caught on the cage of light at the edge of the clearing.

"Hey, Perrill!" Eyre shouted loudly over at the cage, "what do the Blue Mountains have in common with Africa? You guys should know the answer to that one . . . *there's lots of cheetahs!*" Everyone erupted into genuine laughter at the weak joke, the more so when Ben Perrill could be heard shouting death threats at Eyre from his jail across the clearing. The laughter increased, and the Armatura leapt forward in defence, weapons raised, their huge bodies ready to attack.

"Got a limerick for you, Number 95!" Eyre called over to the caged students as her legs quivered, ready to run. She yelled as loudly as she could, eyeing the Armatura nervously:

There once was a terrible cheater
You never would want to meet her
To her immense rage
She got stuck in a cage
Now all of the others will beat her!

Belinda Meaney hollered expletives at her as the students hiding in the bushes smothered their laughter, and the Armatura launched themselves towards Eyre. She gave a choked gurgle as her legs started pumping.

Laughing hysterically, but driven by fear, Eyre, Zanda, and Georgia sprinted along the track, the enraged Armatura behind them, muscular legs clumping and armour clanking as they charged along trying to catch the petrified students. Most of the Armatura were following, bellowing in loud, ferocious voices.

"Oh, hahahaha!" Eyre giggled ridiculously. "Follow me, boys!"

"Me, too, you big vicious soldiers," Zanda simpered. "Just my type!" He pranced a few steps, causing even the terrified Georgia to laugh. Chuckling maniacally, they gasped in fear as they tried to outrun the lumbering Armatura. Despite being very large, the creatures were actually fast, and Eyre started to panic as she realised the fearsome creatures were gaining on them. Choking with gulps of horrified laughter, she rounded the last corner to the sand dunes.

With the sound of the Armatura's sabres rattling in her ears, she hit the sand and sprinted across faster than she had ever run in her life, Zanda and Georgia by her side. The spiders leapt out behind them, springing high in the air and falling back onto the sand, scrabbling across the top of the drifts as they searched for the intruders. Finally reaching the other side, Eyre stood on the bank, laughing her head off madly, and indeed, she felt she might actually be losing her mind; this was so bizarre.

Roaring in rage, the Armatura charged into the sand, their heavy bodies ploughing in up to the knees. They began to wade through the sand dunes with their muscular legs, brushing away the spiders that burst out of the ground in black showers of clicking, hairy podomeres. But the spiders worked fast, winding their silken thread around the legs and up the bodies of the huge warriors, rendering even their powerful muscles useless. The Armatura realised their mistake and turned to run back out, but it was already too late. One of the warriors face-planted in the sand and was quickly trussed up by the spiders, immobilised in seconds. Soon every Armatura was wrapped up like a massive silkworm before they could take even a single step backwards.

The Armatura wriggled around wildly on the sand trying to free themselves, and their bellows of fury thundered across the dunes.

"Quick!" Eyre gasped. "We have to get back. I don't know how long the webs will hold them." While the spiders were distracted with their giant prey, they raced around the edge of the sand dunes and headed back up the track, legs churning and their chests heaving as they desperately ran towards the stone clearing. The wind was howling now, and sheets of rain sliced across their vision, making it difficult to see anything as they stumbled down the track.

When they got to the edge of the clearing, they stopped under the trees, gasping, to catch their breath and to see what was going on. They saw that only a couple of Armatura had remained behind. Obviously laughter was some very serious medicine for this lot, Eyre thought wonderingly, for the majority of them to desert their post.

Peering hard at the metal pole, she could see dim forms up on the platform already, and she felt elated. Their plan had worked: most of the group had made it! Four students were still on the ground, facing the two remaining Armatura, and as she looked blindly through the rain she could make out that it was Jax, Vaughn, Luke, and Vicky—obviously the ones who were best at Ferito. They were ducking and weaving—and mostly reversing—as they tried to get around the Armatura. But the Armatura were quick to block them from the platform. Each time they levitated the Armatura rose with them, making it impossible to pass, and Eyre could see that the students were tired.

Then Vaughn made a corona of lightning, forcing the Armatura to step backwards.

"Go!" he shouted, and Luke and Vicky both shot around the warriors and levitated at mach speed onto the platform. There was a hubbub as students on the platform pointed outwards, and Vicky shot a bright laser beam off into the distance. There was a muffled boom, and Eyre assumed that she had hit the target. A second later there was another blast as Luke's lightbeam found the mark.

The Armatura, obviously enraged that two students had escaped, swung their blades around wildly and thudded their clubs into the ground, trying to knock the last two students off their feet. A glancing blow hit Vaughn, and he staggered, crying out in pain. Jax dragged him away from the Armatura just as the club struck again, and the boys retreated to a safer distance. Vaughn rubbed his shoulder as the warriors returned to their post under the platform, weapons raised.

"Jax!" Zanda called, and Jax and Vaughn squinted at him through the hurtling rain then ran to join them under the stunted trees.

"Thank god!" Jax said, breathing hard. "We've been waiting for you and thought you didn't get away. It's been tough. Those guys have made it difficult for us. But here's what we have to do before the rest of them get back. Spread out far from each other and then get around them and levitate up as fast as you can! That's how everyone else got up there. They can't keep track of us all if we're not close to each other. While they're chasing one of us, another can get around. Once you make the platform they leave you alone. But you have to move fast, or they'll catch you. They got two of us already."

Suddenly it dawned on Eyre that the enraged shouts of the rest of the Armatura seemed to be getting closer. Obviously they were out of their bondage, and she looked nervously over her shoulder up the track, expecting them to appear any second. The noise grew louder, and the five students moved with a panicked energy and spread out around the clearing, keeping their eyes on the Armatura under the platform.

Suddenly Eyre heard loud shouting from the light cage.

"Get 'em! Get 'em!" the students in the cage screeched, and Eyre realised in disbelief that they were actually cheering on the Armatura.

"Don't worry, the zookeepers will be over shortly, Ben!" she shouted back and laughed. The two Armatura looked over at her ferociously and charged towards her. In a flash Jax, Vaughn, Zanda, and Georgia ran around them and raced towards the metal pole. When they were close enough, they levitated up to the platform.

Eyre tried to run also, but found to her horror that her feet were stuck to the floor. She couldn't move at all—why not? Her terror increased as she saw the Armatura almost upon her, when suddenly someone skidded in beside her.

"What's the matter?" Jax said, and she looked at him desperately.

"I'm stuck!" she said. He pulled at her trying to free her. But it was too late—the two Armatura appeared in front of them just as the rest of the warriors charged down the track.

"Sorry, Jax," Eyre said softly and then realised suddenly that she could move again; the force that had been holding her immobile had disappeared. But it was too late for escape; they were surrounded. Back-to-back they faced the fearsome warriors, turning around as the circle tightened.

Eyre thought hard. "Jax," she said. "Don't ask why, just turn around and hold me."

Jax turned and did so with an alacrity that would have given her pause had she had time to think about it. He looked down at her with those brilliant eyes and put his arms around her gently.

"What a way to go," he whispered.

Eyre shut her eyes and willed every bit of energy from every cell of her body to zag outwards around them. She focussed with a fierce concentration dredged from all the hours she had put into meditation and the discipline of the past ten weeks, and suddenly she knew she had masked. The Armatura stopped, looking around blankly. They couldn't see her or Jax!

Reversing quietly, she pulled Jax with her, and they slipped silently between two of the warriors, heading towards the platform. But her head hurt desperately from the intensity of her focus, and she could feel the mask slipping as her energy faded. They were about two metres away from the warriors, walking sideways, when a shout from one of the Armatura made her realise they could be seen again. The mask was gone, and they were still too far away from the platform to levitate, so they started running towards it as fast as they could. But Eyre had used all her energy in the run to the dunes and back, and the mask had exhausted her. The Armatura were gaining fast, and she turned towards them, walking backwards.

"You go, Jax," she gasped. "Don't stay. There's no point!" But Jax stayed by her side as the warriors thundered towards them.

Suddenly the Armatura stopped dead as they rammed into an invisible force. The huge warriors seemed to hit something and bounced backwards, some of them landing on the ground. Confused, Eyre looked over her shoulder at the platform and saw that apart from a small group who were shielding against the lightning, nearly all of the students were leaning over the edge, their hands extended towards the Armatura. Together they had created a powerful barrier that not even the formidable Armatura could penetrate.

"Blocking!" Robeson called over to them in a satisfied voice. "Don't you love it? Come on, before we lose it!"

Eyre stumbled beside Jax until they were close enough to the platform, and then Jax levitated fast off the ground.

"Come on, Eyre!" he called down to her.

Eyre wobbled upwards slowly, and Jax pulled her aboard as everyone cheered. It was very crowded up there, but by holding on to each other they kept themselves from falling off. Eyre looked into Jax's green eyes as he said softly, "Well done, Eyre. That was clever." She felt a disproportionate feeling of happiness—after all, what Jax thought actually didn't count for anything in this examination, but it still felt pretty fine.

A sudden blast of lightning streaked downwards towards the platform, but it struck the shield that four students had created above the group and dissipated with a loud bang. The shielding was working so well, even the rain wasn't falling on her any more, hitting the energy field and sliding off the sides like a waterfall. Some of these students were *good*, she decided. She wasn't surprised to see that 82 was one of the shielders: the girl with enough Viq to hurl a sandshoe up a cliff, girl attached.

"We've all hit the bullseye," Zanda urged, pointing. "Go on, do it!" Eyre moved over and spotted the bullseye in the distance, a target nailed to a tree about 500 metres away. Jax sent a beam of light shooting towards it, and Eyre focussed hard, preparing to launch her Viq.

But just then there was a loud siren, and as Eyre looked up, the world shimmered around her, and she lost sight of everything. A second later she opened her eyes, blinking blindly after the brilliant flash of light, and realised she was back at the lakeside.

Her heart fell as she realised that she alone of those on the platform had not hit the bullseye and completed the test. She had missed the timing by only a couple of seconds; if her feet hadn't been stuck to the ground, she would have made it. She felt incredibly disappointed, but at the same time, pleased for her teammates. Everyone except the five who had been stuck in the cage (now slinking away in shame) and the unfortunate two who had been caught by the Armatura, had managed to get to the top of the podium and hit the bullseye with their Viq. Eyre desperately wished she had done it, too, but was happy that she had managed to mask and thought she had done quite well. . . . Except for crossing the lake, er . . . and the dismal skimming, and the feeble pounding. . . . She hadn't done too badly at Ferito, but she hadn't exactly shone at it, either. Suddenly she began to feel a little less elated. Many of the students here had actually done a lot better at those skills than she had. But realising it was over, whatever the outcome, she headed for the Refectory. They didn't have much time before the mental challenge started in the afternoon.

Sitting with her friends she found it incredibly hard not to talk about the test—both with Beatrice, who had already completed the test, and with Nick and Abby, who were obviously dying to know what they were in for. As she ate her chicken wrap, she raised her eyebrows at Beatrice and simply said, "Well, *that* was interesting!"

Everyone laughed and kept to safer topics—the practise Nick and Abby had done; the book (now *Climatology and Cloud Formations*) that Beatrice was reading; the change in the weather. Georgia Mahoney wandered past and stopped, raising her hand to bump fists with Eyre, then continuing on to sit with Saskia Anderson. Beatrice, Nick, and Abby couldn't have been more surprised if Eyre had suddenly tap-danced on the table. They looked at her speechlessly.

"She's pretty cool," was all Eyre said, taking another bite. And it was true. Georgia had proven that she did have mettle when the pressure was on; it just showed that you could never judge someone too quickly. Eyre felt she had made some important bonds that afternoon with her group (and maybe lost some, she thought ruefully, thinking of Belinda Meaney).

As she ate, Eyre tried not to think about the upcoming mental challenge, but she was fooling no one, least of all herself. After her performance in the physical challenge, the mental was going to be hugely important. Anxiety sat like an immovable rock in the pit of her stomach.

CHAPTER FORTY-TWO

EVENTUALLY IT WAS TIME to head back to the lake and Eyre bid farewell to her friends.

"I'd better head out," she said, and they all gave her a high-five.

"Nail it!" Beatrice said fiercely. "Use a hammer if you have to!"

Eyre walked to the lake, feeling more nervous than before. She hadn't completely failed the physical test, but she couldn't say she'd done amazingly well, either. Not all the students were going to be accepted next year, and at this point she knew she wasn't one of the strong contenders for a place. At least Ben Perrill was in a worse position, she thought with satisfaction. If *she* didn't make it, then he definitely wouldn't. Despite herself, she knew it would really bother her if he got in and she didn't.

Professor Vela was standing at the front of the crowd and looked at Eyre with a frigid gaze as she walked in. She headed to the back of the crowd, unsettled by his unblinking stare.

Soon everyone was there, and he silenced the chatter with one hand.

"You are about to start the mental challenge of your TEPs," he said. "Each part of both sections of the TEPs will be closely analysed to determine whether we would like to offer you a position at our institution. As such, the mental challenge is as important as the physical.

"The lecturers will be close by again, taking notes and analysing your performances. The first part of your challenge will consist of a written test. You will then consult the guide to find your way to the next sections of the exam. There is to be no consultation amongst each other during the mental challenge, and you will undertake it largely on your own."

Four Jotnar appeared carrying a large, clear prism in the shape of a tetrahedron, which they placed on the ground at the front of the crowd, beside Professor Vela. The prism was about a metre high and had steps cut into the side of it leading up to a gleaming crystal formation at its apex. The formation was made of clusters of white hexagonal crystals, with luminous rainbow glints that flashed across its uneven facets. Professor Vela indicated the large structure beside him.

"This is an Iridis Generator," he said. "Most of you will not have seen one before, but some of you may recognise the Anandalite crystals at the apex. Anandalite is a crystal of very high energy that has a multitude of uses and the Generator has been designed by our Master Faceters and often used in our TEP trials. Line up numerically beside the prism. Quickly, don't waste time! We have a lot of people to get through."

The students jumped into line. Professor Vela waved his hands, and the Anandalite crystals began to vibrate and hum, and then suddenly a blinding rainbow shot out the top of the formation and curved over the lake, through the sky, and out of sight. There was a surprised buzz amongst the students, silenced when Professor Vela's sharp gaze sliced through them.

"Ascend the steps to the top of the prism," Professor Vela said in an impatient tone. "As I count you off, you are to jump onto the Iridis." Iridis being the rainbow, Eyre supposed, glad she wasn't going first. Jax raised his eyebrows, looking at the glowing arc of colour. He was Number 81, so therefore going first, and obviously he was just as unsure of what to do as Eyre was.

When everyone was lined up Jax headed up the steps of the prism and waited for the call.

"Number 81!" shouted Professor Vela.

"See you over the rainbow, Eyre with the red hair!"

Jax winked at Eyre and then launched himself up onto the rainbow. Obviously it *was* the Iridis, as instructed, because with a whoop of surprise, he started to slide at huge speed up the rainbow, along the bright banded path of colour, until he disappeared over the top of the arc into the distance.

"Number 82!" continued Professor Vela, and Lindi Jamieson, the dark-haired girl with glasses and the amazing Viq, jumped onto the Iridis. She zoomed off, too, and vanished into the distance, and more students followed until it was Eyre's turn. Feeling the intense dislike emanating from Professor Vela, she was actually quite relieved when he shouted out her number.

"Number 88!" Jumping up, she landed on the Iridis and found it to be slippery but springy like a trampoline. Instantly her feet started to slide at great speed up the arc of the rainbow, and she skidded upwards as the lake and cliffs blurred by her, the mountains and towns below. The rainbow stretched over a great distance, and she covered a vast area in only minutes.

As the Blue Mountains disappeared behind her, Eyre could see the broad Simpson Desert spreading away to her left and patchworks of cultivated farmland in brown and green squares beneath her.

It was terrifying but also exhilarating to travel so far and so fast in such a short time, like a high-speed slippery dip in reverse. She balanced precariously, like surfing or snowboarding, finding that if she kept to the middle of the band of colour (the green band) she could keep relatively balanced. As soon as she strayed to either side of the green band, the Iridis started to bounce and bend and became a lot more unstable, which was terrifying. Imagine falling from up here! She zipped upwards, startling a lone cockatoo that was lazily flying beside the Iridis. The bird screeched and disappeared into a cloud.

Eventually Eyre reached the top of the arc, where she slowed for a second and then stopped as her heart pounded wildly. It was breathtaking! She was so high in the air she could see to the eastern edge of the continent, the Pacific Ocean butting up against the ragged coastline and she watched in amazement as an aircraft flew through a cloud beneath her.

All of a sudden there was a clap of thunder and a blinding flash of lightning, and a searing force knocked Eyre off the Iridis way out into the air. Her feet felt nothing beneath them, and Eyre screamed in terror as she plummeted downwards. No Viq that she could employ was strong enough to save her. She tumbled over and over through the air towards the ground. Wind whipped her hair around her, and tears streamed from her eyes as she windmilled through the clouds, shrieking in fear.

But then something came in gently from the side of her, and like a feathered saviour, swept under her and collected her on its back. Gasping, Eyre looked with sore eyes to see it was a huge pelican, much larger than normal, and it glided along silently as she stretched awkwardly across its broad back. Eyre flung her arms around its neck, hanging on desperately, and it soared upwards through the air, higher and higher, until it reached the Iridis and hovered beside it.

Trembling, Eyre stood up with shaking legs and stepped back on to the unstable band of colour.

"Thank you," she whispered, her teeth chattering, and the pelican blinked at her with a violet eye. Then it soared off in a graceful arc and spiralled down towards the ground. Eyre stood for a minute, unable to believe she was safe and completely unable to move; fear had immobilised her. But the Iridis swayed unsteadily in the wind, and she felt she might fall off again, so she put a foot forward on the green section of the vividly coloured band and tentatively pushed herself into a slide again.

Gravity and the incline caught her, and in a few seconds she was careering down the Iridis once more, at a blurring speed. Faster and faster she went, sliding down the green stripe in a wild trajectory that headed towards a dense rainforest. When she reached the end of it she was launched off like a cannonball and she shrieked as she tumbled through the air.

She landed with a resounding force on something spongy and bounced way up into the air before hurtling back down. She rebounded off the surface again, and again, not as high each time, until eventually she stopped.

Eyre felt the yielding surface underneath her and saw she was sitting on something large and rectangular, like a huge trampoline covered in a soft, textured material. She got up and walked with unsteady legs to the edge and leaned over the side. With a start she realised the trampoline was hovering about two metres above the ground, no legs or structures to support it. It was quite an unsettling sight, and Eyre hoped that whatever force was holding it up there didn't suddenly disappear.

She sat down again, put her legs over the edge, and slowly slid off the side, landing on the rich dark earth of the rainforest floor. Her legs were still trembling after her wild ride and the terrifying fall off the Iridis, and she stood for a moment to recover while trying to figure out what to do next.

As she took in her surroundings, she wished she did have someone with her; she was in a dense green rainforest filled with lurking shadows and strange earthy smells, and it was unsettling being on her own under this dark canopy.

There was no path here or trail to indicate the way she should head. She looked around, at a loss as to which way to go, when in the distance she saw a faint blue light glowing from within the tangled forest. Deciding that was as good a place to start as any, she pushed her way through the foliage towards it, under spiky tree ferns and large elephant-eared plants, and past eucalyptus trees draped with looped and tightening vines. Sunlight crept through the canopy above in dappled abstract patterns that danced along the ground around her, creating an emerald glow through the rainforest.

Eventually she arrived at the source of the blue light and looked at it curiously. It was a perfectly spherical ball of blue crystal sitting on a black onyx base with swirling misty clouds moving within, quite a mesmerising and beautiful object, and it gave off a surprising amount of light. The sphere sat on a table carved out of a piece of a broad tree trunk, with a seat, obviously carved from another piece of the trunk, in front of it. Sitting on the top of the table was a pad of paper with writing on it and a pencil.

Okay, thought Eyre. *This is obviously the written test. I hope it doesn't involve trigonometry, or I'll be sent straight home.* Walking over to the chair, she dragged it out and sat down, looking anxiously at the pad of paper.

Please answer the questions below, the top sheet stated.

It sounded straightforward enough, but unfortunately there was nothing else on the paper. She riffled through the rest of the pad, but all the pages were blank. Eyre sat staring at the pad for a while, hoping that some questions would materialise, but the paper remained blank. She gazed into the swirling crystal ball, searching for questions in the misty clouds, but it glowed quietly, the patterns really quite lovely but not offering any help at all.

She focussed her mind hard on the paper, not sure what she was doing, but hoping that Viq might make some words suddenly appear; but all she produced was a stream of smoke as the paper caught fire. She whacked the flames out with her hand, and a trickle of panic started to curl through her. What if she had to leave the paper blank?

Think, she thought desperately. *Please answer the questions below. . . .* What does that mean? She tapped her fingers on the table, trying to think of what to do as she looked up at the trees, then down at the ground, searching for inspiration. Suddenly a thought came to her and she shoved her chair back.

Below! she thought hopefully. It doesn't have to be on the paper. . . .

Searching under the table she found a small square of paper tacked high up underneath the wooden table. She pulled it out and found two questions on there.

What is your name?

What is your number?

With relief she put down the answers quickly on the pad, writing below the scorch mark. As soon as she had finished, there was a flash and both pieces of paper vanished in a puff of smoke, leaving an empty pad behind and the questions gone.

After the papers disappeared, the clouds in the crystal ball began to swirl around wildly, and then they changed colour, turning a clear green. Looking into the green mist, Eyre saw a sentence suspended within it: *a rag man groover it*

"Oh no," she groaned, rubbing her forehead. "A code. Where's Beatrice when I need her?"

She wrote the sentence on the pad and studied the letters, writing out the alphabet a few times and substituting letters, trying to see if there was a pattern that might make sense. All that emerged was gobbledegook: bsbhnbohsppwfsju; ctciocpitqqwgtkv. . . . She crumpled up the page in disgust. Nope. Racking her brain, she thought back to the day she had met Beatrice and Robeson in the Common Room and the codes they had been practising. One thing they had done was shuffle words around, so she tried that. Man, groover it a rag. It a groover man rag. Aargh! she thought, her head hurting.

What else did they do? She looked hard at the words. Beatrice had also unjumbled letters, making new words. How many combinations could there be, though? It would take her hours. What did she call that again? An anagram, she remembered gloomily, getting her pencil ready to try the hundreds of possible words that could be made from that sentence. Suddenly the first three words caught her attention. "A rag man" could be rearranged to make *anagram*! A clue! That meant she was probably on the right track, and she only had to work out "groover it".

Scribbling fast, she tried many different combinations: giro voter Got revoir. Or give rot. *God!* She started to write faster. It over gor. Grove riot. She tried again and again, using up sheets of paper, nothing making sense until she wrote: go tori rev. Something about that sentence made her pause, and she looked at it again. She rearranged letters in the second two words and finally a sentence that made sense jumped out at her: *"go to river"*. That might be it! She was sweating from the panic and effort of writing so fast, not sure how much time had elapsed but knowing it had taken her some time to arrive at that answer. With a flash of light and a puff of smoke, the papers she had been working on disappeared, which was encouraging as it probably meant she had the right answer. She jumped up, looking around wildly, trying to hear if there was water nearby.

Despite listening hard, she couldn't hear anything remotely like a river running, but with a spark of inspiration, she levitated and wobbled to the top of a eucalyptus, looking out over the canopy. She gasped as she saw the rainforest stretching out in all directions. Where on earth was she? Alone in the middle of this wilderness; it was a bit unsettling. But she saw the glimmer of water flowing beneath the dense leaves about a hundred metres away, and she dropped back down to the ground.

Leaving the table behind, she hurried through the thick rainforest. It was damp and green, and creatures scuttled underfoot as she pushed through the dense foliage—centipedes, beetles, worms, who knew what? Focussing too far down the track she ran face-first into a huge spider's web and did a rain dance getting it off, but eventually she made it to the flowing river.

Okay, so what now? she wondered. Here I am—at the river! Where were the fireworks? Or the neon sign with the next directions? Sighing, she realised she was going to have to work it out herself.

Well, she thought, I guess I have three choices. I can cross it, or I can travel up or down it. Obviously I have to choose. Mulling it over, she finally made the decision to try and travel down the river. It was an excruciating choice, because if she chose wrongly that would probably be the end of the mental challenge for her as she would be heading off in the wrong direction. But she really just had to make a choice and get on with it, hoping that if she did choose the wrong way, she might be able to scramble back again.

She started to push her way through the thick bush at the side of the river heading downstream. She hadn't gone very far before she saw a big log blocking her path, and she went to clamber over it. But as she touched the rough bark, she fell over backwards in fright when the log turned towards her, opening a very large and lethal looking set of jaws. It was a monstrous crocodile that eyed her up with great interest. Scrambling to her feet in total panic, she backed away fast until she was safely out of reach. Just wonderful! *Go to the river and become lunch for a large leathery reptile.* They forgot the second half of the message.

Eyre looked at the massive beast and considered her options. Obviously swimming down the river was totally out of the question now but so was travelling on this side of the river. Should she go up the river? The crocodile flicked its strong tail and took a step towards her on short, sturdy legs.

Eyre moved further back through the undergrowth and looked at it disconsolately.

"You know, I'd really rather you didn't eat me, but I think you're rather magnificent, despite the fact you're ruining my chances at passing this test. How about *you* carry me down the river?"

"Okay," said the crocodile, "hop on my back."

Eyre nearly fainted. She'd had a lot of surprises in the two months, but a talking crocodile was still fairly high on the list of unexpected events. She took a tentative step forward and peered over at it.

"Wow!" she said. "You can talk?"

The crocodile looked at her with unblinking eyes. "I just did, didn't I?" it replied.

Suddenly Eyre couldn't think of a word to say. She spluttered for a minute and then found her voice again. "Well, er . . . would you take me down the river . . . without . . . eating me, please?" she asked, feeling really quite ridiculous.

"Of course," the crocodile replied, slithering through the bush and down to the side of the river. "Get on."

Eyre approached the huge animal cautiously. Any sudden move, and she would be levitating up to Mars. But the crocodile turned away from her placidly, presenting its back to her.

"Hurry up, I don't have all day," it said. As Eyre got on, sitting astride the rough-skinned beast, she noticed that it had very strange purple eyes. Not exactly your typical crocodile, she thought.

The crocodile dove into the water, and Eyre held on tightly, preparing to hold her breath. But the creature just skimmed along the surface of the water, waving its strong tail so that it accelerated down the rapids. Once Eyre got over her fear that the creature might eat her, she actually enjoyed the ride. It was like bodyboarding, with the white water of the rapids washing over her and her reptilian surfboard.

They travelled quite a way down the river until the rapids died away and the water began to get more shallow, ending up in a quiet section with large flat sandstone rocks along the banks, the water flowing gently over them. The crocodile clambered out on to the flat rock, and Eyre hopped off.

"Thank you so much," she said to the great creature. "It was very kind of you." The purple eyes twinkled, and the huge reptile lumbered away over the flat sheets of sandstone before plunging into the rapids and heading back upstream.

Eyre looked around, not sure what to do next. But a cheery voice called out to her, and she saw, sitting on her floral chair on a rock down the river a short way, Madame Overmantle. She had a table set up in front of her with some objects on it and a chair opposite her.

"Come down, dear," she called to Eyre. "Haven't you done well to make it this far? Some of the students are wandering through the bush on the other side of the river, and a couple are still trying to answer the questions on the blank paper, poor things. It's easy to get confused with this challenge."

Eyre ran down the rocks to join Madame Overmantle and sat opposite her at the table.

"Well, I'm very glad to see a friendly face!" Eyre said. "Although I guess the crocodile was fairly friendly. . . ."

"Yes, he hasn't eaten anyone this week," Madame Overmantle said in a sombre tone, and Eyre chuckled feebly, hoping it was a joke.

"Okay then," said Madame Overmantle, indicating a small patchwork bag on the table. "I would like you to select three of the tiles in there and lay them on the table."

Eyre reached in and felt around, eventually pulling out three random tiles. The tiles were made of obsidian, and they had strange geometric shapes on them, marked out with bright golden lines. She laid them down, and Madame Overmantle leaned over them, scrutinising them intently.

"Ah," she said. "I see. Hmm, very interesting runes indeed. Rad, Gur and Daeg. Challenges . . . change . . . an interesting journey ahead indeed for you. Yes, very intriguing."

Eyre was none the wiser, but sat waiting for further instruction.

"Now, could you choose three cards from this deck, please?" Madame Overmantle said, her eyes watching Eyre closely.

Eyre, worrying that she might pick something wrong, looked at the deck anxiously before selecting three cards from different places in the deck. One looked like a wheel, one was a man lying prone but rising up, and the middle card, disconcertingly, was a dark form with a scythe in its hand. Madame Overmantle peered closely at the cards, pursing her lips and musing aloud. "Ah, three of the Major Arcana, interesting," she said. "The Wheel of Fortune, the Reaper, and the Sarcophagus." She looked up suddenly at Eyre, focussing hard. "This may explain why you are impossible to read. I can't see your aura clearly; the energy swirls above you but doesn't settle. These cards show again that you are on a journey that may be difficult and lonely at times. One that is still unfolding. The Reaper doesn't mean death," she said to Eyre, who was looking quite fearfully at the red card in the middle. She had experienced enough death already.

"It means change, my girl." Madame Overmantle's eyes softened. "Often after a period of terrible pain. These are very interesting cards indeed and show that you have a long and sometimes arduous journey ahead. But that you are experiencing an awakening of some kind also. Interesting. Very interesting."

Suddenly she gathered the cards and put them back into the deck, wrapping it up carefully in a blue velvet cloth. She put the runes back in the bag and smiled at Eyre, but her eyes were shuttered, and Eyre worried what the readings had really revealed.

"Well, we're finished here now. Your final task is to find the rainbow and answer its questions." As Eyre looked disconsolately around her, Madam Overmantle smiled kindly. "It's back that way," she said, pointing into the rainforest behind her. "And you'd better hurry," she added as Eyre walked towards the bush. "Time is running out!"

Eyre started to run, heading into the forest looking for the rainbow. How could a rainbow ask questions? she wondered. Her head was hurting from all the concentration; the answers to these sorts of puzzles didn't come easily to her. She raced along, looking left and right and above her, trying to spot the rainbow. Suddenly she came to a halt, stopping in amazement before the most incredible tree she had ever seen.

It was a huge eucalyptus tree but such an unusual one: its bark was a riot of vibrant colours—reds, blues, greens, yellows, oranges—every colour imaginable. It was like someone had taken a medley of paint pots and poured them randomly in bright streaks down the trunk of the tree and along the branches. It was the most improbable sight—a tree as brightly coloured as a rainbow, with hues like melted plasticine running down its trunk. Shards of brilliant bark in many different colours were scattered around the base of the tree.

Eyre studied it from the track, not sure it was real, but realising that *this* was the rainbow she was meant to find. So now to answer its questions. After the crocodile, the idea of a talking tree wasn't so unbelievable.

"Hello?" she said tentatively.

Incredibly, the tree leaned over towards her, its vibrant branches bending, the leaves rustling. "Greetings," it said in a soft bass voice.

"You are very beautiful," Eyre said honestly, and the tree shook itself, obviously preening.

"You have some questions for me," Eyre said politely. "I would like to try and answer them."

"Your courtesy is appreciated," said the tree, and rained speckles of brightly coloured bark on her. This, Eyre supposed, stopping herself from brushing it off, was an honour.

"My first request of you," said the tree in its deep voice, "is to sing the colour yellow."

Here we go, thought Eyre. What? She thought hard, but couldn't even begin to figure out what that meant. How could you sing a colour? She decided to just sing the song her mother had taught her, the song she had sung with the Mimir at her family cabin. "When the world is in a turmoil, and the fighting just goes on," she began, and sang the song through to the end. The tree seemed to shuffle in delight as she finished.

"Lovely," it said. "You have a very harmonious voice. Unfortunately, you just sang the colour red. But it was still very nice."

Eyre felt disappointed, but still had no idea what she was meant to have sung, so she just waited for the next question.

"What colour am I?" asked the tree.

Another impossible question, Eyre thought gloomily. What colour *wasn't* the tree would be more appropriate a question. But that thought triggered a vague idea. If you looked at all the parts of this tree's colour as if it was a spectrum that had separated—the foundation would be white. All the colours of the rainbow came from white light, so perhaps that's what the tree was after.

"You are white," she said confidently, far more certainly than she felt.

"Excellent!" cried the tree. "That is correct. I am white in my soul. All my colours combined create the colour white.

"I have one last task for you," it continued. "I would like you to play me a song."

Play a song. God. Eyre's brain was hurting, and she felt incredibly tired. One more task. No instruments anywhere. Should she pick up some rocks and clack them together? That was hardly a song. Blow through a stick? How to do it? Defeated, she realised she had no idea; her feeble brain had decided to quit.

Disappointed, she walked over to the tree, deciding that at least she would like to touch it before she left. She stroked a yellow streak of bark and the tree seemed to shiver with pleasure. As it moved, a pure sound came from the tree trunk, nearly causing Eyre to fall over backwards in surprise. Recovering, she touched the yellow strip again and once more the bell-like sound filled the air. She knew that the song she had sung was in the key of A, which apparently was the colour red, and it sounded lower than this note. Interested, she touched a blue part of the bark, and a higher note rang out. Trying a green part of the bark produced a note down from the blue. She tested all the colours, stroking the bark softly to make the tones ring out. Eventually she worked out that the colours of the rainbow were arranged in the order of the white keys on a piano.

So A was red, B was orange, C was—yep, there it was—yellow!—D Green, E Blue, F Indigo, and G Violet. Now that she knew what the tree was after, she played a few bars of a song in A minor that she had learned on her piano. It was a short, eight-bar melody, haunting and sad, and she played it through twice, pushing the colours of the bark gently. At the end of the song, a shower of leaves rained down on Eyre, and the tree sighed.

"Thank you," it said. "That resonated with me."

Eyre hugged the tree, feeling a vibration and a warmth run through her body. "Thank you for the experience," she said softly.

Suddenly the air started to shimmer around her, and the familiar white haze appeared. Then the bright light zapped and a second later she was standing, disoriented, by the lake. She blinked her eyes and tried to focus.

Professor Vela was standing with a Felsic, marking off people's names.

"Once I've got your name, you can go," he said officiously.

A few other people were there already—Robeson Paul and Zanda. Both of them were super smart, so Eyre wasn't surprised to see them back already. As Eyre walked over to them, Phillip Outray and Lindi Jamieson also arrived in a flare of light. Another flash and suddenly Ben Perrill was there, smirking as he walked up to them.

"What a breeze," he said. "Too easy!" He sauntered past, and Phillip and Eyre looked at him, open mouthed as he went up to Professor Vela to get his name marked off. Ben might be good at the physical side of things, but apparently at St Jeffrey's he had never been known for his intellectual brilliance. For him to arrive back so quickly when he would have been one of the last to leave on the quest was quite astounding.

Eyre felt a worm of suspicion entering her mind as he arrogantly walked away down the path. And when he looked back over his shoulder surreptitiously at Professor Vela, Eyre felt a jolt of sudden understanding go through her. Was *that* what Professor Vela was doing with Ben Perrill in the Lecture Theatre? Had Professor Vela passed on information about the mental challenge to Ben? If so, no *wonder* they were hiding away from everyone so stealthily in the Hall. It was completely against the school rules, grounds for expulsion in Ben's case. And big trouble for Professor Vela as well, no doubt. Was Professor Vela being paid off? What was in it for him? She was suddenly very glad she hadn't been detected under the podium; she realised now that there could have been very dire consequences.

And she also felt a flare of rage flood through her. The injustice of Ben cheating infuriated her. If he was accepted by the school because of it, it would be depriving someone more worthy of the position of their rightful place. Should she say something? But she had no proof; to speak out could put her in a very precarious position with Professor Vela. And she also wondered how she could even tell anyone without it sounding like sour grapes, her antagonism with Ben Perrill being well known through the student body. With angry resignation, she realised there was really nothing she could do about it.

But as more students returned, her spirits lifted. It hadn't gone all that badly for her, and she felt that whilst it wasn't certain the school would accept her, at least she hadn't flunked out completely. And she wondered what Sector she would be placed in—that was going to be really interesting, whether the school accepted her or not.

As a group, the students all headed over to the Common Room, where a number of students were having afternoon tea.

Beatrice raced over and hugged Eyre. "You're finished!" she shrieked. "Congratulations!"

"How did you do?" asked Abby, her eyes alive with curiosity.

"Average, I'd say," Eyre answered. "But at least I made it through the trials. You and Nick will be alright, Abby. I'm sure you will both do better than I did. I guess I just have to wait and see the outcome now."

"Well, I'm off to shower and then hit the therapeutic pools," Eyre said, yawning. "My body feels like it's been through a meat-grinder. And my mind is like mush. They certainly put you through your paces!"

She headed off, feeling empathetic as she left Abby and Nick, who had rather anxious looks on their faces despite her encouraging words.

CHAPTER FORTY-THREE

THE NEXT COUPLE OF days passed quite quickly. Nick undertook his TEPs on Thursday and seemed to come back relatively satisfied. He said that he thought he'd managed the physical side better than the mental, but that he thought they both weren't too bad.

Abby was a bit dismal on Friday afternoon, saying gloomily that she was sure she'd failed, but she had always been hard on herself, and Eyre suspected she had probably done better than she thought.

In any case, there was huge delight when the last group came back from the TEPs, because finally it was permissible to talk about the exams with each other. Abby went straight to the therapeutic pools to recover, and then joined everyone in the Refectory for dinner. The hall was filled with students, noisily dissecting the TEPs and how they thought they had gone. A great sense of relief pervaded the air—whatever came next, at least the exams were over.

"St Illuminado save me," exclaimed Beatrice, rolling her eyes, "how scary were those big red soldiers?" Eyre nodded.

"Zanda said they're called Armatura. Apparently they're from Incendium, 'the most ferocious warriors in the Overworld'!"

"Didn't like being laughed at, though," Nick chuckled.

"Careful," Eyre said sombrely, "they might hear you!" Everyone laughed, and then Abby's eyes went round in horror.

"What about those spiders!"

"Oh yeah," agreed Beatrice, "not good at all."

Nick looked dreamy. "How awesome was that rainbow?" he said, euphoric at the memory. "It was the coolest ride I've ever had!"

"I found it terrifying," Abby countered. "I was swerving from side to side and bouncing up and down. I thought I was going to fall off and crash somewhere in New Zealand."

Eyre looked at them all. "Did you have a talking crocodile?" she asked, feeling rather ridiculous.

"Yes," said Abby at the same time as Nick said "No." They looked at each other.

"I ran downriver rather fast from one," Nick elaborated. "Huge great thing looked like it was going to eat me!"

"Mine rather politely suggested I walk down the river," Abby shrugged.

Beatrice looked at them all, confused. "I didn't even *see* a crocodile," she said. They all burst out laughing.

"Clearly there is no one path through the challenges," Eyre said. "I think this is a bit like talking about an exam paper afterwards—it usually makes you feel like you've totally failed! Let's not talk about it. We'll find out tomorrow how we did."

Everyone agreed, and they continued on eating, feeling like a huge weight had lifted off their shoulders. The TEPs were finished!

Suddenly Sergeant Tottingham walked in across to the front of the Refectory. Most of the conversation had stopped when she came in, but she thumped her staff to ensure complete silence.

"Well, students," she boomed. "Congratulations on completing the TEPs. It is an arduous examination, and we commend you for your spirit and your achievement in finishing the tests.

"Tonight you should pack up your gear as you will be returning home tomorrow afternoon. But in the morning, you should put on your Lightworker uniform one last time, as we will be having the Placement Ceremony straight after breakfast in the Lecture Theatre.

"Please pick up a robe from the Training Shed tomorrow after breakfast, before you come over to the Lecture Theatre. The robe will be worn at the ceremony, during which time your Sector will be revealed. This is a momentous occasion in your life, and one you will never forget as it will forever define your life's path. Invitations have been sent out to your families, so some of them may be joining us for the ceremony, and you will then travel home together.

"Immediately after the Placement Ceremony, the lists of students accepted to the Academy will be posted on the noticeboard in the Common Room. These lists constitute the first round of offers to the Academy for this group.

"A second round of offers will go out once we determine who accepts the places they have been offered. If anyone has any questions about any of this, please come and see me."

Looking around the room, Sergeant Tottingham gave them all a rare smile. "I've enjoyed getting to know you," she said, "and I look forward to seeing some of you back next year. Thank you for your attention and your effort."

Then she left again, and the noise level in the room became even louder than before, if possible, as people discussed this new information. After a while, students dumped their trays and raced back to their lodges to pack up their gear. Eyre and her friends followed along, going their separate ways as the path branched to the different lodges.

Carly arrived soon after Eyre and she smiled at Eyre. "Well, this is it, roomie, the final countdown!" she said. "I hope you make it in next year, and me, too! It would be great to see you again. I've enjoyed sharing the two metre space with you."

Eyre laughed. "Likewise!" she said. "Good luck tomorrow, too."

They packed up their gear fairly quickly and stored their bags under Carly's lower bunk. Then they clambered into their beds, anxious for the morning to come.

Eyre found it difficult to sleep despite the fact the night was cool and tranquil outside with no wind at all to rustle the eucalypt leaves. She could see the lake shining with reflected moonlight, the calm dark waters holding its secrets close. She stared at it a long time before eventually sleep came and she drifted off with dreams of rainbows and mysteries and talking trees singing to her.

CHAPTER FORTY-FOUR

AFTER BREAKFAST THE NEXT day, Eyre walked over to the Training Shed where students milled around, choosing robes from hanging racks on wheels. The robes were a bright crimson colour and hung on the racks in groups according to size. Eyre headed for the gowns hanging in the middle of the line of racks, trying to find a medium-sized robe. Eventually, after trying on a couple, she found one that fitted her.

It was similar to an academic gown, with pleated shoulders that hung down over her arms to the ground. It looked like the black gowns Eyre had seen before in universities, but it was made of a lightweight fabric that swirled when she took the gown off the rack. Finally satisfied that she had the right size, she fastened the clasps and followed the rest of the students, all wearing the brightly coloured robes, down the stony paths to the Lecture Theatre.

The students crowded around in the hallway outside the Lecture Theatre, full of manic energy and talking to each other madly. Beatrice sneaked a look inside the Hall and came back to join Eyre, Nick, and Abby.

"Mum and Dad are in there," she said happily, "and I could see your Dad, Abby. The theatre is filled with students' families." She hesitated and her eyes softened.

"Sorry, Eyre and Nick, that was a bit insensitive of me," she said awkwardly.

"No, don't apologise," Eyre said quickly. "It's an important day. You need your family here, and I'm glad they came."

Nick nodded in agreement. "It's more fun having a crowd anyway," he said, "whoever they are."

There was a general buzz of excitement in the air as the red-robed students talked and laughed, waiting for instructions. Suddenly Professor

Vela walked out the door from within the Lecture Theatre, and silence descended damply over the hallway.

"Line up numerically," he ordered. "And enter the Lecture Theatre from this side door. Once Mr Ray has finished his speech, you are to go up the steps at the side of the stage, past the Aura and across to Mr Ray. Then you flip your robe back over your shoulders with both hands, like this," he demonstrated the technique, flinging the robe behind his shoulders, leaving his arms bare, "to reveal your Inguz, and Mr Ray will announce your Sector. Once you have your Sector you are to continue across the other side of the stage, then take a seat in one of the empty rows at the front of the Lecture Theatre."

Everyone nodded, and he disappeared back inside the Theatre. Several of the students practised tossing their robe back over their shoulders until they could do it smoothly. Eyre did it, too, getting the hang of it quickly but feeling a bit sad as she looked at her indistinct Inguz. It was going to be a bit embarrassing standing in the middle of the stage with everyone looking at the unorthodox symbol. But she decided that it was better than sitting right now in the middle of an empty room back at the family cabins, and decided to make the best of the occasion.

The students fell silent as they heard Whittaker Ray start to talk.

"Today marks the end of a difficult and challenging two months for your children, our trainees," he began. "Can I let you know that they have worked hard and acquitted themselves admirably during this time, and you should be very proud of them, whether or not they are selected to attend the Academy of Light. We thank you for considering our institution for the education of your children, and we wish every one of them luck and success in their future endeavours.

"Today is one of the most significant days in a Lightworker's life—the day their Sector is determined. I invite our Elevated students to come up on stage and to share with us their Sector and the beginning of their new path in life."

Eyre craned her neck and could see President Zircon appear on stage, dressed in full regalia and carefully carrying a crystal casket from which shone a rainbow of light. The sight was mesmerising, and the Auditorium was hushed as everyone stared at the glowing box.

"That's the piece of the Aura," she heard someone say, and the students crowded forward to try and see it. President Zircon stopped in the centre of the stage and put down the crystal box, sliding the lid off. Instantly a glowing spectrum of coloured light began to swirl out of the box and formed a whirling spiral around it. The shining rays radiated outwards, bathing the stage in myriad colours. After a moment President Zircon stepped to the back of the stage, where he was joined by Jengles on one side and another Mimir on the other. They all watched the crystal box and the Aura intently. It was so precious and rare and Eyre had no doubt that the rest of the Mimir were close by, ready to protect it should the need arise.

Professor Vela moved to the side of the stage, consulted his list and said loudly, "Students, please come on to the stage as you are announced. Number one: Saskia Anderson." Saskia walked confidently up on stage, her long blonde hair curled, looking immaculate. The rays from the Aura swirled around her as she walked towards Whittaker Ray. Then she tossed the robe back over her shoulders, revealing that the centre of her Inguz was a sparkling emerald green.

"Virens Sector!" announced Whittaker Ray, shaking her hand. "Congratulations, Saskia!" Saskia continued off the side of the stage, and as the audience applauded, her Halo turned the same colour as her Inguz. The second student, a boy not familiar to Eyre, came up on stage through the Aura rays, and had his Sector announced by Whittaker Ray: Hese. He shook Whittaker Ray's hand, beaming as Whittaker Ray congratulated him, and headed off stage as his Halo turned shimmering bronze. The boy was followed in a steady stream by others who Eyre vaguely knew, each one receiving their placement after they had walked through the rays of the Aura. The Curtis twins were Rufa, and shortly after, Beatrice nervously ascended the steps and walked across the stage through the coloured light.

"Number 35: Beatrice Edmunsun," Professor Vela announced to the audience. She flicked back her robe, revealing a glittering yellow centre in the middle of her silver Inguz. "Flava!" Whittaker Ray called out, shaking her hand, saying, "Congratulations!" She looked out at the audience, searching for her parents as a proud smile crossed her face. Her Halo turned a dazzling golden yellow as she exited the stage.

The students walked up steadily to receive their placements—Colton, unsurprisingly, was Arant, denoting strong mental and physical skills, as were Jax and Pheria. Warrigal was Tyros, and Carly was Virens. Luke Jordan and Tec Langford joined the Curtis twins in Rufa, and Eyre began to get butterflies as her number was called.

"Number 88," Professor Vela called out, "Eyre Lightward." Eyre walked up the stairs and into the rays of the Aura. A warmth covered her skin as she moved through the rainbow of light, almost as if fingertips were being run over her body. Then she arrived in front of Whittaker Ray and flipped her robe back over her shoulders in anticipation, waiting for him to announce her Sector. But to her embarrassment, there was a resounding silence as Whittaker Ray looked uncomfortable and opened his mouth, speechless.

Panicking, Eyre looked at her arm and saw, to her horror, that the centre of her (pathetically indistinct) Inguz was a dull grey. What was *that?* she thought, in mortification. There was no *grey* Sector! What did this mean? And how quickly could she get off this stage? The audience sat uncomfortably, shocked at the strange-looking Inguz and the unconventional colour in the middle of it. No one knew what to do. Finally Whittaker Ray recovered.

"Well, it looks like Eyre has a form of Hese," he said brightly. "Sometimes the colours can be a little different tonally," he added, obviously lying through his teeth. "Congratulations."

A smattering of awkward applause accompanied Eyre as she miserably walked off stage. She was no Sector at all. Did this mean she was a proper Lightworker? And where would she fit into the community? She was fairly certain that this meant she wouldn't be offered a place at the Academy— there couldn't be a place for a student who didn't have a proper Sector.

She sat next to her fellow students in the front rows, eyes brimming with tears, wanting nothing more than to drag the robe over her Inguz and hide it from all the curious eyes. Beatrice looked across at her from down the row, her face concerned and compassionate. Eyre turned her eyes forward resolutely; she knew if she kept looking at Beatrice, she would completely lose it. To have worked so hard for ten weeks and then have this happen? She would rather have been Unlit than go through this excruciating embarrassment.

She barely noticed the rest of the students as they crossed the stage, although she did register that Nick was Tyros and Abby was Sappir. Finally the interminable ceremony concluded, and Whittaker Ray bid everyone farewell. She watched vaguely as President Zircon stepped forward to seal the Aura back inside the crystal box and take it away, but her mind was numb with disappointment, and she sat rigidly in her chair as a resounding wave of applause and cheers filled the Lecture Theatre. Students jumped up and hugged each other, their Inguzes and Halos shining with the colour of their new Sector. Parents and family members crowded down the stairs to congratulate their students, and in the hubbub, Eyre ran as fast as she could out of the Hall, down the hallway, and away from the joyous awfulness.

Tears streaming down her face, she tore along the pathways and through the Compound until she stood at the side of the lake, her shoulders heaving with wrenching sobs. She looked at the horrible dull grey Inguz on her arm.

and wept harder when she saw reflected in the surface of the lake that her Halo was an indistinct black line, like the outline of her Inguz.

Finally she took a shuddering breath and rubbed her eyes with tired hands. Why was everything so difficult? If only her parents were here. And then she was suddenly glad that they weren't as she thought of the awful shame she would have caused them with her odd placement colours. That thought made her sink to the ground in wretchedness, her heart feeling like it was going to break.

Suddenly there was a loud splash in the water, close into shore, and Eyre looked up in fright, the memory of the Bunyip forever in her mind. A dark form was swimming in fast towards her, and she sprawled backwards on the bank, trying to get away. A huge reptile splashed out of the water, and her heart nearly stopped as it came towards her rapidly. But then she recognised it: it was the crocodile from the TEPs. It stopped and looked at her, the strange unblinking purple eyes taking in her tear-streaked face.

"Hello again," she hiccupped, wiping away her tears. The crocodile regarded her silently, then with a strange flip and morphing of colour, its shape changed until standing before her was a man. And not just any man: Ranger Chrysanthe, as casual as ever, regarded her calmly with his curious purple eyes.

Eyre smiled wryly. "Ah, so it was you," she said, nodding. "I guess that makes sense. You didn't seem like a *real* crocodile." A thought occurred to her. "You were the pelican, too. . . ? And the tree?"

Ranger Chysanthe smiled. "I was the crocodile and the pelican. But not the tree. The Rainbow Eucalyptus is an ancient being."

"I didn't know that Lightworkers could change shape."

"It's called therianthropy—you'll learn about it at the Academy."

Eyre looked miserably at him, her eyes welling with tears again. "I don't think I'm coming," she said, "look!" and she showed him the shameful Inguz on her arm. "I don't even know what that is," she said. "I won't be selected."

"Have you been to look?" Ranger Chrysanthe asked her kindly.

"I'm not going in there," Eyre said, crying anew. "It's too embarrassing, I can't bear it. Everyone is looking at me." Suddenly she felt something in her lap and nearly jumped in the lake with shock. But then she looked down and saw a small lavender form circling around to get comfortable, and realised it was Lenny sitting in her lap, snuggling down for a cuddle. She stroked the velvety creature, smiling between her tears.

"You have got to stop doing that," she said to the long-eared, soft little being.

"Lenny always knows when someone needs a Hug," Ranger Chrysanthe said softly. "Go on up and say your farewells, Eyre," he said gently. "People will be leaving soon, and you'll regret it if you don't say goodbye."

Eyre looked up at him, her mouth turned down. But she stroked Lenny one more time and then handed her carefully back to Ranger Chrysanthe. She sighed deeply, shuddering with the depth of her sorrow.

"Yes, you're right," she said sadly. "I would regret it. I'll go and get my stuff. At least I can travel back with Beatrice, Nick, and Abby. Thank you for trying to make me feel better," she added, her sapphire eyes magnified by the tears. "And thank you for your help over the past two months."

Moving like an old woman, she walked slowly up to the Training Shed and hung her robe back on the rack. Other students were there, returning the crimson garments, and they looked at her with a mixture of curiosity and pity that made Eyre feel like her skin was burning. She left the shed quickly and got her bag from Water Lodge. Carly was there, and she immediately enveloped Eyre in a comforting embrace.

"I don't care what Inguz you've got, Eyre," she said. "You are a special friend, and I'm going to keep in touch." Carly's family were there, trying not to look at Eyre's arm—two big strapping handsome boys older than Carly, a kind looking mother, and a red-faced, weather-beaten father. People of the land, she thought. Good people by the look of them, just as she would have expected, knowing Carly. She smiled a wobbly smile at Carly's mother.

"Thank you for my blanket, I love it." Carly's mother came over and hugged her, her lined face fierce.

"Everyone is special, Eyre." she said, "You will find your gifts!" Eyre smiled gratefully but didn't reply, afraid she might embarrass herself by crying again. She took her bag and headed down to the Common Room to find Beatrice, Nick, and Abby so they could travel home together. The sooner the better, she thought painfully. So many people were staring at her, she felt like a circus freak.

As she entered the Common Room, she was nearly knocked over by an elated Beatrice who shouted excitedly, "We're all in!"

Eyre smiled crookedly, feeling a deep sadness. "Congratulations guys." she said, looking at her friends. "I'm so happy for you!"

"I'm so happy for *us*!" shouted Abby. "You're in *too*, Eyre! Look!" She dragged Eyre over to the student offers pinned up on the noticeboard, and there, way at the bottom of the list was her name: Eyre Lightward. Eyre leaned forward in disbelief, scarcely daring to hope. She *was* on the list, but how? Why would she be offered a place when she didn't even have a proper Sector?

But as she saw the beaming faces of her friends around her, a sudden happiness flared within her. She was in, she was *in*! Unfortunately, Ben Perrill was in, too, halfway up the list above her, but she wasn't going to worry about that right now, she was too ecstatic about this unexpected turn of events to let anything spoil her joy. She was in, she had a chance to prove herself, and she wasn't going to be separated from her wonderful friends. She was going to the Academy with them; she would be *back* here for first year! The joy welled up inside her like a physical force, and she danced around jubilantly with the rest of the students selected for the Academy.

As students gathered their belongings, and after consulting the list and saying their farewells, they started to depart. All over campus people were disappearing rapidly; there were flashes of light as they travelled home with family members. Gradually the campus became more and more deserted, until there were only a few students left.

Mr and Mrs Edmunsun and Mr Wilson, Abby's father, joined them, saying nothing but smiling in congratulations at them all.

Eyre looked around her, savouring for one more moment the unexpected joy that came from realising she would be back here next year. Then she linked hands with the Edmunsuns, Nick, Mr Wilson and Abby.

There was a high-pitched squeal and a blinding flash of light, and they all disappeared, heading for Highlight—*home*.

She only just made it into the secret school. Will she survive the terrifying assaults and make it through her first year?

Barely scraping through the challenging and dangerous Lightworker Trials, Eyre Lightward works hard to bring her new powers under control. Struggling to complete her first task at the Academy, the crystal-powered staff she produces still won't work. And worse still, the campus comes under attack by Earth's vicious enemy intent on the planet's destruction.

But Eyre learns of an ancient prophecy foretelling only those with special abilities can restore the world's protective Aura and save the human race from doom. And with the shield's shattered pieces hurled into otherworldly realms, time is running out for Eyre and her fellow Lightworkers to locate the precious fragments before her foes return to strike a lethal blow.

Can Eyre unlock her hidden skills in time to save humanity from a malevolent menace?

Terra is the second book in the sweeping *Quest for the Aura* YA fantasy series. If you like determined characters, nail-biting battles, and intricately crafted magic systems, then you'll love R.S. O'Neal's gripping adventure.

Buy *Terra* to defend the vulnerable today!

Follow the link or the QR code below to grab your copy.

https://thequestfortheaura.com/terra

About the Quest for the Aura

Discover more exciting facts about the Quest for the Aura and download a free glossary from R.S. O'Neal's website here:

https://thequestfortheaura.com/

www.ingramcontent.com/pod-product-compliance
Lightning Source LLC
Chambersburg PA
CBHW031937110726
47902CB00001B/210